TALES OF THE UNITED STATES
SPACE FORCE

BAEN BOOKS
edited by C. STUART HARDWICK

Tales of the United States Space Force

TALES OF THE UNITED STATES
SPACE FORCE

Edited by

C. Stuart Hardwick

BAEN

Disclaimer: Views expressed in this publication are those of the authors and do not necessarily reflect the policy or position of the U.S. Department of Defense or the U.S. government. All stories are works of fiction, as are all persons, places, events, threats, and technologies therein. No spacecraft or alien life forms were harmed in the making of this work. That ought to just about cover it.

A Baen Books Original

Baen Publishing Enterprises
P.O. Box 1403
Riverdale, NY 10471
www.baen.com

ISBN: 978-1-9821-9345-4

Cover art by Kurt Miller

First printing, June 2024

Distributed by Simon & Schuster
1230 Avenue of the Americas
New York, NY 10020

Library of Congress Cataloging-in-Publication Data

Names: Hardwick, C. Stuart, 1966- editor.
Title: Tales of the United States Space Force / edited by C. Stuart
  Hardwick.
Description: Riverdale, NY : Baen Publishing Enterprises, 2024.
Identifiers: LCCN 2024004731 (print) | LCCN 2024004732 (ebook) | ISBN
  9781982193454 (trade paperback) | ISBN 9781625799661 (ebook)
Subjects: LCSH: United States. Space Force—Literary collections. | BISAC:
  FICTION / Science Fiction / Hard Science Fiction | FICTION / Science
  Fiction / Space Exploration | LCGFT: Science fiction. | Short stories. |
  Essays.
Classification: LCC PN6071.S33 U7333 2006 (print) | LCC PN6071.S33
  (ebook) | DDC 808.83/8762—dc23/eng/20240212
LC record available at https://lccn.loc.gov/2024004731
LC ebook record available at https://lccn.loc.gov/2024004732

Printed in the United States of America

10 9 8 7 6 5 4 3 2 1

Dedicated to the memory of Mike Resnick,
whose "pay it forward" generosity touched all us Writers
of the Future newbies lucky enough to sit up with him
in the bar, sipping equally of soda and wisdom.

Acknowledgments

Special thanks to Kyle Russell, who gave me my first editing job, and to the officers of the United States Air Force Command and Staff College and the United States Secretary of the Air Force Public Affairs office, for invaluable assistance in the course of this one.

Thanks also to Arlan Andrews and the membership of the Sigma think tank, Lieutenant Colonel Peter Garretson, and Alex Shvartsman, each of whom gave assistance, and especially to William Ledbetter and Martin Shoemaker for years of friendship, support, ideas, and commiseration without which this work would certainly never have happened.

Illustration attributions

"Look at My New Space Force" by Phil Hand, used by permission.

Roswell balloon and wreckage, courtesy, *Fort Worth Star-Telegram* Collection, Special Collections, The University of Texas at Arlington Libraries.

"Mission Failed" by Pedro De Elizalde.

"Romulan Piracy" by Dave Granlund, used by permission.

"Space Captain" by Ed Bickford.

All materials not otherwise attributed are the work of your editor.

Contents

✵

"Some people don't want to hear this . . .
but—absolutely—we're going to fight in space.
We're going to fight from space,
and we're going to fight in space when
[U.S. and allied assets on orbit]
become so precious that it's in our national interest."
—General Joseph Ashy, CINCSPACE, 1996

Foreword

✿

"Star Wars" Program Chief Space Laser Engineer
William F. Otto

In 2011, Perseo Mazzoni from the Italian music group Lunocode contacted me for help with song lyrics about a set of primates launched into space in 1948–51 aboard V-2 and Aerobee rockets. Having grown up in Huntsville, Alabama, where every manned space flight was broadcast over the school's public address system, I thought I knew the space program, but this was the first I had known of early Air Force and Army flights.

People of my generation are familiar with the Navy feeling pressure to launch a small satellite on the mostly untested Vanguard-derived three-stage missile. We remember because we witnessed the failure on live television in 1957.

The following year, President Eisenhower established NASA to coordinate civilian space exploration and be the public face of the space race. At the time, the U.S. was very concerned with the space environment and its effect on ICBMs. A number of nuclear tests in space were carried out by the Defense Nuclear Agency with assistance from the Navy in Operations Argus and Hardtack II which explored the effects a nuclear blast would have on military hardware, including satellites.

In that same time frame, the Air Force funded the Atlas missile, the Army developed the Redstone, and the Navy the Polaris missile. NASA may have brought civilian space exploration under one roof, but the branches of the service were each going their own ways in the ICBM arena.

It wasn't just ballistic missiles, but satellites, antiballistic missiles, navigation, communication, and weather. And then the CIA got involved with reconnaissance, and the Advanced Research Project Agency with potential space weapons like lasers and particle beams.

The successor to ARPA, DARPA (the Defense Advanced Research Projects Agency) was researching the space-based laser when I came into the workforce and I got involved in 1979. Reagan was elected president and soon established the Strategic Defense Initiative. The high-tech world of a "missile shield" exploded into an intense effort that was transferred from DARPA and the Air Force to a new SDIO (the Strategic Defense Initiative Organization, the "Star Wars Office" to the press).

A lot of things were happening. The Air Force centralized their space activities within the Air Force Space Command, but people were mentioning that maybe the services shouldn't be duplicating efforts and that space activities should be brought under one Space Agency. Others felt that the independent efforts had a higher probability of success despite the duplication.

In the 1990s, GOP leaders spearheaded by Newt Gingrich, Dick Cheney, and Donald Rumsfeld sought an effective missile defense. There was renewed interest in various interceptors like EKV (the Exoatmospheric Kill Vehicle), THAAD (Terminal High Altitude Area Defense), and the Aegis missile. At the time, however, all of these mostly failed to hit their targets.

Congress directed the Air Force to pursue the space-based laser (which would have scuttled the Outer Space Treaty against weapons in space), but the Air Force didn't believe the technology was ready. Gingrich and Trent Lott responded with a clear threat: If the Air Force had other priorities, then the time had come to set up the U.S. Space Force and shift the budget from the existing branches. I thought this was pretty bold, and it started to look like I would be writing some proposal material after all.

Boeing made me technical lead for their bid to be part of the program. We went through a competitive phase, but after a lot of good work, the Air Force (acting for BMDO, the Ballistic Missile Defense Organization) directed that Lockheed Martin, TRW, and Boeing team up to do the work. I ended up as the systems engineering, integration, and testing lead for the program, or in short, the "chief engineer."

At a conference in Oxnard, California, on large space optics at the time, I was shocked by a presenter from the NRO (National Reconnaissance Office). The existence of the NRO had been a highly guarded secret, but he openly announced that not only did they exist, they had worked out an agreement with NASA and the Air Force to share technology. Since I'd worked for all three, I had seen three independent developments of much of the same technologies, a colossal waste of effort.

Times were changing. The idea of a unified Space Force came up again and again, but when it finally happened under the Trump administration, I found a lot of people confused about what the Space Force would do. Was it a bunch of space rangers flying in space, shooting at aliens or their Russian and Chinese counterparts?

That was not entirely out of the question. In 1965, the Air Force had secretly selected astronauts for its planned Manned Orbiting Laboratory (MOL). You might recognize the names Richard H. Truly, Robert L. Crippen, Robert F. Overmyer, and Henry W. Hartsfield from NASA's Space Shuttle era. Another, James A. Abrahamson, I knew later when he was the first head of SDIO.

By now the reader will have noted a pattern: despite the Outer Space Treaty which prohibits the development of space-resident weapons, there is a long history of delivering weapons to space, through space, or from space. As soon as innovations allow, they are applied to new weapons—by inventors all over the world. And so, new weapons will continue to be added to the growing U.S. military presence in space, helping prevent attack, support national interests, and ultimately benefit us all. Remember, even the Global Positioning System was originally designed to guide missiles and bombers to pinpoint surgical strikes.

Of course, once valuable hardware is up there, we have to protect and defend it. Imagine if Russia or the United States suddenly lost their early warning satellites. Each would feel vulnerable to surprise nuclear attack, and that insecurity would make hostilities more likely. A large role for the Space Force is in defending the defense assets in space for monitoring and intelligence gathering. But it goes beyond military interests. Much of modern life is space based. Automated teller machines, credit card verification at point of sale, airplane navigation, tour guide navigation, entertainment, news... almost everything you can think of depends on space assets. Farmers program their harvesting machines to follow a GPS track. If satellites were attacked by some rogue power, much of modern commerce would grind to a halt. People would starve. *We must defend our space assets with every bit as much diligence as our airspace.*

And there's no doubt that some of the concepts and technologies to do that were inspired by science fiction. One of the more talked about space resident weapon concepts is Jerry Pournelle's "Rods of God" in which orbiting tungsten rods are de-orbited over an enemy and allowed to strike a target with kinetic energy roughly equivalent to a tactical nuclear warhead. Although there are significant technical challenges with this concept, it shows how science fiction and technology spur each other forward. I know I was inspired by countless science fiction movies in the fifties and sixties along with shows like *Star Trek, The Outer Limits, The Twilight Zone,* and *The Time Tunnel,* and so were many others producing defense concepts and ideas over the course of the past fifty years. We still call SDI "Star Wars" after all!

But science fiction doesn't only generate ideas, it also gets us to think about the world in new ways. The 1985 Canadian movie *Def-Con 4* comes to mind, and illustrates why we will probably always have a military presence in space. This anthology is in the same vein, with a mix of fact and fiction to inspire both reflection and innovation. There are articles about the Space Force, its origins, trappings, and mission, and stories that inspire and that present new ideas and concepts that can find their way one day into experimental or even everyday operations—for space defense and everyday life.

It was Arthur C. Clarke who, in a 1945 letter to the editor of *Wireless,* suggested that geostationary satellites would be ideal for global communications. That attracted the military, but it ultimately revolutionized everything from logistics to weather forecasting, to delivery of entertainment on transoceanic flights. How many ideas in the volume you're holding will one day be equally transformative?

Let's find out.

—William F. Otto
Albuquerque

✤　　✤　　✤

After consulting for DARPA on chemical lasers, **Bill Otto** was the technical lead for Boeing's Space-Based Laser Integrated Flight Experiment, and later lead systems engineer for the Air Force Space-Based Laser joint venture that formed the backbone of President Reagan's "Star Wars" Strategic Defense Initiative. A Boeing Technical Fellow and member of the Missile Defense National Team, he enjoys science fiction and can often be found listening to Feynman's Lectures on Physics while doing projects around the house.

Preface

✴

The idea for this anthology sprang from my first introduction to what is now the United States Space Force back in 2017, when as guest of FenCon XIV in Dallas, I was to moderate a panel called "Join the Space Corps: Improvise, Adapt, Overpower." Sounds pretty badass, right? And the other panelists were heavy hitters, including a veteran NASA astronaut and a Lockheed Martin engineer working on Air Force weather satellites. I would be asking the questions and I'd never heard of this "Space Corps," so I needed an education—fast.

The panel description told me that in June of that year, the House Armed Services Strategic Forces Subcommittee had voted to create a Space Corps as a subset of the U.S. Air Force, similar to the way the Marine Corps is set up. Google opined that the new Trump administration opposed the measure, that Defense Secretary Mattis had taken the unusual step of writing a letter in support of a Republican amendment to kill it, arguing the idea was premature and in need of more study.

In fact, though, while perhaps new to most voters and to staffers within the new administration, this idea had already been studied to death. I'd not given the defense of satellites much thought since my school days, when it had occurred to me that bold as President Reagan's Strategic Defense Initiative might seem, in practice it would have been a trillion-dollar sitting duck to anyone with a cheap sounding rocket and a bag full of gravel. Little did I know, smart people were way ahead of me.

Satellites have become critical not only to the military, but the entire economy, providing an ever-growing range of services for which substitutes are inferior, uneconomical, or downright impossible. The need for an independent military organization to protect them had been suggested long before Ronald Reagan, and had been proposed in earnest by bipartisan commissions and panels under both Presidents Bush (George W.) and Obama. The reasons were several and included the growing importance of space to defense and the economy, the scattering of existing space defense responsibilities across various military organizations, and the Air Force's perceived bias toward airplanes at the expense of procurement for and attention to space.

Thus enlightened, I led my panelists in a lively debate and we went on with our lives. Then a few months later, I attended the 2018 International Space Development Conference in Los Angeles to receive a writing award. This conference was an amazing display of space-related entrepreneurship and energy: programs to help college students launch science payloads into space, Cold War cannons promoted for blasting propellants into orbit, serious work on space-elevator design, shiny scrap from the manufacture of rockets turned into skateboards and coasters, inspiring stuff. Everywhere were hopeful idealists and promoters eager to ride the impending wave of commercial space exploitation to be ushered in by plummeting launch costs.

I got my picture taken with Dr. Frank Drake (of the Drake equation fame), and Freeman Dyson (famous for his work on atomic pulse propulsion). I met actor Harry Hamlin and lent a cell phone charger to Rod Roddenberry, son of *Star Trek* creator Gene. Then on the last day, after the last session before my cab came to take me to the airport, I met Lieutenant Colonel Peter Garretson, then director of the Space Horizons Task Force at the Air Force Command and Staff College.

Peter was not one to mince words. Sooner rather than later, the Space Corps was going to happen, he said. The time had come, and while it wouldn't exactly be a space navy anytime soon, wherever people and their interests go, the military and the law must eventually follow. He said that around the college, he liked to say they were building the "real Starfleet Academy," and he told me he'd thought of producing a science fiction anthology to help get the word out.

That piqued my interest, and Peter and I batted the idea around over the next few months. I let the matter drop after he moved on from the Air Force, and in December of 2019, the independent space-defense service branch that had been recommended under Reagan, Bush, and Obama finally got the nod, though the man in the Oval Office by then wanted to call it a "force" instead of a "corps." The name made no difference. Political theater aside, to those of us in the know, this was expected and largely a non-story.

Then in early 2020, when the nascent service branch started making announcements, my social-media feed lit up with confusion and outrage. It wasn't surprising that late night talk show hosts made light of the new military branch—that's literally their job. Nor was it surprising that Netflix rolled out a workplace comedy inspired by such a high-profile event. Or really, that taxpayers unaware that the DOD's Space Command had already existed in one form or another for twenty-five years would balk at the news of a new space-related defense force. If you didn't know any better, you could be forgiven for imagining space stations teaming with Velcro-receptive combat boots.

> The 2020 Netflix television series *Space Force* was created by Greg Daniels and Steve Carell, who previously worked together on the hit TV show *The Office*. Both have said they were inspired by announcement of the creation of the United States Space Force in 2018, but only because they were looking for ideas for a new workplace comedy at the time. In interviews, they've said the show was not intended to make any political statement or to belittle the real U.S. Space Force and that actual members of the U.S. Space Force were consulted in order to make the show more authentic and respectful of the real branch.

All of this was understandable, and after all, the announcement came through an administration if not a uniquely polarizing force in American politics, certainly a lightning rod for existing polarization to align and compound around. Among Donald Trump's detractors, no decision was beneath derision, not even one with bipartisan support grown over six administrations that he actually had little to do with. The Internet memes were as cynical as they were profligate. Several featured images of Trump's face pasted onto Pixar's Buzz Lightyear character over the caption "To insanity and beyond."

The jokes were understandable, but they reflected a certain naïveté about the need for space defense in particular and the military in general. Would the Pentagon really rip off *Star Trek*? Would it really create a whole service branch just to waste money sending Marines into orbit? Was all this really just saber rattling by an unpopular president, boondoggle of boondoggles, the dreaded "militarization of space" where no such thing was warranted? Or had smart people looked into the matter and learned things the jokesters and meme-makers didn't know? Clearly, there was a perception problem.

No rational person wants war, but most people understand that as someone once said, a nation too civilized to fight will soon be conquered by its less civilized neighbors. The more I investigated, the more reasons I found for taking space defense seriously.

In 2019, India conducted a missile test that resulted in the creation of space debris, posing a risk to other spacecraft in orbit. Russia and China have both successfully tested antisatellite missiles. In 2018, a Russian satellite approached a U.S. government satellite close enough to conduct a close inspection or attack, forcing evasive maneuvering. The same year, China launched a satellite that analysts believed was equipped with a robotic arm that could be used to manipulate and disable other satellites.

Why does it matter? For a start, it's worth pointing out that GPS satellites are what make modern precision bombing possible. You might hate war, but when someone else decides to start one, GPS is the biggest single aid in reducing collateral damage. And satellites aren't just up there guiding explosives and pizzas to their destinations; they play a critical role in everything from weather forecasting and disaster response to agriculture and environmental monitoring. Taken together, satellites contribute nearly $200 billion a year to the U.S. economy, which is more than the individual GDPs of half the states.

That's a lot riding on 1,300 high-tech machines, many costing twice their weight in gold even before launch and operating costs, all as lightweight as possible and with delicate optics, sensors, antennas, and solar arrays utterly exposed in the vacuum of space. It would be foolish to pretend they don't need to be protected. So, as the son of an Air Force Cold Warrior myself, I thought the nine thousand or so real, live human beings serving their country within the new Space Force and all their families and dependents deserved a little bit better than dismissive Internet memes. And since I had edited a few small anthology projects and was looking for something more challenging . . . and having achieved some success as an author and, as the great Edward Abbey once put it, an "explainer," I decided to do as Gandhi advised us, and "be the change you wish to see in the world."

Thus, after many false starts and dead ends, it was coincidentally on the last day of the 2022 International Space Development Conference at which I was receiving another award, after my last session before the taxi whisked me away to the airport, that Baen Books editor Toni Weisskopf pulled me aside to say she'd publish the anthology if I'd just go ahead and do it already.

Thus, ladies and gentlebeings, I give you this anthology in the hope it will enlighten, entertain, and inspire. Enlighten you as to the true origins and mission of the Space Force and its accouterments and paraphernalia. Entertain you with thrilling adventures in space and here on the ground, some of which give a taste of what real-world space defense is all about. Inspire you, as science fiction always has, to see something important beyond your own life, to walk in another's footsteps, and perhaps, just perhaps, to one day take a chance and thus find wonders beyond present imagining, maybe even beyond the stars.

And so, inspired by one notable schoolmaster, I enjoin you in paraphrase of another: Let us step into the great vast night, and pursue together that flighty temptress, adventure.

—C. Stuart Hardwick
Houston

The Eyes of Damocles

✵

Brian Trent

"Thought you guys only worked in space."

The old joke floated in the cold night air. Bruce Tennessen, orbital warfare captain with the United States Space Force, didn't feel the need to acknowledge or correct it. He was still looking at the crash. The vehicle lay a hundred meters below the road, crumpled like a tin can.

At 4:12 a.m. on the outskirts of Colorado Springs, the stars were numerous and bright. Bright enough that they auto-triggered his constellation app. A faint overlay appeared on his optic lenses. It connected the dots of the Little Dipper and Cassiopeia in the sky, bringing them to imaginative life. With a flick of his fingers, he could call up information on any of them—their distance from the Sun, stellar classification, and composition—but Bruce was hardly in the mood. He dismissed the image with a wave of his hand.

"This is a dangerous bend," the police officer was saying. "If you drive it too fast, it's easy to lose control."

Bruce stared down at the car's wreckage. The occupants—pronounced dead at the scene—had been taken to the morgue. A tow truck idled nearby. Two police cruisers, and Bruce's own car, were the only vehicles on the road.

It was unusual for anyone from USSF to interface directly with local law enforcement. But the crash had occurred less than ten miles from Peterson Base. Colorado Springs PD had been first on the scene. The base was notified, and so was Bruce.

The cop was watching him. "Do you know what they were doing out so early?"

"I don't."

"Did you know them personally?"

"No," he said, not caring to share the rest: he knew of the deceased. Everyone did. The man in the driver's seat—whether or not he'd been actually driving the vehicle—had been Gavin Palmer, mission commander for the upcoming asteroid landing. The car's other occupant was Kia Ortiz, pilot for the same mission. It was a poorly kept secret that the two had been in a relationship. Like the rest of the mission crew, they'd been home for the New Year holiday. As to why they'd been driving around so early, Bruce couldn't say. The crew was returning to base for training today. Maybe they'd wanted to get an early start. Maybe they'd gone for a romantic drive to watch the starry sky that, in a few short months, would be their workplace.

Bruce's earpiece chimed with an incoming call. The caller ID displayed in a corner of his vision: Major Markowitz from base.

He touched the icon floating on his visual field. "Yes, sir?"

"You're at the scene?"

"Yes, sir."

"What can you tell me?"

He strayed from the police officer, touching his ear in the common etiquette to indicate he'd received a call. "The car went off the road. Palmer and Ortiz were pronounced dead."

He heard the major let out a deep breath. "Were they driving the car themselves?"

"I don't know yet. The car's data recorder was downloaded, but they don't generally share that . . ."

A pause. More than that—a total silence like cotton stuffed into his ear. Bruce knew that his commanding officer had muted him to relay a command to someone else on staff—almost certainly to clear the way for him to get what he needed from the police. Working with law enforcement could be prickly at times.

On the other hand, the upcoming asteroid mission had become a national obsession. It made Bruce feel good to think of it; too often, USSF missions flew under the radar of public awareness. That went with the job, of course. In its forty years of operation, Space Force guardians had earned their name. The high frontier had always been a dangerous place. The so-called Resource Rush made it worse. A new Cold War, the press called it, but it really wasn't so cold: there had been hostilities, sabotage, satellite hijacking, peculiar "accidents" in orbit, espionage on the Moon, and cyberwarfare that could strike like a knife in the dark. The asteroid mission had cranked geopolitical tensions to the breaking point.

No, Bruce thought, looking at the ruined car. It isn't a Cold War. It's an Invisible War, and it just might have gotten worse.

The major's voice came back on the line. "We're talking to the police chief now. Head directly to the station. Ask for the traffic-services unit—they'll be expecting you by the time you arrive."

"Sir?"

"We'd prefer this be done in person," Major Markowitz explained. "You're not far from the station."

"Actually, I was wondering why . . . well . . . can you tell me why . . ."

"Page 13 of your report." He heard the shuffling of papers. "'In the event of threat profiles triggered, an active response should be immediately engaged, to avoid any delays that could have disastrous ramifications.'"

Bruce remembered writing the words. "The Damocles Report?" he asked, astonished.

"The one and only."

He felt his breath catch. He'd nearly forgotten about it, and assumed that everyone else had too. Five years ago, the Department of Defense had asked the Space Force to put together what amounted to a kind of readiness-and-vulnerabilities assessment. It was part of a larger initiative touching all JSOC columns. Bruce had been tapped for the work. He'd held meetings over coffee. Virtual conferences. Lots of emails. He worked steadily for a month, typed up his report, and filed it. That was the end of it.

Bruce glanced more to the stars. There was an unfamiliar light up there—the asteroid Ebisu. It was the destination of the upcoming mission. It was where, in a few months, the two deceased astronauts were supposed to be landing.

"The White House chief of staff has called a meeting in five minutes," the major said. "I need you there to talk about Damocles."

"I won't have the data recorder by then."

"That's okay. He wants something to bring to the president. Just in case."

In case the accident was really an assassination, Bruce thought grimly.

In the front seat of his car, he set the vehicle to auto-drive and went into conference mode. The windshield opaqued and displayed the briefing room of Orbital Warfare at Peterson Space Force Base.

There had been lots of jokes from family and friends when Bruce enlisted, about how he'd be working in some futuristic place full of holograms and robots. The truth was more mundane; Orbital Warfare's operations center wasn't so different from that of other military branches, with a heavily computerized space filled by individual stations and monitors. Even the large screen hadn't changed from the kinds of screens used by the Navy and Air Force decades ago.

The briefing room was even more mundane than that: a small chamber with a rectangular table, and chairs wired for augmented reality so that personnel from around the world could see each other as if they were in the same room.

The White House chief of staff was apparently a more traditional fellow: his bulldog face loomed from the room's wall screen in all its 2D glory. He was sitting far too close to his desktop.

Bruce's image appeared in one of the chairs. Seated across from him, Major Markowitz nodded amicably at him. A handsome, square-jawed man in his fifties, the major was dressed in his USSF blues.

The White House chief of staff leaned even closer to the screen and, without preamble, said, "Talk to me about Damocles."

Bruce straightened in the backseat. "The Damocles Report examines potential threats posed by asymmetrical warfare in our battlespace," he began.

The assignment had initially seemed strange. Five years earlier, Bruce had begun his military career with the USSF's Cyberwarfare division, which had grown out of its earlier incarnation of Cyber Operations. He'd excelled in the post. When the DOD tasked its military branches to write reports on asymmetrical vulnerabilities, Bruce was chosen for Space Force's contribution. He'd spent the first few days scratching his head.

Gradually, though, he warmed to the concept. And the more specialists he spoke to—his fellow guardians in the fields of intel, cyber, nuclear, technology and innovation, strategy and analysis—the more he appreciated why out-of-box tiger-team thinking was important. There was a danger in insular thinking. It was easy to get complacent. To believe that you knew all the variables. That had always been true in the history of warfare, but it was paramount in an age when an entire conflict could be decided in the first few minutes.

The Damocles Report cast a wide net. By the very nature of the thought experiment, it was sometimes vague, focusing on statistics, hundreds of variables, and data-mining correlations. Nonetheless, it recommended the expansion of existing threat profiles, so that if certain conditions were met...

"Two leaders of a high-value asteroid mission died under mysterious circumstances while driving in the same vehicle," Bruce said, jostling in his car. "This close to launch, their deaths could cause disruption, even delays."

"Couldn't it have been a genuine accident?"

"It's possible, but not probable. The timing, the variables, the mission's strategic value to national interests... the calculus suggests the involvement of a hidden malefactor."

"He's saying," Major Markowitz added, "that these factors would make for an extremely inviting target of opportunity for a rival nation."

The Chief of Staff's frown deepened. "So you're thinking that... what? They were driven off the road?"

"There's no evidence another vehicle was involved," Bruce said.

"But you think they were murdered anyway?"

"I do."

In the past, missions involving asteroids had fallen under the auspices of NASA. That changed quickly during the Resource Rush. It had been known since the 1970s that asteroid mining could supercharge national fortunes. Trillions of dollars in precious metals lay waiting to be extracted. So did water ice—useful for making rocket propellant as well as for human consumption, and which would drastically reduce the need for costly supply launches. All this was enough to make "sky estate" the next major rush. The very concept of asteroid mining was cleared of legal hurdles as far back as 2015; nonetheless, it remained a pipe-dream—a prohibitively expensive one—for a long while.

The asteroid nicknamed Ebisu was a game changer. Catalogued in the 2030s, a subsequent probe landing confirmed it contained—among other materials—vast repositories of lithium and cobalt. Earthside, the demand for both had skyrocketed. The Resource Rush was already pitting the U.S., China, India, and Russia in a mad scramble. Global tensions were high. Proxy wars and industrial sabotage were increasing throughout Africa, Asia, and South America. The newest technologies—and national defense—hung in the balance on a knife's edge.

Ebisu promised incalculable advantages to whoever could set up mining operations. Of course, by terms of the 1967 Outer Space Treaty, no one could claim the entire rock for themselves. Nonetheless, whoever got there first would benefit first . . . and that had enormous ramifications for the global situation. The Race to the Rock was on.

"So you see," Bruce explained, "there was ample motive and opportunity for a double assassination."

"What about the means?" the Chief of Staff demanded. "If they weren't run off the road, and there was no physical sabotage to the vehicle . . ."

"We should consider the possibility that the car was hacked." Autonomous vehicles relied on GPS satellites, which were fully within USSF jurisdiction.

The man blinked. "You think someone hacked their car and remotely drove them to their deaths?"

"We need to consider the possibility."

"I've been assured that hacking a self-driving car is impossible."

Bruce considered his next words carefully. In the Damocles Report, the word "impossible" was a recurring antagonist. Assuming something couldn't be done, that certain ideas were not worth investigating, was itself a problem. It created blind spots. Unsinkable ships sank. Unhackable systems got hacked. Sure, there were things that were probably impossible, like faster-than-light communications and teleportation and other things that certain overly enthusiastic people had suggested to Bruce when he was writing the report.

Nonetheless, Damocles didn't shy from outside-the-box thinking. It discouraged knee-jerk dismissals of what was or wasn't possible. On page 91, Bruce had summarized this perspective with the Sunbeam Example: Imagine that someone openly wonders what it might be like to ride a sunbeam. A naysayer might callously dismiss the idea, since it was obviously impossible for a person to ride a sunbeam. Yet ruminating on that "impossible" notion had led a patent clerk named Albert Einstein to discovering general relativity, which had a significant impact on the fate of nations.

The Chief of Staff was still waiting impatiently for his response. "Captain? Is it possible to hack a self-driving car, yes or no?"

"I'm hoping the data recorder will shed light on that," Bruce said evasively.

"I want an update every hour until we know what the hell's going on." The man ended the call. The wall screen went black.

Major Markowitz looked at Bruce. "You didn't answer his question. Can a self-driving car be hacked?"

"It's probably not impossible."

"Christ, you'd make a good politician. Are you at the station yet?"

Bruce dispelled the opacity of his window with the touch of a button. "Just arriving now."

"By any chance, Captain, is your own car in auto-drive?"

"Um. Yes, sir."

"Well, here's an idea: maybe drive it yourself for a while, okay? And I'll advise the rest of the mission crew to drive manually, too—they're all scheduled to be on base within the hour."

"Of course, sir." He ended the call. His car pulled up to the Colorado Springs Police Department. Exiting the vehicle, Bruce hurried inside, glancing back only once to watch it circle around and park itself in a 15 MINUTE PARKING spot further down the road.

The problem, he mused as he entered the police station and was escorted to the traffic-services unit, was that cyberwarfare was an ever-present, ever-advancing threat. In the half century since the USSF's founding, it had become the new artillery. State-sponsored hackers in China, Russia, India, North Korea, and Pakistan waged an unrelenting war—an invisible war—against U.S. operations in space. Bruce had devoted an entire section of the Damocles Report to cyberwarfare, going beyond the usual "what if Russia hacks a U.S. satellite" to "what if Russia sends an orbital drone to physically drill into a satellite and hijack it, bypassing the firewall directly."

So from cars to spaceplanes, hacking was in probability's ballpark.

"They were driving the car themselves," the traffic officer said.

Bruce's jaw hung open. "They were?"

The traffic-services unit was a modest space filled with desks and smartboards. Current traffic-accident investigations were displayed on most, but one board was already devoted to this morning's accident: the mountain bend, the point where the car had gone off the road, the final resting spot. Data glinted at the margins.

The officer handed him a sheet of paper still warm from the printer. "That's from the data event recorder. Car departed at 3:45 a.m. It was under human operation the entire time. The driver obeyed the speed limit. At the bend in the road, he jerked the wheel to the right and went off the cliff."

Bruce scanned the report quickly. "Why would he do that?"

"We're still investigating. And we don't have the results of the bloodwork yet."

"Bloodwork?"

The cop hesitated. "It's standard procedure."

"He wasn't drunk," Bruce insisted, more aggressively than he'd meant to. All cars had been installed with breathalyzers since the 2030s, so it was inconceivable that Palmer had been intoxicated if he'd been at the wheel.

The officer looked uncomfortable. "A breathalyzer wouldn't show if the driver was compromised in other ways."

"Other ways?"

"Mr. Tennessen, if he'd taken pills or other substances, or if there were psychological factors at play—"

"It's Captain Tennessen," Bruce snapped, feeling a surge of annoyance. Astronauts were subjected to strict drug tests. Neither Palmer nor Ortiz would have risked consuming so much as a poppyseed bagel this close to launch. And the implication of suicide/homicide really set Bruce's blood boiling.

He returned to the lobby, signaling his car to pick him up at the curb. Taking the driver's seat, he switched to manual and made for base. His earpiece chimed; he flicked it to audio.

"Your timing is uncanny, Major."

"Well, page 53 of your report advises extra levels of security and monitoring for investigations, so I'm monitoring your car's GPS. Do you have the car's data?"

"Yes. I'm bringing it back to base now."

"Good. I want you to talk to my sister."

"Your sister . . . in space?"

"That's the only sister I have."

There was a long tradition of family members following the same career track; the Space Force was no exception. Major Markowitz had three relatives in the service—his mother was a three-star admiral, his cousin was in IT, and his sister was serving as guardian aboard the Argus V station in geosynchronous orbit above the American Midwest.

Orbital stints served a number of purposes. These ranged from repair missions to the more glamorous-sounding (but ultimately fairly mundane) threat response, which almost always included unmanned foreign spacecraft doing things they weren't supposed to be doing. It had started as early as 2018, when a Chinese device grabbed a defunct satellite. Having USSF personnel in orbit had lessened the frequency of such hostile actions. As a result, guardians on their "high fly" tour were fonts of information. And five years back, Bruce had interviewed the major's sister as part of his research. She was smart, capable, a real credit to the branch.

She was also a bit . . . well . . . loopy in some of her ideas.

Much of the old mockery against the USSF had dissipated over the years—but not all. It always seemed to be lurking in the margins. Bruce wasn't the only guardian to be annoyed by this irritating fact. Other military branches didn't have the same problem; the first suggestions that airplanes might have a place in warfare had been openly mocked at the beginning of the twentieth century, only to have the jokes vanish in the eras of WWI dogfights and WWII bombing runs and air-support and recon that followed. Yet forty years into the USSF, the media still made the occasional joke at their expense—digs about aliens and "space cadets" and the newest live-action version of *The Jetsons*.

Consequently, Bruce cringed when a fellow guardian became a little too enthusiastic. A few years earlier, a NASA astronaut at the lunar outpost had caused a shitstorm of controversy when he made a slightly intoxicated live-cast, pontificating that if aliens had once visited the solar system, they surely would have left remote-monitoring equipment on the Moon to study the terrestrial surface. Predictably, within minutes of the live-cast, every media headline was some variation of NASA BELIEVES ALIENS ARE HIDING ON THE MOON. And though the controversy hadn't even involved the Space Force, they were dragged into the mess anyway.

Bruce sighed. "I'd love to talk to her, sir."

There was a bell-like tone, and a new icon glowed faintly in his vision.

"Captain Tennessen!" The woman's voice boomed in his ear. "Good morning, sir! How have you been?"

"Good morning, Robin."

"My brother said you had questions about hacking a self-driving car? Well, sir, I guess it depends on what the goal is. See, in order for a hacker to override a car—say, from a satellite—they'd have to maintain point-to-point connection with a moving target. Any disruption to that connection breaks the two-way handshake. Weather can interfere. And there's still the problem of cracking through layers of encryption and verification. Can it be done? Sure, but what's the goal?"

"To kill the driver."

"Then it's a lost cause," she said decisively. "At best, you could only hope to crack the encryption for a few seconds and . . . well . . . I remember you don't like the word 'impossible,' so let's just say it's hardly worth a hacker's trouble. You can't do much in a few seconds."

Bruce reflected on the police report. "You could make a car pull a fatal turn in a few seconds."

"Not necessarily," she maintained. "Again, what's the goal? To cause a fender bender? Sure, you could do that. But if you're trying to *kill* the occupants, that's wildly difficult, because you could hardly be certain a few seconds of control would result in a fatal accident. Real-world conditions are constantly changing. If you wanted to slam the car into another car, well, the other car's self-driver would avoid the move. If you want to slam it into a building, well, even that is no guarantee with airbags and seat belts and crash foam and crumple zones. And remember that self-driving cars have safety features to prevent sudden, violent turns for no discernible reason—they'd slam on the brakes. Seriously, if you were trying to kill the occupant, there's far easier ways."

"Like what?"

"Just hire someone to shoot them."

"Except that wouldn't look like an accident."

"Why would you have to make it look like an accident?"

Because, he thought uneasily, if a foreign power is determined to cripple our asteroid mission, then they'd want to knock off as many astronauts as possible. If your first murders look like an accident, you've got time to perpetrate more "accidents" until someone finally gets suspicious. Send a hitman to shoot up famous astronauts, and your opportunity for further malefaction disappears.

The goal was surely to cripple or delay the mission. Could set our program back by months, letting our rivals get there first.

Bruce was reaching the fork in the road that would take him back to Peterson. He was about to turn right when a truck came hurtling at him. Bruce cried out, realizing he was about to be T-boned; in desperation, he veered to the left, gunned the engine, and watched the truck miss him by a foot or less.

"Jesus Christ!" he cursed, heart thudding painfully. Another truck roared by, followed by another. Looking in his rearview mirror, Bruce marveled at the lengthy convoy of trucks racing down the mountain. They looked like National Guard vehicles. What the hell were they doing this close to base? And driving at dangerously high speeds over such a rough and narrow road?

Shaken by the near impact, Bruce continued driving down the wrong road, partly to get his nerves under control, and partly to let the road clear of the trucks. He could still see their headlights winding down the mountain. There must have been twenty of them, maybe more. What the hell?

In his ear, Robin Markowitz cried, "Captain Tennessen? You okay, sir?"

Bruce blotted his sweaty hands on his pants. "Yeah, sorry." He looked for a place to safely turn around. This side road was poorly maintained, forcing him to steer between potholes and boulders encroaching the shoulder. However, a commuter lot glowed ahead of him, less than a quarter mile ahead. "Robin, what if our hypothetical car was not in self-drive mode? Could a hacker still take control?"

"Ah! That changes things!"

"Why?"

"Because then you wouldn't need to hack the car. You could just hack the human."

"What?"

"I've thought about this a lot," she said excitedly. "Pretty much everyone uses augmented reality lenses nowadays." That was certainly true; AR had become as ubiquitous as smartphones (which themselves had become wrist-phones that transmitted their data to the lenses). Walk past a restaurant, and lunch specials appeared. Approach a department store, and coupons popped up. You had to subscribe to such alerts, and you could tailor them to appear only on your wrist-phone; even so, the majority of people in industrialized countries used AR to see caller IDs, texts, and even to play AR games (which themselves had been around since *Pokemon Go* all the way back in 2016).

"So," Robin continued, "imagine a hacker hijacks the optical feed to your eyes. They could overlay whatever they wanted. You'd literally see things that aren't there. Pretty freaky, huh?"

Bruce struggled with a feeling of peculiar dread. "But doesn't that have the same problems as trying to hack a self-driving car?"

"Not necessarily, because a car under human control isn't subject to the same safety redundancies. If a human decides to turn the wheel suddenly, there's nothing stopping him. That's the only reason self-driving cars became popular at all: consumers insisted on having the option of control."

"But AR optics have security features..."

"You'd need three things to do it right," she said. "First, a satcom device that stays near to the target—say, you secretly stick it on their car. That would allow real-time hacking to seek and exploit vulnerabilities in the software. Secondly, you'd want a field team who controls the satcom device and feeds it instructions. And lastly, a spy satellite parked in orbit—my team on the Argus spends most of our time looking for malicious foreign satellites."

Bruce braked hard. He still had a couple hundred feet to the commuter lot, but he pulled over anyway at far as he could. He parked, opened the door, and stepped out into a chilly predawn.

Then, with one hand, he swiped both contact lenses from his eyes.

It was like flipping a TV channel. The road vanished. The commuter lot glowing in the distance was gone. A few pines and blue spruce surrounded his car. In horror, he saw that he'd parked just meters from the edge of a drop off.

His stomach dropped at the sight. The gorge was dizzyingly far below, and Bruce suddenly recognized it: it was where he liked to go hiking on weekends. He'd glanced up at these precipitous heights, appreciating their beauty from a safe distance. Only a few bulging rocks beneath the ledge interrupted what was otherwise a near-vertical drop.

His line to the Argus V was still open. Mouth dry, he said, "Robin! Someone hacked my optics!"

She laughed. "Like I said, it could be done in theory—"

"Not theory! I almost drove right off a cliff . . ." His blood ran cold and he looked up at the star-bejeweled sky. "My God, they must have been watching me at the scene of the accident! They assassinated two people already. The rest of the crew is returning to base within the hour! Any number of them might be vulnerable to this new kind of hack while en route . . ."

The line went dead.

He checked his wrist-phone. A NC SIGNAL message locked on the display.

Impossible, he thought. He'd hiked the canyon enough times to know that, despite its pristine wilderness, there was ample cell coverage. There was no goddamn way a signal could drop.

Unless it was being jammed.

Again, he looked into the sky, knowing that someone else was looking back. It was an eerie thing to contemplate. Hostile forces were bending their malice toward him even now, like angry gods glaring down from heaven. Stealth satellites were a major focus of the USSF. Some spoofed telecommunications. Others could jam earthside signals . . .

Bruce hurried back to his car. The bastards couldn't hack his vision anymore, now that he'd discarded his AR lenses. But the crew of the asteroid mission were still vulnerable. Enemy intel had surely kept track of exactly where they were. They knew that once they were back on base, the opportunities for attack would disappear. Today presented a dozen targets of opportunity for a dozen deadly illusions.

He was just sliding into the driver's seat and about to close the door when he thought back to what the lieutenant had told him.

You needed three things to pull off an AR hack. One was a satellite. Another was a satcom device near to the target . . .

Bruce exited the car once more, and began a slow circle around the vehicle. it. He studied the doors, the tires, and was rounding the rear bumper when he saw the device affixed there.

It was roughly the size of a hummingbird, and some effort had been made to imitate one. There were blue feathers. A small head with black eyes. At some point in the night, the thing must have alighted here— perhaps when he'd gone into the police station. It would have presented the perfect opportunity. Yet in the thin blush of dawn, he could see it for what it was: a mechanical device with magnetic clamps instead of avian talons. The U.S. military had used Nano Air Vehicles like that for decades. Small, lightweight, and nimble enough to fly around an area of operation without drawing casual attention.

As he noticed it, the "hummingbird" took flight. Despite its outward appearance, it didn't move with either the speed or grace of an actual hummingbird; Bruce easily snatched it out of the air. It buzzed in his hands, servos whining. With no small measure of satisfaction, Bruce broke the wings like snapping a pair of wafers. Then he buried it in his pocket and returned to the car.

On the road above him, a van lurched into view. The tires squealed to a violent stop. The back doors flung open, and three men hopped out with rifles in their hands.

Bruce dove behind his car as they opened fire. Bullets stitched a constellation where he'd been standing moments ago.

Anxiety surging, he glanced back to his wrist-phone.

NO SIGNAL.

"Fuck," he muttered. It was a forgone conclusion that foreign agents were operating on American soil. Especially as the Race to the Rock heated up, the USSF had received its share of briefings from the NSA, FBI, and CIA on increased chatter from Beijing and Moscow suggestive of active operations. It had been a dark fact of life in the first Cold War, and there was no reason to think it wouldn't persist in the second.

Nonetheless, he'd hardly expected to be the target.

Keeping low, Bruce dashed for the cover of a Douglas fir. Bullets whined past him, thumping the ground. A low-lying branch burst like confetti to his left. He flung himself to the ground, rolled twice, and—with his heart in his mouth—willingly went over the cliff.

It was a fatal drop, if not for the bulging rocks he'd noticed a few meters below the ledge. He landed hard on the outcropping.

The Cold War has really turned hot, he thought crazily. These people weren't trying to capture him, or interrogate him, or negotiate with him. He was the only one who knew what had happened to Palmer and Ortiz of the Ebisu mission.

And I'm the only one who knows that the rest of the crew is in danger.

Footsteps rushed about above him. Twigs snapped. Bruce hugged the rock face, trying to keep out of sight, but there was nowhere to go. In seconds, his assailants would lean over the ledge and see him there.

And then they would kill him.

Something about this realization calmed his horror. Bruce had enlisted to serve his nation. Land, sea, air, and space . . . these were fronts to be defended, risks be damned. But if he was going to die, there was still something he could do, to prevent his knowledge dying with him. A way for the Ebisu crew to be spared from further harm, while also alerting USSF to this dreadful new attack vector.

Fumbling with his wrist-phone, Bruce pressed RECORD.

He spilled it all. In a quick, low voice he explained what he knew. The augmented reality hacks. The device still in his pocket. The presence of enemy hostiles a few miles from base.

Then he set the message for auto-delivery to Major Markowitz in the next five minutes. By then, he'd be dead. The satellite would no longer be jamming him. The message would send.

And hopefully it wouldn't be too late.

He glanced toward the few stars that remained in the sky. A man in dark clothing leaned over the ledge. Bruce stared helplessly into the rifle's muzzle as he was lined up in his sights.

Gunshots thundered over the canyon.

In the moments before death, Bruce imagined he was back at his office in Orbital Warfare. He imagined it so vividly that it was as if he'd hacked his own field of vision. There would be hot coffee. Emails to go through. The day's briefing. The operations center, where USSF personnel—his fellow guardians of the high frontier—were each doing their part to keep *Semper Supra.*

It took him half a minute to realize he was still alive. The gunshots still echoed in the canyon, but strangely enough, none of them had hit him. The man above him was gone.

What the hell?

Numbly, with extreme wariness, Bruce climbed the short way back to the ledge. Then he saw his attacker, dead on the forested slope. The two other men had likewise been killed. Two armed soldiers in USSF fatigues saw him.

Bruce's earpiece chimed.

"Captain?" It was Major Markowitz. "Are you all right?"

"S-sir?"

"Page 54 of your report," the major said. "'In the event of suspected hostilities, security should be tightened and surveillance on key personnel increased.' I sent a car to intercept you. Seems they reached you just in time."

Bruce struggled to get his thoughts in order. "Sir! You need to contact the mission crew! The enemy can—"

"Can hack augmented-reality displays? My sister just called me to tell me about your conversation. Do you need medical attention?"

"I don't think so."

"Then get back to base. We have a lot to do, Captain."

"Yes, sir."

The guardians formed a protective escort around him as he shuffled back to his vehicle. They were asking him if he was okay. Bruce heard himself answer them. As he reached the car, his eyes flicked skyward.

The brightening sky had banished most of the stars, but he knew they were still up there. An entire frontier of dangers and hopes waited, beyond his sight.

But not beyond our protection, he thought.

When he arrived back at base, a hot coffee was waiting for him.

✵ ✵ ✵

Brian Trent is the award-winning author of the sci-fi thrillers *Redspace Rising* and *Ten Thousand Thunders,* and more than a hundred short stories in the world's top fiction markets, including the *New York Times* best-selling Black Tide Rising series, *The Magazine of Fantasy & Science Fiction, Analog Science Fiction and Fact, Nature, Daily Science Fiction, Escape Pod, Pseudopod, Galaxy's Edge*, and numerous year's best anthologies. He lives in Connecticut. His website and blog are at www.briantrent.com.

Eye in the Sky

✧

Jody Lynn Nye

"Detaching cargo from the ISS," the mission commander's voice announced over the intercom.

"Roger," said the shuttle pilot. "Preparing to intercept."

From her nondescript office in Nebraska, Space Force Lieutenant Nela Ferrar nodded to herself and watched multiple angles on her tri-screen array as the cylinder with the fixed wing floated out from the open bay of the International Space Station and ambled at *2001: A Space Odyssey* speeds toward the camera over the capture arm of the Gryphon space shuttle. Her job was to monitor cameras from around the world and aboard hundreds of satellites circling above Earth, but her favorite leisure activity was peeking in on the space station's mission.

She could see the small cargo lighter at three different angles. The resolution was so clear that she could read its registration numbers and even see the scratches along the white ceramic sides of the well-used container. Like the shuttle, it had wings, but where Gryphon's was a true spaceplane, the lighter was only a glider, needing help from the shuttle or some other craft to begin its deorbit at the right time and place.

It had paced the ISS through the black shadow of the thermosphere as the blue-and-white planet spun below them, but had just crossed into daylight, giving observers the best possible view.

The banter between the approaching shuttle and the ISS sounded like a couple of people who knew each other pretty well.

"Commander McKenzie, you sure you don't want to hop in? We'll be back on Earth within twenty-four hours!"

A hearty baritone responded with a derisive laugh. "You think I trust you to fly me anywhere? The way you drive a jeep, you shouldn't be at the helm of a kiddie car!"

Snorts of laughter erupted in the background. Nela smiled.

As one of the staff of observers the Space Force maintained, Nela had thousands of feeder cams all over the world, but she felt a special connection with the space station. Half a dozen of her fellow guardians, officers, and civilian specialists were deployed onboard, carrying out experiments and generally training for missions off-planet, when that happy day would come. On the two screens flanking the center one, she had rotating views of the other myriad cameras, making sure that the U.S. and its allies were protected from airborne incursions.

A *ping!* came from her personal pad device sitting on the desk beside her keyboard.

Not now! she thought at it. She glanced at the clock in the lower corner of her screen and realized that her friends stationed in Japan must be awake and ready for her to play the next round in Lightspeed Stars, the MMORPG that had been occupying all her hours that weren't devoted to sleep, food, or duty. There had to be a thousand Space Force members on the servers, only a percent of which she knew by IRL names. Everyone else, herself included, went by a pseudonym. She was DevilInABlueDressUniform. The game stretched dexterity and reflexes to the breaking point, as players had to follow tiny ships through scientifically unrealistic asteroid fields and keep them from crashing into heavenly bodies or each other at blinding speeds. Sometimes, though, you just had to smash up your ship for the fun of it. The effects were spectacular. In fact, the graphics had advanced to the point where she had almost come to believe in some of the game-based planets as much as she believed in Earth. Her favorite ship, *Orion's Kneecap*, had battle scars from surviving dozens of close calls. She had flown with the same team of players for months now, and had only met one of them in real life, a gunnery sergeant from Canada.

She glanced back to the image of the shuttle, just in time to hear the pilot speak.

"Oops!"

"Oops?" the commander's voice demanded. "What do you mean, 'oops'?"

"Sir, I mean, it's the glare—I'll fix it!"

But anyone could see the problem. The floating cargo lighter had missed the open claw and was moving away beneath the ISS. It was decelerating, rapidly falling behind both craft. Voices shouted in Nela's ears as the mechanical arm flailed after it.

"What the hell is wrong with you?" the commander bellowed.

"It's . . . it's venting, sir!" the pilot said. He sounded aghast, and Nela felt sympathy. As the shuttle broke away from its matching orbit, Nela switched to the feed on the craft's nose.

Only because the ISS was in the forty-five minutes of its passage over the daylight side of the planet could she see the bright narrow plume shooting out from the nose of the lighter, pushing it ever farther away. It often took a day or more for a departing craft to return to Earth, mostly to let its orbit align with the desired landing. With the jet slowing it down, the loose lighter might descend dramatically faster.

Nela's heart turned over. The lighter would survive reentry, and could even land on a runway if it came down over one, but with no control over the retro-thrust and its stubby little wings, it would probably fall into the sea or crash in the wilderness, and the contents would surely be lost.

"Beginning calculations," said a new voice, a woman with a clipped accent. "Posting potential arcs of reentry."

"Dammit!" the commander exclaimed. "You couldn't have dropped a load of dirty underwear! It had to be this one!"

Nela immediately wondered what was in it, but knew it was none of her business. Still, if the commander was this upset, chances were that it contained either the results of experiments, defense department data, or both.

Before Nela realized she had spoken, she heard her own voice.

"Mission Control, this is Argus Observation Post in Omaha. Lieutenant Nela Ferrar, identification number SF-3662. I can help track the lighter."

There was a brief but perceptible pause, owing to the distance from Earth to the space station and back again.

"You?" the commander asked, with the same scornful tones of some of the male gamers she played with. She flinched a little, but steeled her spine. "Who's your CO, Lieutenant?"

"General Stantis," she replied. "I can patch you through to him. But, sir, let me help now while you are speaking. Send me those charts."

She heard him mutter something about females and dexterity. Despite her concern for the payload and sympathy for the pilot, that comment raised her hackles. She had heard snipes like that all too often, but she had fine motor skills most of the men didn't. She liked beating those players through the tight mazes all the way to the goal, and doing a mic drop on the way out. But she couldn't do that to a superior officer.

"It couldn't hurt, sir," said the clipped voice. "We're calculating dozens of potential landing zones, but anything to reduce the number of sites might be useful."

"All right!" McKenzie said. "Let me talk to Stantis!"

"Connecting you now," Nela said, patching the call in, though she never took her eyes from the screen. At the same time, she heard the honk from her email system. Clipped Voice had given her the whole kitchen sink. It was a live function, constantly updating. As the now-invisible lighter descended, the calculations altered, tightening the circle second by second. The target was still hundreds of miles across, though.

Her hands flew over the keyboard. On her side screens, she pulled up all of the earthbound and satellite-mounted cameras in the wake of the ISS.

A musical female voice answered the call.

"General Stantis's office, Staff Sergeant Marelle Baker speaking."

"Lieutenant Nela Ferrar here. Commander McKenzie on the ISS wishes to speak to the general."

"Oh! Let me see if he is in." After a brief but gut-wrenching pause, Baker returned.

"Holding for Commander McKenzie," she said. Nela put the officer through, still glancing back and forth between the screens and the plotted descent of the lighter.

"Commander, good to hear from you," General Stantis said in his hearty voice. Nela knew she ought to close the circuit, but didn't. The voices of the two men floated back and forth between Earth and space.

"General, we've got a situation . . ."

There! Nela found a camera in Sri Lanka and one in southeastern India pointing up toward the heavens. They picked up a streak of sunlight moments apart. Nela entered the coordinates into the spreadsheet sent to her by Clipped Voice. Instantly, three of the trajectories vanished, and the rest updated, shrinking the target area further. She was aware of the conversation going on, catching the occasional word.

". . . Your officer was watching the handover . . . failure . . . interference . . ."

". . . Offer cooperation . . . time . . . competent . . . content . . . ?"

". . . Classified! Need to know . . . effective . . . ?"

"Dammit, Commander!" Stantis's voice came through loud and clear, dragging Nela's attention to the connection. "Ferrar is the best at this! Don't revert to the 1950s, man! I doubt you were even born then. You don't have a lot of time to plan an intercept!"

A lot of grumbling followed, but in the end, McKenzie gave in. What choice did he have? The Gryphon shuttles were contractors. Maybe the pilot had made an error, maybe as a result of SANS, Spaceflight-Associated Neuro-ocular Syndrome, which caused visual impairments, or maybe just butterfingers or a malfunction, but the fact remained an accident had happened. It sounded like the lighter contained classified material, meaning they didn't want it to land, say, in the Australian outback for anyone to pick up.

"Ferrar is assigned to this exclusively as of now," Stantis continued. "She's good. I will assign her to oversee the entire retrieval. This isn't a goddamned video game like the ones I know you play. She is taking this seriously. You can count on that."

Nela's ears perked up. In spite of herself, she wanted to know which game.

"Yes, General," McKenzie said glumly. "I'll be monitoring her progress."

"I'll see to it that you're patched in on everything," the general said. "Stantis out."

A pause while McKenzie "hung up." "I just lied through my teeth about you, Ferrar. Don't let me down. Pull in anyone you need on this. You've got a blank check. Make the Space Force proud."

"Yes, sir!" Nela said, feeling her cheeks burn. But she pulled up her big-girl panties and buckled down. "How often do you want a report, sir?"

"Just tell me when you locate the damned thing. Stantis out."

"Yes, sir!"

The space station had pinpointed the precise location where they had lost control of the capsule. That drew the parameters tighter yet, but the target still covered an ellipse of a few hundred kilometers. By now, she was getting input from a host of other observers, in the Space Force and the Air Force, not to mention allies from around the world.

"What's in it?" came a curious question from a Canadian observation post in Winnipeg.

"None of my business," Nela said, trying not to sound arrogant.

"Gawd, the brass won't even tell you what you need to know," the Canadian said jovially. "Sympathy, Space Force."

"Thanks, RCAF."

Nela consolidated the data as it flooded in. From the best calculations coming from Clipped Voice and a growing host of others putting in their two cents, it looked as though the landing zone was likely to be at the junction of North and South America.

The mark of a good officer, Nela had always had hammered into her, was to delegate responsibilities. She sent a copy of Stantis's orders to her immediate superior, Captain Delavoir. He sent immediate approval, for which she was thankful. Within minutes, her message service was pinging with logins from other Space Force observers from around the world.

She sent a link to a meeting room on a scrambled online service, but diminished the window so she wouldn't have to take her eyes off the trio of screens.

"What happened, Lieutenant?" Staff Sergeant Lou Furimoto asked. He was stationed at Cape Canaveral.

"An accident with the transfer of a lighter from the space station to a shuttle," she explained. Although the moment had been recorded, blaming and shaming weren't her intention. The pilot had to have felt bad enough. "It's venting . . . on its way earthward. I need everyone not on a vital assignment to help track the lighter. Contents are classified." She punched Clipped Voice's content into the chat window. "Here's the calculations on its descent. At the moment, it looks like it's heading for Panama or Colombia."

"Shit," opined Lieutenant Wanda Dieter. Nela knew Wanda from Boot. She was detail-oriented as hell, but blunt in her expressions, hence her present assignment in Nome, Alaska. "ETA?"

"Sixteen hours, maybe less," Nela said. "I'll have to watch the logarithms. Depending on air speed, wind shear, and a hundred other variables, it could start tumbling and fall straight down into the ocean long before that. I need eyes and ideas, people!"

"USAF here, from AFB Palanquero, Ferrar," came a deep voice. "We're all yours."

"Us too!" a lighter tenor put in. "This is AFB Tyndall, Panama City."

"Gotcha!" added a hearty soprano. "Honolulu here. Just spotted the target going by overhead. Here's video!" A file appeared in the chat. "Trajectory continuing as per your data."

More and more stations chimed in. A reluctant acknowledgment came from the ISS. She knew the commander on board was angry, embarrassed, or both, to have to accept help from the Space Force, but that was what it was there for.

"Thanks, everyone," Nela said, feeling honored and humbled by the cooperation she was getting. Air Force bases, ships at sea, observatories on every continent. Even an orbiting space telescope had begun a majestic turn in the skies to focus on the path the lighter was taking. Between the software and the input from every station, she ought to be able to predict the landing zone of the lighter within ten meters by two hours from impact. She sent out messages to each of the bases in the target area to ask about retrieval and negotiations with the governments of the potential target. Panama would cooperate, but Colombia or Venezuela would want some kind of beneficial exchange. That wasn't up to Nela; she would just send the requests up the chain of command and let them negotiate. They had a little time. Her job was just to find the lighter and make sure it got picked up. So far, she had faith in the technology, and the spirit of cooperation between corps.

But nothing good lasts forever. An insistent *ping* came from her personal phone. She didn't recognize the number, nor the numerous ones that followed, each leaving messages. Nela saw previews, most of them beginning with the word URGENT!

Then, an intranet call came in.

"Ferrar," she said, sparing only a glimpse at the screen.

"Lieutenant, this is Lieutenant Briggs St. John," a brisk male voice with a New England accent announced. "Turn on your camera, please."

"I'm in the middle of a very important assignment and need to stay focused on my visuals," Nela replied. She didn't move a finger toward the touchscreen. People were so used to face-to-face meetings on computer these days, when a phone call would do almost all of the time. "How may I assist you?"

"I'm the public affairs officer for the space station. Have you transmitted any information to news media about this incident?"

"No, of course not," Nela said, stifling an inward groan. PAOs were a necessary evil, but she had had run-ins with them before that convinced her that the "evil" could be a more prominent characteristic than "necessary." "I have only communicated with military bases and astronomical observatories, as per my instructions from my commanding officer."

"Well, somehow"—St. John made it sound accusatory—"the media has gotten a hold of the news about the lighter. I'm being slammed with queries about its contents and mission. What have you told them?"

"Nothing," Nela said. She kept her voice level. The call was probably being recorded. PAOs liked to cover their own asses. "I don't know what's in the lighter, and it has no bearing on my assignment. I don't have to have released any information. We're not the only people out there with eyes on the sky, you know. Nothing that happens in space is a secret! Once you launch something, anyone with a telescope can see it. And they're everywhere. NASA has its own feed, and that's public access. I bet a hundred thousand people saw the drop! And they might even have a better idea where the lighter is than we do," she added, with a touch of malice.

"That is outrageous!" St. John said, as if it was her fault. "We need to make this look good for the space station. And the Space Force," he added, making certain that she knew it was a very minor afterthought.

"Sounds like your job, sir," Nela said. She didn't have time to worry about his ego. "Unless you need something specific from me, I need to focus on my mission. May I suggest you get in touch with General Stantis? He's the one who assigned me to observe the descent."

St. John growled low under his breath. "Make sure you clear any release of information through my office. I'm texting you my office number."

"Of course, sir," Nela said. "Ferrar out." She hit the disconnect. Her heart raced. She hadn't been this nervous when she volunteered to trace the lighter, but being held responsible for a potential breach of information security? That frightened her. When the retrieval seemed like a big video game, it felt almost fun. With bureaucracy intruding, she was yanked back into the real world. Her gamer buddies would call it a minor boss battle. Did she "win" in her conversation with the PAO?

No, the only win that mattered was getting the lighter back safely. Nela reached for her coffee carafe and thumbed back the seal. The contents were cold, but a jolt of caffeine gave her a momentary feeling of confidence.

She checked her charts. Its downward spiral meant that, by now, the lighter had circled the Earth and was nearly back at the same point where it had dropped away. Tracking cameras all around the globe gave her momentary views of the little cylinder. She felt sorry for it, and sorrier still for the shuttle pilot.

Calculations on the live spreadsheet from Clipped Voice, whom she now knew was Technical Sergeant Caroll Bissette in Joint Base Andrews, Maryland, updated to the point that Nela believed with some certainty that southern Colombia or northern Venezuela would be the lighter's landing site. The moment she knew it, the rest of the world did too. Space enthusiasts with telescopes and computers were sharing information back and forth all over the internet, and more than one of Nela's correspondents passed along some insanely clear pictures of the lighter as it passed within range. She added that data to her simulation. Yep, Colombia. She passed that information up to Delavoir, asking politely for updates on cooperation with the governments in Bogota or Caracas.

"Going AFK for five," she told the group chat. "Bio break."

"Go for me, too, will ya?" Honolulu asked. "My relief is late, and I gotta go down two floors to the can."

"I'll do my best," Nela said with a chuckle.

When she stood up, her rear was numb, and her legs almost collapsed underneath her. The digital clocks on the wall and in the corner of her many screens told her that more than five hours had passed since the botched handoff. She stretched, trying to work feeling back into her lower body.

But where was her relief? Reese was normally prompt, even early.

When she tried to leave the monitoring center, she discovered a roadblock: two large MPs wearing solemn expressions.

"Do you know where Lieutenant Reese is?" she asked them.

"This area is restricted until the current mission is resolved, ma'am," the first one said.

"Seriously? I'm supposed to sit out twenty hours on my own?"

"It's important, ma'am," the other added.

"I know that! Can someone at least bring me fresh coffee?"

The two exchanged glances. "I think that can be arranged," the first one said, although he sounded uncertain.

She shook her head and headed for the bathrooms, a line of four individual doors across the hall marked for all genders.

"Where are you going, ma'am?" one of them asked, stepping into her path.

"The can," she said, and pointed. They were less than four meters away.

"One of us will have to accompany you, ma'am," the first guard said, with an apologetic glance. "Please leave all technology here."

She rolled her eyes, but strode across the hallway. The guard glanced inside before letting her enter. It was a one-holer, so there was no way to pass anything under the stall to someone else.

The sentries would have been better off checking her technology. When she returned to her desk—and, thankfully, a fresh cup of coffee beside her central monitor—dozens of messages, pings, and other queries had flooded in on the chat. Her phone started dancing across the desk, buzzing with irritation.

Bissette had updated the stats. The wobble Nela had feared was increasing with every sweep the lighter made around the planet. It caused the stubby craft to descend even faster. Heart beating like a castanet, Nela scanned all of the new information. Had it changed trajectory too?

Her phone lit up again. Another call from Briggs St. John.

Before she could speak, he snapped at her. "I've got word that the Russians are communicating with rebels in Venezuela and Colombia, offering them bribes to take the lighter when it lands. The drug lords will cooperate with them. Can you guarantee that U.S.-friendly forces will retrieve it ahead of them?"

Nela, her eyes fixed on her rapidly updating map, clenched her stomach muscles to avoid shouting at him. She felt her nose getting hot.

"Sir, with all due respect, I can't guarantee anything! I'm not there! I can only estimate the lighter's trajectory, and that changes with every minute."

"Well, what do they know that we don't know?"

"Nothing," Nela said, her patience at an end. "I bet if you get off the line and go Google it, you'll see the same video I did five hours ago. In fact, it's almost certainly the lead story on the evening news everywhere. I respectfully request that you get in touch with General Stantis and tell him to order me to fly into the South American jungle with a catcher's mitt and catch the thing just before it hits ground to make sure no Russian agent intercepts it instead. Please excuse me, I have to concentrate."

She cut the connection. She would almost certainly get flak for her comment, but she didn't care. A sip of coffee, much tastier than she usually got from the junior officers' mess, suggested that despite the PAO holding her personally responsible for his increasingly bad day, someone out there appreciated her.

Hour after hour, she rotated between the updating charts and the tiny flash of light streaking across the screen over oceans, mountains, and plains. True to his word, General Stantis had left authority to her. The responsibility felt overwhelming, but she was touched by the number of people who reached out to offer their support. Fresh cups of coffee and even a lunch tray were delivered to her desk by people outside her field of view. Hands moving into her periphery and out again, without disturbing her, were all she saw. She promised herself she wouldn't let them or the Space Force down.

Closer and closer to the Earth the small lighter came. From the original altitude of four hundred kilometers, it had spiraled down to under a hundred. When it hit the stratosphere, its path would be impacted by weather, and by the time it descended into the troposphere, chances are she could lose sight of it among clouds. But she had input from dozens, if not hundreds, of amateur skywatchers alongside the official observers. Someone had shared one of her accounts, so she received scrolling messages from well-wishers, but among them were trolls, and even threats.

"Your government is bringing alien spores to Earth to wipe us all out!" one "anonymous" message ranted. "If it lands, you and all of your coconspirators are going to die!"

Nela just passed all the weirdo transmissions up to the PAO and Captain Delavoir. She had to keep monitoring. She ran a diagnostic to make sure she hadn't actually been hacked. The computer burbled for a minute, then spat out its findings: nothing. She heaved a sigh of relief. No amateurs, then. She couldn't keep out the pros, so she must not let that prey on her mind.

As zero hour came closer, her nerves began screaming at her. What if she lost sight of the device? What happened if, after all her attention, it still fell into the wrong hands? She was dying to boot up Lightspeed Stars and get a little relief by blowing up enemy spacecraft. She had to blink almost constantly, as her eyes burned from focusing on the screens so intently. She no longer felt her body beneath the waist. All that coffee must have been pooling in her bladder. When she eventually got up, gravity would tell her what a fool she had been. She popped vitamins B-12 and C to stay alert. It wouldn't be her first all-nighter, but it was the tensest one on record since her philosophy final.

"How are you holding up?" Bissette asked. Even her precise diction wavered from its earlier perfection.

"I'll get there," Nela said.

How was she supposed to make certain that the lighter was secure once it landed? The tightening landing zone looked to be square in the middle of the Colombian jungle. The PAO was right about invading drug-lord territory. The U.S. would not negotiate with terrorists, and the cartels fell right into that zone. Still, the Russians were playing with fire, thinking that a deal with the cocaine barons would go completely their way. The drug lords were just as likely to take the lighter hostage and play both sides for a substantial ransom.

So, how were the Russians planning to make sure they got the cargo? Surely they didn't actually have boots on the ground. Or not many.

Technology. The only real answer, and the place where she felt sure she had the advantage. She leaned into her microphone.

"AFB Palanquero?"

"Roger," a hearty tenor voice said, after an audible throat clearing.

"This is Argus Observation Post. Looks like ground zero is going to be right in your neck of the woods," Nela said. She zoomed in from an orbiting camera, one capable of more than ten thousand times magnification. Night with a narrowing half-moon painted that sliver of terrain with pale blue. She scanned over jungles, cliffs, and heavy undergrowth, striped with narrow, glinting rivers, bordering square patches of gray farmland that in an hour or less would burst in a thousand shades of brilliant green. "What kind of air cover can you give my package coming in?"

Palanquero sounded as though he sat straight up in his chair. "Well, shit, Argus, if you give the order, I can arrange to blow hell out of miles of jungle until we can see the landing crater."

Just for a minute, she loved the idea just for the visuals, but firmly tamped it down. Real human beings and their animals lived there, not to mention some endangered wildlife. And she could just imagine what General Stantis and Commander McKenzie would say. She shook her head.

"No way. It'll ruin too many people's day. How fast can your forward observation drones move?"

"Not fast enough to track incoming from outer space, unfortunately. But we have got lots of them, and the Spec Force ops on base have the best toys. Want me to patch in the commander?"

Nela smiled at the moving map on her central screen.

"Please do, Palanquero. I'll wait."

After a while, a woman's voice joined them. "Captain Edelman, Argus. To whom do I have the pleasure of speaking?"

The crispness of her tones made Nela sit up straighter herself. "Space Force, ma'am." She gave a quick briefing on the descending cargo lighter, at that moment transiting over Saudi Arabia, and explained her idea.

"You want to line the forests from the coast to the interior with drones?" Edelman asked, her tone harsh with sarcasm.

"We shouldn't have to, ma'am." Nela pulled up the calculations. "I can give you a corridor about fifty meters wide..."

At that moment, the chart started flipping on her. The numbers tumbled over one another, and the map went wild. What was happening?

"Hold on, Argus," Bissette snapped out. "Unclear what's causing this, maybe something to do with that tropical storm in the Pacific? But the target is losing altitude rapidly. We're going to lose a revolution."

Nela watched the video in dismay. She pulled up as many relays as she could on the lighter's track. The little craft seemed to be tossed up in the air, then dragged down, like a fish being played with by a seal.

Nela gasped, staring at the screen. She pulled feed after feed, trying to catch up with the errant lighter. At last, she caught sight of it east of India, at a dismayingly low altitude. "Captain, hold the line a minute."

"With you, Argus."

"Calculating," Bissette said, her precise voice calm. "Changing ETA. I now estimate only one full orbit before landing. On the other hand, it narrows the landing path."

"Got you," Nela said, following the new calculations. "Captain, it's going to come in south of you, near AFB Apy-yay?"

"Apiay," Edelman corrected her pronunciation. "I can arrange for cooperation. How long have we got?"

"One hour fifteen minutes, as near as I can estimate." She sent the revised flight path to Edelman.

"I'll have them scramble all the drones we can send out and notify my opposite number at the Colombian bases, and get some helicopters in the air above your potential landing site. I'll get back to you ASAP. Edelman out."

The channel closed. Nela hung over the scope, willing the little craft not to hit any more surprises.

Between the long night and the adrenaline, she could feel her brain trying to shut down behind her eyes. Touch-typing, she sent out information to Captain Delavoir, Lieutenant St. John, and to the rest of her chain of command updating them, devil take all her typographical errors. St. John must have had as much coffee as she had, and immediately began blowing up her phone. She ignored his calls. Worried every moment she might miss something, she took a hasty bathroom break, vowing it would be the last until all this was over. The hallway outside her office was dark, and two new guards had taken over from the first two. They eyed her warily, but didn't dare to ask how things were going.

With every wobble on the scope, Nela grew more concerned about the lighter's flight path. Edelman copied her in on the communiqués between her and the flights at both Air Force bases. The lighter had started its last circuit of planet Earth. Dawn had broken in full over Nebraska and South America, and she waited for the cargo lighter to burst out of the night terminator to the western Pacific Ocean.

"Scrambling fully charged drones to the new location," Edelman said. "Six on the coast, twenty arrayed at key points within your target location. They can be adjusted at a moment's notice. Just FYI, unmarked craft are also in the area, estimated twenty UFOs. Advise?"

"Are any of our drones armed?" Nela sent back. It was a flippant reply, but Edelman took it seriously.

"Three."

"Can I get linked to the forward cameras on a drone?" she asked eagerly. "At least one of them? I want to follow the lighter in."

"I can do better than that," Edelman said. "Can you fly a drone?"

"Can I?" Hell, yes! she thought. All her weariness and aches melted away. "I'm flight qualified on remotes as well as cargo aircraft. I also play Lightspeed Stars. Level eighty-seven."

Edelman's voice rose in delight. "No kidding? Me too! I'll have to join your server when all this is over. Let me get my operations center to hook you up."

Nela waited impatiently for the feed to open. The lighter emerged from the night terminator and into the rising sun over the ocean. It was moving fast. When it hit, it was going to bury itself deep. Considering the depths of the forest, she had to home in on the lighter and keep it in her sights as best she could. The fastest drone she knew of could go approximately 225 miles per hour. The lighter was coming in at about the same speed. If she could pace it, she could stay with it to impact and, she hoped, stay with it until an American crew could retrieve it.

She linked to all of the other Space Force observers worldwide.

"I've got to focus on this craft," she explained. "I'm turning all of my usual scan programs over to you until further notice."

"Envy, envy," said Tyndall. "It's gonna be a wild ride. I'd love to piggyback on you."

"I don't know if that's possible," Nela said. "But maybe the video can be declassified later."

To a chorus of disappointment, she clicked off and went back to Palanquero.

"Where's the package now?" the captain asked. Nela shared her screens.

"Less than a hundred kilometers off the coast of South America." With satisfaction, she added, "It's right in the zone, ma'am. Latitude 34.0216."

"Drones deploying, Argus. Lieutenant Souter, you with us?"

"Yes, ma'am!" a very deep voice with a Texas accent jumped in. "Patching you into the visuals, Argus."

On her side screens, Nela suddenly had visuals of a swath of green and dark-brown treetops. They were going fast, but not too fast to follow. She picked the left-hand drone and moved the video into her center screen. The cargo lighter and the calculations still occupied the right-hand screen.

"You want to take over now?" Texas asked.

"Give me a chance to try out the controls," Nela said.

"It's easy. They're all based on console first-person shooters these days," Texas added, humor in his voice. "Plus a couple of special commands." He explained those, and Nela typed a note to pin to the right side of her screen. She made the drone rise and fall, then flew an Immelmann, narrowly missing a tall branch sticking out of the forest crown. "You're now designated Drone One. Welcome to the flight."

"I've got helicopters in the area," Edelman said. "Once we pinpoint the landing zone, four MH-6 birds are ready to drop in."

"Heads up!" AFB Apiay barked. "Eight—no, nine uglies just popped up on my readout." He shared the view, obviously onboard another drone. Nela stared. The small flyers were almost invisible against the thick forest, but she could see four rotors whirling at the corners of a central base. Their sleek design and camouflage paint job suggested Russian military drones.

"Where are they from us?" Nela asked.

"Ten klicks," Apiay said. The display showed a terrain map with the U.S. flight picked out in blue, and the Russians in black. "Closing fast. Wow! They can move." Hot red light erupted from the body of the lead craft. "Oh, shit! They're armed."

"So are we," Texas said, his voice level.

Nela kept an eye on the lighter. Not only did she have satellite views, but coastal cameras were tracking the incoming vessel. The lighter had burnt streaks along its side, probably from reentry through the atmosphere, but looked intact. *You'll be mine in a minute*, she thought at it.

The lighter streaked over the shoreline, over the towns on the coast, and into the interior. It was so low that Nela feared it would hit telecommunication towers on the way. Luckily, it missed everything, and plunged through the line of trees.

"Lost you," announced the observer reporting from the GOES-West satellite. "Switching to infrared."

"On visual!" a woman's voice crowed. "Drone Four falling in behind."

Suddenly, Nela caught a glimpse of white hurtling through the trees. The lighter appeared and disappeared, as it played havoc with the local greenery. She imagined monkeys and parrots screaming at it as they scrambled to safety.

She spun the drone and revved the electric motors up to full. She felt fond of it, as though she was seeing an old friend. The last time she had seen the lighter this close was off the monitors on the nose of the Gryphon shuttle. She let it hurtle past her, and thrust the controls to full to stay on its tail. The craft was large enough to mow down trees. Nela had to pull back in order not to have any of the falling timber hit her rotors.

"Incoming!" Drone Four announced.

It felt like a live-action game of Lightspeed Stars. On the infrared scope provided by GOES-West, she saw the bogeys homing in on them from the north. A few blue streaks peeled off to engage them and try to keep them from following the cargo lighter. They circled one another like dogfighters.

By now, the lighter would be hunting for a landing strip to steer for, but it just wasn't going to find one. The farther they flew, the jungle became thicker and thicker. Nela had to do some neat Han Solo moves to stay behind the lighter, turning the drone on its side to slide between tree trunks. A cluster of lianas, set free by the cargo craft's destruction, slithered down in front of her. She spun a hundred eighty degrees to avoid it, then switched back, throttling up to get back on the lighter's tail. At least one of her companions and a Russian fell prey to the vines.

Nela felt sweat running down her back. With the exhilaration of the chase, she forgot all about her full bladder, the numbness of her legs, and her exhaustion from sitting up for over eighteen hours. A suspension bridge rose out of nowhere. The lighter, thankfully, was too low to crash into any of the supports, and too high to drop into the river, but it wouldn't be long now. Its momentum had slowed drastically because of the impacts with branches in the canopy. Her computer estimated the time of impact to under three minutes, maybe less. She started a countdown on her left screen.

"Two on your tail," Texas said. "Comin' up fast."

She gave the infrared map the briefest glance. Now that she knew the trajectory of the lighter, she didn't have to stay precisely on its tail.

Almost as if she could feel the fingers on the trigger, she dropped the drone two meters, and saw a red tracer zing over her head. She laughed out loud. Although she had never been a combat pilot, she'd dodged plenty of similar attacks on her six in the online game. Watching the map for breaks in the terrain, she planned out a series of maneuvers, hoping to avoid strikes. The two Russians came up to meet her. Red tracers pinged past her, above and below. They were bracketing her for the kill.

She narrowed her eyes gleefully. Hadn't she spent too many wasted hours honing her skills for just this kind of encounter? Hundreds of old movies, newsreels from the 1940s on forward, and battle after battle against competitive players worldwide. Maybe one or both of the drone pilots facing her had been in the game as well?

"What are my armaments?" she asked Texas.

"You got two missiles, one under each arm," he replied. "Control-D and Control-K launch. They'll throw you into a wobble."

"Got it," Nela said, her fingers running over the controls, her eyes intent on the screen.

The seconds counted down rapidly. She needed to be there when the lighter landed, so she took off for the treetops. The Russians followed, still firing. She kept shifting, keeping her movements irregular.

Only the falling trees and birds exploding out of the undergrowth heralded the path of the lighter. The faint infrared trace from residual reentry heat was fading quickly. She angled the drone down into the path of destruction. The Russians followed her.

Almost as soon as she dropped into the canopy, she spun the forward left rotor and zipped off through a gap in the trees. The Russians hesitated for a moment, then followed. Nela led them on a merry chase under branches and through nearly imperceptible gaps in the undergrowth. She was all too aware of the countdown going on in the corner of her screen.

The scenery took a major wobble, and her right rear rotor refused to respond to her controls. They'd hit her!

No more time to lose. Nela took several more abrupt turns and angled upward. Her speed had dropped to two thirds of maximum as the battery kept trying to feed the damaged rotor. The two enemy craft closed in, figuring she would retreat. She broke through the canopy.

No.

Instead, she spun on her three remaining rotors, homed in, and hit both missile controls. She was so close the Russians had no time to react. She hit one dead-on. It burst apart in a shower of parts. The other craft took a hit on its two right rotors and sagged lopsided into the canopy. She never saw it again.

Nela angled her drone toward the destruction the lighter was wreaking. The dogfight had taken less than a minute. The lighter was still on the move.

Only fifteen seconds to impact. Ten. She was just in time to spot the lighter through the trees before it disappeared in an explosion of greenery.

"Touchdown!" she cried. She reeled off her location, though it was already on the screen for anyone to read. "Homing in for retrieval." She circled around the site of the impact. No way to see the craft. It had dug itself a trench, then buried itself deep in the jungle floor.

Within moments, three other drones met her circling above the site.

"Helicopter on the way to your location," Edelman said. "Thank you, Argus. Nice work."

"Thanks." She settled the damaged drone on the ground. Its work was done.

"That was some fancy flying," Texas added. One of the American drones dipped its rotors as if in salute. "I caught some of that on my cameras! You want to come work with us? I could use someone with your reflexes."

"No, thanks," she said with a laugh. "I'm holding out for a Moon base assignment."

"Well, they'd be lucky to have you."

Another voice broke into the circuit. "I know that flying style!" a man exclaimed. "Dammit, are you DevilInABlueDressUniform? I'm NoParachute! We were in a tournament together two months ago. Why didn't you tell me who you were?"

It took her a minute to recognize the voice, and she gawked in flat-out astonishment. Not eighteen hours ago, it had been shouting at her. ". . . Commander McKenzie?"

"Call me Mike," McKenzie said. "Sorry about earlier. You can guess how we were feeling. But the Space Force really helped us out. I appreciate your vigilance. And your fancy flying."

"Happy to help," Nela said. She suddenly became aware how much her body ached from holding one position for so long. She let her arms drop and shook them. "That's what we're here for."

"That was above and beyond," McKenzie said. "I've got a call in to Stantis to thank him for interservice assistance. And I'll see you in the next tournament. It's in two weeks, isn't it?"

"Yes, it is." Nela grinned, as she watched the helicopters land in the jungle and Air Force personnel in camo jump out and race toward her cameras. "I'll beat you then too."

✿   ✿   ✿

Jody Lynn Nye is a *New York Times* and *USA Today* best-selling author of fantasy and science fiction books and short stories, many of them with a humorous bent. She's published more than 170 short stories and over 50 books, including her epic fantasy series, *The Dreamland*, contemporary humorous fantasies, medical science fiction novels, and more.

Before breaking away from gainful employment to write full time, Jody worked as a file clerk, photographer, accounting assistant and costume maker, and oh, as part of the engineering team that built a TV station, acted as technical director during live sports broadcasts, and worked to produce in-house spots and public service announcements.

More at jodynye.com.

The High Ground

✷

Henry Herz

Ocean City, FL, Sunday

Julie Harris's stomach rumbled as she finished her run shortly after sunset. She stretched her short, well-toned legs on the front porch of her Cape Cod-style home. The enticing aroma of steak and potatoes au gratin welcomed her as she pushed open the front door and unlaced her Nikes. *The midsoles are starting to compress.* "Dinner smells great, Bill."

After rehydrating and a quick shower, Julie threw on shorts and a U.S. Space Force T-shirt. She smiled upon entering the dining room—nice tablecloth, two lit candles, and her handsome blue-eyed husband uncorking a bottle of Châteauneuf-du-Pape. "Ooh, I'll take a glass of that, please."

Dessert consisted of Betty Crocker fudge brownies, slightly undercooked, just the way Julie liked them. "Dinner was delicious. But I can't help wondering if I'm being set up for some bad news from Hurlburt Field."

Bill sighed. "Am I that transparent?" He ran a hand through short-cropped brown hair. "The National Reconnaissance Office reports massive Chinese preparations for an assault on Taiwan. The works—amphibious forces, short-range ballistic missiles, airborne forces, submarines. The 73rd Special Operations Squadron has been ordered to deploy to Kadena Air Base on Okinawa. We ship out tomorrow."

Julie's throat tightened. The downside of marrying an AC-130J Ghostrider fire control officer. He's often flying into danger.

Bill pointed to the kitchen. "I'm afraid you'll be batching it for a while."

Julie took her husband's calloused hand. A knowing look passed between them, interrupted by her work phone ringing. The number displayed was from her office at Eglin Air Force Base. "Lieutenant Colonel Harris," she answered. "Uh-huh ... Uh-huh." *Crap.* "Very well, Sergeant. I'll see you tomorrow at oh-seven-hundred." She hung up and scowled.

Bill raised his eyebrows.

"A decommissioned Chinese weather satellite in polar orbit disintegrated. My team now has over two thousand more trackable pieces of debris to monitor."

"Is that unusual?" asked Bill, clearing the dishes.

"They're not sure if it was the result of a conjunction. But satellite high-pressure propellant tanks rarely rupture on their own ..." She stood. "Shit."

"What?"

Julie stood. "I get paid to be paranoid. So, given your news, I wonder if someone tested an antisatellite weapon. Knocking out our reconnaissance satellites would cripple our ability to respond to an attack on Taiwan."

Neither of them slept well that night.

Eglin Air Force Base, FL, Monday

Julie strode into the conference room at the headquarters of United States Space Force's 20th Space Surveillance Squadron. Her briefing team stood. "As you were. Any update on the Chinese weather satellite?"

"We double-checked the radar tracks and confirmed it wasn't struck by debris," replied her executive officer, Major Josh Waxler. "And we have no record of satellites of that model suffering spontaneous explosions."

Julie's face tightened. *Making it more likely it was an ASAT test.* "Very well. What's on the board for this week?"

Waxler ran through his PowerPoint, quickly covering routine

squadron operations. "There will be another bit of excitement on Thursday," he concluded. "The Chinese are expected to launch a Long March 9 from Jiuquan Satellite Launch Center."

Julie's eyes widened. "A super-heavy carrier rocket. Does Intelligence think the payload will be military?"

"No, ma'am. Their assessment is a supply delivery to the Tiangong space station."

Julie nodded. "Very well."

On his way out of Julie's office, Waxler turned. "Don't forget, ma'am, you've got that news interview in Pensacola at fourteen-hundred today. ABC local affiliate."

"I thought you got me out of that?"

Waxler shook his head. "Sorry, boss. Couldn't do it. Public Affairs says it's your turn in the barrel. And heads up regarding the guy who'll be interviewing you. He's more of a weatherman than a military-affairs reporter. He knows less about Space Force than my golden retriever."

"Roger that," Julie replied.

WEAR-TV Station, Pensacola, FL

A young, enthusiastic production assistant led Julie to the TV station's sound stage. "Ma'am, this is Fred Burns, our military-affairs reporter. Fred, this is Lieutenant Colonel Julie Harris."

"Actually, it's military-affairs *journalist*," corrected a man with a bushy mustache and receding hairline. Burns impatiently shooed away a makeup person, who barely had time to remove the paper towels protecting his out-of-style tweed blazer.

Douchenozzle, thought Julie.

"Welcome to our studio. May I call you Julie?"

"Since I'm here in uniform in an official capacity, Mr. Burns, it would be more appropriate if you addressed me by my rank."

His face reddening, Burns called cut, "Someone mic the *colonel*."

After introducing his guest, Burns went straight for the funny bone. "Is it true, Colonel, that members of Space Force are called guardians?" He winked at the camera. "As in *Guardians of the Galaxy?*"

Julie offered a made-for-TV smile. "Actually, Fred, the term comes from the Air Force Space Command's motto, 'Guardians of the High Frontier.'"

A scowl flitted across Burns's face. "And the delta symbol on Space Force's insignia looks awfully familiar." He broke eye contact with Julie to deliver his punchline to the camera. "Does Space Force owe royalties to Gene Roddenberry?"

Julie kept her face from sneering with an effort of will. *Do you really want to keep playing this game?* "That was funny when George Takei first tweeted it, but the reverse is true. Some U.S. Air Force unit emblems have featured a delta symbol since long before the original *Star Trek* series."

Burns gave it one last try before transitioning into a more serious tone. "What can you tell our viewers about Space Force that they can't learn from the Netflix series starring Steve Carell and John Malkovich?"

Finally.

Julie turned to the camera. "As I'm sure *you* know, Fred, access to space is critical not just to our national defense, but also to scientific research, communications, financial and economic information networks, public safety, and weather monitoring. Space Force's Operations Command is comprised of a number of Deltas, which are analogous to Air Force Wings. Space Delta 2 includes five squadrons and is responsible for space domain awareness. I have the honor of commanding the 20th Space Surveillance Squadron. Our primary job is to track objects in orbit."

"Kind of like space lifeguards," interjected Burns, "but without the sunblock. Forgive me, but that doesn't sound as exciting as flying space shuttles."

What a turdwhistle. Julie nodded. "Oh, it's very boring . . . until it isn't. Even a one-centimeter piece of junk"—her eyes flicked to Burns's crotch—"will ruin your day if it hits you at seventeen thousand miles an hour. Our job is very much to keep things as boring as possible. That's not easy because there are a *lot* of objects orbiting the planet. Between operational and retired spacecraft, rocket bodies, fragmentation and mission-related debris, and the occasional meteorite, we track tens of thousands of pieces of debris larger than a softball. There are half a *million* golf ball-sized fragments and millions of smaller items we can't track. Even flecks of paint can damage a spacecraft."

Burns spread his arms, attempting to make himself relevant. "But isn't space so vast that the chances of a collision are tiny?"

Julie offered Burns a steely gaze. "The International Space Station has had to maneuver dozens of times to avoid space junk. In 1996, a French satellite was damaged by fragments from a French rocket that had exploded a *decade* earlier. The impact created even more debris. Spacefaring nations need to do more to clean up the mess we make."

"Colonel, tell us about the wonderfully expensive toys you get to use."

Julie took a breath. "We operate GEODSS, AN/FPS-85, GSSAP, and Space Fence."

"Ah, the military loves their acronyms. What do those stand for?"

Julie warmed to her topic. "The Ground-based Electro-Optical Deep Space Surveillance network comprises telescopes in New Mexico, Hawaii, and Diego Garcia. The thirty-two-megawatt AN/FPS-85 phased array radar at Eglin can track a baseball-sized object in orbit at a 22,236-mile altitude. The Geosynchronous Space Situational Awareness Program uses orbiting telescopes to track geostationary objects. Space Fence ground-based radars monitor anything from low Earth orbit out to geostationary."

The director gestured for them to wrap up the interview.

"Well, I'm afraid that's all the time we have." Fred extended a hand. "Thank you for visiting us, Colonel. To infinity and beyond!"

Julie rolled her green eyes. *What a wankhammer.* She squeezed unnecessarily hard when they shook hands.

Jiuquan Satellite Launch Center, Gobi Desert, Thursday
The Chinese Long March 9 rocket towered 350 feet above Launch Area 4's pad SLS-1. After a flawless countdown, twenty-six 200-ton-thrust methane/liquid oxygen first-stage engines lit up, pushing the 165-ton rocket skyward with an ear-shattering roar. Trailing a silver-white column of smoke and flame, the Long March reached an altitude of forty miles. Explosive bolts fired, disconnecting the now-spent first stage, which would plummet to Earth like the metal casing of an enormous bullet. Four 120-ton-thrust hydrogen-oxygen second-stage engines fired, accelerating the rocket to 17,000 miles per hour. The sky transitioned from atmospheric blue to the black of

space. At an altitude of 240 miles, the second stage separated. The single-engine third stage inserted an unmanned Shenlong-3 spaceplane into low Earth orbit.

Over the next few hours, the Shenlong maneuvered next to a decommissioned Chinese communications satellite and matched its orbit. An operator at Jiuquan SLC directed a robotic arm to extend and gently grapple the satellite. After the satellite was stabilized and precisely positioned to the earthward side of the Shenlong, the arm deployed a small thruster pack from Shenlong's cargo bay. Neodymium magnets locked the pack to the side of the satellite.

Command signals from Jiuquan initiated the thruster pack on the satellite, nudging it earthward, where it subsequently burned up upon atmospheric reentry.

The spacecraft fired its thrusters, maneuvering for several hours toward a spent second stage from an old Long March 5 rocket. Over the next twenty-four hours, it successfully deorbited two more large pieces of debris.

The Shenlong deployed its fifth and final package on the inactive Xuntian space telescope. This package was larger and more sophisticated than the other four. Installation by the Shenlong's robotic arm took considerably longer, as it involved connecting the new hardware with the satellite's telescope control and power subsystems. The package's compact nuclear reactor provided electrical power, reactivating the Xuntian and reorienting its telescope earthward. Operators ran the sensor through an exhaustive series of tests. The reactor also powered a 50-megawatt linear accelerator.

Eglin AFB, FL, Friday

Major Waxler knocked on Julie's open office door. "Got a minute, ma'am?"

Julie set a staffing report down on her cluttered desk. "Sure. What's up, Josh?"

"Looks like the Chinese are cleaning up some of their orbital debris."

Julie's eyebrows rose. "Really? That's a welcome change."

"Yes, ma'am. The AN/FPS-85 has been tracking Thursday's Long

March launch. Intelligence assesses the payload as a Shenlong. Over the last thirty-six hours, the unmanned spacecraft docked with five large pieces of low-Earth-orbit debris, starting with a nonfunctional satellite. The Shenlong then executed a controlled reentry, successfully landing on the three-mile-long runway in the salt flats at Lop Nur in southeastern Xinjiang. Spy satellite imagery observed extensive scorch marks on the nose cone and wing leading-edge insulating tiles." Waxler scratched his chin. "The Shenlong's first four maneuvers succeeded in deorbiting junk, but the fifth attempt on a defunct Xuntian space telescope produced no observable effect."

Julie nodded. "Probably a malfunction in the fifth thruster pack or the comms link."

Low Earth Orbit, Monday

Directed by Chinese ground controllers, the reactivated telescope aboard the Xuntian slewed, locking onto a defunct Russian Meteor-1 weather satellite orbiting roughly fifty miles away. Target data was fed to the newly installed linear accelerator, which featured two long parallel electrodes separated by insulating spacers.

Receiving and twice confirming the order to fire, the rail gun formed a plasmoid sheet armature. A current pulse driven from one electrode, through the armature, to the other electrode, generated an immensely powerful magnetic field behind the armature. Since the current flowed perpendicular to the magnetic field, the armature experienced a Lorentz force, accelerating the plasmoid down the length of the rail gun.

The high-temperature slug of ionized particles hurtled toward the nonoperational weather satellite at 125 miles per second. The impact inflicted massive mechanical and thermal shocks, as well as a pulse of high-energy x-rays that would have scrambled the onboard electronics had the satellite not suffered catastrophic structural failure from the strike.

Eglin AFB, FL, Monday

Julie stood in the squadron's command and control center, a fresh coffee warming her left hand.

"Colonel, you're gonna want to see this," said a specialist four seated in front of a large monitor. "We just lost track on the old Meteor-1 satellite."

Frowning, Julie asked, "Could it be a sensor error or—"

"Space Fence detecting new fragments in the vicinity of Meteor-1, Colonel," reported a tech sergeant from three monitors over.

Julie strode over. "Sergeant, check the Space Fence logs over the last twelve hours for possible conjunction."

"Yes, ma'am."

Julie never drank that cup of coffee.

An hour later, Major Waxler rushed into her office. "Colonel, we've ruled out space debris collision with Meteor-1."

Julie's mouth tightened into a thin line. "How close to that inactive Xuntian was it at the time of destruction?"

Wexler sat and checked his ever-present laptop. "Roughly forty-eight miles, Colonel."

Close enough. I hope I'm wrong. Julie typed rapidly on her computer. "I'll have a GSSAP surveillance mission retasking for you in a few minutes, Josh."

Geosynchronous Orbit, Monday

Space Delta 2 regularly employed the electro-optical sensors of GSSAP satellites to view objects orbiting geosynchronously, 22,236 miles above the Earth. Upon receiving new observation tasking, one GSSAP telescope slewed earthward to track the Xuntian in low Earth orbit. The telescope zoomed in, transmitting images to Space Force headquarters in the Pentagon, provoking a flurry of profanity-laced activity.

Eglin AFB, FL, Tuesday

Major Waxler marched into Julie's office grim faced, closing the door behind himself.

"That bad, Josh?"

"Yes, ma'am. Intelligence believes the recent visit by a Chinese spacecraft to the Xuntian attached a weapon...a directed-energy weapon."

Julie's shoulders slumped. "That makes it more likely they destroyed Meteor-1! Christ. The implications are enormous."

Waxler sat. "It would appear the Chinese violated the Outer Space Treaty."

Staring back, Julie replied, "Yes, but I'm more worried that we may soon start to lose our intelligence-gathering satellites, specifically those that monitor the Taiwan Strait. This could quite possibly be a prelude to an assault on Taiwan."

"Shit."

Julie scowled. "But it's even worse than that. A directed-energy weapon in low Earth orbit could be used for more than destroying satellites."

Waxler's mouth dropped open as the implication sunk in.

Julie nodded. "Exactly. It might have the ability to intercept nuclear ballistic missiles. A constellation of directed-energy weapons would undermine the reliability of our ICBMs and SLBMs. Neutralizing our nuclear deterrent would leave the People's Liberation Army free to exploit their conventional numerical superiority in attacking Taiwan." She ran a hand through her blonde hair. "Get me the latest assessment of scheduled Chinese heavy-lift launches." She straightened. "Wait. Do we have an X-39 in orbit currently?"

"Yes, ma'am. What do you have in mind?"

"Something I'll have to run all the way up the chain of command to the Chief of Space Operations."

Waxler stiffened.

Eglin AFB, FL, Wednesday

Over the last twenty-four hours, Julie's office phone had rung frequently, but not all calls are created equal. "Lieutenant Colonel Harris," she answered.

"Hey, Julie. This is Max," replied Colonel Max Martin, commander of Space Delta 2.

"What can I do for you, sir?"

"I'm calling about your request to retask an X-39. That's a big ask. If we divert it for you, Space Delta 8 is gonna be some kind of pissed because one of their WGS satellites is long overdue for a repair mission."

Julie's stomach tightened. "Yes, sir. But the Chinese have a number of Long March 9s on launch pads. That suggests they could launch more ASATs after their successful test. Those weapons would threaten our ability to have eyes on what they're planning in Taiwan."

"Even if you're right, I'm not certain the X-39 will be able to successfully execute the mission you proposed on such short notice. Permission denied."

Julie hung up the phone and scowled. "Shit." *This is more important than my job.* She dialed an old friend at Peterson Space Force Base, Mike Gibbs, who just happened to be Command Master Sergeant for Lieutenant General Thompson, commander of Space Operations Command.

Gibbs sat up. "Are you sure you want to do this?" he asked after Julie outlined her request. "Colonel Martin is not gonna be happy about you going over his head."

Julie nodded. *Understatement of the year.* "I don't see that there's any choice. This is a chance to convince China to cancel its attack on Taiwan. And if the mission gets blown and China figures out it was us sabotaging their system, they can't complain about it because they'd have to acknowledge they put a nuclear-powered weapon in orbit. Anyway, country before career, right?"

Gibb's throat tightened. "You've got some serious balls, Julie. Very well. I'll pass your plan on to General Thompson. I hope you're right—for your sake and all our sakes."

Low Earth Orbit, Friday

Per orders from General Thompson, Space Delta 9 diverted an unmanned X-39 spacecraft from its planned orbit for a surreptitious rendezvous with the Xuntian. The spacecraft's supercomputer-designed shape and radar-absorbing materials rendered it effectively invisible to enemy radar. After maneuvering to within three feet of the Xuntian, the X-39 transmitted real-time video. Space Delta 9 guardians ordered its robotic arm to extend a radiometer to measure gamma radiation, x-ray radiation, and beta-particle flux density. Upon observing levels strongly suggesting the presence of a nuclear reactor, ground-based controllers instructed the robotic claw hand to "reengineer" the Chinese linear plasma rail gun.

First, the claw severed the cable providing electrical power to the Xuntian, returning the telescope to a nonfunctioning state. Second, it pinched the breech of the rail gun's bore, deforming the triple joint seal and ruining the electrical insulation needed for the weapon to function. The sabotage completed, the Space Force ninja glided silently back to its originally planned orbit, while far below, Space Force guardians cheered raucously.

Ministry of National Defense compound, Beijing, China, Friday

Select members of China's Central Military Commission sat around a long mahogany table in a secure conference room. All but one had surly expressions at having been summoned at such a late hour.

"My apologies, General Secretary," began a People's Liberation Army general. Sweat beaded on his brow. "This is a most urgent matter for the Commission. The first of our satellite-based plasma weapons is no longer replying to our commands . . . for unknown reasons."

The General Secretary of the Chinese Communist Party, effectively the dictator of China, scowled. "Do you understand the gravity of the situation, General? We have nine rockets standing by, ready to deploy the full constellation of antisatellite weapons. And Operation Typhoon cannot commence until we've blinded the American military."

"Ye-yes, sir. I recommend we not launch any more of these weapons until we understand what happened to the first one."

"And how soon will that be, General?" he asked softly, but the menace behind the question was palpable.

The general's heart pounded. "We will have to modify the recently returned Shenlong-3 for a recovery mission, then replace the payload of one of our Long March rockets. The Shenlong will retrieve the malfunctioning weapon so we can analyze it in a lab, identify the problem, and determine the appropriate corrections. If hardware modifications are needed, we will have to pull the other Shenlong vehicles from their rockets. The entire operation could take months, sir." He wilted under the General Secretary's stare. Men had been shot for less. *At least I've planned for this. My children are studying in Europe and know what to do if I disappear.*

Eglin AFB, FL, Saturday

Julie called her senior staff into her office. The stress-induced lines on her face from the last few days had smoothed away. "Good news. Intelligence reports the Chinese are standing down their invasion forces. It would seem they don't want to attack with our reconnaissance satellites intact and able to report their every move to Taiwan. Good work, everyone. We prevented a war from starting, at least for now. First round's on me once we're off duty."

A round of cheers erupted as her personal phone buzzed.

A text from her husband read, *Hi Sweetie. Our squadron expects to return home within four days. Whatever you did must've worked. So proud of you! Will be making you fancy dinners for a week.*

✤   ✤   ✤

Author's Note:

The USSF organizational structure is depicted realistically, as are the U.S. sensors and the Chinese Long March 9. The Shenlong-3 is a hypothesized follow-on to China's Shenlong spacecraft. The X-39 is a hypothesized follow-on to the Boeing X-37 robotic spacecraft. The Chinese space-based plasma rail gun is pure fiction (as far as I know), though the most speculative part of this story may be a husband regularly making dinner for his wife.

✤   ✤   ✤

Henry Herz's short stories include "Out, Damned Virus" (*Daily Science Fiction*), "Bar Mitzvah on Planet Latke" (*Coming of Age*, Albert Whitman & Co.), "The Magic Backpack" (*Metastellar*), "Unbreakable" (*Musing of the Muses*, Brigid's Gate Press), "The Case of the Murderous Alien" (*Spirit Machine*, Air and Nothingness Press), "The Ghosts of Enerhodar" (*Literally Dead*, Alienhead Press),

"Cheating Death" (*The Hitherto Secret Experiments of Marie Curie*, Blackstone Publishing), "Maria & Maslow" (*Highlights for Children*), and "A Proper Party" (*Ladybug* magazine). He's edited five anthologies and written twelve picture books, including the critically acclaimed *I Am Smoke*.

✵   ✵   ✵

To Boldly Go . . . Understanding the Space Force Mission

✸

Michael Morton

When the concept of a Space Force was publicly announced, what reactions did you see in the press and social media? That the Air Force was already doing space stuff and it's a waste of money? This infringed on NASA's territory? Maybe you heard jokes about space shuttle door gunners and going after alien bases on the Moon? Or that we should be more concerned with what was happening on Earth?

What these reactions showed was that the public didn't understand what the United States does with its military space assets. The people and equipment that make up the current (and future) USSF play roles in all aspects of our lives. It isn't just the military that benefits from the USSF mission. So let's take a look at what the USSF actually does and how this relates to both military and civilian life.

The USSF mission[1] is to "secure our nation's interests in, from, and to space." This means the USSF will recruit new members, place them in their respective organizations, train them to operate their systems, and equip them with said systems. This is how the USSF provides space capabilities such as Space Situational Awareness; Space Control; Position, Navigation, and Timing; Space-based

---

[1] United States Space Force. (n.d.). *About Space Force.* https://www.spaceforce.mil /About-Us/About-Space-Force/a

Intelligence, Surveillance, and Reconnaissance (ISR); Space-based Environmental Monitoring; Satellite Communications (SATCOM); and Nuclear detonation Detection (NUDET). To enable these capabilities, the USSF also conducts Spacelift and Satellite Operations. But what exactly are these capabilities?

USSF Capabilities

* Space Situational Awareness (SSA) is knowing where things are in orbit around Earth. The USSF tracks active and dead satellites, junk created from launches (such as expended rocket bodies), and debris from collisions. It's also their job to monitor the space lanes, looking for conjunctions where two or more satellites or other debris have the chance of running into one another—and then making plans to avoid a collision. Operations are being expanded to include the cislunar space around the Moon. Knowing where things are in orbit is key to ensuring they don't collide with each other or interfere with ongoing operations.
* Space Control includes offensive and defensive operations to ensure the U.S. and its allies have the freedom to operate in space. This is how we protect our space assets.
* Position, Navigation and Timing (PNT) supplies positional information, the ability to navigate over terrain, and supplies highly accurate timing for banking, communication systems, and the electrical power grid.[2] The most common example of this is the Global Positioning System (GPS).
* Space-based Intelligence, Surveillance, and Reconnaissance (ISR) is the gathering of information to understand an adversary or situation. This is done by either watching a large area for a long period of time to see what happens (surveillance) or watching a specific area at a specific time (reconnaissance). ISR operations support ballistic missile warning, targeting analysis, threat capability assessment, situational awareness, battle damage assessment, and in general helps the USSF understand what is going on in space.
* Space-based Environmental Monitoring supports both the terrestrial and space environments. This is how the meteorological and oceanographic forecasts and assessments of environmental impacts

---

[2] National Coordination Office for Space-Based Positioning, Navigation, and Timing. GPS.gov: *Timing Applications*. (n.d.) www.gps.gov/applications/timing/

are created. It also provides forecasts, alerts, and warnings for the space environment that may affect space capabilities, space operations, and their terrestrial users. The most visible aspect of this are the weather images showing the tracks of hurricanes and other major storms.

* SATCOM—military, commercial, foreign, and civil—provides global coverage which affords the U.S. and allied national and military leaders with a means to communicate no matter the location. This can also include the broadcast of satellite television signals and video conferences like Zoom and Webex. The USSF's Commercial Satellite Communications Office plans to award nearly $2.3 billion in commercial SATCOM contracts over the next two years.[3]

* The USSF operates the space-based portion of the nuclear detection system to provide a worldwide capability to detect, locate, and report any nuclear detonations in Earth's atmosphere, near space, or deep space in near real-time. This is used to enforce nuclear test ban treaties and monitor developing capability in nonnuclear nations.

* To operate in space, you have to get there. Spacelift is the ability to deliver payloads (satellites or other materials) into space. This includes planning, configuring, and range operations necessary to conduct the launch. Every U.S. rocket launch you see is either from a DOD launch range or overseen by USSF personnel.

* Finally, you have to operate the satellites once they're on orbit. Satellite Operations maneuver, configure, operate, and sustain on-orbit spacecraft to ensure everything is working. These operators ensure the satellite itself (the bus) is able to maintain altitude and attitude, is generating and storing electricity (solar panels and batteries), and is shedding excess heat. The payload is the actual capability provided by the satellite, such as SATCOM or PNT (Positioning, Navigation, and Timing).

"That's interesting," you might say, "but so what? Why does it matter to me?"

---

[3] Erwin, S. (2023b, January 23). *DoD Satcom: Big money for military satellites, slow shift to commercial services*. SpaceNews. https://spacenews.com/dod-satcom-big-money-for-military-satellites-slow-shift-to-commercial-services/

Believe it or not, you use many of the same space capabilities the military does in your everyday life. What the USSF provides is much the same as a utility company, such as electric, water, internet, or cell phone.

Most people wake up to the alarm on their cell phone. Your phone gets its timing through the cellular network, which in turn receives that timing from GPS. That accurate timing across networks and computers is critical to providing secure, encrypted communications. When you check the weather for the day, those forecasts were developed from the data provided by weather satellites. Checking the route on your way to work is a form of ISR, with the maps provided by imaging satellites. So is looking for a place to eat. The reviews you read about the restaurant provide intelligence through surveillance, and checking to see if it's open or busy is reconnaissance.

Let's go one step further. Your breakfast was made from food grown by farmers who use radar satellite images to figure out the best time to plant and harvest and GPS satellites to measure the ground to plow. The food was moved to processing plants and grocery stores by trucks who use GPS to find the best routes. You paid with a credit card, and that terminal uses GPS timing to make sure your transaction goes through securely. At work, you may talk with colleagues or business partners on the other side of the planet, and your Internet or phone signal may use SATCOM to get there.

In short, you use space services in many aspects of your life, even if you aren't aware of it. And that's how those capabilities are supposed to work. You don't need to be aware of every aspect of how the information gets to you. As long as your phone can plot your route, you can use your credit cards, and you can look up the weather forecast, it really doesn't matter how it works.

But it's the men and women in the Space Force that ensure you have access to that information. The USSF ensures the United States will continue to have freedom of action in space, without being constrained by another nation. Our space assets guarantee we have a global perspective, able to detect and respond to changing conditions around the world. Finally, the USSF will go on providing us with an unmatched capability to "… act responsibly in space to ensure the safety, stability, security, and long-term sustainability of space activities."[4]

---

[4] United States. (2020). National Space Policy. Retrieved from https://www.space. commerce.gov/policy/national-space-policy/

✸   ✸   ✸

Michael Morton is a retired USAF space officer and wishes the Space Force happened earlier. Still, he gets to work for them as a civilian, so life isn't all bad. He writes award-winning military sci-fi and fantasy and lives in Colorado Springs with his family. When he's not writing, he enjoys camping and exploring the local distilleries and breweries. His books can be found on Amazon at https://www.amazon.com /stores/Michael-Morton/author/B07SB1PXQ9.

A Kinetic High

✧

Gustavo Bondoni

The woman in the FBI windbreaker held out her hand. "I'm Agent Hamilton. Glad you could make it."

"I wasn't given much of a choice," Captain Sal Garda replied. "Or any information. Hell, I don't even know where I am." A dirt road intersected a tarmac two lane with patched-over potholes. His chopper had landed about sixty miles back, where a car had been waiting for him beside a cluster of official-looking buildings in the middle of nowhere. Great, flat plains surrounded them.

"Yeah, that couldn't be helped. Background check." Her voice made it seem like it wasn't a big deal, and he couldn't really read her expression as she was wearing sunglasses despite the cloud cover.

"Background check? Are you kidding me? Did the one they did when I applied for the Space Force get lost in a crack? You know I'm not a security risk."

"It's not national security this one focused on."

"What the hell was it, then?" Garda asked.

"Drugs."

"I'm with the Space Force, not the DEA."

"We know. But we still had to check. Your family . . ."

"I know who my family was. But that was forty years ago, and my dad was never involved in any of that. He was ten when my grandfather went to jail and never came out. That scared him straight."

"Sorry, man," the agent said. "All they told me was that they were checking up on you and to brief you when you got here if you were cleared. I don't care about any of that other stuff."

"Was I cleared?"

"You wouldn't be here if you weren't." She walked toward a group of men standing on the dirt road about a hundred yards away, so he followed. "Just a couple of things. Remember that here in Canada you're not allowed to arrest anyone or shoot anyone."

"I don't do that in the U.S., either. And if we're in Canada, shouldn't I have gone through customs?"

She waved the concern off. "That's been taken care of. The second thing is that you need to be careful around Senator Rennes. He's an asshat, but he can get you pulled off this job with a phone call."

"For all I know, he'd be doing me a favor."

"Just say yes to everything he says. We'll figure it out later, once he's back in Washington."

He wanted to ask what was going on, why he'd been pulled out of a meeting and flown halfway across the country—actually out of the country, in fact—without any information for something that seemed to have nothing to do with the Space Force.

The crowd of people ahead suddenly parted, revealing the dirt road. "Oh, crap," Garda said.

"Yeah."

"Meteor?" he asked.

"Kinetic impact."

"Someone dropped a Rod from God?" He looked around. "On Canada?"

"It was aimed at the U.S.," an older man from the group, dressed in a dark blue suit, said. "And it's not a weapon. The weapon is what was inside." He held out his hand. "I'm Senator Rennes. Thanks for coming on such short notice, son. I'm glad the Space Force is on the job. Maybe you can solve this, since the other agencies . . ." His voice trailed off as he glanced disapprovingly at Hamilton. "The other agencies don't seem to understand just how much of a threat this is."

"Yes, sir," Garda replied. "We'll take care of it. I'm Captain Garda."

"Glad to see a military man on the job. I'm starting to feel confident we'll clear this up."

"I will definitely do my best. The first thing I need to do is look over the area to see what law enforcement might have missed. Do you mind if I take Agent Hamilton with me?"

"Of course not. Do your job," the senator said. He returned to his group.

The crater was fifteen yards further down the road. Several officers in different uniforms stood around, keeping everyone at a safe distance. As soon as they were out of earshot of the senator, Hamilton whispered: "You really know how to kiss ass."

"I work in Washington," he replied. "I spend half my life deflecting unwanted political attention. Who are these guys?"

"Mounties and the CSIS. That's like the Canadian version of the Bureau. They know their stuff, but in this case, everyone knows where the problem came from. It came from up there." She pointed into the sky. "Your job is to figure out how it got up there in the first place."

"And the soldiers?" Garda asked.

"They're just pissed that someone blew a hole in one of their roads and there's no one around to shoot at."

The crater was roughly circular, thirty feet in diameter and about fifteen feet deep. "If this is really a kinetic strike, it's a small one. A tankbuster at best. Maybe not even that." Garda knelt on the rim of the hole and looked down into it, trying to see if he could spot fragments of the payload. "This doesn't make any sense. Lifting weight into orbit is expensive. You don't drop stuff from space for such a small result."

"This isn't an attack," Hamilton said. "It's a failed attempt at smuggling."

"You'll need to explain," Garda said, standing and walking around the crater. "If I keep guessing, I'm just going to waste everyone's time."

"It's a drug delivery system. High-end designer pills with some serious street values. Stuff you can't get just anywhere. Silicon Valley billionaire candy."

"That explains the cops. But why the senator? Is this some War on Drugs thing?"

"No. He's here because these guys are also one of the main conduits for getting abortion drugs into nonabortion states without a paper trail. And Rennes wants them shut down with prejudice. Like right now." She said it with no inflection, and he didn't ask her feelings. She seemed like the kind that would do the job she'd signed up to do, even if she didn't agree with everything it entailed.

"So this shipment was headed to . . . what? Montana? Wyoming? Where are we, even?"

"Nah. This was a screw-up. The info we've got says the payloads usually have brakes and chutes. Something must have gone seriously wrong for this one to slam into the ground. For all we know, it was supposed to land in Texas."

Garda stood. "Since it's going to take weeks to sift through this hole to pull out the scraps of whatever they used to deliver the payload, and since no one is going to be able to tell much from the remains except that they suffered a huge impact, I can give you my verdict now."

"You haven't even seen any of the evidence."

"Won't make any difference. The most likely cause for this"—he gestured at the demolished road in front of them—"is physical damage either during manipulation to get the rocket to the launchpad or on lift-off. I suspect the latter, as you'd probably do a check if it was the former. And I doubt it's a software glitch, because something that would knock out both the guidance of the orbital section and the brakes on the reentry module would probably have caused mission control to abort altogether."

Hamilton snorted. "You think drug smugglers would have aborted? What do they care if it lands on someone's house? This isn't NASA we're talking about."

Garda pointed at the crowd around the crater rim, the officials looking down on them. "Did you know how they were smuggling the stuff into the U.S.? Did you know they were using rockets?"

"A couple of informants mentioned rumors . . ."

"But you didn't know," Garda completed her sentence for her. "And now you do. Which is why you abort the mission. Look, the Space Force knows more about covert spacecraft protocols than anyone on the planet, and the rule of thumb is: If you can't be a hundred percent sure that you'll recover it before the bad guys do, you blow it up. Because if not, it can fall on a road in the middle of nowhere and get surrounded by cops. Granted, if you hit Canada, you're more likely to drop it in an empty field or a forest and no one will notice, but you still need to cover your risk. If you know it's broken, you abort to keep the secret. So this one was bent and battered physically, but they didn't know. Which tells me a lot about their operation."

Hamilton nodded. "You're the expert."

"Yes. But I suspect that conclusion isn't why you brought the Space Force in, is it?"

From above, the senator's voice boomed into the crater. "That's exactly right, son. You gotta find the people doing this so we can send a few platoons of Special Forces to pay them a visit. And it would be really good for you to do it pronto."

"We got one!"

Three weeks after his trip to Canada, Garda turned to see Reina Peters, the petite specialist on Space Fence duty for the evening shift, burst into his improvised office in Vandenberg Air Force Base. She wore a huge smile and waved a sheaf of printouts.

"How certain are you?" he said.

"I checked it four times before I came."

"Show me."

The numbers would take a specialist's eye to read, so he just checked object weight and orbit before flipping to the diagram on page four. A tiny satellite, indistinguishable from dozens of pieces of space debris or decommissioned smallsats, had split into two barely an hour before. One small part had entered Earth's atmosphere in a ballistic trajectory, but there was no sign of a collision, or of any other event that could have launched a chunk in a different direction at high speed.

The only explanation is that it had been launched deliberately.

"That landing projection . . . Kansas?"

"Yes, sir," Peters replied. "A field just north of Ionia."

"Never heard of it. Little place?"

"Tiny. But a good system of dirt roads and easy access to Route 36."

"Perfect to get in and out quickly. Please send this data to the FBI office in Santa Maria."

"Yes, sir," Peters replied.

Garda pulled out his phone and dialed Hamilton.

"Please tell me you've got something." she said. "Because if you're calling to invite me out for tacos again, I'm still recovering from that last batch."

"We've got something. We're sending the data over, but I'll give you the overview."

"Tell me."

He quickly put her up to speed.

"Thanks," Hamilton said. "I'll get this to Washington and Kansas. And I'll be there in an hour."

The drive from Santa Maria to the Space Force Base at Vandenberg was only a few miles and, half an hour after they'd spoken on the phone, Agent Hamilton stepped into his office.

She looked around. "I see you still refuse to get settled."

The office, except for his laptop, phone, and a couple of notepads, was exactly as it had been issued three weeks before. Even the cardboard boxes holding the stuff the previous occupant hadn't bothered to take with him sat where they'd been on his first day. "I'm not planning on staying."

She chuckled. "You're a noob, Garda. One of the first things a real investigator learns is that home is wherever you just got assigned to. So I'm enjoying the delights of Santa Maria, California, and you should be too."

"Nah, you're the noob," he replied with a grin. "I'm a soldier, so base life is part of the job description. But if you have a desk in Washington, you work to keep it." He turned serious. "What's the story on the drop?"

"There are people on the way, but I doubt we'll catch anyone on the site. You told me the drop time is between twelve and fifteen minutes, right?"

"Yeah. Twenty with braking. Half an hour if it's doing something really weird." As expected, the mangled remains of the canister that had dropped in Canada yielded almost no clue as to the functioning of the delivery system. All they knew was that it was made of several metal components weighing ten kilos in total, and that it had carried down a few kilos of drugs of various kinds. Exactly how many kilos, it was impossible to say without sifting through the entire volume of the crater, but chemical analysis had told them that they were mainly super-high-end entertainment pills.

And, of course, the abortion pills. Which was why the senator was on the phone from Washington every single day demanding results and threatening to kill careers if he didn't see a lot of progress very soon.

Having a shipment land in Kansas—from where they could be driven into any number of antiabortion states without much trouble—would not put the man in a good mood.

"So we won't find them there. But we'll have a starting point to chase them. They'll have a car. We'll get footage. Security cameras, stuff like that, and start tracking the cars. There might be fingerprints. Hell, we might get lucky and someone will have been smoking and we can get a DNA sample. There might be footprints. You've given us a place to start." She seemed genuinely excited by the prospect.

"I just hope this will make the senator happy."

She shook her head. "I think that old man is beyond ever feeling happy. His emotional range appears to span from disappointed to furious."

Garda sighed. "Still, we'd better call him."

The call lasted ten minutes. The senator was not happy that they hadn't caught the delivery on the fly and also arrested the dealers, and he also didn't want to hear it when they explained that Garda would be a lot more useful at the Space Force Base than in the field.

An hour later, Garda and Hamilton were on a plane headed for Moritz Memorial Airport in Beloit, Kansas.

It took three days for Garda to get back to base, and he cursed every moment of it. Even though he had an open line to Reina at Vandenberg, who'd been assigned to backtrack the satellite by dint of having been on duty when the delivery happened, he wanted to be where the action was.

The FBI was just doing cop things. Hamilton explained them to him, and they were easy enough to understand—there were footprints and all sorts of forensic clues to the identity of the people who'd been there—but the only thing he contributed was to note the lack of an impact crater and the fact that nothing in the landing zone was a piece of rocket.

But they had to make it look good. The senator called them twice a day to check on progress, and both he and Hamilton had to report on the day's activities, almost as if the senator expected them to contradict one another.

When he finally got back to California, he checked in on Reina so often that she told him, in no uncertain terms, that it was hard enough to backtrack a small object in a sea of orbital debris without her superior officer hovering over her shoulder.

Garda retreated to his office, looked around, and sighed.

So this was where his career would end. He'd been a promising young officer once. He'd graduated with honors from the Air Force Academy and immediately gone to work as an industry liaison for Air Force Acquisition. He'd parlayed that connection with aerospace suppliers—plus a series of excellent performance reviews—into quick advancement and a desk job in Washington in the Space Force.

His superiors saw him as the kind of officer you sent in to stabilize a department in trouble and to prepare them for their next permanent boss while Garda himself moved on to bigger and better things. It was like being a business consultant, but people called you "Sir."

And now this.

Any meaningful chance of further advancement would end in a gray-carpeted windowless office in Vandenberg Air Force Base, nearly three thousand miles from the Beltway. His success had made him the logical choice for this job...but now he was getting nowhere.

Worse, he wasn't the one who could move things along. He didn't have the technical skills to do the tracking needed. He was there to make decisions with data in hand.

The decision to keep waiting while you gathered even more data was the kind that killed careers.

Even if it was the right one.

He turned off the light in his office and went back to his on-base Unaccompanied Housing unit. If he'd been there permanently, he'd have moved into housing in the community, but for a temporary posting, this was deemed acceptable.

And then, as his investigation failed to progress, everyone had forgotten about him. Everyone except the senator, that was. The senator would be the one to ensure he'd be passed over for promotion from here to the end of the world.

He sighed and dropped into his bed without even bothering to undress.

At four in the morning, Reina called to tell him that the night analyst had found a very good match on the probable origin of the launch vehicle.

"That's great. Where did it come from?"

"North Mali."

"What?"

The helicopter hugged the ground. The roar of the wind through the open door competed with the whine of the jet engine and the rotors above his head. Everyone had their goggles down against the sand from outside.

"You sure you want to do this?" the captain of the Rangers asked. "There's no shame in coming out once the shooting stops. Plus, Dillard won't have to babysit you."

"I'm coming," Garda replied. Instead of diminishing, his frustration had kept increasing over the two days it had taken to get the mission organized. Fortunately, the launch site was just across the border between Mali and the disputed territory of Western Sahara. No government was going to send jets out to annoy the Black Hawks. Hell, Garda didn't even remember if anyone in the region even had fighters in operational condition.

"All right, then," the captain replied. Garda thought there was a hint of approval in the man's nod, but maybe it was wishful thinking. The captain nodded down towards Garda's rifle. "You know how to use that thing?"

"The hollow bit points towards the enemy."

"Good enough, I guess."

He'd spent the entire flight explaining the Space Force to the Rangers. Half of them seemed to think the unit was a nonmilitary joke. The others were genuinely curious about what the Space Force did.

But now, all kidding and curiosity was lost in concentration and checklists. The Rangers had been tasked to secure a launchpad, and to keep it secure until Garda said they could leave, or for thirty minutes, whichever came first. The hard limit was placed on them by the amount of fuel the choppers could carry.

The helicopter landed with a thump. The men near the doors poured out into the desert night.

Dillard, the man tasked to take care of Garda, came up close and shouted: "Get your NV on. We go in fifteen seconds." Pause. "All right, follow me."

Garda's boot sunk in the sand. He stumbled but managed to keep his balance and follow the soldier down the sandy slope. To his surprise, his boots scuffed against hard rock at the bottom: the sand had given way to some kind of flat surface. Without color, he initially thought it must be concrete, that they were running across the landing pad, but they soon came to a small rocky ridge about a foot high and he realized it was stone.

Dillard motioned him to stop and listened to the radio. "The team has reached the designated target. One vehicle present."

They'd pored over satellite images for hours, watching people come and go from the launch area. They hoped another launch was imminent, but most of all, they hoped the target people would be there when they arrived. Drone imagery had shown one improvised fighting vehicle beside the base—a pickup truck converted to a machine-gun platform—but they couldn't see if anyone was hiding inside the single building.

Dillard stood and motioned for Garda to follow. They came over a slight rise and the airfield came into view. Two Rangers crouched behind the empty pickup truck, using it as cover while, at the same time, denying it to anyone who might attempt a defense.

Garda breathed easier; that truck was the most dangerous enemy asset in the area.

Shouting emerged from the structure ahead, a building composed of two forty-foot containers with antennae and a small satellite dish beside the concrete launch area. If the intelligence analysts were correct, the containers held an ops room and a bunk area.

They both were insanely close to the launch pad.

"Area clear," Dillard said.

"Did we catch anyone?"

"Let's go see."

They jogged to the makeshift buildings and arrived just as the Rangers were marching two men out of the dorm container.

Garda's heart sank when he saw the captives. The shorts and

button-down shirts they wore were barely a step up from rags, and both men were barefoot. He would have bet his next paycheck that they were just low-level guards who wouldn't know a gyroscope from a yo-yo. "Get them on the helicopter, I'll interrogate them later."

That part of the plan was set in stone. They didn't have time, so anyone found in the vicinity would be questioned on the carrier. Garda suspected it was illegal as hell, but it wasn't his job to worry about it. His job was to evaluate the facilities.

"Is there anyone else here?"

"No, sir," the captain said. As soon as the area had been secured, Garda went from being an annoying bystander to being in charge. At least until they had to leave, when he would be unceremoniously packed up—ready or not—and tossed into the chopper.

"All right." Garda walked into the other container and felt his jaw go slack. *They're launching satellites into orbit with this?* The equipment looked like something from a Cold War submarine. Switches and analog readers on the walls were easy to understand: fuel pressure gauges, flow meters, and the toggles to control each. They were familiar and fit for the purpose ... which only made it worse. This control room was an insult to anyone who'd ever been involved in the complex process of launching a rocket.

After a quick inspection of the equipment—a Ranger with lights and a camera was photographing every square inch of the facility for later review—Garda tried to locate the central computer. If he could get a hard drive, some kind of memory storage, they might glean something useful from this.

If not, they had just made a very expensive and illegal incursion into a sovereign country and kidnapped two of the people they found there with nothing to show for it.

The senator would be delighted.

"Come on," Garda said. "Where are you?"

But all he found was a standard computer rack, threaded with cables but devoid of actual computers.

Garda ran to the captain. "Were there any computers in the bunk room?"

"Nope. Just two phones. I assume they belong to the guys we grabbed."

"Dammit," Garda said. Then he took a breath and got himself back under control. "How much time do I still have."

"Fifteen minutes before we leave. I need you to show me where you want the demolitions charges."

"In the first place, you need to blow up the control center." Garda waited while the captain relayed the orders. "And now come with me."

They sprinted out to the gantry, a much shorter run than it should have been. The launch area should have been a couple of miles from the control room. Three miles was better. Yet these guys were close enough to feel the heat of the engines. If the rocket exploded . . .

It shouldn't have surprised him that drug dealers would be indifferent to safety considerations, but this was ridiculous.

Garda gave a quick look at the gantry, the exhaust ducting in the concrete, and the clamps to hold the rocket in place. He estimated that this pad could launch vehicles up to one meter in diameter, a little smaller than Rocket Lab's Electron, which was the current leader in smallsat launches.

Unlike the control room, the launch area appeared to be state of the art. The column and the fuel tanks wouldn't have looked out of place at SpaceX's facility in Texas. Someone had spent money.

He turned to the captain. "Do we have photos of this?"

"Every detail you could want," the Ranger replied.

"Good, then put explosives on the base of that column there, and on the wall of the gas tanks. Make sure we're far away when you detonate those."

"Thanks for clearing that up, Space Force. We grunts are too dumb to be out of range when things go bang." He turned away to give the orders, leaving Garda's apology stuck in his throat. Then the captain turned back. "Get back to the chopper. Time's up."

Back in California, Garda looked up to see Hamilton standing in the door to his office. "Still on the job, or did you come to say goodbye?"

"I'm still on the job," she replied with a wry grin. "Barely."

"Yeah, me too. The senator is really pissed."

"Too bad for him." Then she shook her head. "I think he's mad at himself more than at us. He made a big deal out of busting the abortion-pill ring because it will get him a ton of votes . . . but it isn't even something he's been a hard-ass about historically. He's a political animal tied to a controversial issue he doesn't even care about. Which is lucky for us."

"Lucky? Why?"

Hamilton smiled. "Because firing us now would make the news. He wants this to blow over while he concentrates on aligning with some other vote-getting scheme. Plus, if we do solve it, he's the one who'll end up looking like a hero."

"Hell, I don't care anymore. I just want to get this thing closed so I can get back to my life."

"Well, I won't be much help. We caught the guys who went to pick up the Kansas drop. They were just couriers who work with a Mexican guy from the Sinaloa Cartel. We know the cartel doesn't produce this kind of stuff. They just distribute it. So unless we send a force into Mexico to grab some top drug dealers, we aren't going to get any decent information out of them. Feel like another chopper ride?"

"I have a feeling Mexico isn't Africa. We can't just fly there and grab people. Not unless the president is personally pissed," Garda replied. "What brings you here?"

"I wanted to get out of the office for a bit. It didn't feel like I was getting anything done."

"And you came here?"

"I figure if anything is going to happen, it'll come from your end," Hamilton replied.

"Yeah. And we'll get to raid another empty launch pad. Probably in a jungle this time. Since you're here, you might as well come along. I was just going to talk to Peters."

The corridor between the offices and the ops center was also gray and corporate. The Space Force, as the newest of the services, had decided to go with a modern look to their office needs . . . but in Garda's eyes, all they'd achieved was to look like some corporate cubicle farm. Except the cubes were mostly empty.

The ops center was a refreshing contrast. When Garda had switched career tracks to the Space Force, this room was what he'd had in mind.

Screens covered an entire thirty-foot wall. Some showed

numbers, but most had maps of the Earth with overlays on them displaying the orbits and positions of satellites, vehicles, and space stations of high interest. The ISS was permanently tracked, as was the Chinese Tiangong. Garda checked for any interesting developments and noted sourly that the X-37 was up again. It must have launched over the past few days, and he hadn't gotten the memo about the mission. It felt like more than a mere oversight.

Four rows of workstations faced the data. Six operators sat scattered around the room. The faint, tinny sound of music emerged from at least a couple of headsets as the analysts worked.

Reina Peters's station was in the second row at the center of the room, a supervisor's slot. She turned when they entered and nodded to Garda. "Just one second, sir." She finished typing a few more commands and stood.

The ops team's conference room brought them back to Corporate America. "What have you got for us today?" Garda asked.

"Three new possibles. One is a smallsat launched from New Zealand. It's probably legit, because it came up on an Electron launch four days ago, but we don't have the mission parameters. I think it's probably a misfile, and I've put in a request from the company. They should be at work in a couple of hours.

"Number two and number three are a little more suspicious, especially number two, which is the same size and weight as our original bogey. We haven't tracked it back to its source yet, so we don't know. It might just be another North Korean spy satellite. Or maybe Indian. Not everyone tells us when they're sending something up.

"The last one is probably a dead end. It's bigger than what we're looking for and the orbit appears to be decaying. I'm not sure who put it up there. Probably a botched launch."

Garda growled. He knew that filtering the enormous—and growing—field of satellites and space debris in orbit around Earth to find viable candidates was a massive task, and that what Peters showed him represented hundreds of man-hours of painstaking work.

He had to rein himself in to avoid telling her that it was pretty much useless. "Thank you. Looks like we need to concentrate on number two, then. What I'd like is for you to keep me updated in real time on when a kinetic launch could land in the U.S., as well as which areas it could conceivably hit." He nodded toward Hamilton. "That way, we can have the FBI on alert."

Peters looked down at her data. "This satellite is going over us every eighty-seven minutes. And in its transit over the U.S., it can hit pretty much everything between Florida and the northern tip of California."

"I know," Garda said. "But it's all we've got." They sat in silence for a long moment before he slammed his fist on the table. "This isn't going to work."

"We're making progress," Hamilton replied. "We already know that whoever is doing this is in negotiation with Sinaloa. And we also know, from the guys that you picked up in the desert, that the rocket engineers are either French or Belgian. There are threads to pick at."

"It's . . ."

"Look," Hamilton continued, "this is how police work happens. You find a clue, you follow it back until you find more clues. You eliminate the ones that don't seem to fit. Eventually, you find something that leads to something you can actually use. And that's where things happen. It takes time."

"We don't have time."

"Actually, we have all the time in the world. No one is dying because of this. These drugs go to high-end parties, and the abortion pills . . . they probably end up at college dorms going for a hundred times what they're worth. The sense of urgency you're getting is because it's politically sensitive. But we'll catch them before they do any damage."

Garda glared at her. "And if the next drop isn't drugs? Or if they're laced with poison and they kill off half of our captains of industry at some blowout?" he breathed, trying to get his voice under control. "Or if the next one is a canister of weaponized aerosol Ebola in downtown Houston? We know drug money has been financing terrorism forever. This just takes that link to its logical conclusion."

Hamilton and Peters said nothing.

"So what are we achieving with this? Can we stop them from dropping?" Garda said.

"Not unless you're authorized to have one of our hunter-killers fire at an unidentified satellite," Peters replied.

"You know I can't do that." This wasn't like an incursion in a conflictive and sparsely populated part of the world. When you blew up a satellite, it created a buttload of debris, and caused major international incidents. "But we've established that what we're doing now is useless against a real attack."

"But what else can we do?"

The question echoed in the conference room. There was no real answer to that with any kind of technological support behind it.

Garda ground his teeth in frustration. He knew what they had to do. "Look for launches," he said. "It's the only way to reach them quickly enough."

Reina Peters sat back on her chair and raised an eyebrow. "Do you think the Russians are launching drugs at us? The Chinese? Because our IR satellite coverage is pretty much focused on them. We're blind to places like Mali."

"It will be somewhere else," Garda said. "And probably in the southern hemisphere."

"Then our early-warning birds aren't going to be much help. They're not pointed the right way, and no one is going to redirect those for a police matter."

"I know, dammit," Garda said. "But we're supposed to have the best space-based infrastructure in the world. I can't believe that we can only detect a launch when the satellite comes into orbit."

"So why can't you?" Hamilton asked.

"We can detect the launches from anyone who really matters," Garda replied. "The Russians, the Chinese, the North Koreans. Hell, if the South Africans were still nuclear, we would have a satellite on them. But we don't spend resources covering things that aren't a threat."

"I suppose that makes sense." She looked around the room. "Come on, you guys. It's not that bad. It might not seem that way to you, but we're making progress. We'll close this. Welcome to police work."

"I'm not a cop," Garda said. "I'm a soldier who got dragged into a political mess."

"Stop thinking about that. The senator is probably concentrating on subsidies for corn farmers and protecting the cattle industry from the global-warming lobby. Treat this like a job. The politicians have forgotten about you."

"I wish," Garda replied. Then he felt his mouth drop. "Wait, that thing you said . . ."

"The corn subsidies?"

"No. The global-warming lobby. I just remembered something I read." He stood. "Reina, do you know if Green Vigilance ever got off the ground?"

"Yeah. Well, mostly. They've got the constellation pointed at the Third World because Russia said that if they even thought about monitoring their territory, they'd shoot them all down. China said they'd help the Russians," Reina said.

Hamilton stared at them. "What are you two talking about?"

Garda stopped. In his enthusiasm, he'd forgotten that Hamilton wasn't likely to follow minor space projects. He turned to her. "It's a program run by HomeBase that—"

"The eco-extremists? The people who blew up a part of Ford's River Rouge plant?"

"They claim the bombers were a breakaway group that has nothing to do with the cause," Peters replied. "And the Green Vigilance project is completely legitimate."

"Yeah," Garda added. "They sent a constellation of cubesats into space to monitor the heat emissions of major industrial sites all over the world, as well as to monitor ocean temperatures. They're basically infrared cameras aimed the planet. When they announced it, the major industrialized nations told them not to point the cameras their way."

Peters nodded. "Yeah. Most countries were quite civilized about it, but I don't think anyone was really heartbroken when the Russians and the Chinese basically told them that if a single report about their countries was filed, they would break all the ecologists' toys."

"Even so, they're perfect for spotting a launch . . . if we can get real-time access to them," Garda said.

"Sounds expensive," Hamilton said. "How can an eco-group afford a billion-dollar satellite constellation?"

"It's not a billion-dollar anything," Garda said. "With the cost of orbital launches for smallsats down to a few hundred dollars a kilo, most organizations can afford to launch things. Hell, that's how our friends the drug dealers stay in business. In fact, with cheap installations and the lack of security measures, I wouldn't be surprised if they're the cheapest launch system on the planet." Garda grew more excited. "So, to keep everyone in the northern hemisphere from getting mad at them at once, the Green Vigilance project is basically making life miserable for the people in the south who are just trying to industrialize Third World countries. The Brazilians really hate them, but they can't do anything about it. Most African countries hate them too." He paused. "But that doesn't matter. What matters is that they have the entire constellation staring at the world below the Tropic of Cancer. If anything launches, they will definitely see it. So, we should forget about the satellite that's already up, and concentrate on spotting the next one."

"And can we ask for access?" Hamilton asked, understanding what Garda was aiming for. "If the Space Force calls saying it's a national security issue—"

"No dice," Peters said. "HomeBase is a Finnish group. They think the U.S. is part of the problem. And even if they liked the country, they'd still hate the Space Force."

Garda smiled. "They can hate us all they want. But I bet we'll be able to access their feed."

"How?"

"Politics." He pulled his phone out of his pocket and called up the contact that he'd dreaded seeing every day since the investigation began.

The senator answered on the second ring. "Do you know what time it is?" he asked irascibly. "At least tell me you've cracked the case."

As always, Garda kept his tone respectful in the face of the senator's anger. "I have an idea that could do it, but I need your help, sir."

"The Pentagon is still all over my ass about your last idea."

"I can imagine, sir. But this one will bring quicker results." Inspiration suddenly struck. "And besides, it will piss off every environmentalist on the planet."

The long silence on the other end of the line could have meant anything. Finally, when Garda thought he might have accidentally disconnected the call, the senator chuckled. "All right. You have my attention."

"Well, there's a group called HomeBase that . . ."

✵ ✵ ✵

This time the helicopter door let in salty spray as opposed to just wind. And his companions were Navy SEALs as opposed to Army Rangers, but at least the raid was legal.

Well, semilegal.

If you got the right lawyer.

"Lights ahead!" the SEAL next to him shouted. "Three hundred meters to the target."

Garda swallowed and gripped the rifle harder.

"Scared?" the SEAL asked.

"Too tired to be scared," Garda replied.

It was true. As soon as Green Vigilance spotted the telltale bloom of bright heat in the middle of the Atlantic Ocean, Garda had boarded a two-seat Air Force fighter for Florida. He landed in Homestead and was transferred to another two-seat fighter, Navy this time, which landed on the *Dwight D. Eisenhower* somewhere in the Atlantic.

From there, a Sea Ranger helicopter took him to another ship where the SEAL team was waiting for him.

Fifteen minutes after that, they were airborne again.

Information about what the team in California was uncovering about the launch and the payload trickled in at each stop.

The launch was confirmed to be a satellite the same size and trajectory as the one that had delivered the Kansas payload.

The launch had not been informed to any national aerospace administration.

China and Russia, who might have been responsible for a secret launch, not only denied any involvement, but also gave the U.S. permission to take any action required. They thought it was a terrorist thing, apparently.

"What are we heading into?" Garca asked the SEAL assigned to babysit him.

"Images show some kind of platform with a ship moored beside it. Not great in this rain, but that's what intel says it is."

"Oh, my God," Garda said, slapping his head. "Sea Launch. It has to be."

"Say again, sir?"

"I know what the objective is. It's a platform from a company called Sea Launch that used to do orbital lifts out of Russian ports before they went bust. The platform isn't going to run from us, but we need to make sure to grab the ship. That's where the people we want are going to be. And the control room."

The SEAL looked him up and down. "You sure about this?"

"Of course I'm sure. Didn't they tell you? I'm with the Space Force."

The man's eyes opened up, whether in surprise or disdain or respect it was hard to tell. "All they told me was to keep your butt in one piece." He turned away from Garda, toward the front of the chopper. "Sir, I think you need to hear this."

The team leader, a fiftyish man who'd been introduced simply as "the colonel" moved down to sit across from Garda, then listened wordlessly to his explanation. "Anything else we should know?"

"Like what?"

"Like can they blow the platform up with us on it?"

"Without a rocket? Yeah, they could, but only if they brought along way too much fuel. On balance, I'd say it's unlikely."

The colonel grunted. "Anything else nasty you can think of?"

"No, sir. Platforms are dangerous when there's a rocket on them. After the rocket's gone, almost all the explosive stuff goes with it. In fact, they're designed to be extremely robust and to avoid blowing up."

That got him another nod. "All right."

The colonel sat back.

"Sir," Garda said. "I have a question. Is there any way we can land people on the ship first? Any high-value targets are going to be there, not on the platform."

"That is a much harder operation. The ship's heliport is too small for this bird. We'd have to jump off a moving chopper, probably into enemy fire."

Garda nodded. "I suppose you're right. It just sounded like the kind of thing Navy SEALs are known for."

The colonel grinned. "Damn right it is. I didn't say we wouldn't do it, just that it was a lot harder. You." He put a finger in the chest of the man assigned to babysit Garda. "Make sure this guy stays behind something armor plated while we're securing the area. It sounds like they might have sent us a useful advisor for once, and we don't want to get him dead."

"Yes, sir."

The SEAL turned back to Garda. "You heard the man. Stand here, away from the door and beside this beam. That should keep you out of the line of fire."

"What if we get shot down?"

"Do you think they might have missiles?"

"I . . . I suppose not," Garda said.

"Good. Then we're not getting shot down. Don't worry about this. Drug dealers, especially the kind of people they send out on a ship like this one, aren't precisely elite troops. We'll be fine. Now stay put."

The chopper's steady approach through the rain suddenly changed as the pilot angled upward away from the waves. Garda wanted to see what was going on outside, but bodies and metal blocked his view. The SEALs were big, covered in bulky equipment and helmets.

"Stay put, sir!" his minder said, finally remembering his rank.

The chopper circled once and the men inside with him jumped through the door, amid shouted commands.

The belly of the chopper—Garda hadn't even had time to see what kind of bird they'd taken—seemed empty without the operators. Even the deafening sound of the rotors seemed muted without the shouting. It was dark in there too.

The pilot rotated and lifted the craft to give the main guns a better angle if needed, but everything on deck appeared calm.

It shouldn't have been. A shipload of drug dealers sending out a multimillion-dollar load should have been armed for trouble.

Garda swallowed. Had he screwed it up again? He leaned despondently against the metal plate of the chopper bulkhead, wondering if the SEALs would let him jump into the sea during the flight back. That would be better than facing the senator.

"Contact!" his minder shouted. "Shots fired!"

"Yes!" Garda said. The SEAL just raised an eyebrow.

"They're calling in small-arms fire and one AK." The man listened for a few minutes. "The guy with the AK is down. The rest of them are surrendering."

"Can we go see what we got?"

"No way. We wait until they call for us. There are a thousand places to hide on one of these boats and it only takes one bullet to ruin your whole day. Sir."

Ten minutes later five SEALs returned to the helicopter. Two of them remained on the deck while two others loaded a wounded man—shot in the leg and cursing like a soldier who'd been shot in the leg—into the chopper, then climbed in after him.

The medic looked up at Garda and the man with him. "You two are supposed to go find the colonel. The ship is secure between here and there, but take care anyway."

"Yes, sir," the SEAL with Garda said.

The two men waiting below led them across the deck, up two flights of metal steps, through a door that led to the galley and then into a mess deck.

Two SEALs guarded a dozen men with zip-tied arms and legs who sat on the ground. The only prisoner not complaining was a bearded man who lay in a pool of his own blood, empty eyes staring at the roof.

The colonel barked a couple of orders and one of the men who'd come with Garda took his place on guard duty. The other man and Garda's minder sprinted away, presumably to help secure the rest of the vessel.

"Captain," the colonel said. "Were you the one who generated the intel on this op?"

"Yes, sir."

The man nodded. "Well, you did a hell of a job. I think you hit the jackpot. I've got a good ear for accents and languages, and you've got at least three Mexicans here promising dire retribution from their cartel. They're so dumb they think we're from a rival gang." He nudged a different guy with his foot. That one looked more Icelandic than Mexican. "And this one is a Belgian mercenary called Kim Norland. Even if these other guys turn out to be chumps, it was worth it to grab this one. War crimes in four different African conflicts."

"And the rest?"

"Drug dealers. Rocket people. I don't know. We've got a bunch more stashed in one of the dorm rooms, but these were the ones that looked important." The colonel shrugged. "I guess it's your job to sort them out."

"You're sure they said they were from a cartel?"

"Yeah, why?"

"Because if they launched drugs, it means my people can do their thing."

"I'm sure," the colonel replied.

He wasn't the kind of guy you questioned twice, so Garda pulled out a satellite phone and approached the window. A moment later, Reina Peters answered.

"Yes, Captain?" she said.

"Take it down. It's a drug payload."

"Please confirm, I'm authorized to launch against the satellite."

"Confirmed. Take it down." He'd received all the necessary authorizations from higher-ups as he made his way from California to the Sea Launch vessel.

"With pleasure, sir. Missiles away." She paused. "If you're near the launch site, you might want to look up. The detonation should be visible from your position in four minutes."

"Thanks," Garda replied. He turned to the colonel. "Want to see something cool? I've seen you do your thing, and I'm impressed. I want to show you us doing our thing."

The colonel raised an eyebrow and followed Garda up onto the deck.

✡ ✡ ✡

Gustavo Bondoni is a novelist and short story writer with over four hundred stories published in fifteen countries and seven languages. He's a member of Codex, an organization of published writers, and an active member of SFWA. He has published six science fiction novels including one trilogy, four monster books, a dark military fantasy and a thriller. His short fiction is collected in *Pale Reflection* (2020), *Off the Beaten Path* (2019), *Tenth Orbit and Other Faraway Places* (2010), and *Virtuoso and Other Stories* (2011).

In 2019, Gustavo was awarded second place in the Jim Baen Memorial Contest and in 2018 he received a Judges' Commendation (and second place) in the James White Award. He was also a 2019 finalist in the Writers of the Future Contest. His website is at www.gustavobondoni.com.

Luna Lacuna

✧

Laura Montgomery

The January sun stood only just clear of the Atlantic Ocean, exhibiting its usual gaudy display of gold flung toward land across the water. The waves coming to shore cut dark horizontal lines across the shining carpet. Where the gold didn't reach, the pewter-colored water shone hard and brilliant, a bright glare to the right of the two dawn runners making their way northward along Florida's Space Coast. Launch towers at the Cape were distant smudges across the flat expanse of beach, water, and causeway.

Captain Jack Rampling, USSF, was a big man with dark yellow hair. By dint of work, will power, Academy requirements, and an overwhelming irritation with himself, he'd shed most of his high school fat, sloth, and growing pains, replacing it with muscle, strength, and endurance. Now he pounded along the sand in shorts and a thin cotton shirt, barely breaking a sweat. He'd been stationed at the Cape for more than a year and the sun no longer burned him. He was dark from it.

Niall Yarrow, his friend from high school and now in charge of his own remote-sensing company, ran at Jack's left, probably using Jack to block the sun. Niall's red hair was dark with sweat, and his pale skin wet with it. Niall didn't live in Florida and wasn't used to it. He'd been the athletic one in high school, naturally lean and an adequate member of the track team. Jack suspected Niall spent too much time at his desk nowadays. Niall wasn't audibly panting, but maybe he was close to it.

Jack considered slowing. It would be an act of mercy. Instead, it seemed more fun to make Niall talk. "Your company's moving out. No more just looking down."

"Sure," Niall panted. "The Moon counts as looking up."

"Like the Space Force," Jack said, deliberately pompous, working to goad his friend.

"Listen," Niall said. "I need to run something"—he gulped air— "by you."

"Is it serious?" Jack asked. He was familiar with Niall's game. If he acted too interested, Niall would take forever to make his latest disclosure.

"It's interesting." Niall gave him the vulpine grin that used to mean he'd figured out something especially evil for the battlebots to do. They'd won that competition their junior year, justifying the smile.

"How interesting?" Jack didn't let up the pace. He didn't believe in pandering to his own curiosity.

"You'll hate it." Niall's voice no longer sagged. He always gained strength from making trouble.

"Then you have to tell me."

Niall waited several seconds, and their feet pounded against the sand. "I'm pretty sure you've got a Moon base."

Jack almost stopped, but forced himself on. "A what?"

"A Moon base. I think the Space Force has a secret Moon base. Probably on the dark side."

Jack refrained from pointing out that the Moon didn't have a dark side. It was just hidden from observers on Earth. Niall knew that perfectly well.

"Is that why you're putting a bird around the Moon?" Jack's voice dripped skepticism, but inside he wondered. He was working launch safety in his current billet. If there was a Moon base, and it was secret, he'd have no need to know about it.

Jack hoped fervently his friend hadn't lost his mind and was putting a satellite in lunar orbit to look for secret Moon bases.

After high school, Jack had won a coveted spot in the Academy and spent his four years in the Springs. Niall had gone on to engineering at Embry-Riddle. Once out, he'd spent three years with Vision, a remote sensing company whose fleet of satellites did Earth imaging, weather, and dynamic AIS data tracking. After three years in the large corporation, Niall had struck out on his own. He'd picked the right time, when venture capital was high and always looking for places to land. At twenty-six, Niall Yarrow had gotten funding for his start-up, Wheeling Remote Sensing, and now, five years later, his company had a small constellation in orbit around Earth. Niall's current visit to the Cape this week, however, was driven by his launch of a new satellite headed for a more ambitious destination, a cislunar orbit.

"Of course not," Niall said. "I've got a solid business case with the water miners and the PGM people. Lots of contracts." He snapped his head around, the grin back, to try for a face-to-face gloat.

Jack was having none of it, and kept his eyes fixed on the long stretch of sand ahead. He pressed left against Niall and away from the water, which was starting to reach for his shoes. It was a fine line, getting the harder wet sand, but not getting running shoes soaked.

Jack hated to indulge Niall and exhaled audibly. "So why do you think there's a Moon base? On the far side."

"NOAA had a rulemaking. When there was no one there."

Jack waited. Niall liked this game too much. He'd dangle obscure tidbits, forcing one to ask for more information. Jack refused to play, even if he couldn't figure what a NOAA rulemaking had to do with a secret military Moon base.

NOAA was the National Oceanic and Atmospheric Administration. It regulated and licensed remote-sensing satellites that took pictures of or otherwise remotely sensed the Earth and the activity on it. Jack had had dealings with the agency in the course of his Space Force career, and didn't need to play Niall's game—didn't ask for more.

Niall ran without his earlier effort, clearly gifted of a second wind. "You know what a rulemaking is?"

"I do." A regulatory agency like NOAA couldn't just announce its rules overnight. It had to publish them as a proposal for everyone's comments. Then the agency might modify the proposed requirements in response, disagree with the comments and issue the new rules anyway, or a combination of both. Rulemaking could take years.

Niall grimaced, deprived of his fun. "Well, in 2019, NOAA said it was thinking about making anyone sensing the Moon get a license. When it was explaining the proposed requirements, it had a long song and dance about how Congress gave it the authority to do so. My lawyer said that authority was not clear—not clear at all—and NOAA was making a real stretch. Maybe, he said, NOAA was trying to help DOD hide a Moon base. Then, NOAA could order anyone who had to get a license to sense the Moon not to sense the base."

Jack felt a measure of relief. "So it was a joke."

"Well, yes." Niall was running well now. "Larry meant it that way, but why else would they've done it?"

"So now you need a license for your satellite to sense the Moon?"

"No," Niall said. "Not at all. NOAA withdrew that part of its proposal. Complete about-face."

"So if you see a secret Moon base, there's no one to tell you to keep quiet about it?"

Niall kept his face forward, but an eye slid over to check Jack's reaction. "I would consider it my patriotic duty," Niall said. "To keep my mouth shut. You know me."

Jack did know Niall and wasn't worried about him going to the press.

"Sounds like there's no Moon base," Jack said. "If there were, they'd be making you get a license nowadays. It's not 2019 anymore, and there's enough eyes up there I'd think they'd want to make you get a license to be able to order you to keep quiet." Jack and Niall had been kids in 2019, but there were more lunar operators now than then. Private companies had robots on the Moon looking for—and even finding—platinum group minerals, but their findings were as secret as anything the Department of Defense might protect. The European Space Agency had a small "village" capable of housing fifteen live humans, but it rarely held more than half a dozen. NASA had its habitat, and it housed around a dozen, despite the cramped quarters and the constant mold issues. China had an ice mining rig, manned by a rotating crew of four. The whole world knew about all of these.

"It sounds like they'd make us," Niall admitted, "but maybe it's like the formula for Coke. Too important to try for legal protection. Even with an order, there's still the risk of disclosure from someone ordered not to sense it."

"Aren't you the one always telling me the government wants more power all the time?" Jack asked. "Maybe NOAA just had a knee-jerk notion that it should be doing something."

"Or maybe DOD asked them to, then changed its mind."

They ran in silence for another minute. At Jack's side, Niall ghosted across the sand effortlessly now.

"I think the fact you still don't have to get a license now is more telling," Jack said. "Pay attention to the parts that don't support your crazy theory." He picked up the pace until Niall was a good shade of red, even protected by Jack's shadow.

Jack finished his review of the waivers for the flight termination system. For once, they were minimal and the rationales sufficient to demonstrate an equivalent level of safety to the range requirement. Sure, the FAA looked at this, too, but he subscribed to the view that a responsibility shared was a responsibility ignored, and didn't want to fall prey to the syndrome.

He shared an office with two others, but they were both at a meeting, so he pushed away from his desk and opened the double-hung window. It didn't look onto the ocean, but in January it was plenty cool enough in the morning. Even if his view of the road and other low-slung buildings wasn't the most glamorous, he could hear the water now. When his office mates returned, Trainor would close the window, and Subs would whine he liked it open too. They'd all agreed at the outset, however, that whoever felt hot got to decide. You could always put on more layers if the arctic hell of southern air conditioning wasn't your thing.

Unfortunately, completing the waiver review and opening the window left him twenty minutes before lunch to be snared by Niall's nutball idea.

It made no sense, and Jack knew it. Also, he was sure a DOD Moon base wasn't allowed. The United States had signed a treaty back in the middle of the previous century agreeing not to put forts on the Moon. He called up the Treaty on Principles Governing the Activities of States in the Exploration and Use of Outer Space, including the Moon and Other Celestial Bodies on his cuff and sent it to his desk's screen. Sure enough, the treaty's Article IV said, "The establishment of military bases, installations and fortifications, the testing of any type of weapons and the conduct of military maneuvers on celestial bodies shall be forbidden." He leaned back. That sounded clear to him. Niall had had his fun, and no one needed to say anything more about it.

His eye fell on the next sentence. "The use of military personnel for scientific research or for any other peaceful purposes shall not be prohibited." Was that a loophole? NASA was the public research agency for space. Could DOD conduct scientific research? Of course, it could and did. DARPA was DOD's. There was the Air Force Research Lab headquartered at Wright-Patterson. The Navy and Army both had research labs and so did the Space Force.

But what would the military research on the Moon? Telescopes? Maybe the Space Force were watching for aliens.

Jack's lips twitched, but now he needed to know. Not technically. Not legally. But personally, he needed to know. He found NOAA's 2019 rulemaking proposal and the final rule in the *Federal Register*. At first, he thought Niall had made it all up because there was no mention of the Moon, but then his eyes landed on the code words: the Earth's moon was a "celestial body." Everyone had their own jargon. The proposal made it sound like NOAA thought no one could do anything in space without a license. Looking at the final rule, where NOAA answered comments on its proposal, it didn't sound like the satellite operators agreed. A lawyer had once told Jack that agencies were supposed to explain themselves when they did anything different. In the second document, where the agency was supposed to do just that, NOAA glossed over what Niall had called the agency's about-face. Although it didn't come out and admit as much, it seemed like NOAA recognized Congress hadn't given it authority to make companies sensing other planets get a NOAA license, but NOAA was pretty vague about it. Why?

Niall had planted a brain worm in his head, that was for sure. Jack decided he needed food. That would get rid of it.

Niall Yarrow, founder and CEO of Wheeling Remote Sensing, Inc., stepped into the company's visitor's office at the Cape. Morning sun poured through the floor-to-ceiling windows. As he did every time he used the space, Niall dropped the blinds to cut the glare behind his screens. The desk faced the window, and when the sun rose high enough, he would open the blinds so he could see out onto the garden and its palms, swirling ferns, and picnic table. He'd planned to take meetings out there whenever he didn't need his screens. He almost never got to take meetings out there.

He'd awoken early this morning. LunWheel's launch two afternoons earlier had gone flawlessly, and he was grateful for that. Unmanned rockets almost never failed anymore, but he didn't want his to be one of the exceptions. The vehicle had stayed on course, with no one like his friend Jack having to issue a destruct command. The vehicle's first stage had flown back to the Cape; the second stage had reached orbit and released the LunWheel spacecraft. Nineteen hours after launch, the spacecraft had carried out its translunar injection maneuver and LunWheel was now headed for cislunar space. It would reach lunar orbit in a little over two more days. That meant two days of waiting: waiting to see if the autonomously programmed spacecraft deployed as designed, freeing LunWheel from its confines; waiting to test that all the instruments functioned in their new environment; then waiting to see if the bird found anything in the Moon's craters, highlands and maria—in its regolith, to be precise.

He could wait. He was patient. In the meantime, his fingers rolled a staccato rhythm across his desk, and his foot tapped the ground. He stared at the blinds, where the slits between each made stripes of the bright green glare behind them.

LunWheel was his newest baby, and he'd got it in the lunar game early. Sure, governmental lunar orbiters had led to maps good enough for NASA to decide where to land; but LunWheel would let Niall's customers look harder for treasure without having to commit to a landing before resolving at least some uncertainties.

LunWheel was the first build of a planned lunar constellation. It was a three-axis stabilized, nadir-pointed spacecraft, designed for continuous operation. He wasn't nervous about the hydrazine propulsion system capturing the spacecraft into a polar orbit at the Moon. That would work. And he'd pored over the calculations himself for the timing necessary to obtain an orbital plane optimized for the best lighting conditions in polar regions during summer and winter seasons.

There were just so many steps where something could go wrong. Additional burns would be needed to circularize the orbit and maintain it at its planned altitude of 50 ± 20 kilometers. Its large solar array would provide power during the sunlit portions of its lunar orbit, and a sturdy lithium-ion battery would maintain bus voltage and operational power during orbital eclipses, not to mention survival power during those rare instances where the Earth itself eclipsed the sun. Wheeling had planned for and thought of everything.

But what if it hadn't? Niall knew this was all nerves and usually set them aside when he couldn't check and double-check everything for the ninth time.

It was better to contemplate the instrument itself, which was a true work of art. The hyperspectral scanner would let geologists identify different minerals and look for water. In addition to its active and passive sensors, it would employ the newer charge-coupled devices that would directly convert the spectrometer's images into electronic signals for transmission to Wheeling's ground stations. It would deploy lidar and radar for detection and ranging, the arrays of sensors measuring whole swaths of the lunar surface at a time. Ultimately, LunWheel would downlink the raw data to Wheeling's Earth station receivers for processing and sharing with Wheeling's customers.

Then it was up to his clients to figure out what was valuable and where they wanted to go to get it. Geologists would pore over the data, looking for water ice, checking basaltic lava for ilmenite for electrostatic separation into oxygen and iron, and sifting and scraping the data for platinum group minerals along ancient crater rims.

He'd maybe been pulling Jack's leg about his imaginary DOD Moon base during their run on the beach. Mostly. Niall had also been gauging Jack's reaction, and he was certain that if there was a secret Space Force Moon base Jack didn't know anything about it.

Niall considered the question. He and Wheeling's lawyer Larry Gordon had agreed that if they were DOD, they'd put any Moon base on the far side. Amateur astronomers didn't need to see it. Heck, they wouldn't have wanted to risk backyard astronomers finding a strange glint where there hadn't been one before. It would be logical to check the far side first. He'd been too busy—and too keyed up, to be honest—for the launch to indulge his curiosity. Now, however, it might be funny to check it out.

He dropped his chair height and pulled the keyboard tray toward him, stretching his legs out nearly flat in a position unconsciously reminiscent of the video game posture from his teens. The desktop synched and sank with the chair to their preset heights. It made him feel like a race car driver.

In keeping with his working theory, he called up the far-side data from the U.S. Geological Survey. It had what he wanted, government data from the pre-Apollo Lunar Orbiters. Lunar Orbiter 4 had photographed about seventy-five percent of the lunar far side, and the fifth orbiter had gotten almost all the rest. But that was long ago, and there'd been plenty more imaging since then. If there were spots that hadn't been updated or given better resolution in the government GIS database, those would be the interesting parts to investigate. Where had resolution improved and where had it not? Sure, there were private satellites showing plenty, as would LunWheel, but if it had a structure on—or in—the Moon, the government would fudge where it could. So, where did it look like it was fudging?

The lunar far side wasn't like the face the Moon showed Earth. With telescope and even naked eye, humanity had long viewed the near side's dark areas—with what the ancients had characterized as lunar seas or maria, walled craters, and evidence of ridges and rays. No, the far side lacked the near side's dark sweeping maria—except for the small one in the northern hemisphere—but had far, far more craters with radiating rays crossed by more craters, craters inside craters, and rays crossing rays.

He was well aware that when the USGS released its comprehensive 2020 lunar map and GIS database, that it had had to reconcile different scales and different methods from different sources. This meant that maps of the same feature that had been mapped by different groups wouldn't match precisely. The government could ascribe any fuzzy areas to the attempt to reconcile those discrepancies. Whatever the logical explanation for them might be, it didn't matter. Niall would have his own bird on the scene shortly, and it could just look at those areas and he'd be able to see for himself. Assuming he could find them.

He opened a new file and began writing code.

It had been several days since Jack Rampling's friend had tried to plant a brain worm in his head about a Space Force Moon base. He hadn't even thought about it. So when late on a Tuesday the wing commander put Captain Rampling on her calendar for 8:30 a.m. the next day, Jack canceled his standing 9:00 a.m. call with the FAA, polished his shoes, and made sure he was wearing clean everything. There was no one else on the calendar invite.

The next morning, he drove to Patrick Space Force Base instead of north to his office on the Cape, and parked in the lot adjacent to the new headquarters building. Even housing both Space Force and FAA offices, it was a modest sprawl of a building, its lack of height reflecting the large tracts of land the Space Force occupied. Vertical heights were reserved for the launch towers that dotted the coast to the north at intervals sufficient to achieve acceptable levels of risk for neighboring launch operators.

The sun had solidly cleared the horizon but still shone straight in his eyes as he exited his vehicle. He checked his cuff and was relieved to see he had fifteen minutes to spare. He slipped his tablet into his front jacket pocket in case he needed to call up any information. It disturbed him that he didn't know what the meeting was about. The late-arriving invite had contained no subject, and he couldn't think what he needed to brief the range commander on. There'd been no safety issues in months, and she'd want to talk to the colonel about such things, not him. The colonel hadn't been on the invite.

He wasn't nervous. He did, however, like to brush up on a topic before meeting with the brass. He'd spent a couple hours last night going over all the safety waivers for upcoming launches, checking them against the regulations, making sure he knew their status. That was all he could think she'd be interested in.

It was early, but the lot was already full of other cars. The pavement was still hot from the day before, and the smell of it mingled with the salt air. The entry faced the Atlantic, so he made his way around the building, avoiding the in-ground sprinklers giving the knee-high hedgerows their morning drink. An arctic blast of air hit him at the entrance, matched only by the cold gaze of the eighteen-year-old at the door who was taking his security duties seriously.

Through security, Jack took the stairs to the top floor, made his way past the general's receptionist, and into her office.

General Melanie Tucker, USSF, was in her late forties, a blue-eyed blonde who'd seen a lot of sun and not worried about it. She was drifting toward plump, and of middle height for a woman, maybe five-five, and Jack would tower over her if she stood. She didn't stand. Instead, when Jack saluted, she gestured to the empty chair in front of her desk. The other was occupied by a civilian in a dark suit, who wore his hair as short as any Marine. He was also in his middle years, pale and gaunt, and clearly didn't live near the Cape.

"Mr. Merritt," the general said, "this is Captain Rampling. Captain, this is Mr. Merritt. He's visiting from Maryland."

Merritt stood and shook hands, and Jack forced air through a suddenly tight chest. He knew what it meant to be "from Maryland" and have no first name offered. This was someone from the intelligence community. Was someone putting up a secondary payload that would require special attention? He should have been intrigued. Instead, something nagged at him.

So Jack said only, "Sir," and sat when the other man did.

They both turned to Tucker.

Her eyes scanned from one to the other. "I'll need you to help Mr. Merritt, Captain. He has some questions for you. I want to be present when he asks them." She gave Merritt a hard look, as if perhaps Merritt had not himself initially thought her presence necessary.

Was the range commander trying to protect him? From what?

Jack swallowed.

Merritt leaned back in his chair, offering no false smile. No one liked him showing up, and he knew it and wouldn't try to improve the situation. "I'd like you to tell me about what you do here, Captain Rampling."

Jack's mind went momentarily blank. "My job?"

Merritt's lips almost twitched. "Yes. Your job."

"What's this about?" Jack demanded. He hadn't appreciated the stab of fear.

"If I don't have to tell you," Merritt said, "I'd rather not. How about you just tell me what it is you do here at the range?"

Tucker nodded at him, her expression unhelpful.

Jack took a long breath. "Sure. I'm the range safety officer on the Space Force side—government and commercial. I oversee launch and reentry safety for reusables, the old expendables, capsules, spaceplanes, the lot—anything that flies out of or returns to the range."

Merritt waited, clearly wanting more than Jack's usual truncated spiel.

"I make sure the flight safety systems are compliant. I work with the civilian safety team here on any design changes in destruct systems, qualification testing, acceptance testing; downrange coordination; briefing and training the flight control officers. A lot of that is done by the permanent civilian staff."

Merritt allowed Jack to continue for several more minutes, only looking at him expectantly whenever Jack stopped to see if the man from Maryland had heard enough. Jack found himself wracking his brain to unearth any scrap of information about his job and how he did it.

Finally, Tucker intervened, pointing out that she didn't have all morning.

"To what extent do you work with the payload operators?"

Jack blinked. "We like to know their fuels, the oxidizers. Any monopropellants. That feeds into the risk calculations for a launch."

"Mr. Merritt," Tucker said, "Captain Rampling can talk about payload safety a long time too. Do you want him to?"

"Any lunar payloads?" Merritt asked.

Jack had to think. "Yes. About a year ago. Parts for the Gateway project went up uncrewed. That was one of ours—a Space Force launch."

"Do you recall the contents?"

Jack didn't. It made him feel like he was failing an oral exam. Then it came to him. "We asked if there were propellants. We always do. But everything else was classified. Above my clearance." He didn't have to know the answer—wasn't supposed to know, in fact.

Merritt leaned forward, sway backed, arms on the chair rest, hands laced together. "Did anyone say anything about it? That you recall?"

"No, sir."

Merritt settled back again in his seat. Two hard spots formed to either side of his mouth. "The rest of this conversation is classified. You are, in fact, not to mention this meeting to anyone."

"Sure." Out of the corner of his eye, Jack saw Tucker flinch. "Sir."

"What do you know about the Department of Defense's extraterrestrial operations?"

Jack knew a lot. Anyone who'd attended the Academy did.

"Mr. Merritt," Tucker said, "the captain knows plenty. Before he starts describing our satellites on orbit and our personnel seconded to NASA's Moon base, perhaps you could just come out with what *you* want to know."

Merritt stared long at the range commander, but she stared right back. "Yes, ma'am. It was a matter of efficiency. I don't want to tell him anything he doesn't already know."

"It isn't looking efficient," Tucker said. "Not from where I'm sitting." Her tone was polite. She even smiled.

Merritt looked away. He plucked his tablet from the small table that perched between the two visitor chairs and studied it.

"Do you know a Niall Yarrow?"

Sweat sparked the back of Jack's neck. What had Niall done? Worse, what could have happened to him? "I do. Is he all right?"

Merritt produced an anemic smile. "He's fine. Did you see him recently?"

"Sure. Just a few days ago. He was here for a launch."

"And did you tell him anything you know of the Space Force's extraterrestrial activities?"

Jack's face scrunched. "I don't think so. He's in the business— remote sensing. He knows as much as I do about a lot of it. What I do is mostly unclassified. Except for the transmissions to the rocket, of course." He'd forgotten to talk about that in his job description.

"Its installations?" Merritt was leaning forward with his back swayed again.

Niall's ridiculous suggestion about one installation in particular came to him in a rush. "We do have a Moon base?" he blurted. "Niall found it?"

"How do you know about that?" Merritt snapped.

"Mr. Merritt," General Tucker admonished her visitor.

Merritt looked at her and paled, realizing what he'd given away, but far too late.

Tucker again smiled politely. "Less tiptoeing. More thinking."

The look Merritt gave Tucker was not one Jack would have ever sent in a general officer's direction.

Merritt collected himself. "Define 'Moon base,'" he said primly.

"I don't know." Jack thought to the Outer Space Treaty's words. "An installation? A fortification?"

"How do you know about it, Captain?" General Tucker asked.

"I don't, ma'am." Jack's brain was racing. "I thought Niall was joking. He was asking if we had one. I told him I was sure we didn't."

"And what made him ask you?" Merritt had himself under control again, his voice calm, his skin color back to normal.

Jack explained about NOAA's aborted attempt in 2019 to regulate imaging the Moon and how that had made Niall think DOD was hiding something. No one had people or bases on the Moon back then so why would a license be necessary to take pictures of it? Unless there was something there?

"Old Daniels'll get a kick out of that," Merritt muttered. "She warned everyone not to try it. Or so she says now." He pushed his shoulders back. "You're to speak of this to no one."

"Will you be talking to Niall?" Jack doubted he'd get an answer, but he had to try. "Did he find it?"

"Not yet." Merritt's eyes shifted between the two Space Force officers. "We will not be talking to him. We'll be watching him."

"Mr. Merritt," the general said, "do you mean to tell me you came all this way to bother my staff, and Mr. Yarrow hasn't even found it yet? How do you know he will?"

Merritt stiffened. "Mr. Yarrow's search has been looking in all the 'dark' spots, the gaps in our public mapping. Now that he has his own satellite orbiting the Moon, our technical staff advises us it's only a matter of time."

"Do you want me to ask him to stop?"

"Captain Rampling, I repeat: you must not say a word of this to your friend."

"Of course, sir."

"And no hinting either," General Tucker added.

Jack swallowed. "No, ma'am."

"We do have one thing we want from you," Merritt said.

The general sat preternaturally still, and Jack felt the cold, conditioned air deep in his skin.

"What's that?" he asked.

"We want you to keep tabs on him. Keep talking to him about it. We want to know if he's doing it for the Chinese."

Jack found himself on his feet. Some autonomous internal system kept him squarely at attention in the presence of a general officer instead of grabbing Merritt by the neck. "No. He's my friend. Also, he wouldn't."

"Captain," Tucker said smoothly. "Do, please, sit down."

Jack sat. "You don't know him. For him, this is all about curiosity. He'll be thinking it's amusing."

"You're perhaps blinded by your friendship," Merritt said.

Jack pounced. "Exactly. I'd have a conflict of interest. Niall's like a brother to me. He was my best man when I got married. I was his. I've known him since high school. I'm not your man."

Merritt's smile was thin. "So he'll trust you. Also, we'll be listening. We won't be relying on your judgment."

Jack looked to his general, but she only gave the barest nod. "It would be good to agree, Captain." Or she'd order him to.

Merritt had let Jack ask questions. He'd even answered some of them, so Jack knew that Merritt's people hadn't been watching Jack or Niall in particular—which questions made Merritt act righteously indignant—but had a program in place that alerted them when particular searches triggered an alarm. Niall had started one of those searches, looking for areas where the federal government's lunar maps had fuzzy areas.

Merritt had assured Jack that not all of Jack's calls would be monitored, just those with Niall. Also, Merritt wanted Jack to get right on it, so after dinner Jack told Lin he had some work calls and shut himself in their study alone.

He made sure the video chat was securely logged in to his personal account, which was the one Merritt's people would monitor, ironically enough. Merritt hadn't given Jack a script, just told him to get Niall talking about his hunt for the Moon base.

When Niall picked up, Jack told him he was on a secure line since he had some questions about Niall's bird and its capabilities. Niall happily retired to a different room away from his wife, and answered all of Jack's questions.

"What's this for?" Niall asked when Jack ran down.

"I can't say yet," Jack told him.

Niall's grin showed a lot of white teeth. "Not yet? I'll take that for an optimistic answer." Niall always complained that he never had government customers. Jack regularly pointed out he was doing fine without them.

"How's everything else?" Jack asked. "Found your Moon base

yet?" It was a question Jack would have asked without the visit from Merritt, purely on the grounds that it was ridiculous; but he was sure his voice sounded strange and hollow, like a man trying to set someone up.

Niall's eyes lit, and he propped his elbows on his desk, leaning into the camera. His thin face was intent. "No, but I'm on track."

"You're instrument's working already?" Jack was surprised. It had only been three days since Niall's launch.

"No, but I'm checking the USGS maps."

"Because they have a little square marked 'Moon Base.'" The sarcasm helped make his voice sound normal.

Niall rolled his eyes. "No, jerkface. It wouldn't be a secret then. The USGS reconciled a bunch of different images in 2020. They were at different scales, and now they're supposed to show everything on the same scale. I figured I could look to see where these so called 'reconciliations'"—he did two-fingered quotation marks in the air—"showed less detail than earlier maps. Looking for the lacuna in the data." Niall's grin grew giddy. "The luna lacuna."

"Hakuna matata, to you too." Jack kept his voice dry. An ironic tone also masked his hollow voice.

"You know what's the best thing?"

"What?"

"I found three today. Three lacunae."

Jack's heart sank. "Oh? Now what?"

"When LunWheel checks out, I'll have it look in those spots. See what I can see."

"Of course, you will," Jack said. He didn't know if he sounded sarcastic or despairing.

Niall kept on sounding giddy. "I'm looking for telescopes because if I had a secret Moon base, I'd have it looking for aliens. Like Oumuamua, the extrasolar visitor."

Jack knew he should say something snarky, but could think of nothing.

"The Space Force," Niall concluded confidingly, "looks up."

When Jack hung up, he waited to see if he'd hear from Merritt or any of his people. No one called, so Jack went and joined his wife for a game of WarCursed, but he couldn't keep his mind off the idea of a functioning Moon base. It was mind-boggling. All the work that had been done to check how the lunar regolith affected spacecraft on landing had taken place recently. How had anyone put up a Moon base while dealing with those issues? And not been discovered? The Gateway hadn't even been launched in 2019, the date NOAA gave Niall's lawyer the big clue.

But all that was just a cover worry, to mask his concern over Niall. He knew Niall wouldn't do anything crazy with the information if he found the base, like take it to the press. Niall was more responsible than that. On the other hand, Niall was looking for the damned thing. It was just like him, but how responsible was that?

Lin beat him soundly and gleefully.

"Well?" Larry demanded. The lawyer's dark eyes were big in his equally dark face. "Show me." He was a slender man, but tall and with big hands. He reached over Niall's desk for the stills.

Niall couldn't keep the grin off his face. "This one. Even you should be able to make it out. Looks like a telescope."

Larry took the flimsy from him and scowled at it. "I don't see anything."

"The glint," Niall said. "See the smooth curve? I think they're watching for aliens. Makes me feel secure."

Larry scowled again. "It's all gray and black."

Niall looked ostentatiously to the heavens for support, but briefly so as not to overdo it. He was still grinning. "How such a genius as you can't see the most obvious stuff. How long have you been working here?"

Larry Gordon handled Wheeling's regulatory compliance with NOAA. It was he who'd made the joke about how NOAA must've been trying to protect a secret Moon base when it proposed licensing Moon imaging despite the fact Congress hadn't told it to. It had been a great idea, and Larry deserved the credit for it.

"You're sure?" Larry sat down and screwed up his eyes to look more closely. He was only ten years older than Niall, but suddenly looked it.

Niall snatched the flimsy back and replaced it with another. "Here, try this one."

Now Larry's eyes widened. "Should have shown me this one first."

Niall had told Larry about his initial hunt for low-resolution spots that might have been left bland on purpose and what he'd set LunWheel to focus on. Niall relied on attorney-client confidentiality when he had to. It was indeed a privilege. It also meant he had someone to share his victory with.

Niall allowed himself a smug smile. "Pretty good, huh?"

Larry was shaking his head. "Still can't believe it. I was just joking."

"Sure," Niall said. "Me, too. At first."

The lawyer tore his eyes from the image. "Are you going to tell them you know?"

Niall shrugged. "Who would I tell?"

"Your friend Jack, for one. He could tell you where to go."

"I don't want to get him in trouble. He's military. And he didn't know when I saw him last."

Larry's head jerked up. "You told him about this?"

"It's fine," Niall said soothingly. "It was before I even tried to find it. But, yes. I don't want anyone thinking he told me."

"And I want full credit," Larry said. "It was my idea, and I never worked for the government, so it would be pretty clear I wasn't sharing state secrets. That's the approach. But, Niall. You've got to tell someone you've found it. They'll want to read you in."

Niall cocked an eyebrow. "Seriously?"

Larry looked sheepish. "It's what they do in shows."

"And you're always telling me not to get my legal advice from video," Niall said.

Larry stood. "I'll go look into it."

With Larry gone, Niall sat quietly, staring at the smooth gleam of his polished desktop. It took him a long moment, but he made the call. The person he wanted wasn't there.

The next day, a sovereign wealth fund called.

It was a little over a week later when Merritt showed up in Jack's office in person. He insisted on using the SCIF. Jack went through the rigmarole of coding and securing the Sensitive Compartmented Information Facility, which was really just a small room hardened against monitoring, hacking, and other activities of ill intent. The round table seated eight comfortably, and Jack had been in there once with twelve while they all slowly asphyxiated, but that had been an emergency and not repeated. Oxygen levels were the least of his worries, however. Merritt's face was grim.

Once they were seated, the door locked, and the air filters hard at work, the man from Maryland wasted no time on preliminaries. "He's found it."

Jack swallowed. "When?"

"Two days ago. Has he called you?"

Jack felt a spark of temper. "You know he hasn't."

Merritt looked affronted. "We only monitor the calls with your friend. And you notify us about them."

Jack didn't believe him. "Right."

"And he's talking to the Chinese."

Jack was on his feet. This time there was no general around to moderate his reaction and his hands flexed and clenched. Also, his stomach roiled. "That's not true."

Merritt shrugged. "It is."

"You're lying."

"Who'd be more likely to know? Us or you?"

Who'd be more likely to be steeped in deceit, was the real question, Jack thought. Carefully, he unclenched his fists and put his hand on the table. He sat back down. "Why," he bit out, "didn't you people ask Congress for authority for lunar licensing? Once all the lunar activity started? Then you could put your secret shutter control conditions into the license and tell anyone who spotted the Moon base to keep their mouths shut. Under legal order."

Merritt's shoulders rose and fell. "That was a decision at the policy level. Someone decided to take Coca-Cola's approach. There's a good argument that keeping something completely secret works better than letting some know about it. And it's not what we're talking about right now."

"So call him up," Jack said. "Tell him not to talk about it. He's got some level of clearances just for the Earth remote sensing. You won't even have to threaten him. He's no traitor."

"That's the question, isn't it?"

"I'll tell him to cut it out," Jack said.

"You will not." Merritt produced a thin smile. "We have something else in mind for you. We want you to follow up, see where he's going with it."

"He's going nowhere," Jack insisted.

"That's the question, isn't it?"

Jack hated himself. Merritt had eventually reached out to the general, who had reminded Jack that she expected him to provide all reasonable assistance required of him.

It was too soon: his wife hadn't finished the first trimester, but it was all he had that was worth making a call for.

"Lin's pregnant!" Jack announced with false, hearty cheer. It wasn't a topic he could run through a sarcasm filter. Lin's pregnancy wasn't a topic he should be using for Merritt, but he tamped down the queasy feeling.

Niall was thrilled for both of them.

Jack didn't have to bring up the Moon base. Once Niall had said all the right things, he leaned toward the camera, his hands wrapping around his elbows. "You on the secure line?"

Jack felt hollow of a sudden. He had nothing to worry about, he told himself for the thousandth time. Sure, Niall was too curious for his own good sometimes, and, sure, he had a slight reckless streak, but he had his company and his employees to consider, his own family, his freedom from incarceration. And he loved his country.

"I am."

"I've got news too. Not as good as yours, but fun."

"Shoot," Jack said.

"I found it."

"Found what?" Jack knew he was dragging things out purely as an avoidance tactic. He didn't care.

"The Moon base!"

"You're kidding." Jack forced himself to look interested, amazed, and surprised. Maybe he even succeeded.

"On lunar far side."

"How do you know it's ours?" Jack asked. "And not Chinese."

"Found it in one of the USGS lacunae."

Why the man couldn't say "gap" was not something Jack pondered. His friend found everything too fun, from language to Moon bases.

"But speaking of the Chinese—" Niall paused for dramatic effect and Jack's stomach clenched. "They reached out."

Jack swallowed. "What did you say?"

"I told them to get away from me." He batted the air with his hands. "Away from me now."

Relief washed through Jack in a physical wave. "Smart. That was smart."

"He's lying to you," Merritt said the next day on the beach.

"Or you are."

Merritt had found Jack on his run, and had insisted he stop and talk. It gave Jack yet another reason to dislike the man. Merritt looked absurd in his suit and dress shoes on the sand's edge. He'd gestured from near the dunes to get Jack over. At least Jack had his back to the rising sun, and it was in Merritt's eyes.

"We want you to tell him there's no harm in talking to the Chinese. See what they want."

"He'd never," Jack scoffed, "believe I'd suggest that."

"It's a way to draw the Chinese out. We'd like to know how they saw what he was doing."

It was incredible that the Chinese would have been watching Niall or the USGS—or both—and been able to tell what Niall had done so quickly. It was even more incredible that the NSA had been watching the right Chinese. He supposed computer programs could follow many things and alert their operators, but still. It was all incredible, and he knew it.

"So ask Niall," Jack said, watching Merritt's face closely.

Merritt shook his head in a way that said he found Jack a little slow. "We don't know if we can trust Niall."

"You can trust him as much as me," Jack said. "You know he told the Chinese to go pound sand."

"That's what he told you."

Jack realized he was standing at attention, and folded his arms. "Do you know any different?"

"You know I can't share classified information, Captain."

"This makes no sense. What you're really asking me to do is trap Niall. Then you can threaten him with jail to keep him from talking about the base."

"Captain Rampling, may I remind you that you are supposed to help us?"

"To trap my friend." The sun burned into Jack's back. "I don't think the general knew you meant to do this."

"I don't think a captain will be asking her to clarify." Merritt's lips pursed into a new kind of smile.

"If I suggest it, he'll think it's okay," Jack pointed out.

"If you trust him as much as you say you do, you shouldn't worry. Right?" Merritt produced another one of his thin smiles, and Jack pressed his arms against his ribs to hold still.

"Right," he said.

Jack spent the rest of his run slick with three kinds of sweat: cold, nervous, and exertional. He seriously considered trying to warn Niall, but the general had cautioned against hinting. He was being monitored when he talked to Niall. He thought about crossing his eyes when he spoke with his friend about the Chinese. Niall could then maybe figure that cross meant "double cross" and not do or say something stupid, but there were three problems with that: anyone monitoring the call would see it; it was ridiculous; and—worst of all—Niall would ask what was wrong with his eyes.

Merritt hadn't admitted to trying to trap Niall, but it was obvious what was going on. If they were really after the Chinese, they'd enlist Niall himself. The claim they didn't trust him was anatomically implausible. No, for whatever reason the NSA had, this was entrapment, plain and simple.

Jack had no good excuse for this next call to Niall. He'd already told his friend about Lin's pregnancy. Since they'd each married, the two didn't talk as often as they had even in the years after school. Niall would think it strange to get a pointless call.

Jack almost slowed down. Maybe that was a good thing. The topic itself should alert Niall to something being off—really off.

That evening after dinner, he texted Niall for a call and went into the study, closing the door and the windows and cutting off the smell of the ocean and Lin's garden flowers. That was fine. He didn't deserve to be smelling the outdoors—not now that he'd entered Merritt's muck.

His stomach clenched, but he placed the call.

"Now what?" Niall's fox smile was as cheerful as his red hair. "I'm hearing from you a lot these days."

"Just calling to say hi. Lin's doing her pregnancy swim."

"That's a thing?"

It was now. Jack riffed on that, asked after Niall's family, and otherwise talked in circles.

Finally, Niall said, "You want to know about the Moon base, don't you?"

"Of course. I've been waiting to hear about it in the news."

"I'd never do that," Niall said earnestly.

"I know. I know. I have been wondering how the Chinese knew to call you."

"It was bizarre. It happened really fast. Like, why would they be watching me rather than looking for it themselves? And, if they already knew it was there, why would they need to talk to me?"

"Spies," Jack said sourly, well aware of his listeners, "have weasel brains. They think in circles. Now they've got you doing it."

Niall showed his teeth. "I'm not losing sleep over it."

"Maybe you should engage with them. Try to figure out how they got through your firewalls."

A pause grew. It grew longer. Sweat sparked on the back of Jack's neck. Niall wasn't an idiot. He was about to figure out that something was seriously wrong. There were regulations requiring permissions to talk aerospace issues with certain countries, and China was one of them. Jack swallowed. He waited for Niall to laugh and mock him for a failed gotcha.

Instead, Niall frowned. "Do you think that's a good idea?"

"Aren't you curious?"

"I'm always curious. But you?" Niall's ready grin had long vanished.

Jack gave a wan smile. "You know me."

Again, there was a long pause. It was almost as if Jack could watch Niall processing the algorithms. "Well, if you think it's a good idea, I'll give it a go."

Jack shrugged. "Why not?"

Niall opened his mouth. Closed it again. "Listen, I've got work to catch up on. I'll let you know what I find out."

They ended the call.

"You asshole," Jack said, knowing someone would hear, and it wasn't Niall.

※　※　※

Jack spent the next two days sick to his stomach. Lin asked if he had sympathy morning sickness, and he assured her that was probably what it was, despite the fact Lin herself had had none so far.

He'd done it. He'd set the trap and Niall had walked right into it. To find out how the Chinese knew about Niall's discovery meant Niall would have to admit to knowing about it himself—and that might be a nail in his coffin, a coffin that Jack had helped build.

Jack had tried to make his suggestion a strange one, but it had come from him and Niall had trusted him. Niall had probably thought that Jack was doing something appropriate because Jack always did what was appropriate.

Not this time. And if Jack himself could do something this wrong, why wouldn't Niall? Only, the consequences for Niall were far worse.

Late in the afternoon of the second day, Niall texted asking if he could stop by Jack's office the next morning. He had something big, really big. Jack forwarded Niall's message to Merritt, and agreed to meet with Niall in the SCIF at 10:00 a.m.

His stomach continued to pain him.

To Jack's surprise, Merritt showed up an hour before the scheduled meeting. "I caught an early flight," he said. "And you need coaching."

Niall's arrival put an end to the coaching, and Merritt vanished into a second-floor office. Jack ushered Niall down the hall and to the special door with its codes and seals. Neither of them said much, which was strange for them.

Someone had left a window open at the end of the hall, and Jack took a long breath of fresh morning air before he gestured Niall into the SCIF. Niall's face was set and still, and he took a chair across from Jack without his usual bounce.

Jack settled in. Maybe Niall had figured it all out and come to yell at him. That would be all right, he told himself. He'd maybe lost a friend—almost a brother—but Niall wouldn't be going to prison. He cursed Merritt.

"So," Jack said. "Something big? Really big?"

Niall gave a short nod. "But I need something from you first. I need to see whoever put you up to this so they can hear it too."

Now that it had come, Jack felt calm. His stomach stopped

hurting. Niall knew. Niall was safe. Niall was furious with him, and Jack knew that what he'd done wasn't something that could be forgiven. But Jack hadn't misplaced his trust.

He set aside his own rage.

"That could take some time," Jack said.

"I'll wait."

"Here?"

"Here's fine. I figure we're being monitored."

"Okay."

They sat in silence for maybe ten minutes. Jack felt no need to say anything. Niall had the ball and he meant to let him run with it. Niall apparently saw no need for chitchat either.

The door finally opened, and Merritt stepped into the room. It looked like he'd obtained any permissions he needed to talk to Niall. His appearance also suggested that the NSA hadn't been monitoring Niall unless he was talking to Jack. If it had been surveilling Niall, Merritt wouldn't need to reveal himself to hear what was "really big." He'd already know.

Jack stood. Niall didn't. "Niall," Jack said, "this is Mr. Merritt from Fort Meade. He doesn't have a first name."

Niall stretched a lean arm over the chair back next to him, effectively blocking Merritt from taking it.

Merritt gave his thin smile and took a different seat. "I hear you have something really big, Mr. Yarrow."

"I do." Niall maintained his aggressive lounging posture. "But it's more about you than the Chinese. Sorry about that."

Merritt stiffened.

"I learned," Niall began but stopped. "No. Let me change that. I figured out—"

Niall was showing off. That was a good sign.

"—that someone was torturing my friend Jack here. Apparently, it was you. I know Jack. He's a good fellow. He does everything by the book, and he follows orders. And suddenly he thinks I should violate all sorts of regulations and talk to the Chinese? That was crazy talk."

"You made a call we couldn't monitor," Merritt snarled. "On a completely dark line."

Niall showed all his teeth. "Just trying to check in with one of your bosses."

Merritt stood. "Mr. Yarrow, you have knowingly misled me about your big news."

Jack couldn't stop his guffaw.

Merritt glared at him.

"Please." Niall gestured to Merritt's empty seat. "Sit down. I'm trying to help."

"You are not," Merritt said, but resumed his seat.

"I am. I want you to think twice before you torture honorable men again. I suffered. I even worried you'd threatened Jack's family to make him trick me. Terrible stuff. What I really don't like is you probably made Jack suffer even more. That's not right."

"How did you figure it out?" Merritt demanded through stiff lips.

Niall scowled. "I already told you. He suggested I talk to the Chinese."

Merritt turned on Jack. "This is your fault. You should have told him the Chinese might have offered him money."

Jack was laughing, maybe with a thread of the hysteria attendant to sudden and extreme relief. He tried to stop, but was horrified to find himself still hiccupping involuntarily.

"That would have been worse," Jack said. "Sir. I picked the best thing I could for him not to see right through me."

Merritt's head pivoted from one to the other of the younger men. "How was what you said the best thing?"

"Look at him." Jack waved toward Niall. "He's all about curiosity. Showing off what he can figure out. It really was the thing most likely to tempt him. For the love of heaven, man, he figured out we've had a Moon base for more than two decades. A secret one. Curiosity would work better on him than anything."

Niall managed to look proud despite his slouch. "It was when he said, 'you know me,'" he offered helpfully, expertly mimicking Jack's wan, desperate words.

Merritt turned on Jack. "You did do it on purpose."

Jack spread his hands, careful not to look toward Niall. There was a mic in the room. "I really couldn't say. Sir. It was a terrible experience for me, and I've been trying to forget it. I suffered."

Merritt stood again. "You, Captain, are not cut out for intelligence work."

"No," Jack said, rising to his feet as well. "The Space Force looks up."

✦　✦　✦

Laura Montgomery is a practicing space lawyer who writes space opera and near-future, bourgeois, legal science fiction. Her latest book, *His Terrible Stall*, is the fifth in her Martha's Sons series, which is set on the lost colony world of *Now What We Were Looking For*. Her most recent near-future novel is *Mercenary Calling*, and it follows one man's efforts to save a starship captain from charges of mutiny. Her fiction website is at LauraMontgomery.com.

Before starting her own practice that emphasizes commercial space transportation and the Outer Space Treaties, she was the manager of the Space Law Branch in the FAA's Office of the Chief Counsel, where she supported the regulators of commercial launch, reentry, and spaceports. There she worked on issues ranging from explosive siting to property rights in space. She has testified to the space committees of both the House and Senate, and is an adjunct professor of space law at Catholic University's Columbus School of Law. She writes and edits the space law blog GroundBasedSpaceMatters.com, and speaks regularly on space law issues.

Whose Idea Was This Anyway?

✴

When established in December of 2019, the Space Force became the first new United States military service since the creation of the Air Force in 1947. On the occasion, then president Donald Trump held a press conference in which he stated, "I'm hereby directing the Department of Defense and Pentagon to immediately begin the process necessary to establish a Space Force as the sixth branch of the Armed Forces." He might as well, he could hardly do otherwise than direct Pentagon officials to obey the law. You'd never have known it from the proceedings, but while an American president may indeed be commander-in-chief of the nation's Armed Forces, the job carries no authority to create a new service branch. That has to be done by Congress, and it was, when the 116th Congress added chapter 908 to the National Defense Authorization Act (NDAA) for Fiscal Year 2020 under the heading "Space Force." All Trump did was sign it.

In fact, The Trump administration had strongly rebuked the idea in 2016 when an Obama-era proposal to do the same thing was removed from that year's defense authorization bill. Two years later, though, Trump had changed his position and put his full political weight behind it. Like him or loathe him, no one can argue he doesn't like to be perceived as a man of action and ideas. Indeed, on March 13, 2018, in comments at Miramar in San Diego, he told the assembled Marines, "I was saying it the other day—'cause we're doing a tremendous amount of work in space—I said, 'Maybe we need a new force. We'll call it the Space Force...' And I was not really serious. And then I said, 'What a great idea. Maybe we'll have to do that.'"

A casual observer might be excused for thinking it was all his idea—at least if they didn't know what Air Force Space Command had been up to for the last thirty-six years and that as he spoke that day, the Center for Strategic and International Studies was distributing copies of its "Space Threat Assessment 2018," from which Trump had almost certainly been briefed on recent concerning actions by China, Iran, Russia, and North Korea among others. What they might not have told him, and what many Americans didn't know either, was that a dedicated space force was anything but a new idea. In fact, debate over the proper organizational home for missile and space defense had been raging for decades, both in the United States and abroad.

Rockets have existed since ancient times, but only in the twentieth century did they become sophisticated aerial vehicles capable of carrying people, cargo, and bombs. By World War II, advancing technology had enabled the mass production of rocket artillery, which in various forms was used by all combatants in all theaters of the war. Artillery is traditionally the domain of an army, but by the war's end, it was clear that rockets were going to play vital roles not only as artillery, but in defense against air attack, as a means of striking from vast distances, in new strategic deterrent roles, and maybe one day in reconnaissance and rapid logistical support roles, maybe even in space. Thus, every branch of the U.S. military scrambled to deploy rocket technology to keep itself relevant and effective in the new age.

* In 1945, the U.S. Army established the Jet Propulsion Laboratory at the California Institute of Technology in Pasadena, California. It initially focused on developing and testing liquid-fueled rockets and played a key role in the development of the Redstone, Jupiter, and Pershing missile systems.

* In 1949, the U.S. Navy established the Naval Research Laboratory in Washington, D.C., responsible for the development of a wide range of missile systems including the Viking, Aerobee, and Talos missiles.

* In 1952, the Army established the Ordnance Guided Missile Center, later renamed the Army Ballistic Missile Agency, which

went on to develop the Redstone and Jupiter missiles and orbital launch vehicles.

✻ In 1957, the Air Research Development Command's Western Development Division, which had become the center of efforts to develop intercontinental ballistic missiles, was redesignated the Air Force Ballistic Missile Division.

✻ In 1960, the secretive National Reconnaissance Office was created to develop and operate intelligence-gathering satellites.

✻ In 1961, because of differences in applicable technologies and relative maturities between ballistic missile and space systems programs, the Air Force split these two responsibilities into separate commands under the newly organized Air Force Systems Command. In 1967, however, they were merged back together into the new Space and Missile Systems Organization. Collectively over the years, these organizations developed and operated a wide range of space systems, from communication and navigation to reconnaissance, missile warning, and weather observation. They oversaw the development of the Air Force Satellite Control Network and the Defense Satellite Communications System, a secure, jam-resistant global communications system for U.S. government agencies. They also operated the Air Force's Atlas, Titan, and Delta space launch vehicles and developed and deployed the original GPS navigational satellite constellation.

✻ In 1982, Air Force Space Command was created to consolidate the Air Force's space-related activities and responsibilities. Its mission was to provide resilient and affordable space and cyberspace capabilities for the joint force and the nation, and it managed most U.S. military space operations until 2002, when along with the older Space and Missile Systems Organization, it was reorganized into a new Air Force Space Command with a different reporting structure.

✻ In 1985, U.S. Space Command (not to be confused with U.S. Air Force Space Command) was created as a Unified Combatant Command to integrate space capabilities across the Air Force, Army, Navy, and the National Reconnaissance Office. Its mission included strategic warning and defense against potential threats from space and the conduct of military operations in space. In

2002, these responsibilities were transferred to the newly created U.S. Strategic Command, one of about a dozen Unified Combatant Commands under the Joint Chiefs of Staff but not in any service branch.

Meanwhile, an elevated vantage point has provided military advantage since antiquity, and there is no higher ground than space. While many today still protest the "militarization of space," the reality is that bridge long ago burned down, fell over, and sank into the swamp. From the moment a Soviet rocket put a battery-operated transmitter into orbit in October 1957, the high ground of space became a battleground, or in the PR-challenged parlance of modern military leaders, a "war-fighting domain."

After Sputnik, Senator Barry Goldwater warned "the Soviets could drop nuclear bombs like rocks from a highway overpass." Memories of Pearl Harbor were fresh and fears of Soviet aggression high. Western leaders knew the last war had been invited by perceived weakness and ultimately won on the strength of intelligence gathering. The next surprise attack might be the last, the end of the nation or even civilization itself.

And the surveillance overflights needed to prevent it were themselves a recipe for conflict. In order to reduce the risk, uncrewed Project Mogul balloons carried microphones over and around the Soviet Union to listen for nuclear tests. Project Genetrix and Project Moby Dick sent skyscraper-sized balloons over China, Eastern Europe, and the Soviet Union to collect intelligence on nuclear and strategic military capabilities. The balloons worked, but they were logistically complex, risked crashing heavy equipment down on civilian populations, raised vociferous objections, and were simply too slow, requiring photographic film magazines to be recovered after a balloon reached international airspace.

> Project Mogul's NYU Flight 4 was an experimental test balloon launched on June 4, 1947, from Alamogordo Army Air Field (now Holloman Air Force Base) in New Mexico. Carrying a three-foot cylindrical metal sonobuoy, weather instrumentation, and a simple radar target, it was part of a series of experiments to test the feasibility of using high-altitude

balloons to detect sound waves from nuclear explosions (the sonobuoy was just ballast, borrowed from the Navy till new acoustical sensors were ready).

Flight 4 was lost and never recovered by the research team, but ten days later, rancher W. W. Brazel found something weird northwest of Roswell, barely a hundred miles downwind. The rest, as they say, is history, but don't go searching the desert for dilithium crystals just yet.

When interviewed for a congressionally mandated investigation in 1994[*], surviving Project Mogul researchers Dr. Athelstan F. Spilhaus, Charles B. Moore, and Colonel Albert C. Trakowski confirmed that photos and accounts from the time and later were all entirely consistent with Flight 4. This was supported by the recollections of Lieutenant Colonel Cavitt who in 1947 was dispatched by Roswell Army Air Field (now Walker Air Force Base) to investigate. Cavitt remembered a small area of debris which appeared "to resemble bamboo type square sticks one quarter to one half inch square, that were very light, as well as some sort of metallic reflecting material that was also very light."

This matches Moore's description of the radar target meant to help in tracking the balloon. Triangles of paper-backed aluminum foil were affixed to a complex balsa wood frame to form something resembling an inverted box kite—a set of retroreflectors to strongly return radar signals coming from all directions. Late in the war, production of these radar targets had been contracted out to toy companies who were not told what they were making. Various sorts of tape were used in their construction, and multiple contemporaneous sources mention "purplish tape printed with flowers and hearts"—the same tape recalled by a civilian witness of the crash site as well as numerous military men on the project who at the time wondered at the "unmilitary" construction.

This is clearly what Brigadier General Ramey is holding in photos taken of the debris at the time. And at his feet is a

---

[*] *The Roswell Report: Fact Versus Fiction in the New Mexico Desert*: McAndrew, James: Headquarters, United States Air Force.

dark rumble of what is quite clearly the remains of a neoprene rubber weather balloon of the type used in clusters for the first seven Project Mogul tests, after which much larger polyethylene balloons were used instead.

Far from a massive cover-up of alien visitation, it's clear what really happened: NYU Flight 4, carrying no sensitive or secret components, was lost as part of a top-secret program to detect Soviet nuclear tests. Tracking down the wreckage would have attracted attention without yielding additional data, so it was left to disintegrate in the blistering desert. And that would have been the end of it had not the locals come along and called the Army, who sent men knowing nothing about Project Mogul but who knew a weather balloon when they saw one and knew that enough Cold War secret squirrel action was going on just then that discretion was in order.

Cold War hysteria, post-war let-down, and human nature did the rest. The sonobuoy became "a flying disk," goofy craft tape became "alien hieroglyphs," and gentle downplay of a nonevent became the conspiracy of conspiracies. Honestly, if aliens really had stopped by, they'd have gone home shaking their heads at our credulity.

Left: Soldiers prepare radar target weather balloon at Ft. Bliss. Right: Brigadier General Ramey examining Roswell crash debris. Courtesy, *Fort Worth Star-Telegram* Collection, Special Collections, The University of Texas at Arlington Libraries.

Then, two years after Sputnik in August 1959, the first fully successful Corona satellite mission, Discoverer 14, orbited a large telescopic camera with a jettisonable film magazine. The recovery capsule, containing nearly ten kilograms of film and suspended from a parachute, was snatched from midair by an Air Force C-119 aircraft. This first successful reconnaissance satellite alone returned more photos of the Soviet Union than all twenty-four U2 spy plane missions that had come before, and the images, although of poorer quality, covered areas of the Soviet Union never reached by any plane.

With the Soviet Union rapidly expanding its nuclear arsenal and developing advanced delivery systems, there were those (generals MacArthur and LeMay among them) who advocated a preemptive attack on the Soviet Union before "it was too late." But Corona showed that if we feared a nuclear Pearl Harbor, space-based reconnaissance was the way to prevent it. Far from a dystopian nightmare, the militarization of space was now the key to peace.

Indeed, in a 1962 interview with journalist Merle Miller, President Truman reportedly said he had been "damn glad" when the Soviet Union launched Sputnik because it had demonstrated the principle of free overflight and made it easier for the United States to launch its own reconnaissance satellites. Whether that's really true, the legal principle has since been instrumental in making impending attack or military buildup increasingly difficult to conceal, from the Cuban Missile Crisis to the 2022 Russian invasion of Ukraine.

And of course, that's not all. In the late 1950s and early 1960s, the U.S. military began to develop and deploy early-warning and surveillance satellites for use in missile defense. The Air Force also began to develop and test antisatellite (ASAT) weapons, which were designed to destroy enemy satellites in orbit.

During the 1960s and 1970s, the U.S. military continued to develop and deploy advanced surveillance and communication satellites, as well as space-based missile defense systems. In 1983, President Ronald Reagan proposed a bold initiative to use American technical know-how to "render nuclear weapons impotent and obsolete." Never mind the trillion dollar price tag, the over-ambitious goals, the vulnerability of such technology to on-obit attack, the risk of disrupting the balance of power that for over thirty years had staved off the next world war or the fact that an adversary, deprived of intercontinental missiles, might be tempted to use sleeper agents with delivery trucks instead. Never mind all that, the nation had yet another space-defense-related component to staff, fund, and manage.

And observers started to see that as the real problem. By the end of World War II, air combat had developed in breadth and import to a point that made the need for a dedicated service branch obvious, but space technology and defense concerns emerged slowly. Control of missiles was given to the Army, because the Army used rockets as long-range artillery. Then it moved to the Air Force, which used missiles in place of strategic bombers, and the Navy, which used them in a whole new class of strategic weapon, the ballistic missile submarine.

Today's U.S. space defense efforts descend from postwar and Cold War antiballistic missile defense and the Cold War use of space as a high ground from which to conduct surveillance. For decades, government space activity was strongly segregated into three parts, the civil space program run by NASA, intelligence gathering mostly by the National Reconnaissance Office and the CIA, and nuclear missile deterrence and defense, which itself was distributed across an ever-changing mosaic of military organizations.

By the 1990s, the Soviet Union was gone, and with it much of the Cold War threat of a widespread missile attack. But at the same time, technology had marched on, bringing new fears of terrorism, and rogue nuclear states, and making space increasingly central to the entire global economy. Threats, some said, were being missed and undervalued, important work was being lost in the bureaucratic cracks.

Simplifying a bit, the United States Armed Forces consist of six military service branches under three military departments, plus two executive departments and the Joint Chiefs of Staff. At any given time, it also comprises multiple Unified Combatant Commands, each of which consists of units drawn from two or more service branches to fulfill some broad and continuing mission.

One such unified combatant command was the Air Force Space Command formed in 1982 to handle various aspects of procurement, launch, operation, and defense of space assets and access required by the various service branches. AFSPC comprised 26,000 personnel at facilities all over the world, launched satellites from both coasts, maintained a worldwide network of satellite tracking stations, and operated ground-based radars, optical tracking stations, and all manner of advanced sensors to protect the United States and its interests from ballistic missile attack, orbital space attack, and threats from deep space (asteroids).

Space Command itself was formed from space-related units scattered across the Armed Forces as rocketry matured from advanced artillery to strategic deterrent, and space from the province of science fiction to a vital theater of military and commercial interests. These units principally included Aerospace Defense Command (established in 1968 from units involved in Air Defense since World War II), Air Force Systems Command (established in 1951), and the Strategic Air Command (established in 1946 with the creation of the United States Army Air Force).

So much for the history, which convoluted and somewhat arcane though it may be, illustrates clearly the decades-long debate over how best to incorporate rapidly progressing space and rocketry capabilities into existing military organizations. And in this, the U.S. was not alone. Russian space defense has jumped from the old Soviet Air Force to a dedicated space defense and antisatellite force, back to a more general aerospace defense force, and more recently back to a dedicated "Space Force." Similarly, Chinese space defense has at various times been combined with, or split from, its civilian space science programs and national cybersecurity efforts.

The first proposal for a U.S. military service branch for space defense was in 1957, when in the shadow of Sputnik, congressmen joined then secretary of the Air Force Donald Quarles in proposing the creation of a separate military service branch for space, known as the "Space Corps." The proposal, in hindsight significantly ahead of its time, went nowhere, and instead the Air Force was given primary responsibility to develop and manage the military's space capabilities.

Then, during the Reagan administration in the 1980s, calls were again made for a dedicated Space Corps. Chief among these came from Air Force General James Hartinger, then commander in chief of U.S. Space Command. He argued that given the increasing importance of space as a domain of military operations, the Air Force was not giving it the attention it needed and that a separate space corps would better address the problem.

Then in 1986, a report by the Defense Science Board Task Force on Space, headed by then secretary of the Air Force Edward "Pete" Aldridge, also called for creation of a space corps. The report argued that the Air Force had failed to develop a coherent space strategy and that a separate space corps would better address the problem. These proposals too, however, went nowhere.

The idea resurfaced in 2001 while George W. Bush was in the White House. Air Force Chief of Staff General John Jumper and other senior Air Force leaders again proposed creating a Space Corps as a way to better organize and manage military space operations. The idea, this time formally presented by the Rumsfeld Space Commission, was to create a separate service branch within the Department of the Air Force responsible for military space operations, similar to how the Marine Corps is a separate service branch within the Department of the Navy.

The proposal again failed to garner support, but in 2016, the final report from the congressionally mandated, Obama-era National Defense Panel made essentially the same recommendation yet again, and Republican Representative Mike Rogers added a provision to act on it into the National Defense Authorization Act (NDAA) of 2017. However, committee negotiations dropped the provision from the final bill. Instead, the NDAA tasked the secretary of defense with conducting yet *another* study on the establishment of a Space Corps within the Department of the Air Force. The study was to assess the potential benefits and drawbacks of creating a separate military branch focused on space, as well as the feasibility and costs associated with doing so.

The next year, Republican Representative Mike Rogers, on the House Armed Services Committee, again proposed an amendment to the NDAA for 2018 creating a Space Corps within the Department of the Air Force. Florida Democratic Senator Bill Nelson did, too, but the new Trump administration, which had taken office in January 2017, wanted nothing to do with it. In fact the new secretary of defense, James Mattis, spoke out against it, and took the unusual step of intervening to request removal of the proposals, saying the sixty-one-year-old idea needed yet more study.

But by now, threats to America's space assets were becoming less theoretical. The Chinese and the Russian Federation had both created huge orbital debris clouds by testing direct-assent antisatellite weapons. China was known to be developing a wide range of military space technologies, including direct-ascent kinetic kill vehicles, co-orbital satellites, directed-energy weapons, jammers, and cyber capabilities. China had tested a satellite system believed capable of grappling another satellite, towing it to a new orbit, or cutting off its solar panels. A Russian satellite, Kosmos 2499, had approached a U.S. surveillance satellite close enough to force it to take evasive action.

Representative Jim Cooper (D-TN), then ranking member of the Strategic Forces Subcommittee on the House Armed Services Committee, had worked with Representative Rogers for years on legislation to establish a space service and on efforts to convince others in government, arguing that the U.S. military was not sufficiently focused on space and that the country was falling dangerously behind in space defense capabilities. In this environment of heightened concerns, the two lobbied other members of Congress and promoted their ideas to the public and the new president, negotiating the details of the new service with other legislators and together, agreeing to call it a "force" rather than a "corps." This negotiated proposal made it into the final version of the National Defense Authorization Act (NDAA) for Fiscal Year 2020 that was passed by Congress and signed into law on December 20, 2019.

After that, Jim Cooper, who'd originally been skeptical of the idea, issued a statement congratulating the Air Force and Space Force on their successful collaboration in the creation of the new service branch which, he said "should make America stronger and more competitive in space." Mike Rogers, who'd been a vocal proponent of the Space Force for years, praised the establishment of the new branch as "ensuring our strategic advantage in the final frontier." Both Cooper and Rogers acknowledged the bipartisan nature of their efforts to establish a separate military branch focused on space, and expressed optimism for the future of U.S. space policy.

In the final analysis, however you feel about the man who signed the paperwork, the Space Force was created not by Mr. Trump but by Congress, and after literally decades of consideration and debate.

It's Classified

✣

Martin L. Shoemaker

"Moron," I said to myself under my breath as the latest test run once again glitched.

I don't know why I said it under my breath. It's not like there was anyone else around to hear me. The guards were around somewhere, and certainly cameras were recording anything I said. But I doubted the guards cared that I called myself a moron when chasing down a really difficult bug in the code.

What code? Sorry, it's classified. As a fully cleared contractor to Space Force, I know what I'm not allowed to talk about. The nature of my assignment is not subject to disclosure.

There are things you could pick up from public records. It's not like our enemies can't. But still . . . The phrase "I can neither confirm nor deny" is one they trained us to use often.

I'm a software contractor at the Space Force facility in Nebraska, which specializes in orbital object detection, identification, and tracking. It's public record that my thesis was on the mathematics of multidimensional variances and moments as applied to shape recognition.

So no, if I didn't just spell it out for you, I can't spell it out for you. But in general terms, our latest software was crashing. I can tell you that without telling you what it was. There was something that only happened with real data. No matter what test data I used to validate the code, I never saw this crash in test. But after five, ten, or fifteen minutes of a real data stream, the whole system would crash, and take nearly thirty minutes to set up for another run. As you might imagine, the base commander was not happy with that—nor with me, nor my company. So I was working as many extra hours as the military would let me. It was a sign of Colonel Hale's frustration that he authorized me working so late—under constant guard, of course, but it was still unusual. It wasn't a threat to national security, but it was making his command look bad, and he wanted that to stop.

I added diagnostics all throughout the code, but to no avail. Wherever the bug hid, it wasn't someplace I could even imagine to put diagnostic code. Out of frustration, I stopped trying to diagnose the code, and I started trying to diagnose the data. Set by set, entity by entity, I started looking for patterns in the test data that weren't in the real data—or vice versa.

Something was different between the test entities and the real entities. No, I can't tell you what an "entity" is in this context, the definition is classified. It's a thing in a data stream gathered by a classified system using classified instruments pointed at classified targets within a classified field. From the code's point of view, it's just a hunk of data in a larger sea of data.

I spent another two hours with two screens up, one with real entities and one with test entities, trying to discern the differences. I'd put significant effort into randomizing the edges of the test entities so they weren't smooth like an artist's creation. My girlfriend Kylie might've looked at representations of the entities and picked up the differences. She has that artist's eye that I lack. But as best I could tell, by eye or by data analysis, the character of real data and the character of test data were fundamentally the same. I just couldn't see what was different, and the math couldn't either.

Well, except for one object in the real data. That one was . . . different. Size, cohesiveness, albedo . . . No, scratch that, you never heard me mention albedo. But there were a number of factors that made it different from the other entities in the data field. I tried to visualize it from the data, but it didn't match my experience. Was that anomaly the cause of the crash?

I couldn't say it wasn't, not without tracking the exact moment when the anomaly emerged within the data and comparing it to the timing of the crash. I spent another hour playing the data stream back and forth, looking for any correlation.

After an hour, I still had nothing. I was falling into the common debugging trap: assuming that because I saw one anomaly, it had to explain another anomaly. That two different anomalies don't happen at the same time without reason. Assuming that can bite you in the ass.

But the other thing that can bite you in the ass is ignoring that coincidence might equal cause. And that's why I love my job. So many easy answers, so many wrong answers. I live to find the right answers.

I was scrolling the video back to view the anomaly's passage one more time, when I heard the crisp clack of boot heels on tile. I checked my clock just as Lieutenant France's voice said, "Mr. Simpson, it's time to pack up."

"Roger, Lieutenant," I answered before he could even come around the partition wall and into my work area. "Let me just make some notes here."

"Now, Mr. Simpson," he said.

I spread my hands. "Now?"

He gave a small smile and nodded. "One minute, Mr. Simpson. Pack it up."

France had escorted me from the premises on many long nights in the past month. He was a good officer. He followed orders, but he knew just how much liberty he had to interpret them to fit the situation. The colonel really wouldn't care about a couple minutes here or there in the schedule, not when I was trying to save his project; but by being firm, France ensured that he was covered in his reports—and then by giving me an extra couple of minutes, he knew he wasn't interfering with my work, either.

So I made some notes in the metadata for the test set and the real set, and I particularly noted the timestamps where the anomaly came in. I could pick up with those tomorrow, but I didn't want to forget.

Not that I was likely to. Kylie said I was obsessive about the data, that I had to understand everything I didn't want to say she was right, but she was close. I was no good at letting go of a puzzle. I probably wouldn't sleep well that night.

I was still thinking about the anomaly when I got home. I hated letting that anomaly just sit there, unresolved, even if only for one night.

And it wasn't just my obsession that was driving me. The glitch in the system had almost eaten through our bonus, and soon we would be into charge-backs. The longer the system was delayed, the lower our profit margins got. In another two weeks, we'd be into the red. My bosses at Warriner would not be happy about that.

So when I walked up the stairs to our apartment, I was still thinking over the problem. Oh, only in my head. I had no data to work with. The Space Force systems were kept in a secure chamber within the base. My work computers were in there; and there they would stay, permanently, paid for property of the U.S. government. Their data never left there through any channel I had access to. And God help me if any of the data ever left with me, on any sort of mechanism! You had to leave phone, Fitbit, Bluetooth headpiece, even USB desk toys all in a secure drawer outside the quarantine zone. Every contractor who went in there received a lecture that if we ever were ever caught taking any data out, even accidentally, we would be subject to a strip search every time we exited or entered for the duration of the contract. And if that didn't get through to us, they'd move up to cavity searches.

So I didn't have any data with me; but the one thing they can't make you leave in quarantine is your brain. Your memories, your experience, your intuition . . . You get to keep those.

"Kylie, I'm home!" I shouted as I closed the apartment door, but I got no answering shout. I went into the kitchen, and I noticed a note stuck to the refrigerator. *Peter, Professor K is taking us to an art exhibit. Sorry you couldn't join us. Next time?* But she followed it with a smile. She knew the chances of that were slim. There was one final bit at the end: *Roast beef in the fridge is for you. I hope you found your glitch. WE deserve a break.* She underlined we. She'd been saying lately that we needed things when she really meant I did. I found it annoying, but also endearing. She meant that I was overworked, and she wasn't wrong. I just didn't see an answer for it; and being reminded of something I couldn't fix only made me more irritated.

I opened the fridge to find a platter of thin-sliced roast beef, just the way I liked it, next to a covered bowl with fresh buns. This after I had stood Kylie up for the seventh time in two weeks. I didn't deserve her.

✿ ✿ ✿

I like to say I'm not smart, I'm just persistent. I don't let a go of a problem until I understand all the pieces. In my business, that's the functional equivalent of smart . . . except when that obsession with knowing things, with being right, makes me do stupid things like decide that maybe I could simulate the anomalous entity, and then learn something from that. I didn't have any data to describe the anomaly, but I had something almost as good: my expertise. I had pioneered multidimensional variances and moments, and I knew those forms of analysis almost intuitively. I could even look at a data set and predict the moments and their magnitudes. My naked eye was almost as good as the best algorithms I'd ever seen—before mine.

Of course, moments and variances are aggregate data, the sum of thousands of data points. Knowing the answers necessarily loses the inputs. If you have a hundred-pound bag of rocks, that doesn't tell you anything about the individual rocks within the bag. Without the input data, the moments couldn't tell me precisely what the original measurements had looked like.

But maybe . . . ? I could examine existing, known data, and see if anything produced similar moments. That was what my method was about, after all, recognizing statistical similarity to—

Sorry, it's classified. I was getting away with myself there.

But to simplify: I could take a large, public collection of existing entities, analyze them with my thesis algorithms—which are public knowledge—and look for any results that matched. All I really needed was a bunch of test entities to which I could apply the algorithms and filter out anything which didn't have substantially the same variances and moments. That became an interesting, fun challenge.

I had the analysis filter built in under an hour. I could feed it entities—geometric shape models—and it would spit out any that had characteristics like the anomaly. I just needed a source of entities.

I was still pondering the best web search when Kylie came home from her exhibition. "Hey, Paul," she said, wrapping her arms around my neck from behind and planting a kiss on my cheek. "Sorry I couldn't wait, but . . ."

"No," I said, staring at my latest search results. "I got home two hours after your exhibition started. You did the right thing."

"Yeah, I suppose . . . But still, you would have enjoyed it."

"I'm sure I would've," I answered. "But I . . ."

"You can't explain, I know. Can't explain, it's classified, need to know, clearance . . . I am so fucking sick of this," she said, plopping down behind her desk and powering up her Mac.

"Kylie . . ."

"I know, you don't have any choice . . . Same old, same old . . ."

"Kylie, do we have to fight about this now?"

"When else are we going to fight about it? You're here, you're home, you're awake. Let's celebrate with a good fight!"

I sighed. "Look, you're not wrong, but I don't have any choice. I have to find this glitch, or we could lose the whole contract that pays my half of the bills around here. Don't you understand what the penalty phase means? When we start paying them?"

Suddenly she tilted back in her chair, looked up at the ceiling, and screamed for five long, loud seconds. When she was done, she leaned forward and looked at me.

I looked back. "Better?"

She grinned back at me. "No, but venting is good. They say what can't be changed must be endured, but I think what can't be changed must be screamed at."

I understood. Past fights had taught me this: while some people might escalate, Kylie had a good sense for when further argument was futile, when desire was at an impasse with reality. When she saw that point, she gave a good scream. It didn't change her mind, it just let her release her frustration and move past the fight. She wasn't over it, but she would let me know when we were good again.

In the meantime, I could turn safely back to my work. I had my obsessions with data, she had her screams of futility. We were each broken in our own unique ways, and we made it work.

I was deep in building entity models when I knew that Kylie was over her anger. She stood behind me, looking at the screen. "What'cha doing?"

I failed to hide my grin. The tone in her question told me she really didn't care about what I was doing, she cared about what we might be doing. That was another coping mechanism. After we hit a wall that we couldn't change, some time in bed would remind us that we were worth putting up with each other.

But while she might've passed her crisis, I was still stuck with mine. So I answered the question within the bounds of security. "I need to study shapes. Lots of shapes. I'm looking for something—"

"—but you can't tell me what."

"But I can't tell you what," I said, grinning at her. "And I don't even really know how to look for it. I just need to feed the computer lots of shapes and let it do its work."

"Is that all?"

"'Is that all?' I need . . . tens of thousands of shapes. Hundreds of thousands, even millions might not be enough."

"Is that all?" she repeated in the same tone. "Paul, I'm a graphic artist. After all this time, do you have any idea how I work?"

"You . . . um . . . you render images. Lots of rendering, computers always rendering."

"Paul, you have no idea about anything two inches outside of your data. What do you think I render?"

After a pause, I said, "Models!"

"Models, honey. Digital shapes. And I've got a million of them."

"I knew you had a lot, but—"

"A million," she said. "I collect them like Imelda Marcos collected shoes. You never know when you'll need a particular model, and they're usually cheaper in bulk. I'm always adding new models."

Finally I saw her point. "Send me a model file."

"All right, if you say so . . ." Again I heard her suggestive tone, but I couldn't pay attention. When the file arrived, I started tearing it apart. It was so simple. I could convert the artists' models into entities with a simple algorithm, hundreds per second, and then feed them to my filter. "Baby, you've got the jackpot!"

"Are you sure?" she asked. "Hey, Mr. Obsession, I'm trying to seduce you!"

"After you share your model folder, you can have my full attention. I've got nothing but time while the computer works."

"Good. I want some of that time."

I was sleeping lazily in a tangle of bedclothes, Kylie's leg under my head, when suddenly I was instantly awake. My computer had chimed for attention.

I tried not to wake her, but we were too intertwined, and I was too excited. By the time I padded naked out to my desk chair, Kylie was wide awake. She followed me, naked as well, but I barely noticed. "Look!" I said, pointing at my screen. "Zero point nine eight three confidence. This shape has the perfect moments!"

She didn't ask what a moment was. Early in our relationship, that sort of question had come up often before we realized: She didn't speak math, and I didn't speak art. Not even computer art. Instead, she simply asked, "What is it?"

I looked at the filter output, and I read out a file name: "DE_2371_2591_QC_ASTR.SVG."

"That don't tell me nothing," Kylie answered. "Send it to me." As she sat at her Mac, I sent over the file name. I also brought up a data visualizer to give me an idea of what the entity was. It wasn't a rendering, more a graph of the shape. I saw signs of a central mass, and lobes branching off from the mass: two long lobes at one extreme, two shorter in the middle, and the smallest at the other extreme. The long lobes reminded me of limbs, except they were too wide, almost stumpy. But then, artists work with imaginary creatures all the time. Was it some sort of fantasy monster? An orc or something?

But Kylie had gone conspicuously silent. She twisted her screen around so I could see it. The model was an astronaut in a puffy spacesuit.

Despite the long, passion-filled night and the exhaustion that followed, I couldn't go back to sleep. Now that we knew where to look, Kylie sent more models of astronauts and fighter pilots, anyone in a suit with a helmet. The only ones that pinged the bell on the filter were astronauts in their suits.

"What does this mean, Paul?" But before I could answer, Kylie added, "It's classified. Never mind. But does it mean the contract is saved?"

"Hon, I don't know what this means. It's—I don't know if it's an artifact of my algorithm, or if it's just there."

"If *what*'s just there?"

I didn't say, "It's classified." I didn't answer at all. But in the back of my mind, I was coming up with new tests to run on the real data.

Showered and shaved a full three hours ahead of my usual schedule, I sat in my blue Dodge Dart, waiting for my turn at the gatehouse. I'd never had to wait so long before, but I usually came in after the morning commute. I had no idea the gate ever got backed up like that, with seventy-four cars, three trucks, and a white panel van in line ahead of me.

Eventually I pulled up at the gatehouse, rolled down my window, and smiled at Guardian Wayland. "Good morning, Wayland."

"Good morning, Mr. Simpson," Wayland answered. After months, I knew the routine. Verify identity—again. Answer questions about my purpose—again. Answer who I was working with that day, and then wait while Wayland called them to confirm. Then one of the guards would leave the gatehouse, get in my passenger seat, and ride with me to the classified building. The guard would then escort me inside and hand me over to another guard, who would escort me to my station.

At least that was the usual routine; but this time . . . After checking his clipboard, Wayland dropped his arm back down to his side. Near his sidearm. "I'm sorry, Mr. Simpson, you have to turn around."

"What?"

"Your base access has been revoked, sir." Before I could ask, he continued, "That's all I know, sir. Instructions are that you can check in at the Administrative Center. Do you need directions?"

"No, I know where it is, but that's not where I work. I have a computer in there, with all my work. In there."

Wayland shook his head. "I wouldn't know about that, sir. And unless there's need to know, I would prefer you not discuss it further. If you left behind personal property, I'm sure you can make a claim when you go to the Administrative Center."

"But—"

Wayland stood straighter. I noticed another guard step out of the door behind him, with a rifle unshouldered. "Turn around, please, Mr. Simpson," Wayland said. "Other people need to get to work."

As I headed across town to the Administrative Center, I found myself sympathizing with Kylie and her need to scream.

I didn't know what they did in the Administrative Center— administrate, obviously, but that covers a lot—but the security was tighter. There wasn't a chance for civilians to enter the fenced area at all. Instead I was instructed to pull off into the Visitor Center parking lot, go in, and wait for someone to come to me.

What else could I do? I was playing Space Force's game, and on their court. I could play by their rules, or I could go home. I'm sure the bosses would love that. So I entered the Visitors Center, which was at least less boring on the inside than the government-beige-painted bricks on the outside. Everything within was shining metal and glass, with an overriding theme of blue. This was what Space Force was supposed to look like: modern, even hypermodern. A goddamned *Starship Enterprise*.

But though the style was modern, the procedures were as old as time. Stanchions and ropes guided me to a three-windowed waiting area where receptionists male and female sat behind bulletproof glass. Armed guards at each end of the bank of windows were a clear indication that this was a secure military facility, not a tourist trap. They took security seriously.

A young guardian behind the first window on the left said, "Can I help you, sir?"

I walked up to the glass and spoke into the microphone. "Mr. Paul Simpson, here to see Colonel Hale."

"Regarding?"

But I was far too experienced to fall for that one. "It's a classified matter, Guardian. He's expecting me." It was a bit of a lie. I had no appointment to see Hale, but he had to expect me to come looking for him. He was Warriner's contract liaison, and so I was supposed to talk directly to him or to whomever he designated. Not to a random receptionist.

The receptionist didn't miss a beat. "Very well, Mr. Simpson. Take a seat. When I hear from Colonel Hale, I'll call you up."

I turned away with a shrug. There was really nothing else to do. Again a scream moment, when you just have to tolerate the hand you're dealt. If there were right motions for this situation, I was going through them; and if there weren't, I would find that out eventually. But only here.

The guardian pointed toward my right, so I shuffled over to a well-appointed waiting area. I didn't know what else Space Force spent money on, but they were definitely getting the best when it came to decor.

I might as well have stayed in bed. Getting in early had done nothing for me. Sitting there, stymied, my long night finally started getting to me; and unexpectedly for a government facility, the guest chairs were really comfortable. I found myself fighting to stay awake—and losing.

I must've dozed off. I found myself staring down at a pair of shiny black shoes beneath crisp blue pant legs as a hand touched my shoulder. "Mr. Simpson?"

I looked up. A young lieutenant was looking down at me. The rest of her was as crisp as those pants creases. She wasn't a person, she was Space Force. A part of the machine.

"I'm Paul Simpson," I answered, rising. "Can I see Colonel Hale now?"

The lieutenant shook her head. "Colonel Hale will not be seeing you, Mr. Simpson. He asked me to give you this." She held out a thick legal envelope. "And then to thank you for your time, and to let you know that your services will no longer be needed by Space Force."

"No longer—"

"And one more note: He said to tell you that you did a fine service for your country, and you should be satisfied with that."

"Satisfied?"

"Yes. Good day." Before I could say another word, the woman, the machine officer, spun on her heel and strode away.

I waited until I got into the Dart before I opened the envelope and perused the contents. I probably should've waited longer, until I was back in the office: a lot of the papers within were stamped CLASSIFIED. I didn't like examining those out in public.

They were acceptance forms, every single form required by our contract with Space Force; and every one had been stamped COMPLETE and signed by Colonel Hale. I was starting to get nervous. I reached for my phone to call the colonel's office.

But my phone was ringing even as I pulled it from my pocket. The screen said Richard. My manager at Warriner.

I jabbed the green button. "Paul here."

"Paul!" Richard said. "Good work at Space Force! You must've put the glitch to bed."

"Richard! Open line!"

"Oh ... Yeah ..." I had never understood how Richard could rise to management in a company that dealt with so much classified information and still have so little understanding of what security meant. Yeah, I could slip up once in a while, but Richard was just plain sloppy.

Richard continued, "Great job fixing the thing."

I stared at the phone, not sure how to respond. But I couldn't stop myself from saying, "No, I didn't fix it."

"Paul, I've got the electronic copies right here. It says you fixed it, and all the tests passed after that. Colonel Hale specifically attached a note that said you did good work, and they were letting us keep most of our bonus."

"That's—" I almost said *crazy*, but instead I said, "nice. But there's more to do."

"Don't worry about it," Richard said. "I can tell you what happened, though the colonel will never admit it. The whole thing was starting to make his command look bad, so he decided to bury it. The scan—"

"Richard!"

"All right, 'the system' isn't that vital for his overall upgrade plan. He'd rather have it officially done and just not use it than have it dragging on and delaying his target date. He just redefined 'done' as 'We can live with it, even if it's broken.'"

I stared at the beige building for several seconds before answering, "You're right, Richard. That has to be it." I hoped I was convincing him, because I wasn't convincing myself. Not at all.

I told myself to walk away. I didn't have to prove what I believed. I didn't have to.

But I had to. I wasn't going to forget what I knew.

Kylie was thrilled when she came home from her studio and found me waiting, sitting around with nothing to do. She insisted upon going out for dinner, someplace fancy to celebrate the completion of the contract. How could I say no? It was exactly what I had promised her.

But halfway through the meal I could tell she was frustrated because I was distracted. The project had let go of me, but I hadn't let go of it. "Paul," she said, "you're hardly touching your linguine. It's your favorite dish."

I picked up a forkful and shoveled it in. "Really," I said around the mouthful, "it's delicious. I just—" But I stopped. There were too many levels of classified in this and I couldn't explain my frustration.

But apparently I was giving it off in waves, and Kylie was picking up on it. That night she tried to talk me into a repeat performance of the night before; but I couldn't concentrate, my mind was still elsewhere. As we lay under the covers in bed, she said, "It's the astronaut, isn't it?"

"It's classified. Classified, classified, classified . . ."

She slapped me with a pillow. "Look, Mr. Secrets, it may be classified to you, but I never signed no agreement. I can talk about anything I want to."

"I wish you wouldn't."

"And when you clam up, then I'll know I'm close to the truth."

"Then I'll just have to clam up now."

"Oh, the silent treatment? We'll see how silent you are!" Then she ran her fingernails delicately along my short ribs. She didn't have long nails—she said they interfered with her art—so she didn't scratch; but she sure tickled, and I flinched reflexively. She dug more, and I found my skin jumping at her touch. Despite myself, I started to giggle.

That only encouraged her. She wouldn't let up, even when I started to whimper with mirth. "Yeah! Who's the silent one now? All absorbed with your work, but I got your attention now!" And she did. Suddenly she definitely did.

"Two can play at that." I started looking for her ticklish spots.

It was a necessary release. I'd had tension building up all day, and I hadn't even realized it. Now it was released.

But I hadn't forgotten that the project was suddenly cut short. And I wasn't going to forget. So I resolved to get answers.

My company did a lot of contracts for Space Force. Project meetings usually happened in a secure facility; but sometimes, when the meetings were strictly financial and administrative, Space Force came to us. So I bided my time, and I kept an eye on the appointment calendar.

Nearly two months later, Colonel Hale and a number of his junior officers came to our site for a budget meeting. I arranged to be nearby. It wasn't my project, certainly not my meeting; but I was there, waiting for my chance.

In the end, the only time I managed to catch the colonel alone and unawares was when he headed into the men's room. Social niceties told me that that wasn't the place for confrontation; but the way the day was going, I wasn't sure there would be another place. I followed him in.

When he came out of the stall, I was waiting. We were alone, so I said, "Colonel, why is there an abandoned astronaut in orbit?"

He walked past me as if I weren't there. As he stood at the sink, washing his hands, he stared directly at his own reflection as he said in a low voice, "Mr. Simpson, you shall not ask me that again. If I ever hear you say anything like that again, you will lose more than your security clearance. More than your performance bonuses or your contract. You shall be locked up so deep in a federal prison that you won't even remember what the light of day looks like." He stepped away, pulled some towels from the dispenser, and dried his hands as he finally looked at me. "Are we clear?"

I couldn't find words to speak. He walked past me, dumping the wadded-up paper in the trash by the door. "I thought so," he said. "I have a meeting to get back to. This encounter never happened." He pulled open the door and left.

I was shaken. I was infuriated. The colonel thought he could threaten me like that?

But I was also stymied. He could threaten me like that. I understood full well how confidentiality regulations worked. He had me dead to rights. What I knew—knew!—was the result of a classified project. If I were aware of something classified, I had signed paperwork that required me to divulge it only on need to know and only to authorized personnel. I was stuck. Legally, I was obligated to keep my mouth shut, and the colonel had made it abundantly clear that it was in my best interest. So I would have to keep my nose clean and my mouth shut.

Then I came home and found Kylie sitting in an empty living room, staring at the spot where her Mac had been. My computer was gone as well. I didn't get a word out before she yelled, "Is this your project? And don't tell me it's classified!"

"I don't understand."

"Guardians showed up with guns. They handed me a subpoena." She stretched out a piece of paper to me. "A blank subpoena. When I asked what it was for, they said that it was classified. They were very polite as they packed up our computers and then thoroughly searched the apartment for USB drives. They took the fucking DVD library! Who even watches DVDs anymore?"

"Wait . . . They searched the place? Thoroughly?"

"Every inch of every room."

I stopped talking. Every inch of every room gave them a lot of places to hide listening devices. "I'm sorry, Kylie," I said.

"Sorry! This is about you and that entity."

"Shhh! Kylie, shut up, or you're going to land us both in federal prison." Her jaw dropped. She started to reply, but I held up a hand. She stopped.

Space Force people are damned smart. There'd been more than enough spoken in that conversation for them to figure out that Kylie knew something too. I wondered if that deep dark hole in the federal prison allowed conjugal visits. At least I got a dark laugh out of that.

Then my phone rang. I looked at it, and it said UNKNOWN CALLER; but with the timing, it wasn't unknown at all. I pressed the button. "Good evening. I know who this is."

"You're learning," Colonel Hale said. "Make her understand: She has to forget this. Just like you. When our technicians are done, you'll get your equipment back, and as much data as we choose. Until then, just pretend that everything's ordinary."

I almost called him "Colonel," but that would have been a mistake. I didn't want Kylie to know anything more than she already did.

After the call, Kylie was furious, as angry as I'd ever seen her. Screaming it out did no good. Oh, she screamed, all right. At me. At Space Force. At astronauts in general. At the dresser drawer as she hauled it out to pack clothes in a bag. At the medicine cabinet as she pulled out her toothbrush and comb and deodorant. At the door as she yanked it open, only to be stopped by the security chain, which I had fastened. As she opened that, I said, "Come on, Kylie, where you going?"

"It's classified!" She stormed out and slammed the door behind her.

✿   ✿   ✿

I sat in an empty apartment.

Oh, it was still furnished; but for me it was empty. No computer to distract me, no Kylie to care. I was left only with my swirling thoughts, around and around. I had to learn to let go. This obsession wasn't doing anyone any good. It was only harming me. And Kylie, who had never asked for it. I kind of deserved it, but not her.

But I was lying to myself. I said my obsession did no one any good; but up until the anomalous entity, it had been my bread and butter, my livelihood. Never giving up on a question had given me everything. Way back when, it had even helped me to figure out Kylie and how she saw the world. Her artistic point of view, her mercurial temper, eventually these all made a kind of sense to me. Her way was not my way, but a way.

But never before had my two worlds collided like that. Never before had she been caught up in one of my bugs. And of course, the consequences had never been this severe before.

How could I get her back? Did I want to get her back? I mean, I wanted her back, that was more clear than ever; but did I want to put her through all this? I was looking at some bad times ahead. Maybe she was better off out of them.

So I didn't chase after her. I didn't know if that was the right decision or the wrong; but I told myself that in this case, not knowing was okay. Whatever she decided was her right decision.

I was still trying to sell myself that line when I heard a knock at the door. Had she stormed out without her keys?

I rushed to the door, practically tripping over my own feet to unchain the door and open it.

But it wasn't Kylie standing there in the early Nebraska night. It was Colonel Hale; and from the smell of him, drunk as a skunk. "Colonel, I—"

"Shut up, Simpson. You're coming with me."

"I'll do nothing of the sort. You got no right to—"

"I said shut up. You've caused enough trouble as it is. Now are you going to walk, or do I fold you up and carry you out of there?"

I looked at the colonel. Twice my age, shakily drunk . . . I wouldn't stand a chance. Maybe falling down drunk, but probably not even then. The man was steel.

I walked.

We went down the stairs to the parking lot, and he pointed me to a big white Buick sedan. "Get in," he said. "You're driving."

"Driving where?"

"I'll let you know."

We stopped high on a ridge north of the city. I'd never been in the area before. It was dark, very calm. Peaceful. It struck me as a really good place to dispose of a body.

My, I was a cheery sort . . .

"Get out," the colonel said.

"Look, man, if you're going to shoot me, you'll have to do it in here and fuck up your interior."

"I don't shoot anyone, I have people for that. Now get out. Go sit on the trunk."

So I wasn't going to get shot. That wouldn't stop him from roughing me up. I got out of the Buick. As I jumped up onto the trunk, the colonel climbed out, opened the back seat, and pulled something out. When he joined me, he had two things in his hands. In his left, he held my laptop. In his right, he had a flask. He held the latter out to me. I took it, and he leaped up, somehow twisting in midair to land seated on the trunk. Yeah, I could forget about taking him in a fight.

He produced another flask, and he took a pull. "You know the drill," he said. "We were never here."

"What?"

"It's classified. Need to know, and there ain't nobody needs to know this. We were never here, this night never happened. Forget everything."

"I understand. Compartmentalization."

"Like fuck you understand. If you understood, you'd have left it alone. Gotten the clue. There are some questions you don't have to answer."

"Look, I've dropped it already. I get it."

He shook his head. "You're in it now. We're going to finish it up here. And then you and me, we don't know each other."

I didn't know what to say, so I said nothing. The colonel had his own agenda, and he would reveal what he would reveal when he would reveal it. I was tired of asking for explanations.

He stared up at the sky as it darkened and more stars came out.

"They called us Unit 12," he said as he looked up. "Nothing more specific. You'll never find the name in any T/O. We were all military, of course, from different branches. That was before the Space Force. I was Air Force, and the brain of the group. My specialty was orbital mechanics, rocket-science stuff. Izzy's was demolitions. Things that go boom.

"You don't have to know how we got up there. There are spacecraft no one knows about, missions hidden within missions. Things that look like one kind of payload but are another entirely. It's one hell of a rough way to get to space, but we were young then. Tough. Not soft like I am now." If he was soft, I couldn't imagine him when he was younger.

"So we have assets, classified." He turned and looked at me. "Classified. You ever mention this, and you're going to be in a hole deeper than the one I promised you. So deep the only sound you're going to hear will be me in the cell next to you.

"We rendezvoused with the transport to take us to the enemy station."

"Enemy station?" I asked before I could remember that I had decided not to know.

"A weapons platform. Hard to see from the ground, the way they'd configured it. I give them credit for ingenuity. The thing had the radar cross section of a communications satellite, even though it was nearly ten times as big. And a million times as deadly."

"A nuclear platform?" I asked.

He took another swig, and he shook his head. "Rods from God."

"Huh?"

"What kind of a geek are you that you don't know Rods from God? Thor? Guided hammers dropping from orbit with as much power as a nuclear blast but without the messy fallout? Jesus, man, have you never read your Pournelle? Heinlein? It's a kinetic energy weapon. Simple, cheap, and damn effective if you can get it to orbit. And they did."

"Who are they?"

He just glared at me. "We didn't need to know that, and neither do you. We just had to stop it, without drawing the sort of fuss an antisat missile would. We wanted to stop them from launching World War III, not launch it ourselves."

I said nothing. The implications of what he was saying . . . Secret programs, and not just ours, on a battlefield that everyone talked about as if it were hypothetical. Technology the public never knew about, on both sides. It was real, and the fighting was already there.

Hale continued, "We had two objectives: render it inoperative, of course; but first, we wanted their comm protocols and any electronics we could find. The next time they launched, we wanted to be able to disable it from the ground."

"And can you?"

"It's classified. But I rest easier at night." He took a sip. "Most nights.

"So we needed hands and eyes and brains on the scene. And that was us. We rode the sleds in close . . . Oh, wait, forget sleds, they're—"

"Classified," I said.

"Yep. Single-operator space transport, with tools and small arms and enough air for maybe half a day in the worst case. And good tracking gear—not that it helped us any. To this day, we still haven't figured out the enemy's jamming technology. We had no idea of the precise size of the platform . . . Nor that it was defended. Robots. Not as sophisticated as ours, but killing a man in a suit isn't that difficult. The bots killed Gaines and Tso before we knew about them."

Hale handed me the laptop. "Don't look at me like that. Civilians! You think dying is the worst thing possible. Failing your country is worse! And we weren't going to do that. Two of us were already lost, but the mission wasn't. We revised our tactics. Their robots didn't have lasers like we did. We could sit back and snipe at them. Oh, they were fast. Damn near impossible to hit without a tracking computer; and it took long seconds and a lot of battery power to do real damage to them. They would scramble out of the way and hide in the crannies of the platform before you had a chance to hurt them.

"So that became our tactic. I analyzed the structure and found the control module, and four of us used lasers to herd the robots away from that zone, pin them down, while Izzy made for the control block on his sled.

"I'll give the enemy programmers credit. The bots kept improvising new tactics, and we had to zip around on our sleds to find new angles to strike from. Then the damn bots actually started tearing off small bits of their own superstructure and throwing them at us. They took out Brown that way before we wised up.

"All the while, Izzy was trying to tear apart the control module. He carried a load of an ingenious new shaped explosive. In a pinch, he could slap it on the module, blow it, and only get tumbled by the shock wave. He would survive, bruised but not broken. So we could stop the station, but we needed the electronics first. That took more time.

"Meanwhile, the bots had yet another new strategy. In the confusion, it was never clear how many there were. It looked like five, but the way they darted about . . . One would strike out from the platform, draw our attention, and then dive for cover. While that one fled, another would come out. They kept us hopping. So we never saw the one crawling through the superstructure.

"Izzy saw it, though, just seconds before it smashed his left arm. I heard him scream, and my eyes flicked toward the control unit just as three bright laser flashes picked out a robot. I shouted to Izzy.

"'I blinded him,' Izzy said, with a shrill note in his voice. 'He's flailing around, but I'm dodging.' I turned and concentrated laser fire on the bot near him. Between the two of us, we drove it back to cover.

"But I checked my charge gauge. Don't believe what you see on TV. Lasers burn power fast. We couldn't keep that up for long. I asked Izzy how he was doing.

"'The damn bot's timing couldn't be worse. I had the cover loose, and I was cutting the connectors. Now . . . Left arm is broken, numb. I can still work, but I'm slow.'

"'Should I relieve you?'

"'Negative. I'm on it.' There was a pause. 'Hell, I think I see this platform's weak spot. I can break it apart if the bots will leave us alone long enough to hit that. As soon as I get these CPUs . . .'

"'One job at a time, Iz.' I saw a bot creeping around the station toward him, and I drove it back with a laser blast—a short one, conserving power.

"Then Iz shouted, 'I got it!'

"'Get out of there, Izzy,' I said. 'That's what we need. Get out of there and let the missile boys take out the platform later.'

"'I don't think so, Hale,' he answered. 'I saw a fail-safe circuit. Their last defense, I guess. If this thing is off-line for too long, it'll launch the rods. We have to take out the platform now.'

"'And how do you figure to do that?'

"There was a long pause. 'I've strapped the computer to my sled, and it's homing in on your signal now. And I've spliced my computer into the control circuits. I have to keep fighting the countermeasures. It's enough to hold off the fail-safe—for now—and to nudge the guidance system.'

"'Guidance system?'

"'Come on, Hale, you're the orbit guy. You know an orbit this low isn't stable, not without occasional correction. My investigation says this platform has enough fuel to hold orbit for three or four years without servicing.' He chuckled. 'That's enough to boost it to high orbit, but only if I override the controls and steer it.'

"'Can't we steer it remotely?

"'Not enough time, Hale. I'm in the circuit now. I won't stay in if I wait too long. I salvaged air from Brown and Tso, and I've conserved my own. That'll give me enough air to ride the bird up the hill. Then when I'm high enough . . . Well, I've got my charges, and I see the best spot to detonate them. I should have enough explosives on me to break this platform up into a hundred pieces, maybe more, all orbiting so high that any debris will burn up on reentry. It'll spread the pieces out in a cloud too large to recover, probably too large to track reliably. That is the only way to neutralize this thing. Tell the team to back off, I don't want them caught in the exhaust.'

"'Iz . . .' I didn't say more. It was suicide, and it was the only way to complete the mission. I caught his sled, and I flew away."

Hale looked at me. "That was the last we heard from Izzy. We backed off, and we saluted as the orbital engines ignited. We kept a respectable distance as the flame dwindled, and then we had to get the hell out. You can only pack so much fuel and reaction mass into a small sled, and our mission still wasn't complete. We had to get the electronics back to the retrieval shuttle. By the time we were back on the shuttle, the weapon platform was invisible to the naked eye."

"And Izzy . . . ?"

"I saw telescope recordings later. He boosted for nearly a day. He must've been pretty hypoxic by then, but he still had enough sense to trigger the explosion. A hundred pieces? Hell, three times that, spread across an upper orbit. Izzy was one of those pieces."

I swallowed hard. "I'm sorry."

He shrugged. "It was years ago. And we accomplished the mission. America is safer today because of it." He stared up at the sky. "Now boot that damn thing up."

I didn't ask why, I just booted. He continued, "Damn good security you got there. It took my techs four hours to crack it. I'm impressed."

"But if you cracked it, why do you need me?"

"Because none of my people can figure out your scanning and pattern-matching code. We can barely get it to run, and we don't know how to tune it. If you look in the back, you'll find an SD card with some classified data." He looked at his watch, then up at the sky. "I want you to run that through your routines and confirm for me what you think you saw up there."

At last I was seeing the whole picture. I found the data set, and I started the analysis. We sat in silence for several minutes as it ran. I didn't want to disturb Hale in his thoughts. I didn't feel any danger anymore, just sympathy.

Then Hale said, "It's getting to be about time. How's it going?"

On another night, I might have grumbled about how you can't hurry the calculations, but I was trying to preserve our new détente. So I just said, "Another couple minutes."

He looked at his watch again. "Okay, we got a couple."

The machine continued processing, and then the indicator panel flashed. "All right, we have an analysis." Hale leaned over and looked at my screen.

The detail was much better with a real data set than with Kylie's models. I made out a distinct suited figure, floating spreadeagled in space. It tumbled slowly, giving us a good look at arms, legs, and backpack . . . and eventually a helmet pierced by some long, narrow object.

In a very quiet voice, Hale said, "Thank you, Simpson." Then he laid back against the rear window, eyes turned upward. "Close that damn thing."

I closed the laptop, grabbed my flask from where I'd set it beside me, and settled back beside him. I didn't know what we were looking for, but I had no doubt he did.

It was not quite a minute later when Hale's watch gave a small chime. He unscrewed the lid of his flask, and he held it up to the sky.

I held mine up as well, and we clinked them together in memory of the orbiting hero.

Hale drained his flask. "That's for you, Iz."

※   ※   ※

Martin L. Shoemaker is a programmer who writes on the side ... or maybe the other way around. Martin published *UML Applied: A .NET Perspective* with Apress, but a second-place win in the Jim Baen Memorial Writing Contest earned him lunch with Buzz Aldrin! In addition to *Writers of the Future: Volume 31*, his work has appeared in *Analog, Clarkesworld, Galaxy's Edge, Digital Science Fiction*, and *Forever Magazine*. His novella *Murder on the Aldrin Express* was reprinted in *Year's Best Science Fiction: Thirty-First Annual Collection* and in *Year's Top Short SF Novels 4*. His short story "Today I Am Paul" was nominated for a Nebula and won the Washington Science Fiction Association Small Press Award before appearing in *Year's Best Science Fiction: Thirty-third Annual Collection* (edited by Gardner Dozois), *The Best Science Fiction of the Year: Volume One* (edited by Neil Clarke), *The Year's Best Science Fiction and Fantasy* (edited by Rich Horton), *Year's Top Ten Tales of Science Fiction 8* (edited by Allen Kaster), and seven international editions (and counting).

More at shoemaker.space.

A Tight Fit

✵

Marie Vibbert

The Lunar Orbit Gravity Interferometer Assembly (LOGIA) was nearing completion and Stephanie Kovacic hated it. She hated racking in a zero-g bunk in a tiny tin can that smelled like everyone's farts, and she really hated being grunt labor on the project. LOGIA was the kind of thing she'd always dreamed of building; not literally, one screw at a time, but sitting at a design station. That was why she'd signed up with the Space Force. To make great things, not lug a wrench. Still, a successful tour as a tech, with all the logged space time, and hopefully an honorable discharge, meant she could score her pick of engineering programs dirtside. For now, she braced herself against the wall of Lateral Tube A, drilling insulation into place.

It was a dark and featureless workspace, like a mine shaft barely wider than the length of her body. When they finished assembling the interferometer equipment, this area would no longer be pressurized and heated, and would have barely enough room for a rat's ass to squeeze through around the calibrated mounts and wiring for the tube in the center of the tube, all to make the perfectly protected space for a laser to pass unmolested by anything other than gravity.

Her team member, Christa, gestured excitedly down the long, empty tube. "Did you read the brief? The first mirror assembly arrives next week. The reflecting surface is going to be liquid. I can't wait to see the magnetic suspension. We're going to be able to say we hung a liquid mirror on nothingness. It'll be able to record a fly walking on Proxima Centauri."

"On the star? That would be one dead fly." Stephanie finished her panel and kicked off the wall to float to the other side of Christa. "We're building a tube. A fancy, sciency tube. And there're two more just like it." She gestured vaguely toward Lateral Tube B. Unlike terrestrial interferometers, this bad boy was going to have three axes of measurement, which Stephanie refused to admit out loud was awesome.

Oblivious, Christa gestured. "That's the point. By comparing the photons in perpendicular—"

"You already gave that lecture," Stephanie cut her off, lifting the next section of insulation into place. And she knew how interferometers worked, thanks.

"Excuse me for loving engineering," Christa said, which made Stephanie more annoyed, because she loved engineering more than Christa could imagine, and she should have picked up on that by now. Christa shifted the panel she was attaching and sighed, frowning at it. "Sorry. That came out wrong. Truth is, I'm worried about the Cryptons and I'm trying to keep my mind off of it."

Stephanie snorted. The Crypton Colony on Mars, stupid of name and stupid of mission, had been making threats for almost a year now. "Angry Martians aren't going to come all this way to attack three big, empty tubes." Stephanie grabbed a support strut so she could bop Christa on the head without flying away.

Christa had to catch herself on the outer wall of the tube. Instead of laughing the roughhousing off like usual, she gave Stephanie a murderous look. "I can't just forget about the danger. I've got two boys at home."

"Aw, I'll tell Ralph you called him a boy."

"Hell with you. Ralph and two boys. The Cryptons are building rockets and we're one of the nearest military-controlled sites."

Stephanie bent to pat her friend on the shoulder. Christa was highly strung. It came from being a mom. "You know any information we get is months out of date. Why worry?"

Christa shook her head. "Can you think of something more likely to be flagged 'bad for morale—censor' than working rockets?"

When she wasn't waxing poetic about physics, Christa loved to make herself more on edge. Stephanie blew a raspberry. "The Cryptons are just a bunch of whiny rich dudes who discovered they couldn't breathe market research and eat ad revenue."

"You should be more empathetic. There was supposed to be a government base on Mars before the Moon Base ended up taking all the resources. They planned on regular supply shipments they could buy into. What else could they do? They swore to attack military targets if they don't get a base. Military targets like us."

"How do you even know they said that?"

"Petrov plays back his briefings on echo shift because he thinks we're all asleep. The brass aren't going to send anyone to Mars. They don't care how hungry and desperate the Cryptons get."

Stephanie fitted the next panel. "I don't, either. They're one hundred million miles away. I'm more scared of garden—"

The steady light overhead flashed, and Communications Officer Tim Perez's voice intoned, "General quarters. General quarters. All hands to battle stations."

Christa gave her a cold look—"Gnomes?"—before kicking off down the tube toward the command module. Stephanie quickly strapped down her tools to follow.

Commander Petrov was floating over the communications station, which was already staffed, so Stephanie strapped in at tactical. She'd trained on all of the stations, but Stephanie felt itchy sitting down at her secondary station when it wasn't a drill. The USSF had to make do with fewer people than stations because of the expense of flying bodies into orbit. At least it wasn't her tertiary station.

Christa strapped in at engineering, calmly taking in the displays. "Operations nominal, Commander."

"Confirmed, we have authority to fire on incoming object," Tim said from the communications station.

"Kovacic," Petrov called to Stephanie.

There it was on her display: A projectile heading straight for them, a massive rock. How had this not been seen days ago?

She had a blank moment of fear, then shoved it down. The target was far enough away, they had minutes. The telemetry was coming from a ballistic mount on the lunar surface dark side. And Christa wasn't the sort to say, "I told you so."

Stephanie tapped confirmation as the computer honed in. "I have a lock."

"Luna confirms telemetry," Tim said.

"Someone stuck a signal scrambler on that rock," Commander Petrov said, answering Stephanie's silent question. "Keep an eye out. There may be others."

Stephanie's fingers wanted to shake. How many times had she sat in this chair? Twice? Just like training, she told herself. Pretend it's a training run. She clicked through different simulated strikes, the International Moon Base and the nearest artificial satellites outlined in bright yellow. "Computer says all debris from explosion will miss civilian targets. Ready to fire."

Petrov said, "Take the shot."

She held her breath and fired. There was no sound, of course, no feedback from outside the screens, but Stephanie felt the thrill of it, actually firing, the video feedback, the radar menace vanishing, replaced by many scattered inert objects.

"Neutralized!" Tim cheered.

Stephanie felt her shoulders drop. She smirked at Christa. "Told you those Cryptons were punks."

Then her alerts for Luna habitats blinked out one by one, and an alert flashed in the corner of her screen. "Wait . . . what?"

Tim snapped, "Debris from the explosion hit International Moon Base."

"But I ran the simulations . . ." Stephanie's world slowed down. She'd had to guess the composition of the rock, and had gone with the default all-stone, because it was a rock, right? She reran the simulation for half ice. There it was, her mistake, clear as piss. "It . . . it was a combination of rock and ice. The debris scattered wide . . . I'm reading hits." Sterile text and plain lines drew out the damage, helpfully bringing up the Moon Base schematic and coloring sections red. "Debris hit the power plant, a greenhouse, and the battery depot." That wasn't so bad, was it? Not the living quarters.

All eyes turned to Tim, who was the only one moving frantically now. "No on-site damage reports yet. Not getting a distress . . . comms down . . . trying to contact Lunar Control." Tim looked up. "They're completely dark."

Power plant and batteries. "They'll be okay, right?" Stephanie didn't believe it as she said it. She'd goofed. Catastrophically. Tragically. She'd saved her own life and three "science tubes" at the cost of however many people were down there. "They'll get the power back online?"

Commander Petrov hung from a handhold over their external view monitor, staring at the stark gray lunar surface. "They've got twelve hours before they're in the lunar night. They'll freeze to death."

Tim said, "Contacting Pentagon. Nearest other station is Array Alpha. Hailing them."

Petrov turned to Christa. "Chun, confirm our transport pod is operational."

"On it." Christa unsnapped her harness.

"Perez, find a place to take the evacuees."

Tim shook his head helplessly. "Array Alpha communications down—they were targeted."

Stephanie unhooked her harness. "I'll help Christa."

Commander Petrov held up one finger. "Stay there, Technician. We don't know what else is coming our way."

Stephanie itched to leave, to do something other than stare at her screen and rerun the simulations, finding eighty different ways she could have done her job without taking out the International Moon Base and dooming everyone there to a slow freezing death.

Tim reported in a flat tone, only the speed of his words showing his stress, "Array Alpha neutralized two bogies, lost some solar panels in the debris, now operating on emergency power. Contacting Solar Observation. After them, there's just James Webb Station at L2 close enough to help out."

"We can bring the evacuees here." Stephanie turned to face Petrov. "We can get down and back in time. Everyone else is at least ten hours out."

"We only have six racks. There are fifty colonists."

Fifty. That was the cost she'd incurred by not slowing down one fucking step. "We have the tubes. They're heated and pressurized."

"I know you want to help, Technician, but that's scientific equipment."

"Not yet, now it's just insulation and mounting brackets."

Petrov's fists twisted on the handhold over the comms station. "It's not approved for civilian habitation."

"Sir," Tim said, "Solar Observation has no transport currently, also no interior space for more than five people. James Webb is scrambling to assist, but they only have a two-man capsule, and their ETA would be thirteen hours to our six."

"This is Chun," Christa's voice came. "Transport pod's powered up."

Petrov let go with one hand to wipe his face. "Good, turns out we need it. Looks like we're putting them in the tubes."

Thirteen hours was considered their closest neighbors. Because space. Imagine if their station had been at one of the Lagrange points, like it should have been if they hadn't all been taken.

Petrov asked, "Comms, trajectory?"

"Already computed. Looks like we have a window for deorbit burn to IMB in ninety-two minutes."

"Not bad. Chun, are you go to launch in ninety-two minutes?"

"Should be. I'd like a hand pulling the seats to make more room."

Their space station—really just the command module, the hab module, and the docking module linked together off the crux of the science tubes—was so dinky Stephanie could hear Christa grunting and the bangs of the torn-out seat assemblies floating into walls as she chucked them out of the pod. It felt mean, selfish, listening to the grunts of effort, her only struggle to stare as hard as she could at the screen.

"I can help," Stephanie said.

Petrov shook his head. "Maintain your post."

A few more bangs and Christa radioed, breathless, "That's gotta be enough. Don't want to take too long. I'm starting the preflight checks."

Stephanie twisted in her harness, lifting to face Petrov. "Let me go with her, sir. It's my fault. I should help evacuate the colonists."

Tim said, "I can signal Morse code toward the colony using our safety lights, let them know we're coming."

Petrov said, "Do that," to Tim, and to Stephanie, "Stay where you are, Kovacic."

"But I screwed up."

"Not a reason to send you out there, Technician." He let go of the ceiling hold and his hand landed heavily on her shoulder, squeezing briefly. "This is where I need you. Every seat we fill on that craft is a colonist not saved."

Stephanie turned back to her display, feeling like a wet bag of failure.

For the next three hours, Stephanie manned tactical while listening to updates from Tim. With only his words to know what had happened elsewhere, everyone froze in place every time he inhaled to start speaking. "Array Alpha back online. Lost four crew, two are in their lifeboat heading earthward. Confirmed hit was a rock, not seen until too close. Webb crew still on their way, ETA too late but they wish to continue." Then, with a relieved sigh, "Another target was neutralized en route to ISS. Confirmed—similar rock composition, stealth module recovered." He pushed back, looking up at Petrov, "That's six rocks now accounted for. Pentagon suspects two to three more, but it's unlikely they'd have enough resources to launch more."

Petrov frowned thoughtfully a long time, then let go of his handhold. "Keep me updated. I'm going to the hab to report in."

"Yes, sir."

Stephanie felt stillness descend in Petrov's wake, just she and Tim strapped into chairs. None of the various displays she could call up said anything different than they had two hours ago. She'd rerun the simulation for every combination of rock and ice and crystal the system knew how to model. Christa was in the pod on her way to the Moon, three hours out and three more to arrive.

"Okay, Kovacic, hit the rack." The next shift technician poked her arm with a foot.

"Just a minute." She flicked through all the screens again. She was exhausted, and she hated sitting there, knew she wasn't accomplishing anything, but going to rest felt like giving up.

"I'd take your break if I could, drama queen," the tech said, poking her again.

So she unhooked herself and pulled her way slowly to the hab. Stephanie drew her sleeping sack around herself, tying herself in, thinking about Christa, how she could be earnest, honest, love the science without feeling like a faker. How she had two kids at home. Stephanie had never done anything so big as bring a whole human into existence.

"You joke all the time because you're afraid," Christa had said, three days into their tour together, looking at her with that flat, calm sureness, so infuriatingly knowing, so infuriatingly right.

They were assembling their living pod, the head, specifically. Stephanie had made the vacuum poop hose "kiss" Christa, and then had mimed making out with it when that didn't get a rise out of her.

"I'm not afraid," Stephanie said, after too long a pause and with the wrong inflection. Christa swam down to the floor, screwing the hose in place.

"I'm not afraid to be here," Stephanie clarified, louder and surer.

"I know." Christa nodded at the hose in her hands, twisting hard. "You're afraid to be seen."

"Uh . . . you've all seen me naked because I do not go without washing everything."

"You know what I mean."

Seen. All the stuff inside that she covered up with humor and crassness. Something about that moment, this competence and calm from this slightly older woman, made Stephanie drop the act and confess. "I wanted to get into engineer training. The recruiter said I could . . . but I didn't make the cut. I was always good with tools, with math. That was what I was, in high school. Now . . . I'm worried I'm not anything."

And Christa looked up at her, a long, hard-to-read look, and then snorted. "Dude. Recruiters LIE."

"Thanks. If they lied, it's not that I wasn't as good as they hoped, I was never good enough."

"That's not what I meant." Christa frowned, giving her this serious look like she was about to impart the secret of the universe. "I mean they had a number of techs to fill and were never going to look at your scores. You don't have to tell dumb jokes around me unless you really want to."

To her own surprise, Stephanie felt . . . relieved. Let off the hook. It wasn't the end of Stephanie making dumb jokes, of course it wasn't, but later that week, when she figured out a way to get the microwave mounted when they'd been shipped three fewer screws than needed, Christa had said, rather pointedly, "Good with tools and math," and patted her arm.

Stephanie was good with machines. She could do everything that comms station allowed and a few it didn't. She could screw a bolt flush anywhere on Earth or in orbit. She'd turned seven screws into ten with two improvised braces.

So why did she feel like a waste of space?

The duty officer's voice came over the general address, "Engineering crew to docking."

Stephanie wriggled out of her sleeping sack. No way she was missing this.

She caught a handhold outside the docking airlock. "What's going on?"

Commander Petrov was there, and the first engineer. "Chun got over half the colonists in the first run by stripping the secondary fuel tank and landing couches, but the change in weight and configuration made it list on docking. We're not getting a seal."

Stephanie stared at the comms station. How useless she would be there right now. The chatter in the room continued, going nowhere.

"Shuttle firing steering thruster four . . . no change."

"Any other ideas?"

Stephanie thought about bending braces, turning two screws into nine. "Sir, I can go EVA."

Petrov gave her a narrowed-eye look. "We're not sure how to solve this."

"Sir, I am confident I can get the lock to join."

Stephanie held her breath. Was she? Did she really believe she could do this?

Petrov slowly nodded. "Okay, Technician. Move. We can't keep them in there all night. They're on stored oxygen, and it's calibrated for a crew of sixteen maximum."

Stephanie called Christa as soon as she had checked her radio and fastened her helmet liner. "How's it going in there?"

"I never wanted to know how a sardine felt."

Stephanie took the helmet from the crewman helping her dress and ducked into it. "Ah, I wish I was there. I'd unleash a long fart straight from the sulfurous pits of hell."

From the aft airlock, Stephanie had to hand-over-hand along the top of the habitat module to get to the shuttle, which was itself a module. It was what they had lived in while building the habitat. It should have joined up the same way. She could see already that the shuttle was listing port.

She got around the top and saw that the joining assembly was smashed, having hit at an angle, too hard. "Jeez, Chun. What did this dock say to piss you off?"

"My elbow is in someone else's spleen. Less joke; more get me out of here."

Stephanie stared at the damage and felt, suddenly, stupid and alone. She hadn't brought enough tools. She hadn't considered not having the full ring at all. She lowered herself next to the damage and felt herself beginning to hyperventilate.

Christa's voice crackled in her ear. "Hey, sorry for making you save the stupid science tube."

Stephanie closed her eyes and gripped the ring through one thick glove. "I fucking love this stupid science tube."

She pictured the parts and miscellaneous leftover junk in the assembly prep area. The bits that hadn't fit and waited. Then she opened her eyes. "Command, I need some parts moved into the service airlock."

"Standing by," Tim said.

Stephanie clipped her tether closer and floated even with the crumpled side of the dock. She slid her glove between the capsule, measuring the width in glove breadths, the point at which it got wider. She had to do this perfectly, or at least perfectly enough the shuttle could undock again and go get the last twenty colonists. So mashing the metal to fit wasn't an option.

Christa spoke, her voice strained, "You're good with tools and math. You can do this."

Stephanie counted handspans and did some quick calculations. About two and a half spare struts should do it. Her lip curled into a grin. "Girl, I can make this dock stand on its ear and bark."

Exhausted, it took longer to get out of the EVA suit than it had to get into it, and Stephanie only heard the bustle of settling the evacuees temporarily in the laser tunnels. She then had to go over the improvised rigging she'd done with the chief engineer, and participate in a long, annoyingly time-lagged, discussion with mission control about what materials would be needed to make proper repairs once the rescue ship came.

So, it was hours before she got a chance to check on the evacuees herself. Tim was already on his way back with the second group.

The evacuees were rolled up in silver heat blankets which they'd torn and tied to the wall support struts to keep themselves in place as they slept along the Vertical Tube, which was an empty cylinder, lacking the minimal run of equipment they'd started in Lateral Tubes A and B.

And then there was a plaintive howl, and Stephanie rushed to find a guilty-looking man holding a little orange kitten.

"That's not allowed," Stephanie said.

Christa floated over from distributing tubes of food. "Could you have told him to leave it?"

"I would have. Death to kitten."

"Right," Christa said, and bumped her shoulder.

They both knew she was lying. "Can I hold him?" The man curled the kitten tighter to him, glaring at her.

"The death thing was a joke. I was joking. I joke too much. It's an insecurity thing."

Slowly, he nodded, and Stephanie gently helped unhook the catching little claws. She lifted the kitten and stroked the soft little throat, feeling a purr that went right through her. She cleared her throat. "I don't know if anyone told you all about the place you're sheltering. When gravity waves hit this structure, they'll stretch or compress it, and we'll measure the difference in the distance with light beams." Stephanie smiled and met Christa's eyes. She was smiling too. They were united, in love for their science tube. "We'll be able to detect subtle, tiny things. Like a kitten's purr near Alpha Centauri."

❖   ❖   ❖

2023 Nebula Award Nominee **Marie Vibbert** has sold over seventy short stories to top magazines including *Analog*, *Fantasy & Science Fiction*, *Nature*, and *Clarkesworld*. Her debut novel, *Galactic Hellcats*, was long-listed for the British Science Fiction Award. By day she is a computer programmer in Cleveland, Ohio.

Zombie

✸

Karl K. Gallagher

"Sir, I request permission to shoot the body."

Commander Winchell glared at his executive officer. "No. That's desecrating a corpse. I won't have it."

"It's becoming a morale issue, sir." The exec, Captain Franklin, was as close to attention as he could manage in free fall, his feet tucked into the loops before the commander's desk.

"It's been a morale issue since Gardelle got himself killed. The fate of the remains is just a . . . reminder."

Franklin's mouth twitched, then clamped shut.

The commander said defensively, "We had to bury him in space. He requested it. He put it in his will, damn it."

"Master Sergeant Gardelle's will was a collection of jokes," said Franklin flatly.

Franklin was career Space Force. Winchell had transferred in from the Navy. Franklin suspected the late Master Sergeant Gardelle only wrote the burial in space request to poke at the Navy tradition. The last update to the will was after Winchell took command of Polar Support Station One.

"Joke or no, it's what he asked for, so we gave it to him. Now it's just a matter of waiting for it to reenter. Yes, I admit, that's taking longer than it should."

"It's becoming a danger."

"Space Surveillance Center puts the odds of a collision at twenty thousand to one."

Franklin refrained from pointing out that the odds had been zero, then a million to one. "Very well, sir."

As the executive officer turned to leave, Commander Winchell asked, "How were you going to shoot it, anyway?"

"There's a pistol in the escape capsule survival kit."

"Oh, right, right."

Franklin had missed lunch, so he went by the crew lounge for a sandwich. It was more crowded than usual for between meals. Half a dozen spacers were gathered in the observation dome.

"Thirty seconds," said one.

Franklin turned from the sandwich cooler to see what they were waiting for.

"Ten seconds. Five."

"There he is," said another. "Right on time."

"Can't be Gardelle then. Son of a bitch was always early, looking for a chance to plant one of his surprises."

"I'm amazed he managed to hold his gas in."

"Have some respect." The rebuke was from Technical Sergeant Castro. She was senior NCO on the space station since Gardelle skipped three items on his EVA checklist.

"I am being respectful, Sergeant. If it was you out there, Gardelle would be making fart jokes every time you went by."

"If he was here, he would. But I'm here, so we're going to be polite. You've had your look. Back to work."

The spacers dispersed, a couple trading jokes, the rest solemn.

Franklin moved up into the empty dome. The glint of the tumbling space suit stood out against the black. "I hadn't realized it was close enough to see."

Castro nodded. "The last delta-V boosted his apogee enough to be visible. The orbit phasing only brings him close enough every three or four days."

The burial at space had gone as expected for the first month. The space-suited body was launched with enough force to lower its perigee. Drag pulled the orbit down. SSC predicted it would reenter in three to six months, depending on how solar activity heated the upper atmosphere.

A month after Gardelle's death, putrefaction gasses began to escape the suit. This was foreseen. The suit's pressure relief valve had been mounted on the shoulder, far enough from the corpse's center of gravity that the escaping gas torqued the body into a spin. The unintentional rocket thrust went in all directions, canceling itself out. SSC tracked the spin by satellite observation and smugly proclaimed its predictions were accurate.

Then the vent stopped letting gas out. Presumably some gunk had blocked it. The suit kept drifting down, still spinning.

The first delta-V alarmed every observer. Space Force called in outside experts to figure it out. They concluded that gas building up in the suit ruptured a seam. Once the pressure was relieved, liquids boiled away in the gap, leaving a solid residue to seal it. Pressure would build up again until the process repeated.

Every spacer who knew Master Sergeant Gardelle insisted he would have wanted to fart his way through space.

Unlike the continuous venting from the relief valve, the ruptures imparted a noticeable velocity change to the corpse.

That didn't worry the analysts at the Space Surveillance Center. The direction of such delta-V was completely random. A rupture was as likely to push the corpse toward an early reentry as to send it back toward the space station.

Analysts worked out the odds of multiple ruptures causing a collision between Gardelle's body and Polar Support Station One. They were so unlikely that everyone relaxed.

Until a month later, when four of five ruptures had caused stationward delta-Vs, canceling out most of the drag the corpse had experienced. Now it was coming close enough to PSS1 to see with bare eyeballs.

The analysts were tired of superstitious explanations being offered for what was just a natural, if improbable, event.

Captain Franklin, watching Gardelle's corpse pass by, was starting to feel the tug of superstition.

On its next orbit PSS1 was far enough ahead of the corpse's orbit that its apogee was out of sight. Franklin and Castro focused on their top priority, enforcing checklist discipline. Master Sergeant Gardelle, when not springing practical jokes, had pushed the troops for speed and efficiency.

He'd set a record for changing out a solar array bushing, up to where an electrical arc opened his oxygen line and an unchecked retaining valve jammed on some grit.

Now spacers checked each other's gear as well as their own. Full inspections were done on airlocks before an EVA, even if the last use had been only hours before. Discolored parts were replaced and sent to maintenance for examination, instead of being accepted as "only a cosmetic issue."

All the checks doubled the average time for a recon or service robot to be recovered, overhauled, and sent on another mission. Headquarters didn't complain. They'd been thrilled with Gardelle's rapid turnarounds. There weren't any complaints about the new approach from above.

Crew complained. The extra work cut into their free time. Crew rest regulations protected their sleep time, but personal time was reduced to meals and hygiene.

Mutters calling them "tyrant" or "dictator" didn't bother Castro and Franklin. They'd rather hear that than talk of Gardelle as a zombie creeping up on the station.

The officers discussed banning the crew from watching the corpse flybys. Commander Winchell decided against it. There were more ways to see out than the observation dome. Making it forbidden would cause even more discussion.

For the next pass, there were more spacers wanting to watch than could fit in the observation dome. One asked, "Did you hear? Gardelle ripped off a big one!"

"Glad I don't have to smell it. What's the vector?"

"SSC hasn't said yet. Still collecting data."

"Let's hope he's early."

If the rupture lowered the corpse's orbit, by the laws of orbital mechanics, it would travel faster. Therefore, arriving ahead of the scheduled close approach meant the rupture had lowered its orbit. Arriving late meant it had been boosted up. Again.

"Not early," muttered a spacer.

The predicted time passed. Two spacers cursed.

"There he is. Twenty-eight seconds late. Crap."

One of the junior spacers said, "This is like that movie Gardelle would show us. With the shamblers. They're slow, but they won't stop. You can't escape because there's nowhere to go. Just like we don't have anywhere to go. Ow!"

He twisted to look at the hypodermic the station medic had stuck in his arm. "What did you do that for?"

"You need a rest, son." The medic turned to Captain Franklin, hovering by the sandwich cooler. "Sir, I'm taking Johnson off duty until further notice."

Franklin answered, "Very well, Doc."

He brooded as the medic towed his patient out. The medic was authorized to take action in emergencies. Was Johnson freaking out, or just spouting off harmlessly? Either way, how would the rest of the crew react if he'd kept going? He decided to trust the medic's judgment and pray for the next rupture to lower the corpse's orbit.

The prayers weren't granted. He was summoned to Commander Winchell's office at midshift.

The commander belted it straight out. "There's been another rupture. It's coming close enough SSC is giving us one-in-four-hundred odds of a collision. I'm activating the station-keeping thrusters to reduce that. You are directed to use any means necessary to ventilate that space suit and prevent further collision danger."

"Yes, sir." Franklin saluted, rocking sideways as the momentum of the gesture pulled in the slack in his foot loops.

Later, Technical Sergeant Castro found him practicing with the pistol in the wardroom. Franklin wore a pair of space suit gloves. The pistol was intended to fight off bears or sharks after an emergency landing in the wilderness. The trigger guard was too small to let a finger of the space suit glove fit in.

Franklin aimed the pistol with his right hand. His left hand held a screwdriver. He pulled the shaft against the trigger, making the hammer snap down on the unloaded chamber.

He looked up to see Castro watching. "It works, but I'm jerking it too hard. I'll have to shoot at point-blank range."

"I'm more worried about the aiming, sir."

"Oh, that's fine. The suits have enough range of motion to line the sights up with my eye. Takes some effort from the shoulder muscles, but I can do it."

"More specifically, the direction you aim, sir. I'd like to request that you not fire normal to our orbit plane." Castro brought up an orbit diagram on the wardroom's screen. PSS1's orbit was a green circle running north-south around the Earth.

"If you do, the bullet will be in our orbit with a plane change." She added a slightly rotated red circle, intersecting the green one at two points 180 degrees apart.

Franklin studied it. "It'll come back in fifty minutes, at the same speed I fired it. What if I get above it and fire toward Earth?"

Castro tapped a few keys. The red circle lined up with the green one then stretched out, first passing under the green one, then above it for the other half of its circuit.

"Still back in fifty minutes. Okay, we launched the body against our velocity vector, how does that work for a bullet?"

This time the red circle shrank, one side still touching the green one. "Lowering the perigee changes the period, so by the time it comes back to our altitude we'll have moved on. But the orbits still intersect, so if it ever passes through the intersection when we're there . . ."

"Right," said Franklin. "Wasn't an issue for the body because drag pulled it down enough to be clear of us. But a bullet is too dense to be slowed much by drag."

He shoved the pistol into its storage case. "What would you suggest instead?"

"If you'll come with me, sir?"

PSS1's machine shop was the domain of Specialist-4 Turro, a short, fierce machinist. She gave Franklin a nod as he came in, which was as much respect as he could hope for.

"What do you have for us?" demanded Castro.

Turro pulled out some aluminum rods. "You have to understand, I'm improvising here. What you really want for this job is a glaive-guisarme, but best I can do is a poleaxe."

She snapped the ends of the rods together. "Off the shelf connectors. Squeeze both sides to release them. That'll let you fit them into the airlock."

Separated, they were each six feet long. One had a metal triangle bolted to its end. "Be damn careful handling this. Sir. It's steel, so it'll hold the edge. This side and both corners are sharp. The way Gardelle is spinning, you should be able to just hold it out and let him brush against it."

"Thank you, Specialist," said Franklin.

"The other end has a bracket with twenty meters of cord attached, so you can chuck it like a spear and reel it back in." Turro folded some thick plastic sheeting around the blade. "I can't make a real sheath for it, but this should keep it from causing too much damage."

"Good. Thanks."

"Good hunting, sir," said Turro as she ushered them out.

In the corridor, Castro asked, "Good enough, sir?"

"Yes. I'll take a Manned Maneuvering Unit out on the next close approach."

"With your permission, I'll be your backup."

He nodded.

Franklin returned the pistol to the survival kit. He took the knife from it, as a backup to Turro's monstrosity.

There wasn't a "zombie fighter" version of the EVA checklist, but the "Mission Specific Equipment" portion of the standard checklist covered the weapons adequately.

Castro read off, "MSE secured for airlock."

Knife in belt sheath. Pole in two pieces, held together by twisted wires. Blade covered.

"Check," answered Franklin.

"MSE lanyard secure."

The coil of cord sent one end to the base of a pole, the other to a D-ring on Franklin's left hip. A four-foot cord went from the right hip to the haft of the knife.

"Check."

When the EVA Preparation checklist was done, they moved on to the Airlock Egress checklist. Franklin, mindful of Turro's warning, watched the triangular blade. With a little force behind it the plastic cover would only slow it down. It could rip a hole in the wall of the airlock as easily as a spacesuit.

Once outside the station they went through the Manned Maneuvering Unit checklist, once for each of them.

The MMUs were oversized backpacks, sprouting frames which went around the wearer like a basket. Castro tugged on the five-point harness to ensure Franklin was secure. When she donned hers, he couldn't return the favor. With both of them in MMUs, he couldn't reach her without the frames colliding.

The plan said Castro would wait on the hull of the space station until it was over. But if things went according to plan, they wouldn't be doing this.

Gardelle's body flew into sight at the time the SSC predicted. The intercept course was programmed into the MMU. Franklin watched the countdown on his HUD. At zero it shoved him off to meet Gardelle.

The programmed course left him forty meters from his target, too far away even for the pistol, but it gave him space and time to see how the corpse was moving.

The body should be in a flat spin, limbs outstretched. The last rupture must have given it a kick on another axis, because it was spinning head over heels. The unstable mass distribution made it flip front to back every few minutes. The arms were waving, stretching up as the spin pulled them out, then back down as the springiness of the joints reached their limit.

Trying for the torso didn't look like a good idea. He'd have to make cuts on the limbs. He closed on his target.

Five meters was the most he could reach with the pole, and that required holding it by the end. Poking it toward the body made contact for an instant, knocking the pole from his grasp. He grabbed the cord and pulled it back to him.

He'd penetrated the suit. A streak of crystals glittered before him, ice frozen from the venting gas. Dark droplets were mixed in with them, barely reflecting the direct sunlight.

It was a short streak—the cut he'd made was already sealed by vacuum-frozen liquid.

He needed to make bigger cuts. A few taps on the MMU controls nudged him a meter and a half closer.

Spreading his hands apart for leverage, Franklin swung the blade against a passing leg. He held it against the recoil. The MMU hissed as it countered the spin he'd stolen from the body.

Gas sprayed from the cut on the suit's shin. It kept spraying.

Good. Now to do more of it. He cut at the other leg, then went for an arm. The waving arms were harder targets.

As one arm flopped up, he saw a chance to cut the torso. A jab punctured it. A spray of—stuff—came out, shifting the body's spin axis. The arm on the other side came around, hooking over the pole. He yanked back. The back corner of the blade dug into the suit's arm. The body kept turning, pulling the pole out of Franklin's grip.

"Shit."

The retention cord slid out of its coil, following the pole. Cord wrapped around the spinning body. It caught the arms and tied them to the torso. Conservation of angular momentum increased the spin as the arms were pulled in.

He cursed again. The cord pulled taut. The corpse spun along the cord, wrapping up the few meters stretched between them.

Franklin held up his hands. If he could force it to bounce off, the cord should unwrap as it spun away.

The body slammed into him. A leg wedged between his leg and the MMU frame, jamming them together.

Vertigo hammered Franklin as the corpse's spin twirled him with it. The MMU hissed and popped as its thrusters tried to stabilize them.

The corpse's helmet lay beside his. Through the spatters on the inside of the faceplate Franklin could see Gardelle's face. It was still recognizably him. With the dried lips pulled back from the teeth, it looked like the braying laugh he'd let loose for his own practical jokes.

"Yeah, you'd love this, you son of a bitch," snarled Franklin.

He shook his head, trying to get the blood back where it should be. The fuel alarm went off. He slapped the thrust cut off button. The MMU needed a better moment arm to fight this spin.

The poleaxe was useless like this. Franklin pulled out the survival knife from his belt. He slashed it across Gardelle's chest. It took three cuts to open it to the inner lining which then bulged through the gap.

He shifted his grip on the knife. A cut the other way started an X on the torso. The lining burst, spraying gunk onto Franklin's suit. He took deep breaths to control his stomach. It was already upset from the spin. Seeing that . . . spray . . . wasn't helping.

He had enough problems without throwing up in his helmet.

Worst of all, his imagination was suggesting what it must *smell* like.

Damn it, Space Force wasn't supposed to deal with this. Everything in space was dry and sterile. If he'd wanted muck and goo and bad smells, he'd've joined the Army.

As the spray died down, he went back to cutting the second stroke of the X. When he finished, four flaps folded back from the torso.

That wasn't going to reseal.

More knife cuts opened the thighs and upper arms. Shifting the corpse to the right angle made the head bob back and forth, the way Gardelle laughed when he'd really gotten someone.

He'd laughed that way the time he'd drawn an eight-inch spider on the polarized visor of Franklin's suit. It had been Franklin's first EVA on PSS1. He'd nearly pissed himself when he pulled the visor down to cut the sun's glare. It had sounded like Gardelle nearly pissed himself laughing over it.

The suit was now as ventilated as it could be without cutting it to ribbons. Franklin pried it out of the frame and kicked it away. Hard.

The corpse spun away, unwinding the cord. The poleaxe held fast, stuck deep into the right arm.

As it receded, the spin slowed. Earth was no longer flashing past his faceplate. Head and stomach felt easier.

He turned the MMU thrusters back on. They took the last of the spin off. The LOW FUEL warning flashed in his HUD.

"Need a lift, sir?" Technical Sergeant Castro's voice came across the radio.

"I'll take one."

She brought her MMU up next to his. "That looked exciting."

"You could call it that. I'm going to have to ask the crew to clean this suit."

He could see her face moving up and down as she studied the mess. "We'll try, sir. May have to scrap it."

"I won't argue."

"Toss me that cord?"

He unhooked the carabiner at the end and tossed it to her. He would have had to cut it loose in a few minutes anyway. The corpse was almost done unwinding it. He didn't want the cord going taut and pulling it back.

Castro produced a roll of Kapton sheeting and vacc-taped the cord to the end of it. She tossed the sheeting to start it unrolling.

"What's that for?"

"A sail. The more drag, the faster he reenters. Wanted to do that the first time, but I was told it would make him too visible."

Franklin laughed. No one would make that objection this time.

"Want to say any last words, sir?"

He eyed the receding body. "Rest in peace, jackass."

✲   ✲   ✲

"Zombie" first appeared 2022's *Tales Around the Supper Table: Volume 2*, a collection of stories from North Texas writers.

Karl K. Gallagher is a systems engineer, doing data analysis for a major aerospace company. He writes both science fiction (the Torchship Trilogy) and fantasy (*The Lost War*). His novels have been finalists for the Prometheus Award for Best Libertarian Science Fiction Novel of the Year four times. His most recent book is *Swim Among the People*, Book 5 in the Fall of the Censor space opera series. He publishes a free short story monthly on his Substack, gallagherstories.substack.com.

When joining the U.S. Air Force, Karl sought to be assigned to Space Command, having been a space fanatic ever since pulling his first Heinlein story off his father's bookshelf. The Air Force obliged by assigning him to the Defense Meteorological Satellite Program, where he led operations crews and programmed the satellites to deliver higher-resolution imagery of areas of interest. After the Air Force, he designed weather satellites as a contractor, later working on rockets and other defense programs. He also served as a member of the Texas State Guard. Echoes of some of his DMSP crews can be seen in "Zombie."

The Kessler Gambit

※

Matt Bille

**U.S. SPACE FORCE
BOTTOM LINE UP FRONT (BLUF)
SUMMARIES: ARCHIVED**

USSF BLUF DAILY SUMMARY – 0600 9 June 2034
\<CLASSIFICATION\>
At 1625Z on 7 July, China launched a spacecraft which appears to be in the Shǒuhù ASAT family. Satellite and transfer stage remained in Low Earth Orbit (LEO), but imaging from ground and space indicates it carries the large transfer stage used in flights to Geosynchronous orbit (GEO).

At 1330Z on 8 July, Pakistan launched a spacecraft of unknown type. This may be the first of their Talwar satellite inspectors/killers intended to counter Indian satellites.
\<CLASSIFICATION\>

USSF BLUF DAILY SUMMARY – SUPPLEMENTAL – 0600 10 June 2034 \<CLASSIFICATION\>
The USSF issued a preliminary warning that what we believe to be Talwar-1 will pass within 10 km of Transport Layer Satellite No. 1935.

Pakistan was cautioned to avoid causing a collision. Pakistan has not registered the satellite or formally claimed ownership.

A collision event was reported concerning an old Iranian test

satellite, Fajr-3, and a tracked object believed to be a French satellite fairing: inclination 39, altitude 430 km, over West Africa.
    <CLASSIFICATION>

USSF BLUF DAILY SUMMARY – SUPPLEMENTAL – 1600 10 June 2034
    <CLASSIFICATION>
Transport Layer Satellite 216 appears to have had a collision event. This event is probably but not certainly related to the satellite Pakistan still has not named or registered in accordance with the Registration Convention.
    At 1400, the U.S. advised China, the International Tele-communications Union, and the Global Space Clearing Center that a Shǒuhù spacecraft may violate the reserved slot for USSF space station Guardian One. China acknowledged receipt but did not reply.
    <CLASSIFICATION>

USSF BLUF DAILY SUMMARY – 0800 11 June 2034
    <CLASSIFICATION>
No final resolution on the June 9 collision event.
Still examining details and debris from collisions on 10 June.
    <CLASSIFICATION>

USSF BLUF DAILY SUMMARY – 0800 12 June 2034
    <CLASSIFICATION>
No resolution of previous collision events.
    Guardian One carried out a routine maneuver to avoid known debris.
    Russia reported an event, with its commercial Yabloko 5 slightly damaged by two very small objects (debris or micrometeoroid).
    Analysis by the Space-domain Brilliant Recognition Artificial Intelligence Neurosystem (SpaceBrain) indicated a 20 percent chance a of limited (Type 1 autotrophic self-replicating chain of events) Kessler event in low-inclination LEO from 600 to 1200 km, centered on inclination 39 degrees, is underway.
    [UNCLASSIFIED NOTE for release to Public Affairs: Kessler Syndrome, proposed by NASA's Donald J. Kessler in 1978, is a scenario in which the density of objects in low Earth orbit (LEO) is

high enough that collisions between objects could cause a cascade in which each collision generates space debris that increases the likelihood of further collisions. In the worst-case scenario, entire orbits could become unusable. The portrayal in the 2013 movie *Gravity*, while inaccurate, popularized the term.]

U.S. and allied planners directing a total of 15 Space Domain Awareness (SDA) constellation avoidance maneuvers so far: commercial firms and all nations notified.

Other nations also taking precautions, but most of the objects in this orbit are uncontrolled debris or dead satellites.
<CLASSIFICATION>

USSF BLUF DAILY SUMMARY – SUPPLEMENTAL – 1330 13 June 2034
<CLASSIFICATION>
Collision of Chinese and Russian objects reported, no official pronouncements. Space Fence reports debris cloud spreading, centered in orbital inclination 45.5 and altitude 855 km.

Iran says it will demand damages from France under the Liability Convention. France immediately responded they do not think fairing involved in 10 June event was theirs, also that the Fajr-3 had been inoperative for three years.

USSF BLUF DAILY SUMMARY – SUPPLEMENTAL – 1420 13 June 2034
<CLASSIFICATION>
U.S. issued warnings to China over suspected Shǒuhù ASAT: spacecraft is on a trajectory bringing it close to Guardian One in GEO. Guardian One has eight USSF crew on board.

Chinese intentions unknown: may be there to inspect, attack, or intimidate. <CLASSIFICATION>

USSF BLUF DAILY SUMMARY – SUPPLEMENTAL – 1440 13 June 2034
<CLASSIFICATION>
Cyber Command reports an upsurge in routine penetration attempts into Space Command and Control (SC2) and other systems. Specific targets appear to be USSF, Missile Defense Agency (MDA),

and links connecting ground-to-ground and ground-to-space. Degradation so far is minimal, but this is assessed as a serious attempt to disrupt SC2 and related systems. Origins still unknown at this time.

<CLASSIFICATION>

THE CRITICAL DAY
0000Z
Joint Space Operations Center, Vandenberg Space Force Base
0240Z, 13 June 2034

In the softly lit expanse of the JSOC, Major Laura J. Wallace of the U.S. Space Force looked at the console and shook her head. "This just keeps getting more complicated, sir."

Wallace sat in the center seat of the main Space Control Console, the nexus within the coordination center of American space power. She was tall and slender, and she took a second to find a comfortable groove in a seat chosen by some general to look like it belonged on a starship bridge.

Around the SCC stretched semicircles of computer stations with neat signs labeling stations such as "Launch Range Coordination," "Operational Intelligence," or "NATO Liaison," staffed by USSF personnel with a sprinkling of other services and allied nations. Screens and holographic projectors dominated the front of the gym-sized room, along with Space Force emblems and the official motto, *Semper Supra*. Wallace knew a couple of people who had tattoos of the unofficial motto: *Sumis custodes costellatio licisci*, butchered Latin for "We're the Guardians of the Galaxy, bitches."

On her right sat Major Tom Neufeld, a stolid, neatly mustached officer of the Canadian Forces, as space tracking and prediction expert. Wallace's station was meant to be in the left seat, but brigadier general and ex-astronaut Tony "Gorilla" McGill liked to take the traditional pilot's position and see how his junior officers handled the center spot with its always-changing array of screens and holograms.

"Think it through, Major," he said. "Give me the key events from the top."

Wallace nodded. She blinked, a habitual signal to her brain to clear the decks, and focused in on the facts.

"Yes, sir. First, TL 1935 and the Pakistani satellite collided. We assume it's a Talwar ASAT due to general characteristics and two orbit-raising maneuvers in quick succession. Pakistan says it was a test satellite for Iran, so anything that happened is Iran's fault. Iran says it's doing nothing and suggested we're tracking an old Russian stage. Russia says no and this must be either Pakistan's or Iran's fault. We did have a couple of substantial debris objects on the High-Interest Event Tracker. There's a point where the Space Domain Awareness birds couldn't be sure because three objects about the same size were in such close proximity."

"Visual," McGill said. "Replay it."

Wallace twisted her hands in front of her screen, as if kneading dough. Video from one of the SDA satellites came up. The satellites involved appeared in the air in front of them, and he studied the moving objects. "Two objects can collide, but three? In space? Major Neufeld, it looks like a half-dozen objects now that were or may have been involved in collisions in low-inclination LEO orbits within an altitude range of three hundred kilometers. Correct?"

"Yes, sir. That's before we even add in this Iran-French collision."

Wallace looked at the video again. She had the inkling something was off, but she couldn't form the thought.

"Major Wallace. Speculate. Do you think Pakistan, Iran, and Russia are telling different stories because they want the liability to be on someone else, or because there's something more complicated going on?"

"There's something more complex going on that ties this all together, General. I'm certain of it. But I'm still trying to generate a more specific hypothesis."

Major Neufeld spoke. "Pardon me, sir, but Japan told us their radarsat spotted a new collision, and now we've got it too. Looks like a fragment. First guess is it's from the 1935 collision and a spent kick stage from the Pakistani launch. It was within a tenth of a degree, 50 kilometers altitude, and only about 150 kilometer slant range from where the last event happened."

The jabbing in Wallace's brain intensified. What are we missing?

"Major Neufeld, your branch has run these kind of sims a thousand times in the 3Vid," McGill said, using the common shorthand for the AI-run 3D Virtual Reality simulation systems. "Where does it go from here?"

"Countless variables, sir, but with that slice of LEO getting crowded, just a few collisions might set off a Kessler event."

"Be careful using the *K* word, Major Neufeld, it panics people. Major Wallace, how bad is the debris from 1935 so far?"

"Worse than we would have expected, sir. Space Fence has 214 objects, plus whatever is too small or nonreflective to pick up. Collision was at an acute angle and works out to about sixteen thousand kilometers an hour."

"Do we have any other likely collisions forecasted?"

"Not yet, sir."

"Major Neufeld, get the 3Vid gang online to run continual updated scenarios as observation data comes in. I'm starting to think someone here is on our six, and we don't know who."

Two hours later, Wallace, McGill, and Neufeld were replaced on console to meet with other analysts in the briefing room. From here they watched the Tracking Layer Satellite 935 incident replayed on the 3D wall, this time from the satellite's point of view. There was a collective gasp at the violence of the collision and the way debris scattered like fragments from an exploding warhead.

"So now, we've got four LEO collisions," McGill said. "China claims something hit what they call a 'military satellite conducting peaceful materials and technology tests.' What's the inclination on that one?"

Neufeld answered, "Sir, only three degrees higher than our 1935, and it looks like the debris clouds will overlap. There's more coming at us."

"That's our view, sir," said Jack Haaren, the white-haired contractor lead analyst, an ex-officer with more space ops experience than any of them. "We need to shift some of the Transport Layer and Custody Layer birds. We have to stop feeding the fire of these collisions."

McGill looked at Major Neufeld, who said, "Sir, I agree, but understand that we'll burn up the fuel on some of the satellites we move."

"Burn them," McGill said. "General Riordan needs to approve that, but that's what he'll say. Deorbit them if there's no other way. And we need to find out what that Chinese spacecraft is doing headed for Guardian One's GEO slot. We don't have any traffic in last few minutes from USSPACECOM Headquarters, so let's see who's got the stick right now."

The contractor brought up a picture on the secure comm on the room's control console.

A thin-faced, graying two-star general appeared. "This is Hux." Hux was the Operations chief, J3, under General Riordan.

"General, Tony McGill. We need to brief General Riordan and review possible warfighting options if our situation is not accidental. Is he in yet?"

"On his way in. Go ahead and brief me."

"Yes, General. First, I'd like to recommend we get one thing out of the way and go to Space Condition 3."

"Agreed. Go to SPACECON 3."

"One other thing can't wait. I need approval to lose some satellites in the layers. We believe it may take that to avoid a Kessler event."

"Send us your projections, best case to worst. If anything becomes critical before we send new orders, you have authority to take the actions required to avoid that situation."

USSPACECOM BLUF DAILY SUMMARY – SUPPLEMENTAL – 0748Z 13 June 2034
<CLASSIFICATION>
A Shǒuhù spacecraft was confirmed to enter the slot reserved for Guardian One and that Armadillo refueling depot. U.S. reissued warning: as in the last incident, China signaled receipt but did not respond.
<CLASSIFICATION>

USSPACECOM BLUF DAILY SUMMARY – 0940Z 13 June 2034
<CLASSIFICATION>
China's Xi'an Satellite Monitor and Control Center announced they believe a Kessler event is imminent and are shifting six Earth-imaging satellites and four experimental satellites to slightly different orbits.

The Center had no comment on the Shǒuhù spacecraft.
<CLASSIFICATION>

JSOC
0945Z, 13 June 2034

Major Wallace, on the second way-too-interesting stretch in her shift, briefed General McGill on the latest.

"The infrared track has it launching twenty-one minutes ago from the Iranian launch center, the new site they built with Chinese help. Not on a ballistic trajectory like an ICBM. Projecting it as an orbital launch."

"What's the inclination?"

"Around thirty degrees, sir."

"If it's orbital, we should know soon," McGill said. "Who'd have thought the Iranians would be such a potent space power? When I was a lieutenant, they could barely fire a model rocket."

"This could be more of a joint Iran-Pakistan-Korea pact launch, sir, or even a Chinese one." Wallace turned back to her screen and studied the 3D image and accompanying alphanumerics.

"Okay, sir, It's definitely orbital. Inclination 29.9, initial altitude 320 kilometers. Eccentricity and parameters TBD, but we should have them in less than two hours. SpaceBrain is updating now."

"Now, what do we have, in your opinion?"

"General, with an orbit that low, either tactical comms or an imager."

McGill considered the possibilities. "Also could be something a lot nastier. Let's see if we can arrange a visit from CORVUS."

"CORVUS is in routine orbit and not currently tasked, sir, so that should be doable. Only other activity is spaceplane Rook-3, *General Bruce Medaris*, approaching docking with Guardian One."

"Any reason that last is important to us, Major?"

"Uh, no, sir, just routine information."

"Carry on."

She refocused on her console, just a bit rattled. She could swear McGill had flicked an eyebrow in what might have been a humorous way.

Pakistan Space Center, Rawalpindi
1122Z, 11 June

Colonel Mukthi Batra inserted the flash drive in the console. In the fifteen years since the Center had been opened, originally as part of the civilian-focused SUPARCO agency but hosting an ever-larger military wing, its network had not been updated with any consistency. The old civilian computers remained highly vulnerable to attacks. Transferring equipment from his own military research branch to Iran labeled as propellant tanks hadn't been noticed yet, thanks to some altering of records, and the component swap two of his co-conspirators had made on the Talwar satellite had likewise gone undetected. It amused him his country was going so far as to disclaim ownership of the Talwar as experts tried to sort out what had happened.

U.S. Space Force Experimental Station, General Michael Collins, aka Guardian One
1144Z, 11 June

The six modules, giant solar panels, and forest of antennas making up the USSF's space station hung together in the velvet black, prepared to receive visitors. The station's 190 metric tons of mass, with 348 cubic meters of habitable space, had been completed only a year before using a series of Osprey and Sigma commercial boosters. Now the *Medaris* approached Docking Port 2.

The docking was routine. The station commander, Colonel Rick Schlosser, watched impatiently until the inner airlock hatch opened. Three men floated there: the *Medaris's* copilot, the flight engineer, and the new intelligence officer, Major Martellus Jenkins. "Major Jenkins, with me please," Schlosser said. Jenkins, a tall black man, glanced up at the airlock threshold as though afraid he'd bump his head on it, then reoriented himself from Earth to space and floated through horizontally.

The two "flew" through an equipment-encrusted corridor to the dark, small, but critically important space called the Warfighter Information Center. Jenkins had his first look at the liquid-crystal display walls and holograms that projected the environment around the station in all directions and dimensions.

"Major, I hope you'll pardon me for not giving you a chance to get organized, but I don't like what I'm hearing. China seems to intend a visit, but give me a quick update on Iran while we're waiting for data."

Schlosser pointed to the WIC's tiny waist-high conference table behind the two seats of the central control console. The two men tagged their feet onto Velcro pads to "stand" in place. Jenkins, on only his second trip to space, took a moment to orient himself again. *This is the floor, so that's the ceiling. Got it.*

"Well, sir, this all started three years ago when the mullahs couldn't keep Iran under control and General Mossadeq had himself declared a caliph and instituted a military government. He poured money into the space program for more military satellites. Then came the IPK space pact, where they found common ground with Pakistan and North Korea. China is supplying some help and some tech under their 'Space Silk Road' initiative. Mossadeq said once the last two attempts to renew a caliphate failed because the opposing coalitions had space power and they didn't."

"I've heard the part with Iran and Pakistan called a caliphate, but can it be? Pakistan is three-fourths Sunni, while Iran is Shia."

"The intelligence community consensus is that they somehow papered all that over, sir."

Jenkins hesitated, and the colonel caught it. "Major, that's a gigantic bit of 'papering over,' and I don't think you're buying it. Give me your personal opinion."

"My best friend in CIA hinted that CIA people think it's some kind of international military action that's added enough theocratic elements to give it cover. But CIA is still in bad odor since the Siberian nuke mess. No one's listening to them."

Schlosser closed his eyes a minute and pondered.

"Set that aside for a moment, Major. What else?"

"Yes, sir. That first stunt of theirs was a good one, flying the giant aluminized balloon everyone in the world could see when it passed over. They took the idea from our Echo communication balloonsats, which we stopped launching seventy years ago because they didn't have much utility."

"Sure made good propaganda, though. Do the spooks trust what we know about the military side of the IPK confederation?"

"Right now, yes, sir. It's a loose coalition, not a military alliance, but they managed to shoot down—no pun intended—in the UN the strengthening of the Missile Technology Control Regime to tighten the controls on space boosters. Side note is that Pakistan has been edging away a little from the others lately."

"We still haven't seen any ASATs from them, right?"

"Not from IPK nations, sir, but we know China and Russia can reach all the way out to GEO and some distance into cislunar. China has tested four Shǒuhù co-orbital inspectors slash ASATs, three successfully, the last one transiting GEO, although it stayed within a slot assigned to a Chinese satellite."

Schlosser looked out the window, although the Chinese craft was far too distant to be visible, and called back to the JSOC. "Tony, what's with that thing? We sure as hell didn't order takeout!"

Over the South Atlantic
1210Z

Six hundred and forty kilometers above the planet, the CORVUS 1 inspection craft cruised in a low-inclination orbit, complementing the polar-orbiting CORVUS 2. On Earth, the JSOC validated the appropriate order and channeled it to the 4th Space Control Squadron. Major Wallace reported the commands had been relayed from an Earth station through the Transport Layer of smallsats— unofficially, the Woodstock layer, thanks to all the chattering it carried—to CORVUS 1.

The eighteen-meter delta-winged CORVUS 1 activated its propulsion systems and began to shift its orbit. The Priority 1 USSPACECOM had assigned to the mission authorized burning the main engine as well as the ion thrusters.

"We were lucky CORVUS was on an inclination only two degrees off," Wallace said. "SpaceBrain says contact in forty-two minutes, unless the target tries to avoid us."

McGill smiled at the report. "Well, if it does, that'll tell us something right there."

USSPACECOM BLUF DAILY SUMMARY – SUPPLEMENTAL – 1249Z 13 June 2034

<CLASSIFICATION>

After no response to repeated warnings U.S. informed China we will protect Guardian One and other spacecraft by all means necessary, including the use of force.

CORVUS 1 is closing on an unidentified satellite in LEO.

<CLASSIFICATION>

Over the Central Pacific
1252Z

CORVUS 1 acquired the target after two deviations to avoid debris. The visual and infrared feeds went to the commanders at JSOC, the USSPACECOM HQ, and various other points around the Earth and off the Earth. General McGill had his counterpart on Guardian One patched in.

The image of the satellite came through various filters and AI-driven error correction to show up on the various screens as a medium-sized spacecraft, perhaps three hundred kilograms, with a central bus, broad solar panels, and three cylindrical objects about a meter long housed in protective covers.

JSOC

Lieutenant Colonel Gauthier, the sharp-featured Senior Intelligence Duty Officer (SIDO), spoke first. "Sirs, that resembles an unconfirmed design leaked on the Web for a satellite housing three close-inspection vehicles, which double as kinetic ASATs. But the bus looks adapted from Shamshīr, the IPK's joint space surveillance satellite launched last year."

A holograph appeared in a frame next to the JSOC console. It showed General Riordan and his shift lead, Chief Master Sergeant Kris "Sally" Ride.

"Major, that's what I'm hearing here too. Who built the interceptors?"

"We can't see enough to tell, General. The unconfirmed data would say Chinese, although it's possible one of the other actors managed to steal it or parts of it."

"It looks like a polyglot," said Major Wallace. She and Neufeld would normally have left console by now, but they were the most experienced crew and McGill had asked them to stay on, splitting some duties with their replacements. McGill himself was doing the same thing. "But is it designed that way so it's hard to identify, or is this a garage build by someone who got hold of a few parts from different countries?"

"While we're answering the major's excellent question," General Riordan asked, "what's it there for?"

"Unknown, sir," General McGill replied. "Something like that could take out any satellite it could reach, and we don't know the range or delta-V of the interceptors."

"And wouldn't that add to our debris problems," Colonel Schlosser said. "It could cause a Kessler Syndrome all by itself."

"Holy hell!" Wallace exclaimed to her audience of colonels and generals.

"Care to translate that, Major?" General Riordan asked with a raised eyebrow.

"Sorry, General, sirs. But debris. Kessler. I think I just figured something out. It's on the first scenario Major Neufeld's buddies did on the 3Vid. Let me call it up."

Wallace waggled her fingers to bring up the images.

In the main holographic projection space in front of the console, a densely populated image of low orbital space appeared, with the congested area in LEO from 630 to 1450 kilometers around thirty to forty degrees highlighted. The first collisions from recent days appeared as red spheres, then as modeled fields of spreading debris. The affected area grew until several other collisions occurred in a matter of the next twelve hours, shown in two minutes in the simulation.

Feeling her pulse race under the scrutiny, Wallace added the satellite just imaged. "Tom, you're faster than me with this thing. Add the three interceptors we saw spreading out from what I just tagged as Object 1. Show them colliding with three satellites in nearby orbits. I don't care which three. Hurry!"

"Doing it now," he said.

The simulation showed three red trails to other satellites. Then the red collision spheres appeared again. Next came the debris fields, spreading out until they overlapped with the ones from previous impacts. The red spheres blossomed all over the larger sphere of the space projection as impacts with all types of objects tracked by the Space Fence and the satellites occurred. The debris fields became an almost-solid organism, like an ever-growing amoeba devouring the screen as the orbit continued.

Wallace grabbed a pointer made to light up spots in the hologram. "Now. Run it back to the 1935 collision, zoom it in. Forward slo-mo, and show tracks with delta-V on the ten largest pieces of debris."

Neufeld made the inputs. "What are you looking for?"

"I wasn't sure at first," she said. She used the pointer to highlight two chunks of debris. "Sirs, look. This piece of debris, and this one? After the collision, these accelerated. That can't happen unless they were still being propelled."

"There's a lot of uncertainty in this system, Major," Gauthier said, his southern accent growing stronger. "Let's go through this more slowly and check your data."

Wallace responded before her seniors could and more strongly than she meant to. "Sir, do we have time for slow? Our data is good and the interpretation is correct. Sir."

McGill raised his hand a few inches from the console and slashed it left to right in a gesture only Wallace could see. "Sir," she said with forced calm, "we have triple phenomenology and know the velocity down to oh-point-two meters per second. Sir." She sat down hurriedly, her mouth closed.

"Colonel, my officer was a bit abrupt, but 'Holy hell' is right. This is a Kessler event, but it's an artificial Kessler event. Cause a few collisions in the right orbits, put little minimotors on a few pieces you deliberately separate, and watch the results. And I'll bet that Iranian bird didn't hit that old fairing by accident, either."

"Sir, it's worse than that," Neufeld said. "Look at debris item 1935–9. It and the one nearest to it. They fragment. They fragment without hitting anything. Dozens of new hazards!"

"So we're under attack," Riordan said, with a well-practiced calmness neither he nor anyone else felt. "Who gains the most from something like this?"

On Guardian One, Colonel Schlosser nodded to Major Jenkins to answer. "General, the IPK powers have thirteen operational satellites between them, nine in the hazarded zone. The U.S. and allied militaries have nine hundred sixty-eight. I think the number for the other space powers is around five hundred. Commercial firms have over six thousand."

Another holographic face appeared in front of General McGill. "Sir, Colonel Stark in J2. We've decoded traffic from Pakistan asking Iran and North Korea what the hell is going on. If this is real, someone screwed the Pakistanis and SUPARCO over and is using their systems without permission. Their Talwar satellite got away from them, this new launch is a complete surprise, and they're still getting major cyber interference with their space C2."

Riordan consulted with someone outside his holovision frame. "If this is really an IPK plot, it's beautiful. Trade nine assets for hundreds or thousands? We always assumed our ability to strike both spacecraft and spaceports created deterrence, but we forgot something. You can't deter when the enemy has a lot less to lose than you. AND thinks we're not even going to know who did it."

McGill said, "General Riordan, we also assumed the threat to orbiting global utilities would deter anyone who used them. These clowns—and we're not really sure yet whose clowns they are—decided they could live with that. But the attribution's still muddled. Someone may be using Pakistan and even China as cover. I recommend we ask the president to approve an immediate warning to IPK nations—including Pakistan for now—to cease any maneuvers in space and all launches."

Riordan nodded. "He'll need to get the allies on board and do it jointly. Let's check for context here. J2, what do we have on the ground? Anyone ginning up for war?"

"No one is set for immediate hostilities, we don't think, General," Stark replied. "But Iran has gone to a higher defense posture. There are some air-unit movements, and they kicked off a drill yesterday where half their army reservists reported to their units."

"Thank you," Riordan said. "What we need to do is blockade space for those countries. Somewhere back in my Academy education, we talked about that. Technically it might even be legal. I'll speak to Washington. In the meantime, we need to take every precaution to protect our assets. Now what about this damned Chinese ASAT?"

"Now we've got two possibilities, sir," McGill said. "They either launched before this mess by coincidence, or they knew it was happening and waited until we were focused on LEO problems."

Major Neufeld spoke. "Sir, SpaceBrain is recommending a second wave of moves to protect our LEO satellites from most debris. Also, British are confirming the loss of two comsats and one satellite in the Cook telescope array."

"Acknowledged," General McGill said. "Route a Proteus microsatellite swarm in orbit around that new LEO satellite, too, if there's a carrier that can get there quickly. Make it obvious we're crawling all over them. Split the other one and protect the NASA and CosmicView space stations, if they're in the danger zone. See what we or maybe France can do for the UN station. Chinese station will have to take care of itself. Also make sure the FCC and company notify the commercial folks to implement their Kessler contingency plans."

"Tony, we also have our Guardian One Proteus guards ready to launch," Schlosser said.

General Hux spoke to Riordan. "With your okay, sir, we're adding two more Proteus groups."

"Timeline?"

"Guardian Scout at the Cape is integrating now. They can launch in forty-five minutes if State and Defense waive launch-notification protocols." He tried to stop any trace of a smile, but one corner of his mouth twitched up for just a second.

Everyone noticed. They all knew this was Hux's baby. He'd championed having Space Force keep a rapid-launch capability and rotate guardian officers for hands-on experience in a time when almost all launches were contracted out. Now it was front and center. The Proteus carriers released twelve-satellite groups to shadow targets with inspector nanosats that would also sacrifice themselves to deflect impact weapons or major debris.

General Riordan chuckled. "Bill, don't look so damn smug just because you convinced CSO to keep funding your model-rocket boys. Beers are on me next time. Where are you sending them?"

"One will help protect the UN station. The other will go to a higher orbit to shield the laser."

"Good. I know we're going to have power up our friendly neighborhood Space All-altitude Laser to get some of the bigger debris objects. It'll set some teeth on edge, but we need it. We'll issue the proper warning notice. Tony, as long as it's just debris and you've got separation, authorize SPALL control to fire at your discretion. If you need to take out a satellite, though, call me back."

Pakistan Space Center, Rawalpindi
1300Z, 11 June

Colonel Batra dropped the flash drive into a half-full can of wonderfully acidic American-made cola. He crinkled the can shut and buried it deep in the bin from where it would be crushed further, then melted for reuse.

He pondered the near future. He was a man of action, his boldest ideas stifled by his own country but encouraged by the people creating the new caliphate. He himself was a religious man only for appearances' sake; he didn't care what they called it. Pretending to be devout for one's own gain was al-Kaba'ir, one of the great sins under Islamic law, and the punishment was death. To him, that danger just added to the thrill. Being part of a new empire, one where military professionals like himself held sway rather than the unpredictable clerics, meant power, not just wealth. The network he had helped General Mossadeq conceive and nurture was manipulating religious authorities and three governments to establish that empire. He thought of the "trusted channel" the computers here had to counterparts in China and upped that to four governments.

JSOC

"General," suggested McGill, "we need to authorize Sprint to take out the LEO and GEO threat satellites without debris. According to the recommendations from the last Schriever war game, it's politically safer to use ground-based weapons than the laser on foreign satellites. Russia and China can't complain, since we built Sprint only after they dumped on our proposal back in the Biden administration to limit ground-based ASATs and instead built new ones."

"They'll complain anyway, but I agree," Riordan said. "I'll need to take that up through the channel to SecDef and the president, but I'll light a fire under their—" He stopped to switch to diplomatic language. "I'll make it quick. I'm also directing SPACECON 2, effective now."

"Sirs," Wallace reported. "This is getting redundant, but we've got a problem."

"What now? Klingons?"

"No, sir, it's that cyberattack. SPALL Control Center connectivity is going in and out."

"Hell, that's one of our most secure systems, or I hope it is. Who's in the Cyber Command Cell?"

A wall monitor came alive and a very young-looking contractor appeared. "Sir, this is David Chang in the Cyber cell. We've got an attack along three different paths on the computers connecting SPALL Control Center with the uplinks. Very sophisticated, lots of mutations. Pretty advanced quantum-based stuff. Someone was holding their best tech back until now, I'd say."

"From who?"

"China, North Korea, and Russia are among the countries with this level, sir. We can't say which. Sir, this was all-out."

McGill thought about that a moment. "Does the attack include nuclear command and control?"

"No, sir. STRATCOM Cyber says nuclear systems are good. It's space focused."

"Finally, something to be thankful for. Keep us informed." He shut off the link and said, "We'll transfer SPALL to the backup control system on Guardian One."

"Sir?" Wallace asked. "I thought that was still in testing."

McGill grinned. "No one's read into everything in this business, Major. Not me and certainly not you."

Twenty minutes later, the cyber contractor appeared on his screen again. "General, the video from the Sprint base has dropped out, but we've restored secure audio. If you want it, I can pipe in the launch preparations."

"Do so."

"Have it up in one moment, sir."

Wallace looked up a schedule. "Sir, the voices should be Major Frank Washington and Major Cindy James, 18th Space Defense Squadron at Vandenberg Forward Operating Location-1. That's—"

"I remember," McGill said. "To be sure about treaties, we put the ASATs so they were over a hundred kilometers from the nearest space launch site. General, if you agree we'll go ahead with two Sprint-L interceptor missiles for LEO and two three-stage Sprint-Gs for GEO."

"Meaning we need to go to SPACECON 1," Hux said. "I don't like how fast we're ramping up. I feel we're just barely staying on top of it, if we even are. But they've forced our hand here."

General Riordan nodded agreement. "Go to SPACECON 1. Washington says Sprint launch is authorized."

The voices from Forward Operating Location-1 (FOL-1) came in, cool and professional.

"Step 50: Both officers confirm Zeus has directed SPACECON 1," James said, her voice steady.

"Verify SPACECON 1," returned Washington.

"Step 51: Reconfirm good Enable indication." "Check."

"Step 52: Confirm four launches, two salvos, two targets indicated." "Check."

"Step 53: Reconfirm all status lights green." "Check."

"Step 54: Primary and backup battery lights, all eight green." "Check."

"Step 55: Auxiliary power lights." "Check."

"Step 56: Guidance Go." "Check."

"Step 57: Keys inserted." "Check."

"Step 58: Power Arm." "Check."

"Step 59," James said. "Key turn on my mark. Three, two, one, mark!"

"I have good launch on Sprint 1." "Check."

Thirty seconds passed as the group in the JSOC leaned unconsciously toward the speakers and tried to picture the environment where the first ASAT ever fired in anger had just been launched.

"I have good launch on Sprint 2." "Check."

Two minutes passed.

"I have good launch on Sprint 3." "Check."

A final thirty seconds.

"I have a hold on Sprint 4. Guidance Go indicator has gone red. Recycle at Step 22."

"Agreed, recycling from Step 22."

In the high, cold darkness above the Pacific Ocean, the thrust termination ports on Sprint 1's booster second stage opened. The stage backed off, and the ASAT surged ahead. A few kilometers away, the same actions happened for the Sprint 2. At approximately the same time, the second stage of Sprint 3 separated and the third stage ignited.

In the JSOC, McGill took another look at the ASAT as the Sprint grew ever closer. "They've popped the covers off those interceptor tubes," McGill said. "We'd better get this done quick." He looked again as the visible-light imager captured more and more details. "Majors," he said slowly, "take a good look at the seeker warheads in the interceptor tubes."

Neufeld, who had recent experience with ASATs, looked at the seeker heads. Three concentric circles, the outer one showing within it a gold dish from which projected a cylindrical sensor. "I don't see what you're noticing, General. It looks like I'd expect."

"Exactly. Because it looks like one of our old Exoatmospheric Kill Vehicles. That's either an American Plutronics seeker or a copy, right down to where they placed that little connector on the left side of the dish and what it looks like. On top of everything else, we've got industrial espionage on our hands."

Inside Sprint 1, the computer evaluated the inputs from five navigation satellites, cross-checking with the sensor feed from CORVUS 1 and from the SDA systems, and fired tiny blips of its hydrazine thrusters to adjust its trajectory. Three minutes later, the Sprint's webbed mechanical arms extended into a catch basket as the spacecraft matched course and speed with the target. The collision was managed at just a few meters per second. The target began thrusting, but Sprint was designed to have more thrust and delta-V than likely targets, and the combined spacecraft began their deorbit.

JSOC

McGill said, "Okay, we've launched the first deliberate ASAT attack in history. Now let's see who does protest."

"We just found out, sir," Wallace said. "Apparently someone in China fired off a message that interference with their 'inspection' satellite in GEO would not be permitted."

"Not permitted. Hmmm. Time to GEO intercept?"

"One hour twelve minutes, sir," Wallace said. "Sir, Sprint 4 is hard broke. USSPACECOM is prepping the Jacksonville site for backup." She realized how much she was sweating in her gray USSF fatigues despite the coolness of the room—but then, everyone else was too. Her left hand drifted toward the drawer holding the caffeine tablets as she talked. "New incoming traffic being forwarded from SPACECOM Ops Cell."

"And?"

"Sir, they say Sprint 3 has disappeared!"

"What? How?"

"They lost the feed thirty seconds ago."

"Confirmed," Neufeld said.

"Who got them? Cyberattack?"

"No, sir, ISR sources indicate a Chinese laser from the base in Xinjiang." He looked at a new message. "Sir, we have confirmation it was the laser."

There was a moment of silence as McGill pondered that. It could, technically, be an act of war. In practice, they couldn't let it become that. Not while they lacked full information.

"How'd they do it?" Wallace wondered. "How'd they target that far out to a missile moving that fast?"

"I suspect we'll find they got it when the third stage was still thrusting," McGill said. "Used infrared telescope to read the heat signature coupled with radar." He turned toward another console to his left.

"Mr. Logsdon! Come on up here. Take the jump seat." He pointed to an extra chair on his left with a miniconsole in front of it.

The State Department liaison, Ed Logsdon, took his spot. "Sir, no communication yet from China. The president's consulting with General Riordan."

"Do we have indications of any further force ramp-up—IPK countries or China?"

"State has nothing."

General Hux added, "Intel and IndoPacific Command have nothing new."

Colonel Schlosser broke in from Guardian One. "Sirs, General, our command links with SPALL are green and all SPALL status indicators are green. Do we have permission to retask it target the Chinese spacecraft?"

"Retask SPALL," Riordan said. "We'll warn China one last time, but take no chances. Then resume debris clearance. We are in really, really dangerous territory, and we've got the stick because no one else can take all the actions fast enough. According to Major Neufeld's analysis and what General Hux is showing us from SpaceBrain, we still might be able to strangle this Kessler thing before it gets too big."

"Copy, General."

Major Neufeld said, "General, the civilian SpaceSweeper satellites have been retasked and are cleaning up as assigned by SpaceBrain. The commercial constellations have executed their contingencies, moving satellites and so forth. All except one, Argus."

Mr. Logsdon pulled out an earbud. "Sir, I'm listening on a call with

SecState and SecDef. The Argus CEO doesn't want to implement this, said the value of space constellations is already down ten billion dollars on Wall Street and he'd rather ride it out than look panicked. We're reminding him this was finalized in their license agreements."

General Riordan responded. "Tony, Mr. Logsdon, please inform Argus we will not extend Space Force assets to protect their satellites until they follow their agreement. I think he'll come around."

"Sir," McGill asked, "are we losing much military capability yet?"

Riordan held up crossed fingers. "Not bad yet. The layers' redundancy and the GEO sats are keeping us connected. But it could get worse."

"Message traffic from Washington, General," Wallace announced. "Being repeated from China."

The text appeared on Wallace's screen as an AI translator using a robotic but not unpleasant female voice added a vocal track. "We regret the necessity of destroying your Sprint antisatellite vehicle. Our satellite is on a peaceful inspection mission that is permitted and was being targeted."

Logsdon shook his head emphatically. "Our position since those close passes in 2020 has been emphatic. Inspection within someone else's assigned slice of geostationary orbit is NOT permitted without an agreement." He paused, his brow wrinkling. "They're not there to fight. They're there to push us to see if they can establish a new precedent."

General Riordan nodded and turned to Ride. "Ask State to tell them no. I suggest we say, 'As is well known, the United States recognizes no such right. Any approach within one hundred kilometers of our station or depot will be construed as hostile and we will take all necessary measures. In addition, we protest in the strongest possible terms the use of any Chinese technology or equipment in the provisioning and launching of the ASAT vehicle Sprint 1 destroyed.'"

"General," McGill said, "There's something else. Sprint 3 wouldn't have reached their ASAT for an hour. They were either just showing off their laser, or maybe testing it with us providing the target."

Riordan's face tightened. "One more thing to deal with after we resolve this crisis."

Ride asked, "JSOC, can SPALL safely target something that close to Guardian One? I thought it wasn't tested for GEO at all."

"Yes, Chief," McGill replied. "They can use the Proteus guardians as beacons. You're right we haven't tried it, but LEO to GEO is a tenth of a second. We need to know what safety margin Guardian One needs, though."

"We're on it," Hux said.

"Space Force Basic Course 101, quoting Joint Publication 3-14," Wallace said quietly to her console colleagues. "'Just as the United States would not allow interference with navigation of a ship on the open seas, it will take all necessary measures to ensure there is no interference with free navigation in space.'"

She started as General Riordan replied. She had forgotten his link was still live.

"You don't have to give me the quote, Major, I wrote it," he said. "We put an exception in there for regulating navigation in orbits or sectors assigned by treaty, but I can't remember the last time it came up. Either way, we're going to protect our people."

Guardian One

In space, four Proteus nanosatellites were already maneuvering to get as close to the Shǒuhù as possible while remaining between it and Guardian One. As moving satellites keeping station on a moving target, though, they were burning through their hydrazine quickly. The station's own xenon-fueled ion station-keeping thrusters were activated, but they moved the station off its regular course only very slowly, and the attached spaceplane degraded the performance with its added off-center mass.

JSOC

"Do we have a response from China?" McGill asked.

The AI voice translation came on again, and McGill realized someone had amped up the link so they were talking in text in real time.

"We insist on our right to inspect your station. However, as proof of our peaceful intentions, we are willing to stand off one hundred kilometers during discussion. We will also use our laser to destroy critical debris items threating your satellites as our own requirements permit if you send us targeting data."

"This is acceptable," Riordan said.

"Sir, State agrees," Logsdon said. "I see they didn't mention the 'Chinese technology' part."

"It would make sense, though, that that figured into their whole 'peace out' position," Wallace said to no one in particular.

The Chinese voice track came back on. "There is a cybernetic attack on our control systems. You have betrayed us."

Riordan looked startled. "It sure as hell wasn't us! Tell them we didn't do it and ask what that means for their ASAT."

The reply was swift. "Your reckless attack has broken links with our inspection satellite. It has defaulted to a routine directing it to pursue and collide with its surveillance target, which is your Guardian One."

"We did *not* do this. This is not an American attack. Ask why we would create a risk to our own station!"

This time, someone in China took a half minute to think. "The cybernetic attack may be from Pakistan, in which case we will retaliate. Can you defend your Guardian?"

"Yes." McGill looked up, as if he could see his comrades in orbit. "Guardian One, direct Proteus satellites to make minimal-speed magnetic contact with Shŏuhù and try changing its course. Activate the Proteus beacons and SPALL!"

Guardian One

"Acknowledged," Schlosser said. "Going to protective posture and arming SPALL."

All over the station, covers extended over sensors and windows while nonessential equipment shut down. "Doesn't look like the nanosats are affecting it much. Shŏuhù must have a lot of juice. This close, SPALL might fry something on *Medaris*, but no other choice," he said grimly. "Wait, is Major Kukral still on board?"

"Yessir," the spaceplane copilot said from behind him. "She didn't like a propellant gauge. She decided she was going to recheck the propellant tank safing steps and check the valves manually."

The colonel looked at his display and that of the SPALL controller next to him, Major McCoy. "One minute to collision. Get her out *now!*" he called.

"Yessir!"

The last act began in high LEO, where SPALL rotated to train its laser. The compact reactor inside fed in a megawatt of power, and the SPALL tracking antennas picked up the Proteus signals.

"Where's Kukral?" Schlosser barked.

"Headed for the airlock."

"Dammit, hurry her up! We're going to die in about thirty seconds." He gritted his teeth and punched in a code as he nodded to McCoy to make the last control inputs. "Fifteen seconds to impact, authorizing SPALL to fire on best solution NOW!"

The AI controller on SPALL had aligned itself using signals from Proteus, Guardian One's radar, its own low-power laser ranging device, and SDA sources. In less than a second, the beam flashed from LEO to GEO.

The Shŏuhù was pushed away by the photon pressure and outgassing of its surface under intense heat even as its structure began to melt and collapse. In a few more seconds, it was a lump of melted metal and silicon, with debris spinning off, most of it spreading away from Guardian One.

Two loud pings reverberating through the station, one startlingly close to Schlosser's command console, told them they hadn't been entirely missed. Within the space of seconds the station shuddered, first as if punched from the left, then as if punched from below. A third, more muffled, impact sound came from the area of Docking Port 2. Half the lights went out, a built-in action when power levels dropped. Their LCD panels blinked, but came back. Schlosser could hear thrusters going on and off as the autopilot stabilized the station.

"Status!"

"Airtight integrity's looks like high nineties, sir," the engineer floating up behind Schlosser said. "We can handle that. Structural integrity looks good so far." He asked the panel near him for a different set of readouts. "At first look, reflected energy and debris took out one telescope, two unprotected cameras, and the backup quantum transmitter. Solar Array 1 took a big one. Batteries are taking up the slack."

The copilot spoke up. "Sir, the Medaris took a bad debris hit. Atmosphere's dropping to zero and most readouts are dead. "

"Did Major Kukral get out?"

The engineer spoke hesitantly. "Sir, one more second and we'd have all been destroyed."

"What are you not telling me?"

The copilot floated closer, his face white. "She waved off the airlock crew. She left us intact and took her chances."

JSOC

2003Z, 13 June 2019

Major Neufeld tried his best to speak over the excited voices and applause for SPALL's success which resounded from all circuits. "General Riordan, General McGill, SpaceBrain's projections of the Kessler event indicate we reduced damage enough that most debris bigger than a marble is being cleared."

McGill saw wavering in one of the holo displays and traced it back to Major Wallace's suddenly unsteady fingers. He leaned close.

"Major?" he whispered.

"Sir." The word dragged itself out between her teeth. "General, request ten minutes off console."

"Granted."

She vanished.

McGill waved another officer into her spot and rejoined the main conversation.

"More good news," General Riordan was saying. "We see China's acting with its laser as promised."

Neufeld maneuvered his display with his hands. "We'll likely still lose several more satellites in the Transport Layer and below, General. We'll need to keep up all the cleaning efforts as long as we can."

"Acknowledged," Riordan said. "Our future launches will need a lot of replanning, but we're still in business. Mr. Logsdon?"

"General, State and Defense are coordinating response to China over their role in our officer's death."

Neufeld winced as the pen in McGill's hand snapped like a matchstick before the general could compose himself.

"It's going to be touchy," Riordan continued, "but my assessment is we won't go to war. The demonstration of SPALL and our other capabilities caught everyone's attention at just the right time. A little shock and awe never hurts. Their 'inspection' gambit happening during this event was a coincidence in timing. But they or the Iranians, we don't know which yet, need to answer for that seeker head too."

Neufeld felt the fatigue wash over him. McGill had supported his and Wallace's request to be on console whenever McGill was, but caffeine and adrenaline could only do so much. "I'd hate to be Iran right now," he said.

"Or North Korea," a voice he recognized as Chang came on.

"We've neutralized the attacks and traced them to the culprits. Cyber Command approved a strike on a cyberwarfare and satellite control center and the air defense around it."

General Riordan nodded. His holographic face, wearied by the events of the last day, turned toward the JSOC crew who were in turn visible to him. "Good work to you and your crew, Tony. The fallout here will keep us and the diplomats busy for a while. Pakistan has arrested a rogue officer in cahoots with Iran. Everyone's gunning for Iran: I'd expect sanctions and probably a lot worse. In the meantime, we'll break the relay links in North Korea they use to complete their satellite control connections. General Hux, what do we have on the North Korean site?"

Hux traded nods with his intelligence officer and looked at his watch. "I'll answer that for everyone in about forty-five minutes."

USS *Enterprise* (CVN-80)/Carrier Air Wing Nine
Korea Strait
2140Z, 13 June 2034

On the Northerly Threat Axis at 50 kilometers and angels 15, Captain Jon "Irish" Flannigan, Commander Carrier Air Wing Nine, circled with his package of twenty-two Super Lightning strike fighters plus their electronic warfare and tanker drone companions. His aircraft had launched, completed in-flight refueling, and rendezvoused with hardly a glitch. The brass made it clear they didn't just want to damage this target: the strike plan was meant to leave a lasting impression.

His earpiece beeped. "Champion Lead, Hummer 13. Cougar Strike passes you are cleared to push. I say again, you are cleared to push. Switch Tactical and happy hunting, Champion Flight."

With North Korea's C2 air node out of commission thanks to the cyber geniuses, plus the Air Force fighters out of South Korea flying cover and defense suppression, this would indeed be a show to remember. The General Satellite Control Center near Pyongyang was deemed too sensitive, but an installation northwest of Kuupri airbase, with satellite control and relay antennas plus buried cyberwarfare centers, was having visitors.

Irish called "feet dry" to the Big E and pushed his throttles up to reach his ingress airspeed.

JSOC

"That's it," Logsdon said as they watched the smoke and explosions from the satellite control base.

"I wonder if the Navy or the Air Force might have broadened the strike plan a little bit," Neufeld said dryly, noting more smoke rising from the direction of the airbase itself. "Sir, why did they risk the planes? They could have used the Skybolts for a kinetic attack from orbit."

"The titanium 'Rods from God'? The SecDef thought it best to keep those in reserve and not show anyone we have them. Besides, the Space Force can't have all the glory. Let the other branches think they still matter," McGill added with a tired wink.

"And the First Space War is over," General Riordan proclaimed, more relief than triumph in his voice.

McGill looked thoughtful. "For some of us," he muttered, in a voice no one heard.

He knocked on the privacy cubicle. "Laura, let's talk."

She let him in. "Sir, I don't mean to be disrespectful, but I was on a personal call. I was—"

"I know why you were here," he said. "Kukral's family."

Wallace snapped her phone off. "You knew we were—"

He closed the door. "You were top-secretly engaged. You going to be together as soon as she divorced Dr. Stewart." He raised a hand and covered up the rank board on his right shoulder. "Laura, I don't care who my people marry or sleep with, but I hear almost every fact and rumor whether I want to or not. Off-off-*off* the record, that's why I've spoken to Colonel Gauthier once about hitting on younger officers including you. He was going to oppose anything you said, which is why I let you get away with that. Besides, I've seen you and Major Kukral in the same room. You're in love. I'm sorry. I know how you feel right now."

Something snapped in her. "How would you? General—sir"—she looked at where he still had his rank covered up—"no, you don't. Your family's safe in Dallas. I know you mean well, but you haven't lost anyone like this." She fought back tears and didn't quite succeed. "I'm sorry, sir, I'm sorry."

A spark of anger flashed in McGill's brain for a moment, and he bit his lip to shut it down. "Laura, I know why you say that. Now this no-rank thing is good for one more minute while you look up the last conflict they called the 'First Space War.' The Persian Gulf. Look up the B-52 that went down over the Indian Ocean."

She picked up her secure Spacemilnet comm unit and spoke quietly into it. "B-52, 8 February 1991, call sign Hulk 42, three men lost, navigator Captain Eric McGill . . . Oh, my God, he was your father."

"I was a kid. But I know what you're feeling."

She straightened her back and met his gaze. "I understand, sir."

"Major Kukral willingly risked her life. A hit like that with an open airlock could have killed us all.

"Laura, you can take time off, or ask for anything else you need." He took the hand off his rank. "However, you've got two jobs to do, one now and one later. Later will be escorting Lieutenant Colonel Kukral's body to meet her family at Arlington for the award of the Silver Star and her burial. Right now is we have a changed world to adapt to and a nation to protect. And this conversation never happened. So get back on console and do shift change. Ready?"

"Yes, sir."

✧   ✧   ✧

Matt Bille is a former Air Force ICBM officer and now a science writer, historian, and novelist living in Colorado Springs. He is the author of the NASA-sponsored history *The First Space Race: Launching the World's First Satellite* (Texas A&M, 2004) and numerous papers and articles on space. He is also a defense and space consultant for the firm Booz Allen Hamilton and an early advocate of microsatellites and responsive launch. This story was written by the author in his personal capacity. Matt can be reached via his website www.mattbilleauthor.com.

This story is dedicated to L.J. Hachmeister: science fiction writer, humanitarian, rescuer of puppies, and my friend to infinity and beyond.

Did USSF Steal the Seal?

✳️

Seals, emblems, logos, and insignia are important cultural elements in any organization, especially in the military, where they carry special significance in ceremony, as part of official channels of communication to the service personnel and to the public, and also in efficient day-to-day interpersonal interaction to convey rank, unit, ability, and role.

In various forms, iconography for America's Navy and Marine forces have long featured the anchor, its Army the shield, and its Air Forces, wings. All are abstracted and simplified to varying degrees, both to meet typographic and stylistic requirements, and also for universality; the best icon is the one that is equally recognizable across time and space, independent of changes in technology or situation.

Silver border signifies "defense and protection from all adversaries and threats emanating from the space domain."

Black interior "embodies the vast darkness of deep space."

Four beveled elements "symbolize the joint armed forces supporting the space mission: Air Force, Army, Navy, and Marines."

Two inner spires represent "the action of a rocket launching into the outer atmosphere in support of the central role of the Space Force in defending the space domain."

A central star, Polaris, "symbolizes how the core values guide the Space Force mission."

Space Force iconography centers around "the delta," a symmetrical triangle and star meant to represent the USSF's mission to defend America's interests in space. In science and mathematics, the Greek symbol delta (Δ) represents change, appropriate for a service branch called into existence by political and technical change and concerned in many ways with rocketry, in which the mathematical underpinnings of the symbol feature so prominently. But in other forms, the same basic glyph has long served military iconography as an abstract representation of an arrowhead or spearpoint. Both meanings are relevant for the Space Force, which has adopted it "to represent the organization's role as a 'force of change' in the military and in space exploration" and also to pay tribute to historic military antecedents going all the way back to the Second World War.

The arrowhead has been a staple of military heraldry for as long as there have been organized military units. In modern times, the delta symbol used in Space Force unit insignia and central to the USSF Seal honors a heritage leading (at least) back to World War II. According to the 36th Wing Heritage Pamphlet 1940–1994[5], the emblem approved in June 1940 for 36th Group was: "An arrowhead

5 Meyer, Jeffrey, 36th Wing Historian, April 2019. 36th Wing Heritage Pamphlet 1940-1994.

point upward gules, in a chief, azure, a demi wing agent . . . The shield is blue and gold, the colors for the Air Force. The arrowhead is a deadly swift weapon of offensive[sic]. The silver wing in the upper part of the shield is emblematic of aerial protection and vigilance."

Subsequent to the war, the Western Transport Air Force (a high-speed airlift logistics service) adopted a stylized delta similar to that now used in the NASA logo. New missile defense units of the Army and Air Force continued the use of stylized arrowheads, often combined with lightning bolts and/or triangular "shockwave" lines representing rapidity of action. As missile technology developed, stars symbolized operation at the edge of space, and actual rockets were often represented with varying degrees of artistic success.

Thus, "the delta" is far from new to military iconography. Yet in July 2020, when the fledgling service announced the designs for its new seal and delta emblem, social media influencers pounced on similarities between the new graphics and those familiar from *Star Trek*. George Takei, who played Sulu on the original series before settling into the social mediasphere as lovable provocateur, took famously to Twitter to opine over an image of the new USSF seal, "Ahem. We are expecting some royalties from this . . ." Nationally syndicated cartoonist & illustrator Dave Granlund joined in the fun with the following (used by permission):

And fair enough, the similarities are there, but is this life imitating art, or is it the other way around?

The sets and costumes of the *Star Trek* franchise are littered with pseudomilitary iconography, but those most recognizable today are the "delta" uniform insignia (later the combadge) of starship personnel, and the seals of Starfleet and of the United Federation of Planets. This last, we know, was directly based in the original series on the seal of the then still-young United Nations. That leaves the delta and the Starfleet seal which incorporated it as the alleged source material. But is it?

According to *Star Trek* creator Gene Roddenberry, the delta symbol was chosen to represent Starfleet because it was a simple, bold shape that would be easily recognizable and memorable. Indeed, documentary evidence[6] shows he had discussed selection of such a clear symbol suitable for trademarking and merchandising at least as early as the summer of 1964. The exact genesis of what Roddenberry came to call "the *Star Trek* emblem" is lost, but we don't have to strain too far in search of its roots. He'd flown in the Army Air Corps during World War II, and would have been familiar with military emblems based on the delta and spearpoint motifs. He'd flown for Pan Am after the war, and would have known that the Greek letter delta, which represents change and evolution, had been used by Delta Airlines since the 1930s; and this usage would have appealed to his *Star Trek* vision of a future where humanity has evolved and is working together for the betterment of all. Then again, in surviving memoranda he also called the emblem "the flying-A," probably in reference to a popular West Coast gas station logo featuring pilot's wings flanking a neon letter *A* with which he'd have been long familiar, and which in turn was heavily influenced by the "shield and wings" emblem of the old N.A.C.A., predecessor to NASA.

> For years, many *Star Trek* fans believed that the iconic "delta" insignia ubiquitous in the franchise identified members of the *Enterprise* crew specifically, and that the

[6] August 10, 1964 memo from Gene Roddenberry to Pato Guzman, Subject: Star Trek Emblem. UCLA, Gene Roddenberry *Star Trek* television series collection, 1966–1969.

crews of other ships wore other insignia. But a memorandum sent December 18, 1967, from producer Robert Justman to costume designer William Ware Theiss proves otherwise. In it, Justman points out that the insignia created for an earlier episode's "merchant marine" crew had erroneously inspired creation of yet another insignia for the uniforms of a crew from a different starship in the episode in production at that time. "I have checked the occurences [sic] out with Mr. Roddenberry," he said, "who has assured me that all Starship personnel wear the Starship emblem that we have established for our Enterprise Crew Members to wear."

By the time Justman saw the mistake in dailies, of course, a correction would have required expensive reshoots. This was in the earliest days of off-network rebroadcast syndication and years before the home video recorder, when TV episodes were only expected to be aired at most twice. Thus, Justman continued, "Please do not do anything to correct this understandable mistake in the present episode. However, should we have Starfleet personnel in any other episodes, please make certain that they were [sic] the proper emblem.

Under penalty of death!"

This was after all, 1964: seven years after Sputnik; six years after the founding of NASA; and five years after the Ford Galaxie, an old-fashioned gas-guzzling sedan born of the space age, had been embellished with the same delta motif slashed across its flanks in gleaming chrome. The "boomerang" graphic adorning the primary hull of the original starship *Enterprise* and her shuttlecraft was meant to be futuristic, and so was absolutely the product of the times. Whatever its exact origin, the *Star Trek* delta was history smearing into the future, part artistic flourish, part midcentury logo perfect for selling lunch boxes. It was literally iconic by design.

Which brings us to the Starfleet seal, bearing the same delta but set over a field of stars and wrapped in an orbiting spacecraft. *Star*

Trek lead graphic designer Michael Okuda[7] has said this emblem, perhaps surprisingly, did not appear until a *Deep Space Nine* episode in the 1990s (nearly a decade after the founding of U.S. Space Command). To make it, Okuda's team just grafted "the *Star Trek* emblem" into a background patterned after the NASA seal, so . . . mark another down for art imitating life.

At least in the case of NASA, we know the exact origin of its official seal and logo. The NASA seal was designed in 1958 by James J. Modarelli, an artist-designer at the N.A.C.A.'s Lewis Research Center in Cleveland (now the NASA Glenn Research Center). When the decision was made to absorb the facilities of the old National Advisory Committee on Aeronautics into NASA, N.A.C.A. employees were invited to submit designs for the new agency's official seal. Modarelli, a division chief with an undergraduate degree in art, submitted the winning design.

And we know exactly what inspired him because he told the story in a 1992 interview with NASA historian Glen E. Swanson.[8] Two months earlier, Modarelli had toured the Ames Unitary Plan Wind Tunnel at Langley Research Center, where a radical new Mach-3 wing design was being studied. The cambered, twisted arrow wing and upturned nose of the model impressed Modarelli, who later stylized its radical features in his NASA seal design, though he unknowingly drew it upside down. After the design was selected, this mistake was corrected and the design was further simplified for mass color reproduction. The "ball and wing" design was then used in the official seal and the original NASA logo we now call the "meatball."

So there you have it. The seal and emblem of the U.S. Space Force, like all military iconography, are the product of historical context. Steeped in symbolism intended to meet the future, they take inspiration from, and pay homage to, the history of those who blazed the trail, most directly the Air Force Space Command, but also the long line of air-logistics and missile-defense units going all the way back to the Second World War and earlier.

That's a fitting legacy, too, since far from some jack-booted

[7] https://www.ex-astris-scientia.org/inconsistencies/sf_command_emblem.htm

[8] https://www.thespacereview.com/article/3947/1

imperial space navy drawn from dystopic science fiction, the Space Force actually has a pretty "down-to-earth" mission to safeguard space and ensure the nation and its allies enjoy the unfettered benefits of this remarkable age. Even Captain Kirk needed shields and phasers and laws and diplomats. Neither the community of nations nor our deepest wishes will stop those who would creep through the endless night to sabotage and weaken us; only strength and vigilance are the universal price of peace.

Bubbles from Beneath

✵

Sylvie Althoff

Lieutenant Elizabeth Webb's eyes shot open, but it was still pitch black. The air was cold and dry, and her ears were filled with the thundering of her heart beneath an insistent, high-pitched beeping.

Breathe, soldier, she told herself, clenching her fingers into fists. She forced away images of snow, of a turtle, a monster awakening beneath a sheet of ice. *You're needed. Leave the dream behind.* Webb sucked in a gulp of recycled air and remembered.

Tearing off her sleep mask and blinking at the perpetual daylight of the transport ship *Pinckney*'s shared sleeping quarters, she peered at the screen positioned by the head of her coffin-sized berth. It took her longer than it should to decode the nature of the unfamiliar alert—a medical emergency in the main passenger compartment— and even longer to unstrap herself and push her way through the air to the ship's central corridor.

Her limbs groaned at the effort of navigating down the corridor, of the long glides and infinite momentum and sudden stops required to travel in a zero-g environment. For a stomach-flipping instant she felt sure she was plummeting down a vast metal well headfirst, and she swallowed bile as she forced herself to keep steady. She blinked hard, her mind still a tangled mess of dream and memory. She could still see the frozen pond on Aunt Barb's farm, see the turtle crashing through the ice, jaws like daggers rushing toward her face.

You're getting soft, Webb thought, gritting her teeth and following the flashing red line running along the wall. Between swings of her arm against the metal handles that lined the corridor, she used one hand to stuff her ash-brown braid back down her collar, to straighten the lapels of her uniform, the same one she'd worn for thirty-six hours. It was a futile gesture, she knew—she'd never achieve the regulation-perfect appearance that she always strove for on Earth. Even the artificial gravity aboard USSF vessels, while occasionally unreliable, was better than the perpetual zero-g on this civilian vessel.

She shivered as she neared the end of the corridor, wishing she'd taken time to pull a hoodie over her uniform. This damned rattletrap was as cold as it was deathly boring.

Cold and boring. No wonder I'm dreaming about Missouri.

Webb heard two voices before she reached the juncture between the central corridor and the passenger compartment. Their tone was unlike any she'd heard in her eight long months as an unwelcome observer among the *Pinckney*'s crew—there had been plenty of grumbling, gossiping, picking, even shouting. But never anything with this kind of deadly urgency.

"—got here! I hit the alert as soon as I noticed!"

"Meaning it didn't go off automatically?"

"I swear, the readouts looked stable, nothing changed since B shift!"

"Tell us something good, Oleg."

"Nothing," said a third voice just as Webb swung herself into the room.

The Hotel, as the crew of the *Pinckney* called the passenger compartment, was a long, quiet room that always felt dark to Webb despite the same glaring lights that adorned every wall in every paste-white room on the ship. With the two rows of thirty-six identical person-sized pods stretching down to the ass end of the spacecraft, the room felt like a morgue.

Three figures stood around Pod A3, feet fastened to the floor by their magnetized boots. Rudenko and Park were focused on the pod while Rubin wrung her hands and looked on in that helpless way that Webb couldn't stand.

"Sitrep?" Webb asked in a clipped voice as she glided over to the center of activity.

Supervisor Park looked sidelong in her direction for half a moment. "Pull the connection to the SEV system, Oleg," he snapped.

"Already done," Rudenko answered.

"Whatever's going on, we can't have it affect the other pods."

"I did it, I said. Christ."

Even in an emergency, no discipline, no respect, even for one another, Webb thought with a shake of her head. It killed her to see how poorly this vessel was run in the absence of proper protocol. If her position as military attaché aboard the Ellipse Corporation vessel had come with any power over the day-to-day, she would have whipped these shitbags into a proper crew ages ago. At least that would have been better than sitting around and trying not to look as useless as she felt.

Webb engaged her boots and struggled her way to the side of the pod, looking over Rubin's shoulder. The display was lit up with a constellation of warnings and alerts surrounding a silhouette of a human body pulsating red. It had been a long few years since her first aid training in Basic, but this looked bad.

"He's dying," Rubin said in a quiet voice. Webb turned to look at the woman, staring blankly at the pod. "By the time I saw something was wrong, it was already too late."

Webb eyed the men standing over the pod, sizing up the situation and instantly sorting through potential courses of action. This could be the moment she'd been waiting for. She could take control of the situation, maybe even save some lives.

Stand down, soldier, she told herself, breathing slowly. *Until this is a full-blown crisis, Supervisor Park is still in command here, however ineffectual he may be. Don't blow your wad just because you're bored of sitting around. Just because they don't respect the chain of command doesn't mean you can haul off and play cowboy.* Those lessons she'd been taught in the Force had been hard ones; she wasn't about to let herself forget them.

Rudenko stepped back from the pod with a huff and wiped his brow with a handkerchief.

"What are you doing?" Park snapped as his outstretched fingers clenched into a fist. "Save him!"

Rudenko shot him an unimpressed look. His eyes were red and bleary, hands shaky, mouth twisted in a stomach-acid frown. Fairly normal for Rudenko, really. "You want him saved? Bring a saint. Or at least real doctor, not just a medic. Ellipse doesn't pay me to resurrect the dead."

Park gave a wordless grunt of frustration and began tapping frantically on the panel.

"What happened, Mister Rudenko?" asked Webb.

The Ukrainian shook his head. "Not paid to do autopsies, either."

"Best guess?"

He sniffed. "Embolism. Oxygen bubble in his brain. Was dead before I got here."

"No way," Park muttered. "It can't be. Not possible."

Park began a lengthy lamentation of the grand unfairness of his situation while Webb sidled up to the pod for a closer look at the display. Most of the passengers' biographical information was locked, but her USSF login let her in without a problem. She scrolled through the available data, trying to take in as much as she could for as little as she understood. "Passenger A3, Leonid Toropov," Webb read aloud.

That name stopped Park midmonologue. Out of the corner of her eye she saw Rudenko shift his bulk almost imperceptibly.

"Fantastic," Park was now grumbling. "Just great. First time a pod's been lost on an Ellipse craft, and not only is it on my watch, it's Leonid Toropov. Wonderful."

"Toropov?" asked Rubin. "The . . . the business guy?"

"'The business guy.' As if he—" Park snarled, then stopped, breath catching before he said something else. After a beat he continued in a scolding tone, "With an attitude like that you're going to be stuck wiping down manifolds forever. The man bankrolled half the infrastructure advancements in Europe over the last ten years. Autonomous vehicles, space navigation, universities . . ."

Rubin cursed under her breath. "Some kinda big deal." She paused. "What's a guy like that doing heading out to the middle of nowhere? I didn't think Ulysses Station was bringing in anybody but engineers and drone mechanics."

Webb went on scanning her way through the menus on the pod's screen, half listening to the conversation. As soon as she accessed the activity log, she felt a familiar tickle in her stomach. There was a series of soft *ch-kunks* as Webb unlatched the cover of the pod and its environmental locks disengaged, preparing to swing open.

"What the hell are you doing?" Park yelped. "In case you haven't been paying attention, the Ellipse manual makes it very clear that the pods remain cl—"

"'Pods remain closed for the comfort and health of the guests as well as to conserve oxygen and other resources for the duration of a long space flight,'" Webb quoted, keeping her tone even. "I remember, sir. But I don't think any of those are concerns for Mister Toropov any longer."

The hinges glided open, revealing a slight man in his late fifties, dressed in a crisp gray jumpsuit and lying on a sterile white bed. Despite his small frame he was the picture of terrestrial health, boasting a tan and a lean, muscular physique. Other than the stillness of his chest, he looked like he could just be asleep, or still in the chemical stasis that he'd enjoyed for the last eight months.

"So that's him, huh?" asked Rubin in a small voice.

A smoky voice from the doorway called, "Wait, don't tell me something actually happened for once?"

"I'm sorry, Sophie, was there something confusing about 'All Hands Alert'?" Park snapped at the newcomer. Webb glanced over her shoulder to see Sophie McMillan in a tank top, a sweaty towel tucked into her waistband.

"Figured Keller just leaned on the instruments again. I wanted to finish my workout before starting my shift." The tall woman leaned in to get a look at the opened pod. "Whoa, that's not Leonid Toropov, is it?"

"Yes," Rubin answered. McMillan snapped her head in Rubin's direction, and the two shared a look.

"Talk to me, Oleg," Park sighed as he rubbed his eyes. "How could this have happened? How does an oxygen bubble make it into the SEV system?"

Rudenko took a sip of water from a bottle. "Technical malfunction."

"But how? The synchronized environmental system's got fail-safes to prevent that, and fail-safes in place if those fail-safes fail!"

He shrugged. "Those failed, too, then."

Webb straightened, her eyes roving over each of the room's occupants. The math clicked into place—this situation demanded leadership, and for once she was empowered to deliver it.

Cowboy time.

"Is there any chance this wasn't just a glitch, Mister Rudenko?"

Webb asked in a steady voice. "That someone or something intentionally put that oxygen bubble into Toropov's bloodstream?"

As expected, the questions threw the room into chaos. Park threw up his hands and began a new, elaborate objection; Rubin's muscles slackened, the zero-gravity environment gently pulling her limp form away from the floor; McMillan said something under her breath as she stepped closer to Rubin. Webb only paid attention to Rudenko's nonchalant answer.

"Possible, yes. Mechanical, manual, electronic—many ways to do it, for someone who wants Mister Toropov dead discreetly."

McMillan snorted. "You seriously think somebody killed this asshole?"

Rudenko waved his hands dismissively. "Not for sure. I only said: maybe natural, maybe not."

"But who would even—" Rubin blinked, the implication hitting home. "Wait. You think one of us did it?"

"Jesus, Liz, you can't just throw around—"

"Without examination by licensed physician you can't—"

"All right, that's it!" Park snapped, hitting his palm against the bulkhead with a low metallic thump. "Everybody back to your duty rotations immediately. Oleg, seal up that pod and keep it that way until we pull into Ulysses. All of you—no more breaks, no more slack. When you're not working or exercising, you're alone in your berth. No fraternizing, no talking even a word of this until I figure out what's going on here."

"Oh, sure," McMillan said with a sneer. "One of you assholes is a murderer and you want us to just pretend like nothing's going on. Right away, Chief, you got it."

Park thrust a finger in her direction. "This is not the time for your attitude. You don't have to like it; you just have to do what you're told."

"And just who made you king of this boat?"

"I'm the manager on duty, Sophie, in case you've forgotten."

Webb felt her shoulders rise. *The man has no idea how to give orders. Even if nobody else dies, he's going to have a mutiny on his hands if he starts cracking down now, when everyone's panicked and paranoid.*

Park and McMillan were brow to brow, and Webb saw no

awareness in Park's eyes that the taller woman's fingers were clenched into a massive fist. "Maybe you need another reprimand on your record to refresh your memory. huh?" the supervisor barked.

"That won't be necessary, Supervisor Park." Webb stepped in front of the man, her back to McMillan. "I'll be taking charge of this investigation."

"Excuse me?" said Park. "What gives you the right?"

Webb tapped her rank insignia. "Sir, I'm empowered to take charge according to the same regulation that brought me to this vessel in the first place. USSF guardians are charged with taking jurisdiction in the event of any military, criminal, or disaster situation occurring in neutral space on spacecraft with U.S. registrations. This incident qualifies."

McMillan scoffed. "Sure, that's just what we needed. A tool of state violence, here to save us all."

"We're civilians," Rubin pointed out. "Why should we have to follow orders from the military?"

"You're only a lieutenant," Rudenko muttered.

"I am the only Space Force guardian in the vicinity, which puts me in charge." Webb straightened, keeping her face serious though she could feel a smile blossoming inside her. "As far as the operations of this ship are concerned, I'm captain of this vessel and commander in chief of the whole fleet. I'll be in touch with my superiors about everything related to this incident, up to and including how cooperative the *Pinckney*'s crew have been with my investigation. Is that understood?"

Four heads nodded. None of them looked happy about it.

Webb steadied herself with a breath. "Good. I'll be interviewing each of you and Mister Keller in the next few hours, right after I file my initial report. For the time being, I'm ordering you all to follow Supervisor Park's directions and clear out of here. Until I determine otherwise, this is a crime scene."

Maybe I really can be of some use on this assignment, Webb thought with a proud lift of her chin as the crew unhitched their boots and floated their way out. *Maybe my career isn't dead in the water after all.*

Then her eyes fell upon the corpse, and that pride shattered like an icicle.

✿　✿　✿

Webb bumped gently into the ceiling of her office, frowning as she pushed herself away with her index finger and continued floating aimlessly around the room. It wasn't really an office; just a cramped cubicle between storage compartments that she'd commandeered for her work aboard the *Pinckney*. Such as it was.

Her eyes flitted to her screen, but it still only displayed the thinking animation over the icon for SF HQ in Huntsville.

Wiping her palms on her uniform, she looked down at her notes once again, not seeing the handwriting she'd reviewed a dozen times already. She had the evidence necessary to make her arrest and close the investigation. All she needed was her superior's authorization to formally place a civilian under arrest. Then all would be well—her job would be done, and she could stop looking over her shoulder at every suspicious noise. She swallowed a mouthful of stomach acid.

Webb stared at the blank gray bulkhead, picturing the infinite stars just beyond arm's reach. Her mind went to the one unanswerable question she was sure she'd be asked: Why did the killer wait until now, eight months into a nine-month journey? Why not kill him the day after liftoff? Or why not wait a little longer? Another few weeks and they could've disguised it as an accident during end-flight procedures, maybe even gotten themselves lost in the shuffle at Ulysses Station. What was the hurry?

Her stomach growled, and she started to trace how long it had been since she'd eaten anything when her screen lit up and a tone sounded in her earpiece. Even in zero-g, Webb's salute to the camera was crisp and professional. "Major."

She held her salute, waiting for her order to be at ease. After a few moments the still image of her commanding officer's rank on the screen still hadn't winked into Major Forman's craggy face. Then, barely perceptible in between scrambled syllables: "—able video feed, Sear—peat, t—ff your—"

Webb broke her salute and hurriedly tapped at her screen to try to improve their connection. "Piece of shit," she muttered under her breath, then stopped with a flare of embarrassment as she remembered her audio feed was enabled.

"—atch that, Lieutenant, please repeat?"

"Sir, I asked if you can hear me clearly now that I've disabled my video feed?" *Get it together, soldier. Don't let this crew rub off on you.*

"Clear enough, at least." The voice cutting through the static was Forman's, terse and sleepless as Webb remembered. "We've received your initial report, Lieutenant. What progress has been made in your investigation?"

"Sir. Since my initial report I've conducted interviews with all five crewmen and cross-referenced with ship's logs." Webb glanced down at her notes and grimaced. "With all candor, sir, it's a cluster up here. All five had the opportunity to inject something time-released into the EV system of Mister Toropov's pod, and the available civilian data uncovered potential motives for everyone but Mister Keller, the pilot."

She paused to invite a reply from Forman. The silence stuck in her throat, and she couldn't help but picture the major glowering at his screen, that same glower that she'd run into headfirst a dozen times since her assignment to his wing.

Webb sucked in a breath and decided to take the silence as an invitation to continue. "Crewman McMillan has numerous ties to radical antigovernment and anticorporate movements, and her disciplinary record with Ellipse documents both threats and actual physical violence. Crewman Rubin was attending DePaul University at the time of its purchase by one of Mister Toropov's organizations and subsequent closure, and she encountered considerable personal turmoil in the aftermath. Similarly, Crewman Rudenko's home state in Ukraine has been mostly bought up by a Toropov property with an eye toward aggressive, large-scale mineral extraction starting next year. And Supervisor Park had a family member killed in a crash involving a malfunction of autonomous vehicles produced by—"

A burst of warped language broke into her report. "—nection is poor and failing, Webb. I read your rep—concur with your findings. Has an a— been made?"

She swallowed. "N . . . no, sir. I haven't made an arrest yet, no. The activity log confirms which crewman was responsible. I was only waiting for confirmation of—"

"Stop w— care of it, Webb, immediately, and r— only when you've done your job." Forman's heavy, disappointed sigh came through with perfect clarity. "Eyes are on how we'll —dle this. Don't screw this up, Webb."

"No, sir."

"Since you've been —ssion there's already —een talk of pulling our men off civilian ships in the absence of another Sino-Russian Alliance attack," he growled. "Keep anything from getting worse on th— and we may be able to get the support we need. Drop the ball and the legislature's liable to c— altogether."

"I understand, sir. You can count on me."

Webb didn't know if she heard or imagined the snort that came into her earpiece. "I'd rest a lot easier if you weren't on your own out there and we had a real o—".

Another chirp in her ear, a minor-key tone announcing that the link had collapsed.

A real officer on the job, she finished for him. *Instead of you.*

Webb felt her muscles slacken as the screen shimmered into idleness. She put a hand to her eyes and rubbed, feeling every ounce of the weakness and exhaustion put into her by eight months of space travel.

"On your feet, soldier," she said under her breath. The words felt faraway, hollow as an empty turtle shell. "Come on, time to do your job. You heard the man."

Webb's body moved her into the central corridor as her mind swam with conflicting emotions about the arrest she was about to make. After seeing how Ellipse treated its employees, especially its women, Webb couldn't help but feel guilty for what she was going to do, even under the circumstances. Space wasn't a kind place, in the Force or anywhere else.

All those feelings were shut out easily enough as Webb floated down to the aft cargo bay, her mind retreating to a cold and familiar distance. The background context didn't make a difference; not when she had her evidence. Her superiors were counting on her to close this promptly. That was all that mattered.

The *Pinckney*'s vast cargo bays were stuffed to the gills with huge plastic crates containing a staggering array of banal industrial components and consumer goods. Webb had spent much of her second month aboard checking the contents and condition of the cargo against the ship's manifest, mostly just for something to do. It was mind-numbing make-work, and after a few weeks she gave up even pretending the task was necessary.

Her brow furrowed at the memory, plunged back into her anger at being shipped off on this assignment. Forman had barely tried to keep the smile from his face when he'd given Webb her orders—he finally had an opportunity to get his biggest problem guardian out of his hair, something that her perfect service record had made extremely difficult up to that point. This cargo bay still felt like a jail cell to her, even all these months later.

"Crewman Rubin?" Webb called into the cavernous room.

A head peeked out from behind one of the massive plastic crates. Even at this distance she could see the fear in Rubin's eyes, felt the same midwinter fear gnaw at her insides.

"Would you come with me, please?" Webb asked in a steady voice. "And I'll ask you to keep your hands where I can see them."

"This is *bullshit* and you know it!"

McMillan was across the crew lounge and within arm's reach before Webb could look up from her tube of dinner. Lightning danced through her muscles, but she kept her head and refused to flinch as the other woman stopped half a yard away from Webb's face, her boots sealing neatly to the ground just before they made contact.

"Is there something you'd like to say to me, Crewman McMillan?" Webb kept herself perfectly still as a vein throbbed in McMillan's red-tinted temple.

"Nothing you don't already know," McMillan snarled.

Webb's nose wrinkled, the woman's breath stale and hot against her face. She glanced over to Rudenko, who wordlessly tucked his tablet under his arm and floated his way out into the corridor, leaving the two of them alone.

She took a breath. "I'll tell you what, crewman..." she said stiffly, pushing herself gently backward to put some distance between herself and McMillan. "...instead of guessing what I do and don't know, why don't you tell me what's on your mind? Better use of both of our time, don't you think?"

"Alicia didn't kill Toropov and it's asinine to pretend that she did," McMillan snarled.

Webb clocked the woman's lean, ropey legs flexing through her shapeless gray Ellipse jumpsuit. Subtly, she put out a hand to alter the trajectory of her movement. *Don't let her get your back up on the wall,* Webb thought. *It's probably not more than the usual bluster, but...*

"Crewman Rubin is only being detained in her berth until we arrive at Ulysses Station," Webb said coolly. "At which point she will be remanded to the next arriving USSF vessel for a civilian trial."

"Sure. We all know how much fascists love a good show trial. Especially of an innocent woman."

"The evidence shows—" Webb started to explain, stopping as McMillan spat a clear globule into existence between them. She tried not to let her disgust show.

"That's what I say to your evidence. If you'd bothered to actually get to know Alicia, you'd know she could never hurt anybody, not ever. If you only knew what she's been through." Webb didn't have to look closely to see the blush on McMillan's cheeks beneath the righteous indignation. "Her mom getting sick, losing out on her degree, the things her monster of an ex-husband put her through… Goddammit, are you really going to take even this last little crumb of life from her too?"

Webb folded her arms, eyes quickly scanning over the lounge for anything she might use to defend herself if McMillan fully lost it. "I'm not about to talk about an ongoing investigation with you, Crewman."

"I'm not here to listen to you anyway. I'm here to tell you you're an idiot." McMillan's eyes glittered with anger. "Are you really going to have her put away because her access code was used right before Toropov ate it? Anyone with half a brain could spoof her code, and that includes most of us here."

"I think you should return to your post," Webb growled. "Park was right—you don't need another black mark on your record. Don't throw your career away over a crush."

Webb's muscles were iron bars waiting for the response to that, but McMillan didn't lash out at her. Instead Webb watched as McMillan's anger curdled into cruelty, and her eye ran up and down Webb's frame in an all too familiar way.

"You know, Liz," McMillan said as she reclined against empty air, stretching out her limbs with the strength of a lioness. "I've seen some pretty ugly stuff in my day. But I don't think there's anything uglier than the sight of someone like us helping the system grind helpless people into the dirt. Not a good look, girl."

Webb felt her heart pounding in her teeth. *Keep it together,*

Guardian. God, why couldn't she have just tried to hit me instead? "Okay," she managed at last, craning her head to see if she could squeeze past McMillan out into the corridor.

"You can french that boot all you want," McMillan sneered, positioning herself to block the doorway. "Push comes to shove, you're expendable to them. Same as me, same as every working-class person out there, even the cis ones. Your bosses and mine—same oppressors with a different coat of paint. All the fancy government hormones in the world won't convince them that you're any different than the rest of us. You'll never be a real woman to them."

There it is. "I think we're done here," said Webb as she launched herself toward the door into the spaceship's central corridor.

McMillan didn't move, though, and Webb bumped roughly into her. "Civilians have to wait for years in the med queue to get access to hormones. Always the same excuses: supply-chain interruptions, clearance issues, problems with sourcing. We're not a priority. Nobody's a priority if they're not rich or well connected."

"It sucks, Sophie. I never said it doesn't. But that doesn't—"

McMillan didn't budge, didn't wait for her to finish speaking. "How long did you have to wait to get your first dose, Liz? Your first surgery? Did they just give it to you right away as a reward for drone-striking a daycare or hospital? Only the best for their pet tra—"

A fist clenched, reached out. Webb held it together in time and sealed her boots to the floor to stare McMillan in the eye. "I enjoy a certain degree of privilege, I know. That includes medical care, yes. But that privilege isn't something I was just given. I earn that privilege every single day with my service in the Force."

"I know girls who've died in that queue, Liz." McMillan had tears in her eyes though she was still wearing a cruel smile. "Girls who couldn't afford to do anything but wait until they couldn't wait any longer. How can you live with yourself, knowing that you live and other girls just like you don't? That only you get the care you need to stay alive?"

"If they're Americans, they can enlist too. It's not easy, but it's better than waiting, and it's sure better than dying."

McMillan barked out an angry laugh. "How many innocent people are you going to get killed before you understand that it's the bosses versus everyone? That you're just a tool they use to keep all of us down, and they're going to throw you away when you're no longer useful?"

"Have you seen me killing anybody?"

"I see you trying your best to get Alicia killed, yeah."

A headache rampaged behind Webb's eyes. She took a slow breath. "Rubin isn't going to get killed over this. Certainly not if she's innocent. When we get to Ulysses the autopsy will uncover DNA or other forensic evidence that proves her guilt. Or it won't, and she'll go free with my apologies."

McMillan's lip curled. "Traitor."

"That's enough. Get out of my way."

McMillan opened her mouth to spew something else, but Webb wasn't waiting around to hear it. With fluid motions Webb sideswiped McMillan into a lazy spin into the middle of the lounge while kicking herself into the recycled air and sailing out into the corridor. Curses sputtered out after her as McMillan struggled to orient her feet to the floor.

"You can't set her up for this, you asshole! She didn't do it!" Webb heard just before floating out of earshot around the bend.

Back and forth. Back and forth. Ten more before you rest. Come on, you slacker.

With her lack of any real duties, it hadn't taken Webb long to polish off all the available reading material on the *Pinckney*'s intranet—those had only consisted of a Bible, a couple of Tony Robbins books, and a fawning biography of somebody named Elon Musk.

Eventually she got desperate enough to dig a little deeper and found the Ellipse Corporation's recruitment materials, the ones the company used to sucker poor souls like McMillan and Keller and the rest into these interminable interplanetary babysitting gigs. The glossy digital ads boasted "comfortable accommodations including a full suite of modern entertainment and gym equipment."

Webb snorted; if the *Pinckney* had anything approaching "entertainment" apart from Keller's five-string banjo, she hadn't seen it.

At least the gym equipment hadn't been a lie. It might not have been the cleanest she'd worked out on, but it was in good working order, and she was usually able to get in an uninterrupted hour or two before A shift started. Considering how much exercise the human body needed not to break down in a zero-g environment, it would have been a human rights violation if the *Pinckney* hadn't come stocked with gym equipment . . . not that that necessarily meant much to Ellipse.

"Fifty," Webb grunted. She let go of the handles of the rowing machine and grabbed her sweaty towel from where it floated just above her head. She wiped her forehead and checked the time readout on the gym's screen. The seconds ticked into an incomprehensible blur, her thoughts flying off to the same dead end where they'd lingered for the last week.

You're a good guardian, Webb, no matter what the men said to Forman. But you're no detective. You followed a lead to a logical conclusion—is that really enough to confirm Rubin as the killer?

Since making the arrest she'd spent most of her time keeping an eye on Rubin. Supervisor Park had made it clear that the rest of the crew was going to have to work around the clock to cover Rubin's duties, so these days Webb hardly even saw anyone else.

For her part, Rubin didn't have much to say. She protested her innocence, but clammed up under any probing about her motive. More damningly, she didn't even try to offer an explanation for how, from all the digital footprints Webb could find, entering her code was what had prompted the release of those deadly bubbles in Toropov's pod.

It doesn't matter if it adds up or not, Webb thought, turning back to the rowing machine for another set. *Murder doesn't make sense.*

She'd torn through every scrap of data on the ship, from the tech specs that gave her a daylong headache to the protected passenger information. From the available info, the thirty-one sleeping individuals taking this barge to the outskirts of humanity were all just working stiffs, none of them much higher up the food chain than the *Pinckney*'s crew. Some of them had some marginally shady business behind them, and at least one was traveling under a hilarious assumed name, but none of them had any obvious ties to Toropov. Not that it mattered, anyway; they had all been kept in stasis for months. The ship's visual records confirmed that every pod was loaded onto the ship sealed, and no pods had been opened until she cracked open Toropov's.

Webb shook her head with a grimace. McMillan's paranoia aside, there was no other answer to this riddle, which meant her conclusion was the only correct one. Process of elimination. Onboard cameras confirmed everyone else's alibis. Rudenko was sleeping, McMillan was working out, Keller was piloting, Park was eating in the lounge. That left Rubin, like it or not. She was stationed in the Hotel for routine maintenance at the time—that's opportunity, to go with her motive and means.

She grunted, straining at the pull bars as she felt her arms cry out. The sight of her triceps straining brought her mind back to McMillan, filling her with something between resentment and guilt. *Sorry about your shitty life, Sophie. Wish you hadn't fallen for a murderer like Rubin.*

Then there was a muffled explosive sound and the world shifted around her. Webb reached out a hand to catch herself from falling, but lost the horizon again as the ground tumbled back the other way.

Training kicking to life, Webb engaged her boots and fixed her vision on a point on the far wall. A red light was flashing along the edge of the screen. She pushed herself over to it.

"Sitrep!" Webb barked into the comm, zipping up her uniform.

She was answered by a dissonant jangle of metal strings as the cockpit speaker kicked to life. "Say again, Liz?"

"What happened, Mister Keller?"

Another voice cut in. "I'm showing a loss of pressure out our stern. Keller, what's going on?"

"Um . . . good question, boss. Hold on a sec."

Webb tapped open the cockpit camera and looked at the greasy yellow hair of Garrick Keller. The man's perpetual blinding-white smile was gone as he assessed every instrument panel he could get his hands on. Webb opened the ship's electronic activity log without waiting for Keller's answer. Her heart fell at the sight of the most recent incident listed.

Rubin's code. I thought Park deactivated that when she was detained. How the hell could she have . . . ?

She swallowed, the answer hitting her with a thump.

"Supervisor Park, something's off in the Hotel," Webb said in a clipped tone, tapping her way through the digital guts of the ship.

"Someone entered a command string I don't recognize associated with Pod A3."

"Uh, roger that, boss," said Keller. "Looks like somebody ordered up a pod ejection. That would explain the pressure loss as well as the proximity alert off our port side."

"What?" Park squeaked. "Sophie, you're stationed in the aft, aren't you? What can you see?"

"Seems contained enough, anyway, but that pod's moving at a pretty good clip." Keller peered at one of the displays, then whistled. "Not for long, though. Looks lined up to cross paths with something big and rocky a few thousand klicks to our left."

"How long before impact?" Webb asked. "And can you catch up with it before that?"

"Absolutely not, Lieutenant. You're not about to take—" said Park.

Webb didn't let him finish. "I'd think you would be more concerned about your passengers' remains, Supervisor Park. To say nothing of Ellipse corporate property. How long, Mister Keller?"

Another whistle. "Fifteen minutes, maybe? I dunno about catching it. I can get us close, but at that speed you'd need—"

"Get us close. That's an order."

Park's outraged reply mingled with the questions in her head, receding into background noise. Training gave purpose to Webb's movements and propelled her out of the gym. In thirty seconds she was at the airlock. In ninety seconds she was suited up, more or less.

No spacewalks without a partner, she remembered, engaging her helmet's seal and reaching to pull the Hybrid Maneuvering Unit from its cubby. The boat-shaped conveyance was little, but powerful enough to allow her to stop the pod in its tracks and bring it back home . . . at least, that was the idea.

No spacewalks without triple-checking oxygen levels, fuel levels, radio, surrounding environment, she heard her drill instructor say. Absolutely no spacewalks in a hurry.

"We're caught up, Lieutenant, but not for long," Keller's voice chirped in her ear.

"Roger that." Webb's hand clutched the handle of the HMU as she stepped into the airlock.

No spacewalks without a partner, without triple-checking, in a hurry.

The door hissed open, and all sound was swallowed into an endless field of stars.

Webb swung her head around, deafened by the noise of her own breathing. It didn't take her long to spot the silvery-white egg shape. The impossible parallax of it all made it feel like she was stuck in a dream. The pod, the same one she had opened, was right there, barely out of arm's reach. The rocky asteroid was close, small enough to pop into her mouth like a Milk Dud. She reached out her arm toward Toropov's distant pod and she could barely tell if she was moving.

"Don't go anywhere, Mister Keller," Webb said into her helmet speaker. "I'll be right back."

She didn't hear an answer. No spacewalks without triple-checking radio.

Webb attached her tether, frail as a piece of yarn, to the clip next to the exterior door of the airlock, then oriented the HMU's jet propulsion system toward the runaway pod. She gritted her teeth, prayed to a god she'd never believed in, and fired the engine. The force of the jolt nearly ripped the HMU out of her grasp, but she held on with every muscle in her body, and slowly, she saw that silver-white egg grow larger before her. She cranked the jets to the red line, her arms feeling like they were going to rip out of their sockets. Her tether spooled out behind her, or at least she hoped that was what she was feeling.

Come on. Come on, you son of a bitch.

Something red flashed in her peripheral vision, pulling her attention away from the pod. She blinked, hoping she was misreading the display beneath her chin, that her suit wasn't perilously low on oxygen, that there was some mistake. The shaky, unsatisfying breath she pulled in through her nose confirmed it, though—she didn't have more than a few minutes, by the smell of it.

Doesn't matter. One thing at a time, Guardian. Get the pod back first, then you can worry about breathing.

But by now the arc of physics was unquestionable, even to a tiny human speck in the void. The pod juked and twisted, its momentum distorting with the gravity of the rocky body in front of her. At this point even gunning the HMU past the breaking point wouldn't do anything more than drag her along into its cold, dead grave.

"Shit."

Toropov was gone. Consigned to his crypt among the stars, carrying with it any evidence that would identify the killer. And the last scrap of hope for a career for Elizabeth Webb.

Not now, she thought, blinking. First you worry about breathing. Then worry about living.

The HMU was a miracle of military engineering, but it cornered like a parade float. By the time Webb had reoriented it back along the taut white path of her tether to the ship, her O_2 levels were past orange and red and into exciting new colors entirely. She pictured the ghost of her breath leaving her lungs, and for a second she could plainly see the paper-white winter landscape of Aunt Barb's farm in Missouri, as real and cold and airless as when she visited it in her dreams.

Not going to make it.

"This is Webb," she spoke into her speaker, suddenly realizing she hadn't heard the slightest peep of ship's chatter since stepping outside. She swallowed sand. "Returning to *Pinckney* without the pod. Approaching port airlock."

The *Pinckney* was an even uglier ship from the outside than from within, all odd angles and nonsensical bulges. Webb let go of the HMU and let her momentum carry her the final fatal drop to the hull, then used the wee little thrusters on her suit to slow her descent.

"Open port airlock," she said, hearing the fear in her voice.

The airlock was still closed as Webb smacked into the side of the ship There was a panicked dance of limbs against the cold metal and colder void, but somehow she affixed herself to the hull next to the still-motionless door. Stars zipped across her vision, continuing even after she blinked frantically.

"This is Lieutenant Webb," she croaked. "Webb to Keller. Open the door, Mister Keller. Oxygen dangerously low."

Webb closed her eyes as her head sank forward, helmet clinking against the frictionless skin of the hull. She forced herself to take shallow, even breaths, trying not to gulp the precious little air she had in her tank.

"Webb to Keller," she squeaked through a quickly closing throat. "Webb to Park. Can you hear me? Please respond."

They can't hear me. They have to hear me. Oh God, they can't hear me. Is my suit's comm system broken? Did they lock me out on purpose?

Blackness closed around her. She forced breath into her lungs, opening her eyes wide. *In and out. Breathe. Come on, soldier. You're not allowed to lose it. Not now.*

Her head swam between the steady counts of inhale and exhale. She was a little boy again in her dream, just like when she'd really been there when she was nine years old.

In and out. Breathe.

The Missouri cold cut through her padded red jacket, but the LED-bright glow of the winter sun through the clouds had made her smile. She tramped down to the pond and found it was frozen over with a sheet of ice.

Breathe.

"Webb to all hands," she said into the comm, squeezing the manual broadcast button in her glove hard enough to leave a bruise. "Airlock is sealed. Won't open. Request im-immediate assistance. Priority... top priority."

Not really knowing why, in her dream and her memory she chucked a fist-sized rock into the pond and watched the explosion of ice crystals pirouette through the air. She tossed another, and another, savoring the violent movement of her muscles as much as the watery dance that followed every impact.

"Repeat."

She located an old chunk of concrete as big as her head and grunted as she lifted it up over her head. Another wave of ripples disturbed the pond's surface, something bubbling up before she could launch the missile.

In. Out. In.

Something was making the bubbles under the water. She knew what it was, what was about to happen, but she couldn't move her cold, wet feet from that spot by the pond.

"Open... please. Open the door."

Only static in her earpiece. Her thumb slipped off the broadcast switch and refused to move back on, muscles frozen and sleepy.

A shiny dark shape the size of a car jumped from the water right at her, sharp jaws snapping, ice spraying from the pond and pelting her face. She fell backward onto the snow and screamed.

A metallic thump, dim, hollow. Another.

The enormous alligator snapping turtle lunged toward her, beak clacking as it sought bloody vengeance on what had interrupted its frigid hibernation. She would later learn that the turtles of Missouri didn't truly hibernate, but rested motionless beneath the frozen pond, awake and as conscious as turtles could be. She never knew that in her dream.

Bubbles.

Light poured through her eyelids. Webb raised a hand to shield her eyes from the glare, and fingers wrapped around hers. She fell down—or forward, she thought, her stomach flopping unhelpfully. There was another metal crunch, a sucking sound, and then it was quiet and cold as death.

She opened her eyes to teeth as big and white as God's.

"Ope. Sorry to leave you hangin' there, Liz." Keller released her from his grasp with a sudden blush. "We couldn't hear you out there, dunno if it was the comm system or—"

He stopped talking as Webb gasped in a breath and switched on her boots, standing straight against the beautifully solid metal floor.

"I know how they did it. How they killed Toropov," she announced.

The Hotel was crowded with every member of the *Pinckney*'s crew present. The looks everyone was shooting in Rubin's direction filled the long room, and Park's tirade rattled against every polished surface.

"—*knew* she was too lenient, just leaving you in your berth! She should've tied you up and left you in the cargo bay," Park spat, finger shaking in Rubin's direction. "I don't know how you did it after I disabled your access codes, but now on top of murder you're going to be tried for covering up your crime, disposing of Ellipse property, de-defiling human remains—"

"I told you I didn't *do* it, Park." There was a bitter, ashy anger smoldering in Rubin's eyes now, and she looked directly at the supervisor as she answered him even if her posture was still one of defeat.

"Yeah, Jesus," growled McMillan, though her eyes were bleary with tears.

Webb frowned as she clomped into the Hotel, all eyes flying to her as she entered. *I told Park I wanted him and Rubin here in ninety minutes, he brings the whole damn ship when he feels like it.*

"Lieutenant Webb," Park called over to her. "If you clearly can't do the job of keeping an eye on the prisoner, you at least owe us an explanation."

There was something fierce in Rubin's eyes, but she kept as silent as Rudenko. McMillan wouldn't even look at her.

Keller smiled that Keller smile. "Good to see you're still on your feet, Liz. Still think you should take a breather."

Webb noticed all of their reactions but didn't speak, moving right past the cluster of humanity at the front of the room to the center of the second row of pods. She stopped at her goal, her finger brushing against the odd corner of plastic she'd found an hour before on the port underneath the pod. It was still there. She nodded with satisfaction.

"What the hell is this about?" snapped Park as he strode over to her, trailed by everyone but McMillan. "If you don't mean to take action against Rubin for ejecting Toropov's pod, then I will, regulations be damned!"

"Stand down, Supervisor Park," Webb said calmly. "Rubin didn't touch that pod."

Park snorted with derision. "And just how do you know that?"

Webb pointedly avoided looking at McMillan, felt her do the same from across the room. "We can come back to that. What's more important is that we arrest Toropov's killer."

Straight-faced, Rudenko gestured in Rubin's direction. Webb shook her head as she leaned on the pod, fingers tapping on the polished plastic.

"It wasn't Rubin. I know that for sure now."

A wordless expression of relief burst out of Rubin. McMillan took a step toward the others but stayed where she was, tears now running freely from her eyes as Keller reached out and punched Rubin's shoulder amiably.

"If Rubin didn't kill Toropov, who did?" asked Park.

Webb smiled as she stopped drumming her fingers against the

glossy surface of Pod B8. Seeing the confusion on the crew's faces, she entered her code and brought up the display of the occupant's biographical data.

"Passenger B8. Johan Galt," Park read aloud. "I don't get it."

"Oh, ugh," McMillan grunted, stepping over to the side of the pod.

"What does this guest have to do with Toropov?" asked Park.

Another few taps on the screen and the pod's cover shimmered away, its surface made transparent. Lying in the pod was a man who appeared far less peaceful than Passenger A3, and far less comfortable. A doughy man, his eyes roved madly as if stuck in a bad dream, his face red and twitchy.

"Oh my god!" Rubin exclaimed. "Jayden?"

Webb nodded. "Jayden Engelbrecht. Your ex-husband."

"But what the hell is he doing here? How did . . . I didn't know. I didn't . . . oh god." McMillan's arms were around Rubin now, and she leaned into the taller woman's frame helplessly, tears streaming from her fearful eyes.

"We won't know for sure until we reach Ulysses in a week and we place him under arrest," said Webb, "but my theory is that he planned to frame you for Toropov's murder, then catch the next ship out of Ulysses to one of the colonies on Titan."

"And what's your evidence?" Park snorted. "So he was traveling under an assumed name. Not a lot to hang an arrest on, Lieutenant."

"He has been in stasis," Rudenko spoke up softly. "How could he kill Toropov?"

"Hey, yeah," said Keller.

Reaching down, Webb tapped her finger against the stray bit of plastic sticking out of one of the pod's dozens of ports. Park leaned down to peer at it. "I wouldn't pull it now if I were you—no way to know if that'll spike his vitals or wake him up right away. But if Mister Rudenko will confirm my assessment of these readings, our passenger here hasn't been as sound a sleeper as his peers."

The Ukrainian pushed Park to one side and examined the details on the screen. His scowl deepened ever so slightly, and then he knelt down to examine the plug.

"Nothing dangerous, wouldn't have tripped the alarm," Rudenko said at last. "But yes, brain activity suggests he may be conscious."

"This sick SOB spent eight months in a coffin just to frame his ex for murder?" Keller asked, scratching his head.

McMillan piped up, "And what, he injected an air bubble from inside his pod? Is that even possible?"

"Can't know without examining his program," Rudenko uttered. "But if this plug was connected to the SEV, very possible. Easy."

"This is all pretty farfetched, Webb. What kind of man does something like this?" asked Park.

"I believe it," Rubin said in a stiff, faraway voice. "Jayden would go to any length to hurt me. He was so convinced he was so much smarter than everybody else—not only smarter, more deserving of rights, more human. I'm sure he expected he'd get away with this."

The air in the Hotel felt lighter only by an ounce, but that was enough to dissipate the fog that had settled over the ship for the previous weeks. Webb let Park give the order to leave Engelbrecht to stew in his pod until they arrived at Ulysses Station next week— they'd have station security in the room when they delivered his wake-up call. Keller and Rudenko returned to their shifts while Park muttered a nonapology to Webb in between threats to report her to the DOD. McMillan and Rubin went on hugging for a few moments longer.

"Thank you, Liz," Rubin said in an exhausted voice. She blinked up her brilliant green eyes, looking as though she wanted to say something else, then walked out of the Hotel wordlessly.

Webb reached out and grabbed McMillan's arm before she could follow. McMillan looked up in surprise, fear, rage.

"You didn't know I'd go after the pod," Webb said under her breath. "You just wanted to make sure there wouldn't be enough evidence to convict Rubin . . . Alicia. You didn't lock me out there, didn't know the suits weren't being maintained properly."

She stared at McMillan, swallowed. *Right?*

McMillan looked into Webb's eyes—what she saw there Webb couldn't begin to guess. Then she pulled away her arm and stomped out of the room, the metal of her boots ticking quietly away into nothing.

This won't look good for her in my report to Forman. Webb breathed out a sigh and retreated to her office to start writing. *If I decide to tell.*

✵ ✵ ✵

Sylvie Althoff is a writer, editor, and elementary teacher. She has ghostwritten eight period romance novels and helped bring to life dozens of novels, short stories, memoirs, and children's books. This is her first publication under her own name. She lives in Kansas with her wife, Jenn.

Not a War

Harry Turtledove

It was not a war. It was nothing like a war.

They were serious about that. Justin knew of a Space Force major who'd called it a war in an encrypted dispatch, the kind where brevity was at a premium and "war" took up far fewer characters than something like "international dispute potentially involving violence." Didn't help. That luckless, forthright major was now a first lieutenant, and she'd never see field grade again, not if she lived to Moses' one hundred and twenty.

Because nobody in the inner solar system wanted to hear about war. Hearing about the dreadful thing might mean thinking about it, and nobody in the inner solar system wanted to do that, either. There'd been a medium-sized war in the 2050s, and a bigger one in the 2080s that might have been a slate wiper if an American breakthrough in jamming technology hadn't kept a particular Central American rabbit from popping out of its hat.

Even now, forty years later, people on Earth and the Moon bases in craters near both poles and the Mars bases at the edges of the polar caps shuddered to remember what a near miss that had been. And so, just as their Victorian ancestors hadn't cared to mention or even think about the ghastly word *sex*, they didn't want to talk about *war*.

Of course, not talking about sex hadn't kept the Victorians from screwing like bunnies. And, out here in the asteroid belt, where so much industry had sprung up since the turn of the twenty-second century, modern, sophisticated humans and AIs sparred with one another and sometimes killed one another. But Yahweh, Jesus, Allah, and Brahma forbid that they call it war.

Captain Justin Bregman guided the *G. Harry Stine* toward an asteroid that rejoiced in the name 130 Elektra. What that boiled down to was keeping an eye on the computer system doing the actual work. Nothing was likely to go wrong, which didn't mean nothing could or would.

He asked his signals officer, "Any new transmissions from the installation there?"

"No, sir," answered First Lieutenant Maria Canha. The installation was LATAMSEC. Like most Space Force officers, Justin had some Portuguese. Maria's parents had fled to the States following the Barbosa e Souza countercoup in 2089. She'd grown up with the language.

A light on the screen blinked red for a moment: a radar pulse from the factory—LATAMSEC insisted it was just a factory—had touched the *Hank Stine*. They wouldn't get any joy from that. Whatever radar waves the ship's skin didn't absorb, it deflected away from the transmitter. A bullet would have had a bigger radar signature.

Bullets . . . Just thinking of them made Bregman mutter to himself, as it would have with any spacer, regardless of homeland. The *Hank Stine* carried two old-school Ma Deuces and some lighter firearms. They, and other nations' equivalents, did get used in the various international disputes potentially involving violence that were nothing—nothing!—like wars.

On Earth, a thick atmosphere and a deep gravity well limited what bullets could do. Mars and the Moon were less massive; Mars had only a thin atmosphere and the Moon none. Even so, bullets fired from their surfaces did eventually return to them. In space? In space, it was a different story.

Bullets that hit what they were aimed at were bad enough. They commonly punched right on through. With weight always at a premium, no one yet had built a spacecraft armored against .50-caliber slugs. Encounters between ships sometimes seemed too much like flamethrower duels at five paces.

Captain Bregman muttered some more. If someone was shooting

at you on purpose, you could at least try to do something about it—get the bastard first, for instance. But bullets that missed were gifts that kept on giving. Between planets and here in the asteroid belt, it was all hard vacuum, with no objects massive enough to pull in expended rounds. They just kept going at high velocities and in unexpected directions. You weren't likely to run into one, but you could.

Back on Earth, land mines and ordnance from wars that went back to the early days of the twentieth century still killed people every year. As best anyone could tell, the bullet that turned the Chinese supply ship *Tianfei* into a fireball near Vesta in 2117 had come from a skirmish between Indian and LATAMSEC scoutships more than thirty years earlier. Bad luck? Nothing else but.

Anything that can happen can happen to you, Bregman reminded himself. Reminding did not mean reassuring. There ahead lay Progreso, Elektra's middle satellite: a chunk of ice, organics, and a little rock a couple of kilometers thick. The outermost moonlet was Ordem; the inner one, Lasca. So LATAMSEC states called them, anyhow. The International Astronomical Union didn't recognize the names. The first two came from a national motto, while the last one meant "splinter" or "Chip." As far as anyone knew, Elektra was the only asteroid in the belt with three satellites of its own.

With Progreso between the *Hank Stine* and whatever LATAMSEC was up to on Elektra, Captain Bregman breathed a little easier. "Now we wait for Chip to move into position," he said.

"Scooter is juiced up and ready," Ali Riahi told him.

He nodded. "Good." He would have been astonished and furious had the engineer said anything else. Your equipment was supposed to be ready before you needed it, and to work first time every time. It wasn't always, of course, and didn't always, but the Space Force came as close as humanly possible to living up to the ideal.

At its closest approach, Chip came within about 170 klicks of Progreso. You didn't launch the scooter then, of course. You launched it well before, so it could reach that point at the same time as the asteroid's inner moonlet.

Bregman took his place in the scooter half an hour before he was scheduled to leave. He ran through all the checks one more time. The vehicle was a souped-up version of the ones Heinlein had talked about almost two hundred years earlier. It was made of light tubing coated with radar-absorbing material. It had thrusters fore and aft, up and down, right and left. You could pilot it by eyeball and joystick if you had to, but it boasted electronics Heinlein'd never dreamt of.

It also had teeth, sharp ones. The *G. Harry Stine* wasn't here on a reconnaissance mission. The ship had come to make a point. It wasn't a war. It was nothing like a war. Things could get smashed anyhow. People could get killed. Out here in the asteroid belt, it happened more often than the comfortable folk in the inner solar system ever heard about.

A puff of gas pushed the scooter out of the ship. Captain Bregman waited till he was a hundred meters clear to start his first burn. Before long, he came out from behind Progreso and could see Elektra. Of course, that also meant Elektra could see him, but odds were nobody on the asteroid would.

Elektra wasn't big enough for gravity to have shaped it into a sphere. It looked like a giant potato made of ice and a little rock, with gouges and craters here and there simulating places where you'd use the pointy end of a potato peeler to poke out eyes before you baked the spud.

Potatoes, though, didn't have large solar arrays powering... whatever they were powering on Elektra's surface. Out here, more than three AUs from the Sun, you needed a large array to draw useful amounts of energy from its light.

Elektra already had a high albedo. Icy objects commonly did. That meant no one had paid much attention to occasional flashes from the panels for a long time. Justin hadn't the slightest idea how long the installation had been here. If any people in the States did, they were far above his need-to-know level.

He acquired Chip by eye. It looked like a free-orbiting chunk of Elektra a bit more than a klick and a half thick. Progreso and Ordem looked like bigger pieces of the asteroid. They all probably were. People thought Elektra's satellites had been knocked off the main body in one or more cosmic collisions, but not hard enough to escape even its tiny gravitational field.

In due course, he—well, the scooter's computer—matched velocity and vector with Chip. He kept the tiny moonlet between him and Elektra for a while, the way the *Hank Stine* was using Progreso.

But he couldn't stay hidden. He had to see what he was going to do. Piloting by hand, he edged out so he could survey the asteroid's surface.

Elektra's mean diameter was as close to two hundred kilometers as made no difference. On a planetary scale, it was tiny. But it still had a hell of a lot of surface to survey. Luckily LATAMSEC wasn't trying to hide. There was the solar array, and there next to it sat the automated chemical works it powered.

Bregman photographed that at high magnification and gave the scooter computer the image for analysis. It took only a fraction of a second. *Closest match is opioid-synthesis plant suppressed in lunar crater Wargentin in 2121*, the machine told him. Three more near matches came up. All of them were drug cookers.

He sighed hard enough to fog the inside of his suit window for a moment. That was what the USSF honchos who sent the *G. Harry Stine* out for a close look at Elektra had suspected. There'd been too many ODs lately, both among civilians working in the asteroid belt and in the Space Force itself. The shit wasn't coming out from the inner solar system; people seemed sure of that. Somebody was making it locally.

"And now we know who," Bregman muttered to himself. Of course LATAMSEC governments, or people in them, had a hand in this installation, and a hand in the pockets of the sons of bitches doing the dealing. And, of course, those governments would loudly and fervently deny everything, and would sound plausible when they did.

Which meant that what happened next would happen unofficially. The world would little note nor long remember... But, with a little luck, some LATAMSEC bigwigs would be annoyed— again, of course, unofficially.

He waited till Chip came as close to the installation as it was going to, then electronically locked the minigun above the nose thruster on the synthesis facility. When a red light told him the lock was successful, his finger stabbed the firing button.

He gave it about a fifteen-second burst, sending something over a thousand rounds of 7.62mm ammo toward the plant. And that, of course, blew his anonymity to hell and gone. Whoever was down there couldn't very well miss the minigun's muzzle flash. Even with powder specifically made for use in space, the weapon wasn't subtle. And radar would be picking up the incoming rounds.

Whether anybody could do anything about that was an altogether different question. Flight time would be a skosh over three and a half minutes. LATAMSEC didn't have long to react. All the same, Bregman pulled back behind the comforting mass of Chip.

That done, he sent a brief tight-beam message to the *G. Harry Stine:* "Evaluation confirmed. Target confirmed. Target attacked. Awaiting results."

He had to hope the *Hank Stine* was far enough away from Progreso so the middle satellite's bulk wouldn't block his signal. The ship must have been, for the answer came back at one. "Roger," Lieutenant Canha said, and then, "Be careful when you check what you did, sir."

"Affirmative," he answered, in lieu of something more heartfelt like, *Bet your sweet ass!* All transmissions got multiply recorded. They got multiply examined too. You could hope the deskbound types back on Earth would recognize the exigencies of action. You could hope, but you couldn't take it to the bank.

He maneuvered through five minutes by the clock, so when the scooter came out from behind Chip again, it didn't emerge in the place where it had disappeared. The position difference wouldn't be large, but he hoped it would be large enough.

"Well!" he said as his eyeballs and enhanced video picked up the scene down on the surface of Elektra. Not to put too fine a point on it, hell had broken loose down there. A lot of the chemicals these installations used to turn basic organic sludge into drugs were, um, volatile. A lot of the reactions when those chemicals combined in unexpected ways because minigun bullets had slammed into the apparatus were, um, exothermic. Highly exothermic. Flames and clouds of he didn't want to know what had swollen very quickly in Elektra's low gravity.

Then he saw another flame on the surface. That was a minigun shooting back at him. The neighborhood was going bad in a hurry. Lighting off the thruster in the scooter's nose, he pulled back behind Chip again.

Staying around seemed a lousy idea. He told the computer to work out a course back to Progreso. The first one it gave him, which was also the fastest, he rejected out of hand. It used almost all his fuel. He wanted one with a decent safety margin; he had the feeling he might need the extra for unplanned maneuvers.

No sooner had that cheery thought crossed his mind than he got another signal from Lieutenant Canha: "They've launched something toward Chip from Elektra. A bigger heat signature than the scooter, so it probably has more legs."

"Roger that," Bregman answered. Happy days, he thought. He couldn't run away, she was telling him. If he couldn't run, he'd have to fight. He didn't much want to. The LATAMSEC spacecraft likely had more weapons than he did as well as more acceleration. But what you wanted to do wasn't always what you could do. He asked, "Can you tell me where they'll come around Chip? I'd better take the best position I can."

"Wait one," the signals officer said, and then, "Not yet. Chip is so little, we can't be sure. And they can maneuver to change that point up till close to the last minute. Will inform when we have a clearer picture."

"Roger," Captain Bregman repeated. So he'd sit here twiddling his thumbs till just before he urgently needed to move—or till the spacecraft from Elektra opened up on him from some unexpected direction.

Time crawled by. Then Lieutenant Canha came back: "Looks like they're heading over Chip's north pole. ETA is about four minutes."

"North pole. Four minutes. Wish me luck." He used his thrusters to turn the scooter so its nose pointed in that direction. As soon as anything appeared or occulted some of the countless stars strewn across the black-velvet backdrop of deep space, he'd do what he could. Of course, so would whoever was inside the other spacecraft.

He wished it hadn't come to this. As far as he knew, he hadn't hurt anybody down on the asteroid. He'd just messed up the installation. LATAMSEC could have written it off as a business expense. But no. They took it personally. And they wanted payback.

Some stars winked out. A tiny maneuver to line up the minigun, part his, partly the fire-control system's . . . The souped-up Gatling spat flame.

So did the other spacecraft's weapon. But he'd found it first, which was always the most important thing in a duel like this. Their burst went wide. His struck home. Something—probably their fuel tank—blew up in a pyrotechnic blaze of glory.

Back aboard the *G. Harry Stine*, the crew would be wondering whether that had been his fuel tank. "Target is neutralized," he reported. Military lingo was bloodless, no doubt on purpose. It was just a target, not a spacecraft with at least one person aboard. He'd neutralized it; he hadn't killed anybody. If you said it like that often enough, you started believing it. Or you might. He hadn't yet.

"Good to hear you, sir!" Lieutenant Canha said, more warmth in her voice than he usually noticed. "When can you start your burn to come back here?"

He already had a countdown clock running in one corner of his display. "Just over an hour and a half," he answered. "Are you still monitoring the surface of Elektra?"

"Not personally, but through sensors." Now the lieutenant reverted to sounding as precise as she could.

"That's pretty much what I meant. Keep me appraised if they open up on me again from down there. Chances are I'll need evasive action."

"Roger, wilco," she said, which was what he wanted to hear.

They didn't launch anything from Elektra while he waited for the asteroid's moonlets to reach the proper positions. He wondered if they'd had only the one vehicle for moving around. He also wondered what kind of tight-beam conversations they were having with their friends, and how far away those friends might be. Were the *Hank Stine*'s sensors picking up those signals? He could hope so, anyway.

His gloved forefinger came down on the ignition button a split second after the scooter's electronics did the job for him. The odds against his needing to fire up the motors himself were astronomical, but people who worked in space didn't take chances, not if they wanted to keep working there very long.

The scooter came out from behind Chip's protective bulk, tiny though that was. It was even smaller itself, but down on the surface of Elektra they'd been looking for a heat signature. They'd find one too. He wished the scooter were powered by beer, like the spacecraft in the classic "The Makeshift Rocket."

As usual, what you wished for and what you had were two different critters. He hadn't gone very far from Chip toward Progreso before Lieutenant Canha spoke urgently in his earbuds: "Muzzle flashes down below. They're shooting at where you'll be between two and a half and three minutes from now."

"Between two and a half and three minutes," he repeated. "Roger. I'll do my best to evade. How tight is the spread?"

"Pretty loose," she said. "They hosed it up and down when they fired. They want something to hit you."

"I wish I could tell them how much I appreciate their generosity," Bregman said. "Okay. Let's see what I can manage."

He burned his nose rocket for a few seconds, cutting his velocity. If the bullets from the surface passed in front of him because he'd slowed down, he was golden. As long as he had enough fuel to correct his trajectory again, anyhow. For now, the gauges and the computer said he did.

As he decelerated, he asked, "Is the densest part of the spread lined up with my course before I changed it?"

"Hold on," Maria Canha said, and then, presumably after checking the displays she had in front of her, "That's affirmative. Repeat—affirmative."

"Understand. Okay, I'll slide up a bit too, do what I can to give myself less metal-jacketed company."

Before he used the thruster under his backside, he made sure he'd have enough fuel once he'd got past the storm of man-made meteors ahead. Having confirmed that, he made the burn. He made it a bit smaller than he really wanted to, to conserve propellant in case the lovely people down on Elektra sent another present his way.

A few seconds later, Lieutenant Canha told him, "You're entering the area most of the burst should already have passed through."

"Most?" Bregman said plaintively. That burn should have been longer, dammit. He'd hoped everything would have been past his track before he got to the danger zone.

Before the signals officer could reply, something smacked the scooter. It wasn't a bird strike, worse luck. No birds for three hundred million klicks, give or take a few. He hadn't gone out in a fireball, the way the drug cookers' spacecraft had. He frantically scanned his instruments. He wasn't losing fuel or oxygen. He seemed to have control over all the thrusters. But he knew only too well he'd got clipped.

And then he saw the damage. One round out of however many they'd fired from Elektra had grazed the tubing that led out to and supported the nose thruster. It had cut through the antiradar coating and taken a bite—only a small one, thank God—out of the carbon-fiber-impregnated plastic under it.

He reported the damage to the *G. Harry Stine*, finishing, "Everything up there still seems functional. I got lucky. I'll take it real easy unless I've got no choice."

"Roger," Lieutenant Canha answered, adding, "Glad you're okay."

"Now that you mention it, so am I," he said. Somebody a couple of hundred years before—was it Churchill or Stalin?—had remarked, *Nothing in life is so exhilarating as to be shot at without result.* As far as Bregman was concerned, that was BS of the purest ray serene. He'd almost forced his spacesuit to take care of something which, even after a century and a half of alleged improvements, it wasn't particularly well designed to do.

On he went, towards a rendezvous with the *Hank Stine* behind Progreso. When the LATAMSEC contingent on Elektra didn't see the scooter explode and did detect his small course-correction burns, they sent another storm of lead up at him. He was farther from the asteroid now; the bullets took longer to climb up to him. At Maria Canha's advice, he sped up instead of slowing down, so he could get through the region where the barrage would pass before it did.

The advice must have been good—nothing clipped him this time. Then he had to decelerate again. Instead of using the nose motor and testing the damaged tubing, he spun the scooter through a hundred eighty degrees and applied the correction with the tail thruster.

Progreso swelled ahead of him, as much as a lump of dirty, rocky ice a couple of klicks across could swell. And there was the *G. Harry Stine*. He spotted it the same way he'd seen the spacecraft coming over Chip's north pole: by the stars it occulted for him. He made a couple of more tiny course corrections, by eye rather than computer.

A protective hatch on the ship opened. Lights around the airlock shone invitingly. He eased the scooter in with as much care as a cat walking on eggs. The outer door closed behind him. The inner door opened. "You have air pressure," Lieutenant Canha told him. "You can open your helmet."

"I'll do that," he said. He'd been breathing his own stinks all the way to Chip and back. Now he was breathing everybody else's again—the air scrubbers were good, but they weren't perfect. Your nose tuned out the smells when you were in the ship all the time. When they seemed fresh again, so to speak, you noticed them . . . till you didn't any more.

Everyone wanted to shake his hand and pound him on the back and tell him what a great job he'd done. "You whaled the living snot out of that drug-cooker. They won't be able to fix it up any time soon," Ali Riahi said. "We've got the video, if you want to take a look at it."

"I'll need to," Bregman answered mildly. "I have to write the after-action report." If he sounded surprised, it was only because he was. He'd been so intent on doing what he needed to do, he hadn't worried about anything else. He pointed to the damaged tubing aft of the nose thruster. "Can you fix that?"

"I think so, sir," the engineer said. "I'll cut out the damaged section, then splice in some from the spares stock. The bonding adhesive is almost stronger than the tubing. I've got the coating too."

"Good. Too close for comfort, if you know what I mean." No, Justin Bregman didn't care to think about how close he'd come to dying. Who ever did?

It was not a war. It was nothing like a war. But sometimes, when it almost bit you, you had trouble remembering that.

✵　✵　✵

Harry Turtledove is a prolific writer of alternate history and science fiction, including *The Man with the Iron Heart, The Guns of the South,* and *How Few Remain* (Sidewise Award for Best Novel), and enough others to fill this page to combustion pressure. He was born in 1949 and raised in Los Angeles, which may explain why many of his stories involve the destruction of that city. His early interests included Byzantine history and dinosaurs, and he's managed to work both into his writing, often at the same time.

He gained widespread recognition in the 1990s with his Worldwar series, in which aliens invade Earth during World War II, throwing the conflict into chaos. Turtledove's attention to historical detail and penchant for puns earned him a reputation as the "master of alternate history."

About "Aficionado"

This story first appeared in 2012 as a chapter in David Brin's novel Existence. *Set in the mid-twenty-first century, the novel deals with the impact of technological advances and contact with extraterrestrial intelligence, as well as issues related to privacy, surveillance, and the role of the individual in a connected society. It also explores the possibilities and challenges of harnessing resources in space, and of particular note, the potential consequences of unregulated space development and the importance of responsible governance in shaping the future of space exploration and utilization.*

✵   ✵   ✵

Aficionado

✧

David Brin

Meanwhile, far below, cameras stared across forbidden desert, monitoring disputed territory in a conflict so bitter, antagonists couldn't agree what to call it.

One side named the struggle righteous war, with countless innocent lives in peril.

Their opponents claimed there were no victims, at all.

And so, suspicious cameras panned, alert for encroachment. Camouflaged atop hills or under highway culverts or innocuous stones, they probed for a hated adversary And for some months the guardians succeeded, staving off incursions. Protecting sandy desolation.

Then, technology shifted advantages again.

The enemy's first move? Take out those guarding eyes.

Infiltrators came at dawn, out of the rising sun—several hundred little machines, skimming low on whispering gusts. Each one, resembling a native hummingbird, followed a carefully scouted path toward its target, landing behind some camera or sensor, in its blind spot. It then unfolded wings that transformed into holo-displays, depicting perfect false images of the same desert scene to the guardian lens, without even a suspicious flicker. Other spy machines sniffed out camouflaged seismic sensors and embraced them gently—cushioning to mask approaching tremors.

The robotic attack covered a hundred square kilometers. In eight minutes, the desert lay unwatched, undefended.

Now, from over the horizon, large vehicles converged along multiple roadways toward the same open area—seventeen hybrid-electric rigs, disguised as commercial cargo transports, complete with company hologos. But when their paths intersected, crews in dun-colored jumpsuits leaped to unlash cargoes. Generators roared and the air swirled with exotic stench as pungent volatiles gushed from storage tanks to fill pressurized vessels. Consoles sprang to life. Hinged panels fell away, revealing long, tapered cylinders on slanted ramps.

Ponderously, each cigar shape raised its nose skyward while fins popped open at the tail. Shouts grew tense as tightly coordinated countdowns commenced. Soon the enemy—sophisticated and wary—would pick up enough clues. They would realize . . . and act.

When every missile was aimed, targets acquired, all they lacked were payloads.

A dozen figures emerged from an air-conditioned van, wearing snug suits of shimmering material and garishly painted helmets. Each carried a satchel that hummed and whirred to keep them cool. Several moved with a gait that seemed rubbery with anxious excitement. One skipped a little caper, about every fourth step.

A dour-looking woman awaited them with badge and uniform. Holding up a databoard, she confronted the first vacuum-suited figure.

"Name and scan," she demanded. "Then affirm your intent."

The helmet visor, decorated with gilt swirls, swiveled back, revealing heavily tanned features, about thirty years old, with eyes the color of a cold sea—till the official's instrument cast a questioning ray. Then, briefly, one pupil flared retinal red.

"Hacker Sander," the tall man said, in a voice both taut and restrained. "I affirm that I'm doing this of my own free will, according to documents on record."

His clarity of purpose must have satisfied the AI-clipboard, which uttered an approving beep. The inspector nodded. "Thank you, Mr. Sander. Have a safe trip. Next?"

She indicated another would-be rocketeer, who carried his helmet in the crook of one arm, bearing a motif of flames surrounding a screaming mouth.

"What rubbish," the blond youth snarled, elbowing Hacker as he tried to loom over the bureaucrat. "Do you have any idea who we are? Who I am?"

"Yes, Lord Smits. Though whether I care or not doesn't matter." She held up the scanner. "This matters. It can prevent you from being lasered into tiny fragments by the USSF, while you're passing through controlled airspace."

"Is that a threat? Why you little .. government . . . pissant. You had better not be trying to—"

"Government and guild," Hacker Sander interrupted, suppressing his own hot anger over that elbow in the ribs. "Come on, Smitty. We're on a tight schedule."

The baron whirled on him, tension cracking the normally smooth aristocratic accent. "I warned you about nicknames, Sander, you third-generation poser. I had to put up with your seniority during pilot training. But just wait until we get back. I'll take you apart!"

"Why wait?" Hacker kept eye contact while reaching up to unlatch his air hose. A quick punch ought to lay this blue-blood out, letting the rest of them get on with it. There were good reasons to hurry. Other forces, more formidable than mere government, were converging right now, eager to prevent what was planned here.

Besides, nobody called a Sander a "poser."

The other rocket jockeys intervened before he could use his fist— probably a good thing, at that—grabbing the two men and separating them. Pushed to the end of the queue, Smits stewed and cast deadly looks toward Hacker. But when his turn came again, the nobleman went through ID check with composure, as cold and brittle as some glacier.

"Your permits are in order," the functionary concluded, unhurriedly addressing Hacker, because he was most experienced. "Your liability bonds and Rocket Racing League waivers have been accepted. The government won't stand in your way."

Hacker shrugged, as if the statement was both expected and irrelevant. He flung his visor back down and gave a sign to the other suited figures, who rushed to the ladders that launch personnel braced against each rocket, clambering awkwardly, then squirming into cramped couches and strapping in. Even the novices had practiced countless times.

Hatches slammed, hissing as they sealed. Muffled shouts told of final preparations. Then came a distant chant, familiar, yet always thrilling, counting backward at a steady cadence. A rhythm more than a century old.

Is it really that long, since Robert Goddard came to this same desert? Hacker pondered. To experiment with the first controllable rockets? Would he be surprised at what we've done with the thing he started? Turning them into weapons of war . . . then giant exploration vessels . . . and finally playthings of the superrich?

Oh, there were alternatives, like commercial space tourism. One Japanese orbital hotel and another under construction. Hacker owned stock. There were even multipassenger suborbital jaunts, available to the merely well-off. For the price of maybe twenty college educations.

Hacker felt no shame or regret. If it weren't for us, there'd be almost nothing left of the dream.

Countdown approached zero for the first missile.

His.

"Yeeeee-haw!" Hacker Sander shouted . . .

. . . before a violent kick flattened him against the airbed. A mammoth hand seemed to plant itself on his chest and shoved, expelling half the contents of his lungs in a moan of sweet agony. Like every other time, the sudden shock brought physical surprise and visceral dread—followed by a sheer ecstatic rush, like nothing else on Earth.

Hell . . . he wasn't even part of the Earth! For a little while, at least.

Seconds passed amid brutal shaking as the rocket clawed its way skyward. Friction heat and ionization licked the transparent nose cone only centimeters from his face. Shooting toward heaven at Mach ten, he felt pinned, helplessly immobile . . .

. . . and completely omnipotent.

I'm a freaking god!

At Mach fifteen somehow he drew enough breath for another cry—this time a shout of elated greeting as black space spread before the missile's bubble nose, flecked by a million glittering stars.

Back on the ground, cleanup efforts were even more frenetic than setup. With all rockets away, men and women sprinted across the scorched desert, packing to depart before the enemy arrived. Warning posts had already spotted flying machines, racing this way at high speed.

But the government official moved languidly, tallying damage to vegetation, erodible soils, and tiny animals—all of it localized, without appreciable effect on endangered species. A commercial reconditioning service had already been summoned. Atmospheric pollution was easier to calculate, of course. Harder to ameliorate.

She knew these people had plenty to spend. And nowadays, soaking up excess accumulated wealth was as important as any other process of recycling. Her AI-board printed a bill, which she handed over as the last team member revved his engine, impatient to be off.

"Aw, man!" he complained, reading the total. "Our club will barely break even on this launch!"

"Then pick a less expensive hobby," she replied, and stepped back as the driver gunned his truck, roaring away in clouds of dust, incidentally crushing one more barrel cactus en route to the highway. Her vigilant clipboard noted this, adjusting the final tally.

Sitting on the hood of her jeep, she waited for another "club" whose members were as passionate as the rocketeers. Equally skilled and dedicated, though both groups despised each other. Sensors showed them coming fast, from the west—radical environmentalists. The official knew what to expect when they arrived. Frustrated to find their opponents gone and two acres of desert singed, they'd give her a tongue-lashing for being "evenhanded" in a situation where— obviously—you could only choose sides.

Well, she thought. It takes a thick skin to work in government nowadays. No one thinks you matter much.

Overhead, the contrails were starting to shear, ripped by stratospheric winds, a sight that always tugged the heart. And while her intellectual sympathies lay closer to the eco-activists, not the spoiled rocket jockeys...

...a part of her still thrilled, whenever she witnessed a launch. So ecstatic—almost orgiastic.

"Go!" she whispered with a touch of secret envy toward those distant glitters, already arcing toward the pinnacle of their brief climb, before starting their long plummet to the Gulf of Mexico.

✡ ✡ ✡

David Brin is a scientist, speaker, technical consultant and world-known author. His novels have been *New York Times* bestsellers, winning multiple Hugo, Nebula and other awards. At least a dozen have been translated into more than twenty languages. His 1989 ecological thriller, *Earth*, foreshadowed global warming, cyberwarfare and near-future trends such as the World Wide Web. His 2012 novel *Existence* explored bioengineering, intelligence and open-creative civilization.

As a "scientist/futurist," David appears frequently on TV, and serves on advisory committees dealing with subjects as diverse as national defense, SETI, nanotechnology, and philanthropy. He's served on NASA's Innovative and Advanced Concepts group (NIAC), and helped establish the Arthur C. Clarke Center for Human Imagination at UCSD.

Defense of Waygo Port

✨

M.T. Reiten

Trix waited impatiently in the tunnel outside the secure conference room. The war had started and they were busy talking, not defending the home that they had carved from below the lunar surface.

The soundproof hatch finally opened with a dusty creak. Officers spilled out clutching clipboards with scribbled timetables and hand-drawn defensive positions. Nothing could be trusted to the network or computers. Every one of them moved with desperate purpose. Some had already donned their in-station pressure suits. They dispersed to protect the Oasis, the man-made skylight lava tube that let sunlight in and let life grow. They had broken the corporate hold on prime lunar real estate, so their community could be more than a high-tech favela living off discards and trash heaps in the dark.

Trix looked for her commander, who emerged frowning and troubled. Colonel Shivankar came to her and they pushed against the smoothed basalt of the tunnel to let the others pass. The musty organic scent from his vegetable greenhouse clung to the old man's rumpled coveralls, which now served as the official uniform of the defense force.

Colonel Shivankar rubbed the fringe of gray stubble on his scalp. "You're reassigned."

"I'm your bodyguard." Trix patted the gyro carbine slung across her chest. "I go where you go, sir."

"Enough with the sirs. There aren't enough of us for formality."

The anger left Shivankar's tired face as quickly as it had appeared. His raspy voice softened as he shook his head. "Sorry. You were requested by name."

Trix should have been honored, but instead she felt abandoned. "Did you offer me up?"

"No."

But Colonel Shivankar hadn't fought to keep her. Trix scowled. "So what? I protect you. I don't have to blindly obey."

"You do, Trix. The quiet war is getting loud. Not the tit-for-tat sabotage we've been running the past few years. It's a real war now. We're on the verge of recognition by the UN." Shivankar touched her chin to hold her gaze. "The UN, on Earth, will recognize the Luna Republic as a sovereign nation. They vote in two days and we need to hold out."

"We held in Derbtown," Trix said with burning pride.

"That was different. Derbtown is a tunnel complex. It would take a hundred years to dig us out."

"But—" Trix started to object.

"But we inhabit the only Goldilocks zone on the Moon that the Congloms don't control. We made the Oasis and they want it. And here we're open to attack from the sky." Shivankar pointed his finger up to emphasize his point. Black soil matrix from his garden was crusted under his nails.

Trix sniffed and wrinkled her nose. She wanted to play her part alongside Colonel Shivankar in the coming fight. She would follow someone worth following, not hide in a flare shelter. "Who am I babysitting?"

"You're with Cody Hiru." Shivankar gestured with an open hand at the briefing room doorway behind her. "You won't be babysitting."

Trix glanced over her shoulder to see the last occupant of the briefing room march into the tunnel. An Earthborn who didn't have to duck through the standard hatch.

Cody Hiru was a compact cement block of a man in tight coveralls with a wear-faded military name tape sewn over his right chest. Bald headed and with a dark square beard, he looked like a dwarf from the Tolkien books Trix had once loved. Everyone agreed Cody Hiru was a proper veteran, an experienced warfighter. An "Operator." He didn't need an assigned rank among the lunar irregulars to have authority. Special Advisor Cody Hiru had been Space Force before finding his way to Derbtown and settling among the economic refugees. He had proper military training and wikipedic knowledge of the weapon systems the defenders had scrounged.

Shivankar turned to her and whispered, "We need his help. He's the best we have on our side."

Cody Hiru boomed out, "Beatrix, I've heard good things about you" He thrust out his hairy-knuckled fist in greeting.

Earthborn never understood Derbtown etiquette. Noise echoed in confined spaces and there was always someone nearby, trying to sleep or—more often—overhear. He emitted the self-assured obliviousness of a colonist. Trix touched knuckles with him.

"Good luck, sir," Shivankar said with a courteous nod. He squeezed Trix's elbow to keep her from automatically following when he shuffled away to the stairs at the end of the corridor.

Cody took a deep breath through his nose and then looked up at Trix. He gave her a tight grin. "Meet me at the Waygo auxiliary port in twenty. We're going up top. Pack for forty-eight hours with no resupply. I'll brief the operation there."

"Understood."

Special Advisor Hiru spun and went the opposite way up the tunnel.

Trix knew this was going to end up bad.

Trix lugged her combat suit in its hazbag to the abandoned cargo entrance dubbed Waygo. The crude entrance was the first one the community had constructed, before Detonation Day, utilizing existing subsurface lava tubes to access the vertical shaft that would become Oasis. But after they dropped the roof and opened Oasis to sunshine, they bored new tunnels closer to the settlement that weren't a meandering spaghetti mess. The twisty tunnels that took her here were deserted now. All the noncombatants had gone deep into flare shelters or back to the warrens of Derbtown. Unease settled in Trix's stomach as she trudged up the gentle inclines under the weak glow of emergency lights.

She was five minutes early to the cargo lock. The prickly scent of gunpowder and the taste of throat-coating chalk reminded her to put on her mask. She hung her hazbag and peered at the cracked, but still functional, monitor that showed the interior of the cargo lock. An autonomous surface scooter in a cheery blue, white, and orange color scheme, waited patiently at the huge exterior door under a large load. Trix didn't recognize it, but she'd only come over from Derbtown a few months ago. The mongrel scooter was a unique agglomeration of parts: wide, low chassis, sport motors in each wheel, and a cut-down carry-all deck from a mining dumper. In the cargo bed, massive barrels, like fungal spore pods, clung to gimballed mounting brackets. The stress-optimized mounting system from laser-fused titanium, bumpy unfinished metal surfaces and no right angles, made it seem even more organic. The repurposed scooter, with hasty modifications and oversized load, did not look like it was up to fighting a war.

Trix heard Cody before she saw him, huffing through the dim tunnel singing a running cadence about being an "airborne ranger," whatever that was. He bounded toward her with an inefficient loping stride like a tourist. He carried a battered stack of printed signs under his arm. He tossed them to the floor in a clatter outside the personnel airlock entrance. Untreated dust swirled up.

The signage had been for intersection markings toward Oasis proper. Trix asked, "Did you take down all the signs?"

"Most." A manic grin stretched Cody's bearded face. "I swapped a few pointing the wrong directions. Don't want to make it easy for them if they make it past us."

No wireless location service had ever been installed in Derbtown or Oasis for that specific reason. Trix nodded and then pointed at her mask to remind him.

Cody pulled on his filter mask—a new model that sealed through his beard—and shrugged. "I wasn't born here."

"Yes." Trix heaped as much scorn and sarcasm as she could into her single word reply.

Oblivious to her disrespect, he continued directly into his briefing. "Our task is to emplace the Mark 22 Azawakh missiles and defend the auxiliary port. Our purpose is to delay their attack at this entry point. Most likely threat is a full-on assault through the Oasis main shaft. Most dangerous is if they break through here. Nearly all of our defenders are in Oasis proper. We're all that can be spared to cover our flank."

Trix caught the action-movie jargon. She had wondered if operators actually talked like that. Or, maybe, he should spend time learning their way of speaking, since he was the outsider. She followed him into the personnel lock.

Cody continued his banter as he opened his hazbag which was already hanging inside. "Two days until the emergency vote at the UN on our sovereignty. Until then we're just a labor dispute."

Cody unfurled his high-tech suit. The latest issue Space Force Orbital Commando rig. Ceramic trauma plates and reactive fiber musculature. Extra optics hung from the helmet. Attachment points and external pouches by design rather than kludged together from recycled junk. Everything was clean and new, no scratches or wear. The swooshing delta of the U.S. Space Force filled the chest plate in subdued grays. Trix felt jealous, but the little suit wouldn't fit her. She doubted they made them in her elongated size. With a sigh, she stripped and climbed into her dome-made patchwork suit, accepting its familiar and comforting full-body hug. Then she slung her carbine across her chest.

"The Conglom's only hope is to hit us hard and end it right away before the UN can react. The attack will come when the sun rises over North America. No ground-based observatories can watch in real time. There will be a shift change then. The overnight crew will be tired and the incoming crew won't have their heads in the game yet. Closest thing to surprise they can get." Cody didn't slip into his combat suit with well-practiced ease. The Space Force Operator grunted and wriggled his arms. The shell seemed a bit too tight for him.

Trix verified his back weld, as common courtesy, and adjusted the mating closure which should have happened automatically.

He tugged at the neck seal, pulling his slightly too-long beard free. "Expect radio jamming. We won't have voice comms during the attack except for close-range optical." Cody seated his helmet and his words were lost while the omni-voice link regained crypto. "—independent and a top shot according to Shivankar. We may be bored and forgotten or we may be in a fight for our lives."

"Got it." At least now, Trix could control his volume. She thumbed it down a notch.

Cody and Trix cycled through the personnel lock and stepped

into the cargo entrance. The exterior layers of Trix's suit tightened with a plasticky creak in the vacuum. The massive uricrete and metal overhead door lifted slightly and slid back, exposing the black sky above. A slender omni-antenna reached straight above them and seemed to disappear into space at the tip. The hum of the pumps vibrated the floor. Trix checked her dosimeter as they walked to the overloaded scooter. She set two spare oxygen packs in the scooter to fill out forty-eight hours if needed. They hopped onto the rear running board and held the grab bar. The weaponized scooter's suspension barely responded to their extra mass, bottomed out as it was already.

"Scooter, go ahead," Trix commanded.

"Listen to her. Pad Three," Cody said. He sounded like he said "Tree" instead of the number.

The scooter edged forward, swaying under its load. The fat tires whirled up the ramp with the illusion of speed and they emerged onto the lunar surface. The dark rock all around seemed to draw the heat out of her. Her fingers gripping the carbine felt a chill pinch through her haptic gloves as her heaters lagged the changing environment. Her eyes adjusted to the ghostly, earth-lit barren world that was her only home.

Trix oriented herself to the Earth, ever present in the sky and currently half shadowed. She identified the Atlantic Ocean sliding out of the terminator. The great shaft of Oasis opened into the Moon behind them, smooth blackness against the rumpled gray surface. Ahead, accreted regolith landing pads, the color of bone, sat in a hex pattern at the end of the straight paved road leading from the cargo lock. The guide beacons and marker lights were off. Abandoned Waygo gave off a serious cemetery vibe.

She didn't like it. Minimal cover. A few recessed equipment holes were dug near each pad, but the rest of the landing field was wide open. Important for a landing site, but bad for a defensive position. So much open sky for their enemy to come from and the horizon was close.

The scooter whisked them efficiently to Pad Three. It must have been the dedicated scooter for Waygo, since it didn't pause for further directions at the end of the taxiway.

Cody and Trix off loaded the Mk 22 Azawakh launcher by hand, an easier task than she had imagined As soon as the mass lifted from its cargo bed and its suspension recovered, the scooter shot away on its own and jounced over the nearby lunar surface.

"Thank God for the low g," Cody mumbled as they slowly lowered the tripodic mounting legs to the flat pad surface. The framework relaxed into place.

"Shouldn't we stick this in a hole or something?" Trix asked.

"Nope. Need unobstructed field of fire." Cody scrambled up the framework like a kid on playground equipment. He aimed the missile pods, consulting his onboard computers and cycling through various helmet optics. His carbine hung loosely, not rigged properly, and whacked against his hip or the titanium frame as he clambered across the equipment. He kept adjusting the orientation of the missile pods.

Each missile pod had eight sealed tubes, supposedly housing a Mk 22 in each. Four pods meant thirty-two shots. The Conglom, or their mercenaries, couldn't fly more than ten assault craft. Colonel Shivankar had made sure of that two weeks ago with his daring raid. There was a definite chance they could succeed, at least by the balance of numbers. "Anything I can do?"

"Stand guard."

Trix paced around their dome-grown missile battery to generate some body heat. She scanned the horizon and the empty sky with eyes and warning sensors. She used her gun camera on maximum zoom to look at the jagged peaks to the south—nearest straight-line direction to a major Conglom port—and the wide flat mare to the west. Nothing. She checked her time and double-checked the orb of the Earth. Maybe the Conglom had decided it was too costly to fight the self-proclaimed Lunar Republic?

Trix turned to watch the scooter's antics, the only visible activity. The unburdened buggy jiggled across the barren landscape. High rooster tails of ash-gray dust flipped up behind it. Must have a repurposed canine biomimetic of some kind in the control box. How long had it been left alone until called on to fight? Trix whistled for "Scooter" to calm down and come to them. It spun around once and then zipped back to wait obediently, just off the landing pad with rear wheels on powdery regolith.

The sense of exposure nagged at her as she circled the launcher.

There were no permanent satellites peering down at her; the lunar gravity was too lumpy for stable orbits. She doubted any pattern-recognition program could identify the launcher as more than an odd pile of junk even if there were fast-moving cameras pointed at them. Nothing like this ugly unit could exist in any military database, though the missile pods might give it away.

Trix patted the lowest hanging missile pod above her head. These were big and surprisingly light. Harsh plasma etching had left bare patches in the gray coating. Dents from rough handling dimpled the surface now that she looked closer. Were those scorch marks around holes in the outer case? "These missiles are munged up and ancient."

Cody grumbled as he positioned the flat-panel antenna like a folding table above the missile pods. A slight hiss of bleed over static edged in on their omni-voice channel as the radar lit up. He made another satisfied old-man grunt as he held the control umbilical. "The Azawakh has two stages and vectored nozzle, not fin steered. Perfect for LEO defense. Good enough for LLO."

"Why did they get scrapped then?" The defenders of the Lunar Republic only had castoff weapons.

"Prebiomimetic controls. They're vulnerable to electromag countermeasures. Their state-machine controllers drop out for ten seconds on upset."

"Long time to recover." Ten seconds was forever when someone was shooting at you.

"That's because they had a tendency to home in on the launch radar when spoofed."

"On the source radar?" Trix stopped and rotated to face Cody. "Back on us? Fratricide?"

"That's a roger." Then he murmured something about "more like suicide" as he fiddled with the control unit.

"They sold the Azawakhs like that?"

"Sure, passed milspec shock and vibe and was shielded against hostile electromagnetics. In separate tests. On the ground. When you think you know the answer, you stop asking questions." Cody flicked through screens on the display. "Hadn't considered combined environments. When the missile is under thrust, it vibrates. The vibrations flex seams and allow high-power EM to penetrate to the control electronics." Cody spoke with such supreme confidence about things she had never considered. "Hard to predict everything all at once."

"Let's hope the Conglom doesn't know that vulnerability." Trix's sense of possible victory diminished.

"Hope is not a plan," Cody said cryptically.

Trix felt alone and unsure.

An hour later, Cody Hiru still fussed with the Mk 22 Azawakh launcher like he was rearranging furniture, not emplacing a hypervelocity weapon system, their last line of defense for an unlikely scenario. Two of the pods pointed toward the horizon to the north. Half of their shots. Perhaps he anticipated an over-the-pole attack from the Congloms? Cody dismounted the flat panel radar and shifted it to another pad. He played out the cables effortlessly, even though his tactical posture seemed rusty or half forgotten.

"Shouldn't we rig these pads for demo?" Trix decided it would only take a minute or so to get from here to the entrance on the smooth bridgeway. "Set some cratering charges. That would slow anyone down."

"They'll know. They'll suspect. Then they won't come into the kill zone. Congloms and their mercs are risk averse. Any hint that things aren't what they expect, they'll go with the guaranteed solution."

"Most likely threat?" Trix stared into the distance at the shadow that was Oasis. There was no protective cover to slide over the huge skylight, unlike the Waygo Port entrance. There was no way to hide its location. They had broadcast it to the solar system asking for sovereignty and recognition. Most likely threat was an attack from the sky.

"That's a roger."

There was a lot of North America for the sun to rise over. Cody hadn't specified where in North America the observatories were located or who would be watching. How many hours was that from east to west?

Bored, Trix asked, "Azawakh? What does it stand for?"

"Eh? Nothing. Some acquisition guy apparently liked dogs. All the other dog names were taken, like terrier or malamute." Cody chuckled from atop the launch frame. Again. "Azawakhs were desert hunting dogs. Sort of appropriate. Deserts are wastelands on Earth where only a few can survive. Our desert and oasis is here."

"That's why we named it Oasis."

"I know," he said tolerantly. Cody hopped down and resumed messing with the firing controller. "I was here the day we dropped the roof. I helped set charges."

"You did? Just how old are you?" Trix did the math. That was before she was born. Long before the Space Force stood up its orbit-capable direct-action teams.

When armed conflict with the Conglom became inevitable, Trix had read and watched everything she could find about military operations in space with the same focus as she had on her abandoned engineering studies. She consumed everything that their pirated LunaNet bandwidth would let her access. The Space Force wasn't taken seriously as a warfighter until Delta 9 Orbital formed. She knew this as a fact. Cody Hiru would have been behind a computer if he was from the prewar earthbound Space Force. Just an ordinary guardian if anything. He was no "operator." He was a poser. Stolen valor all the way.

And her leadership had believed him! They let him shape their strategy. He knew the whole defense plan. Every little doubt fell into place. No wonder she didn't like him. He reeked of fake. Some Earther come here to live out his video-game fantasy.

"What sort of special operator were you really?" Trix demanded.

"Come again?"

"Have you been in combat?" Trix loomed over him and pressed closer. She couldn't stop blinking as her fury swelled. "We were depending on you and you lied!"

"I never claimed to be a special operator—" Cody protested and acted confused. He backed away, something a true lunar native would never do, unable to see where feet were going. He bumped into the titanium cage of the Azawakh launcher.

"You didn't correct them." Trix pushed forward until only her slung gyro carbine separated them. She stared down through his metallic-coated visor to see the face of the liar. All she saw was her warped reflection. "Did you even serve in a military?"

"I did—" His hand groped toward his external weapon pouch.

"Everyone listened to you. You sound so confident." Trix caught his wrist before he could withdraw his hand from the pouch.

With a dismissive chuckle, he said, "No one knows what this will be like."

His lack of proper shame drove the anger burning in her chest. He was caught and only laughed at her. She yelled, "My parents are down in Oasis! You don't have to be here. Why are you even here?"

"I was an operator—"

"You've got slick gear. Buy that used? Are you here because it's cool? Get off on this?"

"I was a satellite operator for ten years. I served at Schriever. JTF Space Defense. Yes, I was at a computer most of that time. But that was long ago." Cody slowly broke free with his Earther strength.

Trix let go of his wrist when she couldn't stop him.

Cody pulled his fist from his pouch and passed his spare magazines to her. "And why am I here, if you'll listen, is the same as you. A free self-governing lunar settlement. Not a colony."

She clenched the gyro mags in a trembling hand as she stumbled back. "What am I supposed to do with these?"

"Fight." Long pause. "What do you think we should do?"

Stunned at his answer and sudden embarrassment knifing in where she had been enraged a millisecond before, Trix fumbled the extra mags into her ammo pouch. "We need cover," she snapped.

"Roger." Cody Hiru followed her.

The nearest equipment hole would have to serve as their fighting position. An inert landing beacon and the power hub for the safety lights crowded the shallow excavation. The pit was only deep enough to prevent nozzle exhaust from whipping small rocks onto its contents and to keep the electronics shadowed during the hot lunar day. Trix tore the landing beacon out and tossed it away with all her strength. Scooter zipped over to investigate the tumbling box. Doing something, anything, felt better than the nothing she had been doing before.

Cody strung the umbilical over the crusted lip of the pit. The barrel of his carbine dug into the regolith, but he didn't seem to notice. Cody hunched over the Azawakh firing control screen. How much more could he do now?

Annoyed, Trix whistled. "Scooter, go recharge."

Scooter spun in place and paused. Its sensor turret pointed toward her.

"Go!" Trix said.

Scooter scurried along the bridgeway toward the Waygo entrance. The wispy omni-antenna, the lone indicator, marked the location of the cargo lock. Scooter disappeared down the ramp. An alert icon of a charging battery popped in her display.

Trix settled into the hole and glared at Cody Hiru. He had full cover. She had to fold in half to fit. She tried to scrape out the bottom of the pit to improve the position, but she wasn't able to dislodge the rocks trapped in the subsurface crust. It would take a boring tool to bust through the densified sediment. She gave up and hunkered down. She checked the time readout. They had only been outside a few hours. It felt like forever.

Cody started talking. "We had put Mark 22s on some satellites for offensive security. We never used them."

"So what?" Trix said.

"You asked if I had ever been in combat. Not like you. Not like Delta 9. But we were engaged in our own alternate conflict. Creating orbital debris is a war crime now." Cody pointed at his chest with his thumb. "I was responsible for a fair share of that Kessler Syndrome wreckage myself."

He sighed. "The situation in the U.S. went downhill fast when the Congloms got voting rights. I had sworn to protect the U.S. Constitution, not corporate profits. So, I took my medals and bonus pay, resigned my commission and signed on with an orbital salvage crew.

"Tough work, but I was good at it," Cody continued. "Satellite operations had been my entire military life. I had a good sense of which orbits these unused Mark 22 Azawakhs would end up in after the shooting was over. We pulled these babies on board along with a few choice metric tons of useful materials and precious recyclables.

"The Conglom would have loved to get their hands on these. Heavy weapons are hard to get off Earth. Serious big money. But they couldn't pay me enough."

Trix took a sip from her drinking tube, but only enough tepid water to clear the chalky taste from her mouth. "Is that so?"

"Instead, I boosted up to the Moon with my share of the haul, not to make big cash or enhance my personal stock, but to join you. Because we can't get trapped on Earth and die as a species. Who knows if we'll make it past the next self-inflicted disaster down there?" Cody waved his gloved hand at the Earth. "The Lunar Republic is the last chance at a free society that is open to immigrants like me."

The old man knew the right words to say. Trix growled, "Can't let the Congloms win."

"Can't let the Congloms win," he repeated.

Trix was unsure in places where she had been dead certain before.

In a flat monotone, Cody Hiru said, "Inbound."

Instantly alert, Trix tracked to the azimuth he transmitted to her display. West. Toward Oasis and to shadows passing in front of a starry background. Her stomach went sickeningly soft at the sight. She raised her gunsight to zoom in on the distant shapes in time to see the first open bombardment of the war. Netwide warnings flashed from the consolidated command on her message stream. Not a drill!

Bulbous assault craft, long-range hoppers from the Conglom, dropped from a high ballistic trajectory over the blacked-out lava tube a few kilometers away. The hoppers were dark blue, she knew, but looked black at this distance, and unmarked. They hung like fat dragons breathing fire on the town below. Missiles fired from Oasis streaked toward the approaching targets. Some missiles left slowly expanding smoke trails and detonated early, defective. Return fire from the Conglom gunships lit the walls of Oasis with staccato explosions, like silent flickering lights at the far end of a tunnel.

Trix imagined Shivankar's greenhouse at the bottom of the main shaft under a shower of rocks. Shattered. She imagined Shivankar trapped. Asphyxiated.

Trix should have been there with her people, her family, facing the fight directly from their home. Down in the tunnels like before. Not out here waiting for nothing to happen watching from behind her faceplate. Distant and removed. The anxiety of the hours exposed on the surface mingled with the guilt of being safe while others probably died in the first wave and the soul-deep hurt of broken trust. She turned on Cody Hiru to vent her frustration.

The old man had just tilted his body to stare up at the southern sky. The firing control unit blinked hostile red.

Another three hoppers configured as troop carriers had appeared.

Her guilt and anxiety vanished. The fight had come to them. Most dangerous threat. She became a charged wire of adrenaline.

Trix shouldered her carbine and focused with her gun camera at the descending assault craft. The range and velocity numbers dropped as they approached. Jets fired and rotated the ships. Landing gear extended fully, talons reaching to clutch the ground. Cargo doors sat wide open with combat-ready mercenaries visible inside. The three Conglom hoppers were coming in for a controlled soft landing, directly into the range of the vulnerable Azawakhs. Just as Special Advisor Hiru had predicted.

Trix whispered, "As long as they don't know."

"They know," Cody answered.

"How can you be sure?"

Cody launched the entire Mk 22 Azawakh battery with a press of his thumb. "Because I told them."

The Azawakhs leapt out of their pods in rapid-fire grace. A volley of arrows toward the armored flying beasts. The fleeting impression of snub-nosed cylinders, glowing for a second in the fire of their exhaust, was left. The rocket streaks left blue traces in her vision. Blown grit hissed on her faceplate. Metal shavings and plastic bits floated around them. A dozen points of light swirled upward at the invading spacecraft.

Then electromag jamming hit from the lead assault craft. Their omni-voice link turned to static and then squelch silence. All data feeds outside her own suit went blank or flashed last known number. She only heard her own shallow breathing and the whir of her helmet fan. The guided trajectories of some missiles straightened. The hoppers fired engines and juked higher to avoid the disrupted barrage. The enemy's point-defense guns shot down the closest missiles in sparking wreckage. However, the majority of the Azawakh salvo accelerated, unimpeded and ignored, toward the north pole, nowhere near any intended targets, no change to initial trajectories. Shots thrown away. Shots that might have made it through defenses to the enemy ships. The assault craft had slowed their approach, but they were about to land unopposed.

Trix screamed and raised the gyro carbine on reflex at Cody's helmet. Tight range wouldn't get full velocity on the round, but enough to kill. He was a liar and now an admitted traitor. She flicked the safety off. This wasn't how she expected her last act in this life to happen.

"You told them?!" Her own breath smelled sour as Trix screamed and he couldn't hear. She hesitated with her finger on the firing stud. This was wrong. She lowered her carbine slightly. He could have eliminated her at any point before now when her back was turned if he really was a traitor. It was easy to die on the Moon. Maybe she didn't have the right answer.

Cody raised his hands palm out, but he still held the controls for the spent missile battery. Then he pointed behind her.

Wary, Trix keyed her gun camera and kept him in her helmet display as she turned her body to look. She edged to the west and straightened to peer over the rim.

Across the broad flat mare, a swarm of drones rode on jets of compressed gas that kicked up regolith like a cavalry horde on the charge. The low-flying crosses were standard surveillance models from the Conglom, usually posted to debris fields and facility perimeters. Familiar foes to any derb diver. The biomimetics were based on wild-bee neural paths, solitary by nature, but territorial.

These drones had been repurposed into a swarm. The Conglom didn't do that. Ever. They imported single-use equipment. These had been modified. And the invaders above were waiting for the drones to lead the fight. To clear the defenders of Waygo. She had no idea how these drones were armed or even how many were in the swarm, but they were a clear threat.

Trix whipped her carbine around, braced herself on the lip of their position, and fired aimed shots at the leading drones. A few tumbled, broken, but replacements appeared from the back ranks. The lifted dust obscured her sights. The ground felt like blocks of ice below her elbows and against her thighs as she shifted and fired. The next hit sent one drone spurting into the sky with a pierced gas line.

The prominent X shape of the drone chassis grew more distinct as the swarm grew near. Their spherical payloads behind their camera and controller pods hung like black spider bellies at the intersection of the X. The drones reached the far western edge of the landing area where less dust flew up and their cameras focused as one as they converged.

A few probing shots came from hoppers above. Only light-caliber gyrojets. All their heavy weaponry must have been bombarding Oasis. Cody fired a burst of return fire at the hoppers, an undisciplined fan of reddish streaks into the sky, as Trix concentrated on knocking out drones. She felt an immediate jolt of triumph for each drone she blasted and kept herself from counting the ones following behind. She dropped an empty magazine and reloaded.

Drone carcasses littered the landing pads like black shards of broken glass, but the wave barely slowed. Then a red light glowed behind the single eye of the nearest drones as if they had grown angry.

Now Trix knew how they were armed. Tasers. Very limited range of a few meters, although most likely no longer limited to less-than-lethal currents.

The nearest one reached their position and fired its stinger at her. Two needles, spooling out coiled wire, rocketed out of its fat spider-belly.

Instinctively, Trix raised her left arm to shield herself. The needles sank into her forearm. A strobe flashed. The twisted wires jerked. Sharp, muscle-clenching pain penetrated through the tough outer shell of her suit. Malfunction warnings lit on her display. The reactive fabric of her suit failed near the taser hit. The now unbalanced pressure between her internal atmosphere and the lunar vacuum stiffened her elbow, like her arm was trapped in webbing or numbed with poison.

Trix stood and smashed the attacking drone with the butt of her carbine. The spider belly shattered. Her med warnings flashed in her helmet: heart rate racing and a spike in oxygen usage. The suit warnings alerted her to a possible micrometeor strike, but integrity held. For the moment. She didn't want to take another taser hit.

More drones dropped into taser range and their eyes glowed warning red.

Trix backed away, firing into the swarm. Walking backward was drilled in as forbidden on the surface. She had no choice. She dropped another empty magazine and struggled with her stiff arm to reload quickly. She stumbled when her heels banged into the power hub. Floating black Xs descended from the landing pad toward them. Their fighting position was about to be overrun.

A blue, white and orange shape bounded down the bridgeway.

Scooter zoomed past their position, knocking the low-flying drones to the side. It drove over the nearest fallen ones and ground them under its tires. Shards of skeletal ceramic and metal tubing snapped apart. Scooter spun and braked and lifted its front tires off the ground in a dervish frenzy. Something about the drone behavior had clearly triggered hidden biomimetic subprogramming. The surviving drones fired tasers at Scooter, who shrugged off the sparking wires and grew more agitated with each sting.

Trix regained her balance and fired at the closest one still flying. The gyrojet didn't strike hard enough to destroy it cleanly. The drone flopped to the surface on its back. The nozzles at the ends of its booms twitched like little claws. It spun on the pad and righted itself before Scooter trampled it into crushed fragments. Trix hurled herself prone at her original firing point, ignoring the growing number of system alerts from her suit.

Another drone cast its stinger at her. Trix rocked to the side and took the hit on her carbine. The barbed needles glanced off and the floppy wires trailed below the drone. She shot it and then found another target.

Cody scrambled to the wall next to her. The optic voice link connected at close visor-to-visor range. "Get forces shifted to Waygo."

"Let's go." Trix reloaded with her good arm.

"I need to man the launcher. I've got two shots left."

"There's three hoppers!"

"Move out!" Cody commanded.

Trix nearly argued with him. She would have to go to the cargo lock and tie directly into the comm network to avoid the jamming. He would have to delay. She nodded, a useless gesture in a suit, and whistled for Scooter. Also a useless impulse.

Scooter shimmied to untangle a pair of drones that were caught in its tires. It was unaware of her commands, engrossed in its own vengeance against the drones.

Trix jumped out of the hole. Bounding covered ground quickly, but she made herself a visible target. Scooter zipped in front of her when it recognized her. Plumes of dust fountained up nearby—harassing fire from the ships. She climbed onto Scooter's rear running board, kicking broken bits of drone from beneath her boots. A trace of burning gyro exhaust appeared to her left and a jagged hole suddenly penetrated the cargo bed directly in front of her. She felt the impact shock through the grab bar.

Trix crouched—a stupid reflex—and heard the beep of the optic voice link accepted by Scooter's controller. "Inside!"

Trix shot one-handed behind her back as fast as she could depress the firing stud. Most of the swarm jetted toward her, the easily identified antagonist for their insect-like brains. She tried to knock down as many of the black drones as possible, to keep them off Cody, to keep them after her. To buy a few more moments.

Scooter leapt ahead, spraying basalt grit from tires. A chunk flew off its left front wheel where another gyrojet round caught it. Scooter wobbled, but compensated, and settled for a periodic loping as it raced to safety. Trix rode the jolting buggy with flexed knees, unable to return fire from the unstable platform.

The assault craft didn't need the landing pads, but were clearly taking the easy option for a clean touchdown and rapid airlock breach. The electromag jamming abruptly stopped. External signals came back online. Alerts from Cody's suit and Scooter's diagnostics filled her display. But nothing from central command. The omni-voice link was clear again. She didn't need to retreat. She could pass the message now and return to the fight.

"Scooter, halt!"

Scooter came to a skidding stop. Trix held tight with her stiff left arm. She fired at the few drones that still trailed them. "Command, Command. This is Waygo Port. Three hoppers with ground units assaulting Waygo. Need reinforcement ASAP."

Nothing.

"Command, Command…" Trix started to say again. Then she looked up from her gunsight display to observe the scant surroundings.

The slender omni-antenna, their data and voice relay to the rest of the Lunar Republic military, was destroyed. Concentrated gyrojet fire had left hundreds of pock marks in the regolith where the base of the antenna had been. Only the local omni-voice network was active between suits and scooter. No one except Cody would hear her cries for help.

Now the mercenaries shifted fire to the Azawakh launcher. Gyrojet traces lanced in three jumbled streams from the nearing hoppers and converged on Pad Three.

"Launch!" she yelled. Why didn't Cody fire his last rounds? Was he down? No. He didn't fire because there were no Azawakhs left to fire, she realized. Trix now saw the scorched and empty missile tubes torn to shreds under streams of enemy rounds. Cody had already launched the entire battery. He never had two more shots. The drones that remained near Pad Three were caught in the massed fire from the mercenaries. She couldn't see any sign of Cody Hiru. The lying bastard better be digging deeper somehow. He'd better be alive.

Then Trix heard the sideband hiss in her omni-voice link as the targeting radar turned on. The Mk 22 radar, shifted to the adjoining pad, painted the assault craft as they landed. What was this hopeless gesture?

Over the distant mountain ridgeline to the south, near the constellation of Orion, flame trails ignited. A flight of Mk 22 Azawakhs reengaged targets. The missiles' second-stage warheads hit the invaders like a volley of deadly arrows in rapid succession. Molten metal erupted from the rear of the hoppers, sending hypervelocity shrapnel toward the ramp. The attack ships crumpled into the landing pads in slow motion. Surviving mercenaries leaped out before impact.

Orbital mechanics had been his military trade. Cody Hiru had launched Azawakhs into a low lunar pass from north to south pole! He had gauged the orbital trajectories with minimal instruments and raw intuition well enough to predict a full transit. He sent the vulnerable Azawakhs to catch the Conglom mercenaries from behind.

Trix hoped the stupid missiles don't think she was a target. Who knew what machines thought? "Scooter, inside!"

She kept firing from the back of the limping Scooter. Screw accuracy. One drone would get hit and spin before dropping into the dust. Then it would spring up in a splash of fine power and spurt toward her again. Her last magazine came up dry. The drones got closer and fired their twisted wire stingers.

Then Trix felt weightless, falling, and they were down the ramp. The chasing drones overshot the below-ground cargo entrance. Trix hopped off Scooter and punched the Emergency button. "Locking the door," she announced.

She wanted to hear something back in the instant before the

retainer bolts fired. Nothing. The massive overhead door slammed shut, barricading out the attackers for the moment. And Cody Hiru if he still survived.

She hesitated before pushing the atmosphere flood. A deeply ingrained fear of wasting oxygen and knowing that it would delay the opening of the overhead hatch. The attackers would have to breach with thermal lances now. That would buy time. But she wouldn't be able to open it to recover Coby. Time lost. She flooded the chamber without knowing the answer. She could finally move her arm freely as internal and external pressures equalized.

A black cross zipped across the corner of her vision. One drone had managed to follow her inside. It circled the interior of the cargo lock, bumping into the now-closed overhead hatch. A delicate ting-ting of fused ceramic sounded with each strike. A red glow came to its eye as it locked on and descended toward her.

Trix detached her empty carbine and readied it like a club. She eased toward the lock control panels, ready to dash for the personnel hatch.

Scooter spun. Its wheel jammed against the far wall. It readied to pounce, but seemed to hesitate with Trix directly in the path.

The drone's jets gave out, its reservoirs empty. It flopped uncontrolled to the ramp where it clattered and slid to the bottom. The red eye on the spider belly twitched to target Trix from the ground.

Scooter rolled forward and delicately crushed it beneath a wheel.

Trix plugged directly into the comm network and connected. No static. She dropped onto the open channel. "Command, command. This is Waygo. Need reaction force. Three hoppers with mercs. Cody Hiru caught topside."

Scooter left the crushed drone and climbed up the ramp. It rocked back and forth on its damaged wheel at the top, nudging the overhead hatch as if it wanted to go back out.

Colonel Shivankar's calming voice replied, "Roger, Waygo. Help is on the way."

For a second, Trix felt relief. When the answers are known, questions are no longer asked. Coby had told the Conglom about the Azawakh vulnerability somehow. She had assumed treason. The attackers had also assumed their own knowledge was sufficient, that they understood the risks. Coby took advantage of their arrogance to put outdated, easily defeated weapons onto target. To buy a little more time for desperate people struggling after their own freedom. No one else in Oasis or Derbtown could have done that. She had nearly killed him and only a moment of doubt kept her from losing the fight that had barely begun.

Everything shifted for her. Cody Hiru wasn't the special operator, the highly trained trigger puller of action movies and tip of the spear in warfighting. He wasn't what Trix had expected when she had assumed she had all the answers. It didn't matter that Cody Hiru once served behind a computer. He managed to apply what little the self-proclaimed Lunar Republic had on hand and what he had brought to the fight, without regard for his personal safety in an act of noble heroism for their shared ideals.

Coby Hiru was not a dwarf with strength in swinging a battle axe, but a wizard who worked unimagined magic.

Now she had to find a way to hold against the invaders, if any were left, until reinforcements arrived, so that Cody's sacrifice could be built into victory. She whistled for Scooter and opened inner airlock door to prepare more surprises for the enemy in the dark tunnels ahead.

✴   ✴   ✴

M. L. Reiten served in the military, with deployments to Bosnia and Afghanistan, and worked as a scientist at a national lab (proving that there *is* such a thing as too much research for writing science fiction). A Writers of the Future and Jim Baen Memorial Short Story Contest winner, he has published stories in *Analog* and *DreamForge* and several anthologies, including S.M. Stirling's *The Change* and, recently, "Higher Ground" in *Robosoldiers: Thank You for Your Servos*. He practices aikido, makes pizza, and now lives near Washington, D.C., with his wonderful wife and daughter. More at: www.mtreiten.com.

The Pattern

✵

Avery Parks

Alex Farmakis checked her incoming requests once more, idly clicking through on her interface. Nothing. She had finished her assignments for the day—monitor the newest crop of microsats for proper integration into the orbital network, clear the queue of potential collisions marked by the AI.

Hours left on the clock, she leaned back in her seat and groaned, stretching her shoulders before reaching for her mug of instacoffee and popping the heating tab. She hated idleness, and in the eleven months since the AI had finished being trained for, well, *her* job, she had been idle more often than not.

Maybe it was time for a new career. She had wanted to be involved with space without actually going there, but providing the human overwatch for an AI was not what she had envisioned when she applied to the International Space Surveillance and Coordination Center five years ago.

She blew on the now-steaming surface of her coffee and chewed her lip reflectively. It would be easier if she didn't love what she did so much, love managing the ordered complexity of thousands of satellites all spinning around the planet, love searching for the anomalies that might disrupt that balanced system.

Oh well. Working, even made-up busywork to pass the time, was better than stewing over career paths and her future. She reentered her interface and pulled up the data for the satellites in low Earth orbit over the past month to review. She typically worked in much shorter time frames for LEO; so close to Earth, the satellites orbited the planet over a dozen times each day and required close monitoring. Even minute changes could have large impacts when the satellites were moving over 25,000 kilometers per hour.

She reviewed the data over the course of an hour, the visualization of the orbits solid lines at such artificially rapid speeds. She wasn't sure why she bothered. The AI had already reviewed and flagged anything of note. But she welcomed sinking into the data and letting it wash over her, too vast to track things individually.

But as the satellites spun, a pattern began to emerge. She frowned, twitching her fingers to click back, slow things down, and then forward once more. At smaller intervals—a week, instead of a month—the pattern faded, lost in the noise.

She sped back up and found it again, then went back further, adding more data to her simulation. The web of satellites was like a living thing, constantly pulsing and changing as satellites were added, deorbited, or routed around the odd bit of debris.

Lost in the data, she went backward and forward over the past six months, chasing the pattern as it emerged and tagging satellites as they joined it, one after another. Individually, their behavior was perfectly normal.

But together . . . something was wrong.

"Alex, what are you still doing here?" a voice piped up behind her, and she jumped, fumbling at the interface clipped over her ear. Finally untangling it from her hair, she set both it and the rings that tracked her finger movements on the desk before turning to her boss.

Siavash Kazemirad, head of what remained of the Satellite Behavior Tracking department at ISSCC, was a perpetually rumpled and easygoing man, his casual T-shirt just beginning to stretch across his growing waistline.

"I lost track of time," she replied as her eyes finally refocused on the room around her. How long had it been? She rubbed at her temples and grimaced at the cold coffee on her desk.

"That's not like you," he pointed out, settling into the chair next to hers. "Something come up?"

"Yes," she said immediately, then stopped. How to explain? "Can I show you?"

At his nod, she put her interface back on and started compiling a new simulation of the past three months, but without her tags, curious if he would spot the pattern as well. She dropped it into the network for him, and waited.

He watched in silence on his interface. Finally, he spoke up. "What am I looking at here?"

"Don't you see it?" she blurted out, then stopped. Obviously not, if he was asking. "I mean, does anything stand out to you?"

"No, not really. Just a bajillion satellites spinning, like always," he said lightly.

"There's a pattern. Can you watch again?"

Obligingly, he went through the simulation once more. "Sorry. Nothing."

She pursed her lips, then overlaid her tags onto his simulation, marking the satellites in the pattern. "How about now?"

He watched again, then removed his interface. "Why did you mark those satellites?"

"Because of the pattern," she said impatiently. "Can you not see it?"

He shook his head slowly. "No. They're just random satellites. Did the AI flag this?"

At the mention of the AI, her temper flared. "No, *I* did. The human, with a brain."

He sighed. "I know it's been hard this past year. But you're not being replaced by the AI, it's just keeping an eye on things as the satellite network continues to grow."

"I know that," she said with a frown. Why was he telling her what she already knew?

"Your job is safe. You don't need to go looking for things that . . . may not be there," he said.

"Siavash, there *is* a pattern," she insisted. "I'm not making it up."

"Of course not," he said quickly. "But the human brain is sometimes too good at pattern recognition. My nephew loves to find animals in the clouds, for example."

She scoffed. Was he being condescending? Or trying to be kind? She had always been better at reading satellites than people.

"It's late. How about you go home and get some rest, and we'll talk about it more tomorrow."

"Fine." She quickly gathered her things and slung her messenger bag over her shoulder. She could analyze the pattern at home just as easily, after all.

"And let's leave work at work," he called after her. He clearly had no trouble reading her, which just stoked her annoyance further. She waved a hand behind her noncommittally and left. Once she had a more solid analysis put together, he would see it. He had to.

Alex tilted her head back as she walked down an empty stretch of sidewalk toward home, letting the expanse of night sky fill her vision. It was her favorite time of year—late autumn, when the days grew shorter but before the nights became too bitterly cold.

She didn't understand why Siavash hadn't been able to see the pattern. But she was more concerned about how it might disrupt the entire network.

She made mental notes as she walked, letting the rhythm of her steps mark them in her memory: What commonalities did the satellites in the pattern share? Who owned them, who made them, their age? Where had they launched from? What tied them together?

She wished she could simply ask their operators why they had moved their satellites, but every satellite was at least partially controlled by an onboard AI, a requirement of the treaty following the Kessler Incident of 2036. It had taken decades to clean up low Earth orbit after that catastrophic cascade of space debris—decades and international cooperation and unimaginable amounts of money.

She glanced down long enough to not miss her turn, then looked up again, watching for glimpses of the lowest satellites, tiny points of light steadily tracking across the sky. She loved seeing them with her own eyes rather than an interface, tying reality to the office she spent most of her waking hours inside.

A larger point caught her eye, and she squinted her eyes enough to make out a minute circle, all that was visible with the naked eye of the Hub's enormous spinning wheel. She smiled.

The Hub was Earth's largest space station by far, dwarfing anything else humanity had built by orders of magnitude. It was the launch point for missions further into the solar system, a transit hub for the Moon base, even a tourist destination. At any point in time, hundreds of people lived, worked, or passed through there.

As a child, she had dreamed of going up; as an adult, she admired it from afar. It was part of what had inspired her career, and even with the office AI leaving her less work to do, she had to admit she still loved what she did.

She continued toward home, the sight of the Hub almost enough to chase away her worries about what the pattern might mean.

"Alex, I'm sorry, but it's time to move on from this." Siavash leaned against the desk next to hers and raised his hands apologetically. "It's been a week, and..."

And nothing. There wasn't a single common thread amongst the satellites in the pattern, beyond that she saw them there.

"I just need access to their onboard programming," she insisted. It was the next logical step, but Siavash had dug his heels in.

"We've been over this. To get that, I need approval from my boss, and I can't send something up the chain if I can't even see it." He stopped, sighing. "I'm trying here, Alex. You've been exemplary in your work here, and you've never given me a reason to doubt you. Have you found anyone else yet who can see the pattern?"

She shook her head mutely. None of her colleagues could see it, at least not with enough certainty to back her on it.

Why was it just her? She refused to doubt herself, and it was incredibly frustrating that no one else could see it. Was her brain just that different?

She had to admit, patterns soothed her, the same way the complexity of the satellite network did. To pick them out, follow them, predict where they might go next...

She groaned, and only years of practice controlling unexpected hand motions while wearing the interface rings stopped her from slapping her forehead. Siavash looked down at her, eyebrows drawn together.

"What?"

"I'm an idiot," she said. She had been so wrapped up in finding evidence that the satellites in the pattern were connected and prove the pattern was there that she had overlooked the easiest way to actually do so.

"Well, that's not true. What's up?" he asked.

She didn't answer right away, already buried back in the data to see if her theory was right. The network was vast, so it would take time to find them all, but . . . yes. That one. She began to explain, still half-distracted as she searched.

"The pattern. I can predict it. I'll prove it."

"How?"

She found another, and marked it as well. Confident now that she could do this, she reluctantly removed the interface and turned to Siavash. "By the end of today, I'll send you a list of satellites that are most likely to join the pattern next. If I'm right, will you talk to your boss on Monday and get me the access I need?"

"Sounds fair. But if you're wrong, you agree to let this go?"

She nodded once. She wasn't wrong, and she knew it.

Alex watched Siavash as he sat back in his chair and reviewed her list of satellites and her predictions for their movements over the weekend. He snorted and shook his head, then flipped up his interface.

"Are you . . . surprised?" she ventured, and he opened his mouth a few times before speaking.

"Honestly, yeah. I didn't doubt your intellect, but this is crazy. I've never seen anything like it."

"And my access?"

"Yeah, yeah. But even if that gives us the how, I'm more interested in the why," he said, and something she hadn't realized was clenched tight inside her relaxed. He had said *us*. She was no longer alone in this; Siavash's backing meant more resources, enough to find actual answers. To protect everything and everyone in orbit. Or so she hoped.

But maybe it was more than that. Being the only person to see the pattern hadn't set well, and the uneasiness that had lingered in the back of her mind finally dissipated.

"The why seems more like your question to answer than mine," she said.

"How so?"

"I mean . . . I don't understand why people do what they do, how could I possibly figure this out? I'd rather focus on the programming data." She shrugged self-consciously.

"So you think someone is behind this?" he asked, settling back in his chair, and she shrugged again.

"It has to be someone hacking them. It can't be natural, and there isn't an AI who can handle enough data to be responsible." AIs had their limitations, for which she was secretly grateful. She would have been without the job she loved otherwise.

"Fair point," he said, then clapped his hands together. "All right. Access for you, brainstorming for me."

She turned to go back to her desk, but he called after her.

"Hey, Alex. Well done on finding this."

She nodded in awkward thanks and went back to work.

Alex ripped her interface off in frustration and slapped her hands flat against her desk.

It was another dead end.

After waiting nearly two weeks for ISSCC's lawyers to jump through the hoops required to give her access to a dozen of the satellites in the pattern, their code wasn't providing the answers she had hoped for. It was still being reviewed by other departments that had more expertise in that area, but she was losing hope.

The onboard AIs were cataloging routine course corrections, nothing more. Whoever was doing this was covering their tracks exceedingly well. And it was pissing her off.

More of her department was assigned to the pattern now, as well, and as the person who had discovered it, she was required to attend all the meetings. Which also wasn't helping her mood. If she had to waste another hour listening to people discuss the same things over and over again, she was going to scream.

So now, after exhausting all avenues to figure out how it was happening, she was going to have to shift to why. And what the end goal may be. If there even was one.

True to his word, Siavash had been working on it, but he only had unsubstantiated theories, unbacked by data. Useless.

But regardless of his theories, he was certain that whoever was doing this had a goal. If that was true, she didn't need to figure out *why* they were doing this, only what the endpoint of the pattern might be. And that felt far more doable.

She reentered her interface and pulled up her most recent simulation, programming it further into the future. As long as a satellite's velocity didn't change, its position in orbit was easy to extrapolate, based on time. Which satellites would be joining the pattern next, and how the entire network would react to that, was more difficult.

An endpoint. Would they all come together at some point, like one of Siavash's theories? Yes. Some would, small groups that condensed and then split back apart. But no matter the timeline or how she adjusted the variables, never all at once.

She worked for hours, until the smell of someone's lunch made her stomach grumble uncomfortably. She downed a granola bar and an instacoffee, then dove back in.

Continuing to look forward, she decided to focus on one of the largest groups that came together on this coming Thursday. They wouldn't be close enough to collide—another of Siavash's theories—and they separated quickly.

Well, if she was going to focus on this group, she was going to do so properly. None were in the sample they had gotten access to, so she shot Siavash a request for access to whichever of this group that he could quickly get. If any belonged to the same corporation or country that had given access to the others, it should be relatively straightforward.

Was there a resource, something of import that orbited at a similar distance above Earth? This group was in the upper ranges of LEO, above the Hub and other stations. But, no. It didn't share an orbit with anything.

Putting that group aside for a moment, she looked at other smaller groups that came together around the same time. One met a dozen kilometers below the initial group, a minute or two later, on the other side of the planet.

Then, below that, another, this one close enough together to trigger each AI's collision avoidance. Alex swallowed, mouth suddenly dry. There was another group, again minutes later, below.

Was it just a random coincidence of the pattern? Groups had come together before; it was almost impossible not to, with so many satellites in orbit. She looked back at the highest group, then higher still, to middle Earth orbit.

Then back down, to the lowest group, orbiting at the same height as the Hub.

No amount of practice staying still while using the interface could prevent her from jumping to her feet in alarm. The visuals from the interface swirled drunkenly around her, and she stumbled, clawing it off and yelling for Siavash.

He popped into sight, eyes wide.

She took a deep breath, heart pounding. "I know what they're going to do."

Alex had barely begun to explain before Siavash spun, gesturing for her to follow him. Jogging together down the corridor toward the elevator to top management's office, she continued.

"It's XB-20675. It's being decommissioned out of MEO, and its transfer orbit down puts it square in the first group. If their AIs are disabled, they'll obliterate it." She panted, catching her breath as Siavash jiggled the elevator call button. "It's the Kessler Incident all over again."

XB-20675 was one of the oldest and largest satellites, scheduled to safely deorbit into the Pacific in two days. But if it were hit with enough force—say, over a dozen microsats—it would disintegrate into millions of pieces. The Earth's gravity would pull some into the orbit below, where those pieces would overwhelm the satellites' AIs. Too much data to track, too impossible to avoid a collision.

And down. And down. Each group Alex had identified would hit and add to the shrapnel, forming a cascade ultimately large enough to take out nearly everything in LEO.

Including the Hub.

Even if they started now, there might not be enough time to evacuate the station—there were hundreds of lives in danger. But not just there, she realized with a shock. There were hundreds more on the Moon who relied on the Hub for support, and people surveying Mars and Titan as well.

Alex tried to control the fine trembling that emanated from her core as she followed Siavash into the elevator; she needed to remain calm, to work the problem.

"Are you sure?" Siavash glanced at her, as if hoping for her to say no, then shook his head. "Of course you're sure."

She clenched her hands tight as the trembling reached her fingertips, and tried to concentrate on breathing stillness through her body as they went up. The doors opened onto the top floor, and Siavash quickly explained to the assistant at the front desk that it was an emergency relating to the pattern their department had been studying. She overheard the words *Kessler* and *Hub*, and the assistant's face went blank even as his fingers rapidly twitched through a message on his interface.

After a few moments, they were waved through, and she followed Siavash into the head of the ISSCC's office. She had never been here before, and even the panic of the situation didn't prevent her from noticing the view across the city, unspoiled by any breaks in the enormous wall of glass.

"Mr. Kazemirad, yes? And Dr. Farmakis? Please, come in. The other department heads are on their way." Ingrid Klein, the head of ISSCC, was a petite woman, but no less intimidating for her lack of height. "Care to sit?"

Alex shook her head quickly, resisting the urge to look back for the others. There was enough time, wasn't there? Nearly forty hours until the first collision.

Thankfully, they began to file in, a half dozen men and women. Were they annoyed at being called at such short notice? She wondered. Not that it mattered.

Ingrid motioned for them to join her, and they followed her to the large conference table in front of the window. "Dr. Farmakis. Please, begin."

This was too important to be nervous, so she wiped her clammy palms on her pants and spoke to the air above their heads. No one was going to give her a hard time about maintaining eye contact when she was warning about the potential loss of hundreds of lives and the end of humanity in space for decades to come.

She explained what she had discovered as concisely as she could, then gratefully stepped back as Siavash fielded some of their questions. But then, Ingrid turned back to her.

"But the satellites are programmed to avoid collision. This system has worked for nearly a decade. Why is this different?"

Alex wished she had had time to put together a cleaned-up simulation to present, but she had only her words. She could come back later, with her data, but . . . *no time.*

"Whoever is doing this has been laying the groundwork for a long time, and I believe they are exploiting an inherent weakness in the system," she said, looking firmly out the window at the city below.

"Yes, the satellites avoid collisions, but that's because we so effectively cleaned LEO of space debris. They have a limited number of objects to track, the vast majority of which are other functioning satellites. If you introduce millions, if not billions of pieces of debris to that system..." She trailed off, shivering. Everything she loved about the space above Earth, the beautiful intricacy of thousands of satellites moving in concert, would be destroyed.

"It collapses," Siavash finished. "The number of objects will overload each AI's processing power, not to mention there will be too many things to maneuver around. We have to stop that first domino from falling, or we lose it all. Including the Hub."

A hush fell over the room, and Alex watched Ingrid and the others carefully. Did they believe her?

"Well. Even if there is only a small probability of this doomsday scenario, that is still enough to act. We will discover who is behind this at a later date. The priority now is prevention." Ingrid turned to the head of the Eastern European branch. "I understand there have been some issues concerning XB-20675. Can its decommission be rescheduled?"

He shook his head, and Alex went cold. "I can't guarantee that. They've already lost most control of it, and had to move the date up to get it down safely. They're not likely to agree to a reschedule request."

"Even with what's at stake?" Alex blurted out, then shrank back as every head in the room swiveled her way.

"We believe you, Dr. Farmakis. That does not mean everyone will, and as an international group, sometimes we must tread carefully," Ingrid said calmly.

Alex scowled, but relented as Siavash spoke quietly. "We'll fix this, Alex. There's time."

She took a deep breath. He was right. Ignoring the conversation between the department heads for a moment, she saw that the sun had nearly set and the first stars were visible through the crystal-clear window. She wished the sight calmed her, as it usually did.

No one made mention of the time, and Alex realized with relief that everyone was staying until this was sorted out. As the hours passed, others came and went, Ingrid's enormous office becoming the control center of their efforts to find a solution.

The data came in from two of the satellites in the group that would hit the decommissioned satellite, and Alex had been right—those satellites, and likely all the rest in that group, had disabled onboard AIs. The programmers were scrambling to get them back online for manual course corrections, but with the amount of time they had left, it wasn't promising.

A dozen solutions were being thrown around the room, alongside damage control measures if their efforts didn't prevent the first impact. Alex had never seen the ISSCC so busy, a chaotic scramble of people desperate to prevent a tragedy.

She considered joining one of the brainstorming teams, but she knew she did her best work on her own. She stayed buried in the data for hours, until she yawned so hard it felt like her jaw would unhinge. She clumsily removed her interface and stumbled off to find caffeine. Someone had placed a cart of instacoffee near the door, and she glanced up at the clock as she cracked the heating tab on one.

Nearly six in the morning, she realized with a shock. They had worked through the night, losing all track of time.

Time. Alex stared at the clock, the seconds ticking past. Something nagged at the back of her brain, fuzzy with fatigue. She let the room fade away, eyes on the clock as she quickly sipped her coffee.

It was too hot, and the shock of it burning her tongue jolted the thought forward. Clocks!

She elbowed her way into the knot of programmers working on the first group's AIs.

"Clocks. Change their clocks," she said, and watched as realization slowly dawned on one of the men's faces.

"Oh my God. You're right," he said, quickly sitting down to pull on an interface. One of the women turned questioningly to Alex, who collapsed into another chair.

"The onboard clocks are separate from the AIs. Basic hardware. We can access them, change the time by a few seconds. They'll automatically adjust their course to where they should be at that time. And miss XB-20675."

The stately dance of satellites in orbit, all governed by *time*. She had moved time forward and backward, watching the pattern, predicting the pattern. They were trapped by the amount of time left until the collision. But if they tricked the *satellites* into thinking it was a different time...

The rest of the programmers were urgently talking, and Alex noticed one leave to report to Ingrid. She let their words wash over her as she mechanically finished her coffee, slumped down in her chair. She knew they would all keep working on other solutions, and was glad of it—too much was at stake to let it all hinge on one idea. But this would work.

They would stop the first domino from falling and save the Hub, along with everything else. She looked out the window to watch the sun rise, too overwhelmed with relief to do anything else.

As the preparations that morning had turned to evacuating the Hub, reprogramming satellites to protect them from further hacking, and searching for who was responsible, Alex had staggered home for a few hours sleep.

Back at the office, she joined the crowd crammed into Ingrid's office to monitor the skies as the clock ticked down to zero.

The onboard clocks in the most critical group of satellites had been successfully changed, and their orbits monitored to insure that the change wouldn't lead to any unexpected collisions.

She joined the crowd around Ingrid's conference table, where a 3D projector had been set up to display what was happening far above. XB-20675's orbit had been slowly degrading for years, the defunct reconnaissance satellite moving from the upper ranges of MEO to skimming above LEO.

As they watched, the satellite used the last of its fuel to slow its velocity, right on time. Alex clenched her fists as the room went deadly silent and shifted her attention to the microsats. One by one, their staggered clocks brought them under and around the larger satellite as it began its graceful fall toward Earth. And missed it completely.

Everyone erupted into cheers, laughing and hugging in general pandemonium. Alex smiled but kept watching, eyes still glued to the satellite network. The pattern that had dominated her life for the past month disintegrated, each grouping of satellites spreading apart and rejoining the overall network.

Only once she could no longer spot any traces of the pattern did

Alex truly relax. Siavash found her in the crowd, offering a fist bump in celebration. She grinned and tapped his fist with hers, then looked back at the display.

Someone pulled up XB-20675's charted path; it was on target to crash into the Pacific. The Hub still orbited, its stately wheel spinning. Safe.

"Did they figure out who did it?" she asked, still watching the satellites. Siavash hooked his thumbs in his belt loops, tilting back on his heels.

"Yup," he said, drawing the word out in satisfaction. "Hackers, but we knew that. Anti-AI ones. They apparently thought this would be the best way to protest AIs replacing jobs."

"I don't think we should over-rely on them either, but . . ." Alex trailed off, flabbergasted. They would kill everyone on the Hub and destroy the satellite network, just to take out the satellites' AIs? They were just a *tool*.

But hadn't she herself been frustrated with the AI at the office? She hadn't expected to have anything at all in common with the people who attacked the network, and the connection made her uncomfortable.

"Yeah, I didn't say they were smart. Brilliant hackers, though."

"Do you admire them?" she asked, affronted.

He barked out a laugh. "Not at all. I admire you," he admitted with a grin. "You did a hell of a good job."

She flushed, not looking at him. "Thanks."

"So what now? We still have the network, not to mention the Hub, because of you. Time to celebrate? Go lay on the beach for a month? After what you did, I think we can make pretty much any vacation happen."

She snorted. A vacation did sound nice, just not on the beach. She looked past the projector into the sky outside.

There was the Hub . . .

She should be more afraid of going into space now, not less. But somehow her newfound knowledge of the station's fragility inspired her to go there, not to stay on Earth where it was safe.

It might not always be there, after all. What if she never went? For the first time in her life, that scared her even more than going up did.

"Yes, I think I'll take some time. But not to stay on the ground."

✲ ✲ ✲

Avery Parks is a science fiction writer with stories at *Cossmass Infinities*, *MetaStellar Magazine*, and *Infinite Worlds*, among others. She has also placed in multiple contests, most recently winning second place for the Jim Baen Memorial Short Story Award. She lives in Texas with her family, a variety of pets, and (according to some) too many books.

You can find her online at averyparkswrites.com.

"Sleek, Modern, and Iconic"

✷

How the Space Force Got Its
Out-Of-This-World Uniform

Among many seemingly mundane decisions awaiting the new Space Force was simply how to dress its personnel. But in September 2021 when the decision was announced, public reaction was, shall we say, mixed. A particular focus of attention was the cut of the new service dress coat, the buttoned, slanted closure of which reminded some commentators of the burgundy uniform worn by Captain James T. Kirk in *Star Trek II: The Wrath of Khan*, or the dark blue uniforms worn on the reboot of *Battlestar Galactica*.

So ... did the Space Force steal its uniform from the silver screen? Well ... no. The military is a collection of human beings, each with duties and objectives, tastes and talents, and sure, even literary preferences. But as you might imagine, outfitting a whole new service branch has profound cultural, financial, and practical ramifications. It's not something to be taken lightly, and it's not something some fanboy politico could do on a whim. In this case, it required a collaboration between the Air Force Uniform Office, the U.S. Space Force Office of the Chief of Space Operations, and the Defense Logistics Agency Troop Support Clothing and Textiles—the group in charge of outfitting "every soldier, sailor, airman and Marine around the world, from their first day of service in boot camp, to camouflage uniforms worn on the battlefield, to service dress uniforms."

Some decisions were easier than others. For most everyday purposes, the same camouflaged fatigues worn by the Air Force and Army would suffice. After all, even the new Space Force's two astronauts would spend most of their time on the ground, and even if most earthbound guardians would never need to hide in the woods, it made no economic sense to develop a unique operational uniform for a service branch smaller than most corporations. Nor was it necessary. A military uniform isn't just a piece of clothing, but all the accessories and insignia worn with it. Air Force camouflage ABUs and intra-service OCPs were durable, practical and readily available, and more fit to Space Force service than gas-station coveralls. They fit the bill.

But as the first new U.S. military branch since the Air Force was created in 1947, the Space Force does need to foster its own traditions and culture. One important way of doing that is with a unique service dress uniform for wear in the office, barracks and other nonfield duties, and especially for ceremonial occasions.

In the words of Tracy Roan, Chief of the Air Force Uniform Office responsible for the design, the mandate was to create a service uniform that was "sleek, modern, and iconic." Doing that took a little more than doodling costumes from the movies.

In an interview for this article, Roan and her Pentagon counterpart, Space Force Change Management Team analyst Cathy Lovelady, said that aside from stylistic and cultural considerations, a military uniform must first be manufacturable, affordable to supply to thousands of personnel, comfortable, durable and fit to purpose.

So how did they go about it?

Half the staff of the Uniform Office was assigned to brainstorm, looking for inspiration to historical military and commercial aviation uniforms, drawing from their own interests, and creating anew from their imaginations. One hundred fifty candidate "sleek, modern, iconic" designs were then workshopped with various mixed-rank focus groups. Roan and Lovelady say that because the new branch is so small (originally about nine thousand people transferred from the Air Force) it was practical to incorporate more feedback from service members than in the design of probably any other uniform in history.

A key part of these initial steps was a first-of-its-kind "female first" approach. Why? Because today, twenty percent of Air Force personnel are women, and women are more variable in proportions than men. A military uniform needs to be just that, uniform enough to fit everyone well without unsightly or unserviceable gaps, binding, or anatomically inconvenient pockets or closures. A design that fits the diversity of women will easily fit men too, while the reverse—as the focus groups were quick to point out—is not true. NASA, are your space suit designers listening?

The initial ideas were whittled down to five major options, then after more focus groups and consultations, to the one which, as Roan puts it, "had pretty much been everyone's first or second choice." Prototypes were made, tried out, reviewed, refined, showed off to the press, taken on a roadshow to installations across the country, and refined some more. In response to service personnel feedback, a stripe was added to the retailored pants, the jacket was lengthened, the number of interior buttons was reduced, and pockets were restyled and added, including an accessible inner jacket pocket.

The final design features a midnight blue jacket with a lapel-less collar bearing mirror-silver "U.S." insignia, a closure of six prominent buttons representing the six service branches, and for commissioned officers, platinum sleeve braids. The jacket is worn with a matching midnight blue necktie, a platinum shirt, dark gray pants, and black shoes.

The jacket's asymmetrical cut and closure give it a distinctive style that recalls both the military frock coats of the Napoleonic era and the asymmetrical "swish" associated with rocketry in military emblems as far back as World War II. It makes sense, in context, and if it reminds some of the costumery of Star Trek or Battlestar Galactica, there are two obvious reasons that might be the case. First, most Americans are more familiar with movies than with military history. Second, the twentieth-century peak of mass-production consumerism arguably created something of a stylistic desert from which we are only now emerging. That is to say, these jackets do not resemble each other nearly so much as they stand apart from the mundane cut of the men's suits and uniforms common throughout the latter twentieth century.

Tail fins notwithstanding, the rise of industrial mass production brought with it a shift away from the ornate craftsmanship of some earlier eras toward a modern aesthetic of simple parts stamped out by the million. It gave us Brutalist architecture, injection-molded furniture, tract housing, wall-to-wall carpet, and cheap clothing made on assembly lines rather than by tailors. This is not to say the century was without style or innovation, but in subtle ways and without realizing why, we in the West today have had our tastes strongly influenced by the stripped-down, flat-pack design aesthetic wrought by mass production. That's not a bad thing, it's just part of who we are and when we are living.

But style wasn't always this way, and as advancing technology restores a measure of control and customization back into production without sacrificing all the economies of massive scale, it's becoming less so again. Theatrical costumes, produced in small lots, have always been free from the restraints imposed by the assembly line. Increasingly today, so are the factories that cloth armies, both figuratively and literally.

Furthermore, those who see *Battlestar Galactica* in the new Space Force jacket may not be aware that the same Napoleonic era aesthetic never quite died out. It still survives in the Air Force Cadet uniform, in the uniforms of many marching bands, and in some places, those of valets and other long-standing uniformed civilian occupations. Indeed, its clearly more realistic to say that in this regard, science fiction has long imitated life.

Star Trek is a case in point. For the original series, costumes were created by William Ware Theiss, who'd spent four years in the U.S. Navy and witnessed hydrogen bomb tests at Bikini Atoll before moving to Hollywood. Charged with creating a futuristic military look on a shoestring 1960s TV production budget, he bloused the trousers over the boots to recall the look of naval uniforms of his day, but used synthetic fabrics that were cheap, modern-looking, and easy to keep clean, even if they reminded some of pajamas.

This changed with *Star Trek: The Motion Picture. Star Trek* had appeared in the technicolor sixties, just as color television was becoming widespread, on a network that used a polychromatic peacock's tail as its logo over the catch phrase "and now in living color." Some, including director Robert Wise, thought its color scheme a bit overdone. Theiss being otherwise committed, costume designer Robert Fletcher was brought in with a mandate to tone down the uniforms and let the actors be seen. His design left little but formfitting beltless catsuits, and though the results were arguably more uniform, many found them distractedly bland and unflattering.

Nicholas Meyer, who came aboard to direct *The Wrath of Khan*, gave Fletcher new—and most would argue better—marching orders. Gene Roddenberry had sold the original series as "Wagon Train to the Stars," but Meyer latched on to another cultural prototype—Horatio Hornblower, and the comparison is more than apt.

For those who don't know, the Hornblower books were written in the 1930s and '40s by C.S. Forester, who also wrote *The African Queen* and is regarded as the father of the naval historical novel. Forester got the idea after reading an old copy of the Royal Navy's magazine *Naval Chronicle*, from the early nineteenth century. At that time, long-distance communication was limited to the speed of sail, and it could take months for orders or news of political developments (like the start or end of hostilities) to travel from one end of the British Empire to the other. As a result, sea captains were given extraordinary latitude and so carried extraordinary responsibility, and Forester saw in this fertile ground for spinning a gripping adventure.

So did Gene Roddenberry. It's no coincidence that on *Star Trek*, subspace communication is always out of service, filled with static, or slightly too slow to save the day—it's more dramatic that way. It's also revealing that in the original *Star Trek* pilot (later re-cut into the episode, "The Menagerie") and in early episodes, Spock sometimes shouts from his bridge station as if into an old-style ship's speaking tube, and the captain is seen chatting over drinks with the intercom on so he can worry over every blip of the ship's goings-on. Roddenbery's *Enterprise* is a U-boat in space, her captain as isolated and weighed down by responsibility as Sir George Cockburn in the War of 1812.

Roddenberry, who wrote science fiction to escape the ire of network censorship, emulated the naval adventure stories of his youth—which were inspired by the Hornblower books. Screenwriter David Gerrold, in his 1973 book *The World of Star Trek*, described the series as "Horatio Hornblower in space," and Meyer (who had never seen *Star Trek* before he was asked to direct it) has always described it in exactly those words. It's no surprise then that Fletcher, with Meyer at the helm, was now free to recostume Starfleet in a more recognizably naval mold.

To all three men, Horatio Hornblower could not have failed to recall images of Gregory Peck, who in promotional art for the 1951 film *Captain Horatio Hornblower*, stands *en garde* and saber drawn beside Virginia Mayo, his Napoleonic war–era captain's frock open and disheveled, exposing the white lining inside. Never has a wardrobe choice said more in a glance about a character and his story, and the appeal of the look for what was essentially going to be *Moby Dick* in space could not have been more obvious.

Like the naval uniforms that inspired it (or a modern trench coat, inspired by the same source), Fletcher's new Starfleet uniform featured a double-breasted front that could be fastened on both sides to (perhaps unnecessarily in Starfleet's case) securely seal out the wind, or be left partially open to regulate ventilation, allowing those engaged in daring deeds to both stay cool and look cool at the same time. Of course to "futurize" the design, Fletcher replaced the traditionally large cast metal buttons with hidden hooks more common to girdles, and swept the left breast out at the top, emulating the swoop of the Starfleet insignia and further securing it by a clasp to a modified epaulet.

This is a perfect example of how movie costumes and military uniforms converge and diverge around their similar, but differing requirements. Modern zippered closures only appeared in 1914 and quickly became a central part of the minimalist twentieth-century fashion aesthetic. Buttons therefore became old-fashioned, hidden fasteners "modern." So Captain Kirk got off-the-shelf, mass-produced clasps that were easily sewn into a hidden jacket closure that appeared "futuristic" but retained the flexibility and cut of a nineteenth-century frock coat. The Space Force jacket is a more practical "futuristic" take on the same historic antecedents, only at the scale of production required to outfit the military—long-wearing buttons, easy, practical and deeply recalling military tradition, are cheap to mass produce.

Military uniforms are informed by history for cultural reasons. Costumes borrow from history for authenticity. Sometimes, converging objectives give similar results, like a swooping closure for a jacket associated with rocketry. Sometimes, diverging requirements lead to different solutions—cheap "pajama" synthetics versus comfortable, long-wearing cotton, tiny clasps versus sturdy buttons.

The Space Force didn't steal their uniform from sci-fi, but if it supplied a kernel of inspiration, is that really such a bad thing? The best science fiction is not only entertaining, it's aspirational. *Battlestar Galactica* was about perseverance and hope under threat of extermination. *Star Trek* was about not only defense and projection of power, but the pursuit of peace and discovery for its own sake. Neither is exactly well grounded in reality, yet each in its own way speaks to the very best of humanity. We can only hope that in the conflicts to come, our defenders will aspire to similarly high ideals.

Emergency Supplies

✴

Liam Hogan

It'd take more than a suspect ore carrier for us to call in reinforcements, whatever my instincts were telling me. Nobody wanted the reputation for jumping at shadows. Out past Mars, we were spread so thin that for all intents and purposes we were on our own, and those shadows were vast and cast by a cold, distant sun.

Down in the inner system, the Space Force rule is simple: broadcast your existence, pretty much at all times, or be prepared to be fired upon. The potential risk, if not to the Earth then to the growing number of manned satellite hubs and lunar bases, was too high to have a few rogue megatons of fusion-powered metal aimed down your throat.

Which brought its own problems as the number of craft, from pleasure to industrial to freight, increased over time. The lunar shipyards churned them out as fast as they could shape the raw materials, and as fast as the rarer metals could be extracted by autonomous drones out in the cold, lonely expanse of the asteroid belts.

Way out here, space was mostly empty, and mostly silent. Chatter was limited to daily or even weekly check-ins and to the looped sermons from colonies of religious fanatics, who came all this way to escape the godless hordes and who generally considered the Space Force heathens of the worst (i.e., interfering) kind.

All of it listened to by Ada, our ship AI, who picked over the sparse gossip for hints and rumors, oddities and strange patterns, looking for things to investigate, and who was also ever alert for actual emergencies: Save Our Souls distress calls and May God Have Mercies.

Ada decided a lot of things. Our wide, looping path for one, making the most of what gravitational forces were available. It cut us through the shipping lanes, but also veered us out to the distant edges, where traffic was lighter and things were not always what they seemed.

Like this ancient K-Class, the *Herman Munster*, dimly glinting in the scope as our patrol ship sniffed delicately at her trail. Most ships out this way are old, ours included. The newer, shinier craft get to ply their trade in the busy inner system, but are then, if they survive that long, put out to pasture, spending their twilight years in the belts or even further beyond. The pace out here was slower, all about energy conservation, no one in a particular rush. If the worst should happen . . . well, no great loss. Or so the fat-cat investors back on Earth thought, happy to insure the cargo, but not the ship, or the crew.

"An antique," Rodgers said, eyeing the hulk on the screen.

"A trusty old workhorse," replied Jasmine, who had a soft spot for these stout, elderly ladies.

"A floating scrap pile."

"That has proven its worth, over and over."

"On its last legs. I'll offer odds that even if she's on her return trip, she never makes it home."

Maybe they were both right, based on the engine signatures. But I knew these ships, had grown up on them, the precocious child of a spacer. And though I was the most junior of our trio, it was me that had the feeling about this one, that had us paying close scrutiny, testing the thin vapor that she, and all ships, leave in their wake.

Ada had brought the vessel to our attention, but only that. A ship, a big one, a long way out, though not unheard of. Just pootling along, belly stuffed with ore. There was nothing to suggest illegality, or worse. But Ada trusted human intuition, and so was, on this occasion, happy to listen to what my gut was telling me.

"Let's match paths," Ada announced, having done the astronav calculations. "And give her a friendly holler, to tell her we're on our way."

Which would give them plenty of time to try and hide or even space whatever it was that was playing havoc with my spider sense, but that was better than them thinking we were pirates. It would also give them a chance to alter their course. That didn't bother us much. A K-Class is far from the most nimble of spacecraft. One of the heaviest vessels ever built, except for a few special purpose behemoths. Ponderous. Once we decided to pay it a visit, we'd be like a dog after a bone.

"Ada? How long until rendezvous?"

"Seven hours and twenty minutes."

Albeit a rather slow dog, after a marginally less slow bone. Plenty of time to eat and get some beauty sleep. Make sure we were fully functioning, when we got close enough for that to matter.

The *Herman* didn't do anything to change our ETA, which was almost disappointing. Right on schedule, we were staring at the vast bulk so close we could see the pockmarks. Spend enough time in deep space, and you'd be pockmarked as well. Tiny, and sometimes not so tiny, bits of primordial rubble traveling at frightening speeds, relatively. Sometimes relativistically. Sometimes you heard one go "pock" as you were sleeping, and there was always a giddy moment as you waited to see what alarms it might trigger, and tried to guess how long it would take to get into your survival suit.

"Who wants the EVA?" I asked. Even if, if all went well, there'd be nothing particularly Extravehicular about it. Whoever went would still be suiting up, though. Still be wearing helmets as they went through the narrow umbilical that temporarily joined the two ships. If someone wanted to space one of us, we weren't going to make it easy for them.

"It's your call, Ellie," Jasmine pointed out. Which, given how much she loved seeing these fossils up close and personal, suggested she thought there might be something funky about this one as well. That, or she was just picking up on my vibes. That, or she just wanted me to step up.

"SOP, then," I said, feeling a tingle of excitement and of worry. "By the numbers. You two stay put with Ada. Keep scanning, for all the good it will do, and let me know what you find."

The *Herman*'s solitary crew member met me at the airlock. A stolid, gray, short-haired spacer, wearing dungarees with a Rorschach pattern of oils and scorch marks. She waited as I took off my helmet.

"Space Force First Lieutenant Ellie Rodriguez, of the Patrol Ship *Thelxinoe*," I said, perhaps a little too crisply. "Routine inspection."

"Kait Symons," she said, taking the proffered hand, her skin a patchwork of rough calluses and smooth burn marks. "Of the *Herman Munster*."

I gave her a tight smile. Obviously of the *Herman Munster*, since we were on it. The crew quarters, life support part of it. K-Class freighters were mostly not pressurized. Ore doesn't need it, doesn't really need much in the way of shielding either, since it does that job well enough itself. The crew could range from anything from a lonely one, as now, up to about a dozen or so if you didn't mind fending off other people's feet and elbows. But more usually, out this far, pairs of spacers who bickered like old married couples and spent far more time together than those ever did. With an AI as the third wheel, doing the best to keep the peace.

"Not often you see a K-Class anymore, outside of a museum," I said, pulling out my flimsy. You always look more official, with paperwork.

She grunted. I guessed she wasn't going to make things easy. Or maybe she'd been out here too long, and had forgotten the strange art of conversation.

"Original engines?" I asked.

"No—" She bit off her reply a moment too late.

"Didn't think so. Replaced by Klusky T7s?"

"T5s," she begrudgingly admitted.

"That so?" That much I already knew, Ada had done the pattern matching. "Temperamental?"

"Sure." She shrugged. "But nothing I can't handle."

"And it's just you and the ship AI on board, is it?"

She nodded, but didn't risk saying anything. I liked her. Kait Symons was the sort of fiercely independent loner it took to spend time out on the fringes with nothing but a souped-up chess computer. Able to turn their hands to pretty much anything, because if they didn't, who would? But she was a terrible liar. And it's always suspicious, when a ship's AI doesn't want to talk.

I tapped my comms. "*Thel*? I'm about to inspect the cargo—two hundred tons of assorted rare earths. It's likely to block my signal, so I'm switching comms off. Engage protocol Prodigal Son. One hour."

"Roger that, Ellie. Stay frosty. *Thelxinoe* out."

I eyed the spacer as I unclipped the comms badge, her darting gaze watching my every move. "Do you know what that protocol is, Kait?"

She shook her head—a rabbit, cornered by a fox, but perhaps sensing a bolt hole behind her.

"Basically, if I don't reestablish contact at the end of the hour, then your freighter is to be considered hostile. I don't need to explain what that means, right?"

She frowned, wary as hell.

"Well then." I smiled again, a little more expansively. "Let's go inspect the cargo, shall we? Both of them."

There's not much to say about the ore. The autonomous drones that harvest it take their own sweet time, working away at a decent-sized asteroid for years, picking and choosing and extracting only the rarest, most useful elements. When they have a full hopper, they push it out along with a beacon, and the first ore freighter to pick it up gets the delivery fee. Some never got picked up—the fee wasn't always very generous and depended on the fluctuating values of rare ores. To make any money at all, ore freighters had to compute the most energy efficient paths through the belt, hoping to pass enough full hoppers to make it worth their while. The *Herman* had done well enough, though by Ada's records, it had taken her the best part of three long years to fill her cavernous bays.

The other cargo, though . . . The one in the spaces left behind when a bulky Tolmach fusion engine is ripped out and replaced by twin Klusky Fives. Still lined by the same thick panels the leaky old drives needed, radiation and everything proof, impenetrable to external scans. Not exactly spacious, but roomy enough.

I'd half expected to find a dead hopper, the dual-purpose beacon and ID fried or just utterly drained, something half-forgotten whose contents could be sold on the black market, no questions asked. Or contraband—each space station and colony had its own rules on what was and what wasn't allowed, from soft narcotics like alcohol, to any of a thousand blasphemous tracts at one of the religious settlements out toward the frozen edges, be it in infidel book form or heathen digital format.

I hadn't expected a dozen pairs of eyes, staring wordlessly up at me. Small eyes. Young eyes. Fearful eyes.

Kait was still at my shoulder, breathing heavily. I was horribly aware that she was about twice my size. She hadn't helped as I'd opened up the bay, had only muttered curses that I knew these old birds so damned well. But she hadn't offered active resistance, either, and in my eagerness to root out the smuggler's secrets I'd found myself ignoring her. A potentially dangerous and possibly fatal mistake. For both of us.

"Orphans," she muttered, in weary explanation, opening her meaty scarred hands to show they were still empty. "Destined probably for Triton, though they would never have got there. Not in a leaky shuttle with no crew and not even a functioning AI; whoever set the course must have turned back well before the belts. And whatever signal was supposed to be guiding them has long since stopped. Pure chance I stumbled across them."

"Triton? D'hell!"

Even as I said it, the pieces clicked into place. There were a dozen rarely heard from religious cults set up around frigid Neptune, out on the very edges of the solar system and way beyond our regular patrols. Whenever anyone did make the effort to go check on them, they were met either by extreme hostility, sometimes backed up by aging ordnance, or dead silence. It was an unforgiving place to set up camp, and the cults had a life expectancy not much beyond a dozen years.

The surprise was that any of them lasted even that long. Fervor alone did not make for well-prepared colonists, and they were always too few in number to be viable that far from the warmth of the sun. It's hard to recruit followers when you're a billion miles from anyone and anything. Rumors persisted on how they managed it. Rumors now backed up by a dozen pairs of frightened eyes.

Sometimes, so those rumors went, a cult would put the call out. Splash what remained of their founder's cash to get a shipment of those who wouldn't be missed. That their recruits most likely had no choice in the matter, that they might be treated abominably, both on route and on arrival, that a failing religious settlement at the ass end of the solar system was no place for a young kid, for anyone, really, didn't matter—to the cult leaders.

But while rescuing them was a noble act, Kait had saddled herself, and me, with a thorny problem. Someone might still claim they were theirs, if word got out. And even if the original cult members had collectively gone to meet their maker without even waiting for the new disciples to arrive, any and all of the other Neptunian cults would battle for possession of such a valuable, innocent, blessed cargo.

Space is an expensive business. No one would be willing to pay the exorbitant costs to return these orphans all the way back to Earth or the Moon, and no one would want them when they got there. Just another problem to be shuttled back and forth, until, yet again, some cult with cash came a-calling.

Despite our status as the upholders of law out here, there wasn't much the Space Force could do about it. The standard approach in all matters was to ensure safety, and let the lawyers battle over ownership. But once they were in the grasp of a Neptunian cult, all the civil rights lawyers could do was to send strongly worded messages into the inky void.

Which explained why the *Herman* wasn't singing to the cosmos about what she had found. But not what her plan was.

"Where are you taking them?" I asked, as pale, delicate fingers emerged from the dark to tug at my belt, my hands, trying to give me something.

"It's a stretch," she admitted with a deep sigh. "But there's always the freighter academy."

Definitely a stretch. The ore the *Herman* was carrying would barely pay for the fuel that particular trip into the inner system would cost. Most outer ore freighters only went as far as Mars, where the bulk of the ore was off-loaded and/or further refined, and smaller craft transported the more valuable stuff on to Earth and the Moon. Kait was sacrificing three years of lonely, hard work, for nothing.

Almost nothing. I looked the orphans over once more, and their snug hidey-hole. There was a crate of food and water in there. Supplies were expensive this far out, and I wondered whether Kait had been depriving herself to eke them out for her unexpected charges.

I glanced down at the small hand that kept pushing at mine, at the thing it—she—was trying to give me. An odd, amorphous lump.

Memoputty. This was one of the older ones, the sort that got discarded in the inner belt, the sort of thing a Spacer played with during the long, lonely hours. But for anyone new to them, they were still a wonder. Muscle memory took over and I twisted and pulled it into the shape of a long-eared bunny rabbit, and handed it back. A shy grin was my reward, before the kid was swallowed by her companions, soft excited whispers shared between them.

"So what are you going to do, Lieutenant?" Kait asked, half defiant, half resigned.

"Do?" I echoed, clipping my comms badge back on, the flash of light as I did saying it was active again. "*Thelxinoe*, this is Ellie. The *Herman* is running low on consumables. I've cited the captain, Kait Symons, for having insufficient reserves, and am requisitioning four crates of Space Force emergency supplies. Have them ready for transfer."

There was relief in her eyes, and I could tell she almost wanted to hug me. All I'd done was give away something that wasn't mine. Heck, the bean counters over at Space Force HQ would probably try to bill the *Herman* for them. Or more likely whichever shipping company owned the ancient tug, because Kait was going to end up with empty pockets at the end of all of this.

But neither of us said anything about that, now the comms badge was back in place, Ada listening and recording every word. "Go safely, Kait Symons," I said, in way of a farewell.

"Another hungry freight driver, hey?" Rodgers said with a grin, as I clambered through the patrol ship's airlock, and Jasmine helped me out of my suit.

I didn't say what I'd found. I couldn't, there was no privacy aboard the *Thelxinoe*. We'd taught Ada a number of things over the length of our current tour, including how to swear in Swahili, though she'd rapidly outgrown us in her inventiveness. But this . . . we couldn't teach this. That turning a blind eye was sometimes better than sticking to the rule book.

Rodgers, who had been an officer much longer than I, and even Jasmine, only a half-dozen years my senior, didn't push for details. A conspiracy of silence. Which made me wonder if they too had ever inspected a freighter and found the same surprising hidden cargo. Those rumors, they had to start somewhere.

I did a little light digging, after. Ada, and our base quartermaster, didn't seem to balk at the extra supplies I had to order, to make sure we were properly provisioned for any and all emergencies. Each crate was signed off without comment.

And freighter academy always seemed to have a ready crop of young recruits, for what most considered the least glamorous of nonterrestrial professions. Not a bad place to grow up, if you were an orphan. Not that they all became Spacers, of course. Not everyone takes to the lonely reaches of space. Some of them get recruited into the inner system, as shuttle pilots or lunar engineers. Some even join the Space Force.

So now I had to include Ada, as well as the *Herman Munster's* taciturn AI, in that silent conspiracy. In space, no one can hear you do the right thing.

✸   ✸   ✸

Liam Hogan is an award-winning short story writer, with stories in *Best of British Science Fiction* and in *Best of British Fantasy* (NewCon Press). He's been published by *Analog, Daily Science Fiction*, and Flame Tree Press, among others. He helps host Liars' League London, volunteers at the creative writing charity Ministry of Stories, and lives and avoids work in London. More at happyendingnotguaranteed.blogspot.co.uk.

About "The Return of William Proxmire"

From the 1960s through the 1980s, Democratic Senator William Proxmire was famous for outspoken fiscal conservatism, exemplified by his annual "Golden Fleece Award" for government officials guilty in his eyes of squandering public money. While government pork is an unquestionable blight, one could argue that some of Proxmire's crusades—like many arguments against public investment today—rested more on naïveté than reason. We do, after all, need the government to invest handsomely on important things private industry can't or won't, and there is always balance to be found, nuance and unintended consequence to be considered, all without the benefit of a crystal ball.

Proxmire was not one for nuance, and he was no fan of space exploration either, once declaring (as chairman of the Senate subcommittee responsible for NASA appropriations, no less), "I say not a penny for this nutty fantasy." That attracted ire from those with ties both to science fiction and government, those like Jerry Pournelle, for example, and Larry Niven, who penned this response in 1988 for What Might Have Been? Volume 1: Alternate Empires, *edited by Greg Benford.*

The story has its detractors, but it's as pleasant a romp as they come, and a natural fit for a collection of stories about space and government and politics, and it provides an entertaining reminder—in the way that almost only science fiction can do—to be careful what you wish for.

✿　　✿　　✿

The Return of William Proxmire

�֎

Larry Niven

Through the peephole in Andrew's front door the man made a startling sight.

He looked to be in his eighties. He was breathing hard and streaming sweat. He seemed slightly more real than most men: photogenic as hell, tall and lean, with stringy muscles and no pot belly, running shoes and a day pack and a blue windbreaker, and an open smile. The face was familiar, but from where?

Andrew opened the front door but left the screen door locked. "Hello?"

"Dr. Andrew Minsky?"

"Yes." Memory clicked. "William Proxmire, big as life."

The ex-senator smiled acknowledgment. "I've only just finished reading about you in the *Tribune*, Dr. Minsky. May I come in?"

It had never been Andrew Minsky's ambition to invite William Proxmire into his home. Still . . . "Sure. Come in, sit down, have some coffee. Or do your stretches." Andrew was a runner himself when he could find the time.

"Thank you."

Andrew left him on the rug with one knee pulled against his chest. From the kitchen he called, "I never in my life expected to meet you face to face. You must have seen the article on me and Tipler and Penrose?"

"Yes. I'm prepared to learn that the media got it all wrong."

"I bet you are. Any politician would. Well, the *Tribune* implied

323

that what we've got is a time machine. Of course we don't. We've got a schematic based on a theory. Then again, it's the new improved version. It doesn't involve an infinitely long cylinder that you'd have to make out of neutronium—"

"Good. What would it cost?"

Andrew Minsky sighed. Had the politician even recognized the reference? He said, "Oh . . . hard to say." He picked up two cups and the coffee pot and went back in. "Is that it? You came looking for a time machine?"

The old man was sitting on the yellow rug with his legs spread wide apart and his fingers grasping his right foot. He released, folded his legs heel to heel, touched forehead to toes, held, then stood up with a sound like popcorn popping. He said, "Close enough. How much would it cost?"

"Depends on what you're after. If you—"

"I can't get you a grant if you can't name a figure."

Andrew set his cup down very carefully. He said, "No, of course not."

"I'm retired now, but people still owe me favors. I want a ride. One trip. What would it cost?"

Andrew hadn't had enough coffee yet. He didn't feel fully awake. "I have to think out loud a little. Okay? Mass isn't a problem. You can go as far back as you like if . . . mmm. Let's say under sixty years. Cost might be twelve, thirteen million if you could also get us access to the proton-antiproton accelerator at Washburn University, or maybe CERN in Switzerland. Otherwise we'd have to build that too. By the way, you're not expecting to get younger, are you?"

"I hadn't thought about it."

"Good. The theory depends on maneuverings between event points. You don't ever go backward. Where and when, Senator?"

William Proxmire leaned forward with his hands clasped. "Picture this. A Navy officer walks the deck of a ship, coughing, late at night in the 1930s. Suddenly an arm snakes around his neck, a needle plunges into his buttocks—"

"The deck of a ship at sea?"

Proxmire nodded, grinning.

"You're just having fun, aren't you? Something to do while jogging, now that you've retired."

"Put it this way," Proxmire said. "I read the article. It linked up with an old daydream of mine. I looked up your address. You were within easy running distance. I hope you don't mind?"

Oddly enough, Andrew found he didn't. Anything that happened before his morning coffee was recreation.

So dream a little. "Deck of a moving ship. I was going to say it's ridiculous, but it isn't. We'll have to deal with much higher velocities. Any point on the Earth's surface is spinning at up to half a mile per second and circling the sun at eighteen miles per. In principle I think we could solve all of it with one stroke. We could scan one patch of deck, say, over a period of a few seconds, then integrate the record into the program. Same coming home."

"You can do it?"

"Well, if we can't solve that one we can't do anything else either. You'd be on a tight schedule, though. Senator, what's the purpose of the visit?"

"Have you ever had daydreams about a time machine and a scope-sighted rifle?"

Andrew's eyebrows went up. "Sure, what little boy hasn't? Hitler, I suppose? For me it was always Lyndon Johnson. Senator, I do not commit murder under any circumstances."

"A time machine and a scope-sighted rifle, and me," William Proxmire said dreamily. "I get more anonymous letters than you'd believe, even now. They tell me that every space advocate day—dreams about me and a time machine and a scope-sighted rifle. Well, I started daydreaming too, but my fantasy involves a time machine and a hypodermic full of antibiotics."

Andrew laughed. "You're plotting to do someone good behind his back?"

"Right."

"Who?"

"Robert Anson Heinlein."

All laughter dropped away. "Why?"

"It's a good deed, isn't it?"

"Sure. Why?"

"You know the name? Over the past forty years or so I've talked to a great many people in science and in the space program. I kept hearing the name Robert Heinlein. They were seduced into science because they read Heinlein at age twelve. These were the people I found hard to deal with. No grasp of reality. Fanatics."

Andrew suspected that the senator had met more of these than he realized. Heinlein spun off ideas at a terrific rate. Other writers picked them up . . . along with a distrust for arrogance combined with stupidity or ignorance, particularly in politicians.

"Well, Heinlein's literary career began after he left the Navy because of lung disease."

"You're trying to destroy the space program."

"Will you help?"

Andrew was about to tell him to go to Hell. He didn't. "I'm still talking. Why do you want to destroy the space program?"

"I didn't, at first. I was opposed to waste," Proxmire said. "My colleagues, they'll spend money on any pet project, as if there was a money tree out there somewhere—"

"Milk price supports," Andrew said gently. For several decades now, the great state of Wisconsin had taken tax money from the other states so that the price they paid for milk would stay *up*.

Proxmire's lips twitched. "Without milk price supports, there would be places where families with children can't buy milk."

"Why?"

The old man shook his head hard. "I've just remembered that I don't have to answer that question anymore. My point is that the government has spent far more taking rocks from the Moon and photographs from Saturn. Our economy would be far healthier if that money had been spent elsewhere."

"I'd rather shoot Lyndon. Eliminate welfare. Save a *lot* more money that way."

"A minute ago you were opposed to murder."

The old man did have a way with words. "Point taken. Could you get us funding? It'd be a guaranteed Nobel Prize. I like the fact that you don't need a scope-sighted rifle. A hypo full of sulfa drugs doesn't have to be kept secret. What antibiotic?"

"I don't know what cures consumption. I don't know which year or what ship. I've got people to look those things up, if I decide I want to know. I came straight here as soon as I read the morning paper. Why not? I run every day, any direction I like. But I haven't heard you say it's impossible, Andrew, and I haven't heard you say you won't do it."

"More coffee?"

"Yes, thank you."

Proxmire left him alone in the kitchen, and for that Andrew was grateful. He'd have made no progress at all if he'd had to guard his expression. There was simply too much to think about.

He preferred not to consider the honors. Assume he had changed the past; how would he prove it before a board of his peers? "How would I prove it *now*? What would I have to show them?" he muttered under his breath, while the coffee water was heating. "Books? Books that didn't get written? Newspapers? There are places that'll print any newspaper headline I ask for. 'Waffen SS to Build Work Camp in Death Valley.' I can mint Robert Kennedy half-dollars for a lot less than thirteen million bucks. Hmm..." But the Nobel Prize wasn't the point.

Keeping Robert Heinlein alive a few years longer: was *that* the point? It shouldn't be. Heinlein wouldn't have thought so.

Would the science fiction field really have collapsed without "The Menace from Earth"? Tradition within the science fiction field would have named Campbell, not Heinlein. But think: was it magazines that had sucked Andrew Minsky into taking advanced physics classes? Or... *Double Star, Red Planet*, Anderson's *Tau Zero*, Vance's *Tschai* series. Then the newsstand magazines, then the subscriptions, then (of course) he'd dropped it all to pursue a career. If Proxmire's staff investigated his past (as they must, if he was at all serious), they would find that Andrew Minsky, Ph.D., hadn't read a science fiction magazine in fifteen years.

Proxmire's voice came from the other room. "Of course it would be a major chunk of funding. But wouldn't my old friends be surprised to find me backing a scientific project! How's the coffee coming?"

"Done." Andrew carried the pot in. "I'll do it," he said. "That is, I and my associates will build a time machine. We'll need funding and we'll need active assistance using the Washburn accelerator. We should be ready for a man-rated experiment in three years, I'd think. We won't fail."

He sat. He looked Proxmire in the eye. "Let's keep thinking, though. A Navy officer walks the tilting deck of what would now be an antique Navy ship. An arm circles his throat. He grips the skinny wrist and elbow, bends the wrist downward and throws the intruder into the sea. They train Navy men to fight, you know, and he was young and you are old."

"I keep in shape," Proxmire said coldly. "A medical man who performs autopsies once told me about men and women like me. We run two to five miles a day. We die in our eighties and nineties and hundreds. A fall kills us, or a car accident. Cut into us and you find veins and arteries you could run a toy train through."

He was serious. "I was afraid you were thinking of taking along a blackjack or a tranq gun or a Kalashnikov—"

"No."

"I'll say it anyway. Don't hurt him."

Proxmire smiled. "That would be missing the point."

And if that part worked out, Andrew would take his chances with the rest.

He had been reaching for a beer while he thought about revising the time machine paper he'd done with Tipler and Penrose four years ago. Somewhere he'd shifted over into daydreams, and that had sent him off on a weird track indeed.

It was like double vision in his head. The time machine (never built) had put William Proxmire (the ex-senator!) on the moving deck of the USS *Roper* on a gray midmorning in December 1933. Andrew never daydreamed this vividly. He slapped his flat belly, and wondered why, and remembered: he was ten pounds heavier in the daydream, because he'd been too busy to run.

So much detail! Maybe he was remembering a sweaty razor-sharp nightmare from last night, the kind in which you know you're doing something bizarrely stupid, but you can't figure out how to stop.

He'd reached for a Henry Weinhard's (Budweiser) from the refrigerator in his kitchen (in the office at Washburn, where the Weinhard's always ran out first) while the project team watched their monitors (while the KCET funding drive whined in his living room). In his head there was double vision, double memories, double sensations. The world of quantum physics was blurred in spots. But this was his kitchen and he could hear KCET begging for money a room away.

Andrew walked into his living room and found William Proxmire dripping on his yellow rug.

No, wait. That's the other—

The photogenic old man tossed the spray hypo on Andrew's couch. He stripped off his hooded raincoat, inverted it and dropped it on top. He was trying to smile, but the fear showed through. "Andrew? What am I doing *here*?"

Andrew said, "My head feels like two flavors of cotton. Give me a moment. I'm trying to remember two histories at once."

"I should have had more time. And then it should have been the Washburn accelerator! You said!"

"Yeah, well, I did and I didn't. Welcome to the wonderful world of Schrödinger's Cat. How did it go? You found a young lieutenant junior grade gunnery officer alone on deck—" The raincoat was soaking his cushions. "In the rain—"

"Losing his breakfast overside in the rain. Pulmonary tuberculosis, consumption. Good riddance to an ugly disease."

"You wrestled him to the deck—"

"Heh heh heh. No. I told him I was from the future. I showed him a spray hypo. He'd never seen one. I was dressed as a civilian on a Navy ship. That got his attention. I told him if he was Robert Heinlein I had a cure for his cough."

"Cure for his cough?"

"I didn't say it would kill him otherwise. I didn't say it wouldn't, and he didn't ask, but he may have assumed I wouldn't have come for anything trivial. I knew his name. This was Heinlein, not some Wisconsin dairy farmer. He *wanted* to believe I was a time traveler. He *did* believe. I gave him his shot. Andrew, I feel cheated."

"Me too. Get used to it." But it was Andrew who was beginning to smile.

The older man hardly heard; his ears must be still ringing with that long-dead storm. "You know, I would have liked to talk to him. I was supposed to have twenty-two minutes more. I gave him his shot and the whole scene popped like a soap bubble. *Why* did I come back *here*?"

"Because we never got funding for research into time travel."

"Ah . . . hah. There *have* been changes. What changes?"

It wasn't just remembering; it was a matter of selecting pairs of memories that were mutually exclusive, then judging between them. It was maddening . . . but it could be done. Andrew said, "The Washburn accelerator goes with the time machine goes with the funding. My apartment goes with no time machine goes with no funding goes with . . . Bill, let's go outside. It should be dark by now."

Proxmire didn't ask why. He looked badly worried.

The sun had set, but the sky wasn't exactly black. In a line across a smaller, dimmer full moon, four rectangles blazed like windows into the sun. Andrew sighed with relief. Collapse of the wave function: *this* was reality.

William Proxmire said, "Don't make me guess."

"Solar power satellites. Looking Glass Three through Six."

"What happened to your time machine?"

"Apollo Eleven landed on the Moon on July 20, 1969, just like clockwork. Apollo Thirteen left a month or two early, but something still exploded in the service module, so I guess it wasn't a meteor. They . . . shit."

"Eh?"

"They didn't get back. They died. We murdered them."

"Then?"

Could he put it back? Should he put it back? It was still coming together in his head. "Let's see, NASA tried to cancel Apollo Eighteen, but there was a hell of a write-in campaign—"

"Why? From whom?"

"The spec-fic community went absolutely apeshit. Okay, Bill, I've got it now."

"Well?"

"You were right, the whole science fiction magazine business just faded out in the Fifties, last remnants of the pulp era. Campbell alone couldn't save it. Then in the Sixties the literary crowd rediscovered the idea. There must have been an empty ecological niche and the lit-crits moved in.

"Speculative fiction, spec-fic, the literature of the possible. *The New Yorker* ran spec-fic short stories and critical reviews of novels. They thought *Planet of the Apes* was wonderful, and *Selig's Complaint*, which was Robert Silverberg's study of a telepath. Tom Wolfe started appearing in *Esquire* with his bizarre alien cultures. I can't remember an issue of *The Saturday Evening Post* that didn't have *some* spec-fic in it. Anderson, Vance, MacDonald . . . John D. MacDonald turns out novels set on a ring the size of Earth's orbit.

"The new writers were good enough that some of the early ones couldn't keep up, but a few did it by talking to hard science teachers. Benford and Forward did it in reverse. Jim Benford's a plasma physicist but he writes like he swallowed a college English teacher. Robert Forward wrote a novel called *Neutron Star*, but he built the Forward Mass Detector too."

"Wonderful."

"There's a lot of spec-fic fans in the military. When Apollo Twenty-One burned up during reentry, they raised so much hell that Congress took the manned space program away from NASA and gave it to the Navy."

William Proxmire glared and Andrew Minsky grinned. "Now, you left office in the sixties because of the Cheese Boycott. When you tried to chop the funding for the Shuttle, the spec-fic community took offense. They stopped eating Wisconsin cheese. The San Francisco *Locus* called you the Cheese Man. Most of your supporters must have eaten nothing but their own cheese for about eight months, and then Goldwater chopped the milk price supports. 'Golden Fleece,' he called it. So you were out, and now there's no time machine."

"We could build one," Proxmire said.

Rescue Apollo Thirteen? The possibility had to be considered . . . Andrew remembered the twenty years that followed the Apollo flights. In one set of memories, lost goals, pointlessness and depression, political faddishness leading nowhere. In the other, half a dozen space stations, government and military and civilian; Moonbase and Moonbase Polar; *Life* magazine photographs of the Mars Project half-finished on the lunar plain, sitting on a hemispherical Orion-style shield made from lunar aluminum and fused lunar dust.

I do not commit murder under any circumstances.

"I don't think so, Bill. We don't have the political support. We don't have the incentive. Where would a Nobel Prize *come* from? We can't prove there was ever a time line different from this one. Besides, this isn't just a more interesting world, it's safer too. Admiral Heinlein doesn't let the Soviets build spacecraft."

Proxmire stopped breathing for an instant. Then, "I suppose he wouldn't."

"Nope. He's taking six of their people on the Mars expedition, though. They paid their share of the cost in fusion bombs for propulsion."

☼   ☼   ☼

Born on April 30, 1938, **Larry Niven** is a renowned American science fiction writer with a career spanning decades. Niven is widely acclaimed for his imaginative and thought-provoking works, characterized by their scientific rigor and inventive concepts. He is best known for his Known Space series, which introduced readers to the captivating Ringworld and explored complex themes such as interstellar travel, alien civilizations, and the implications of advanced technology. Niven's storytelling prowess, attention to detail, and ability to blend hard science with compelling narratives have made him a beloved figure in the science fiction community.

The Lurker

✩

Gregory Benford & James Benford

August 12, 2049, 8:33AM

"What the hell is that?" Sabine says.

Her husband, Dilip, frowns at the big screen. They're approaching the quasi-satellite officially known as 2016 HO3. It's a small asteroidal body, a rubble pile most likely, that was only discovered in 2016. It's named Kamoʻoalewa, a Hawaiian word that refers to an oscillating object. The earthlike orbit and lunar-like silicates might be explained as lunar ejecta, a piece of the Moon broken off by some past collision.

Kamoʻoalewa is very small, a fast rotator, about a hundred meters in diameter. It falls into the category of quasi-satellites of Earth. It's the smallest, closest, and most stable known quasi-satellite, which is an object in a 1:1 orbital resonance with a planet, so that the object always stays close to the planet. Outside the Hill sphere, that region where an astronomical body dominates the attraction of satellites, which for Earth is 1.5 million kilometers. So quasi-satellites cannot be considered true satellites. Instead, while their period around the Sun is the same as the planet, they seem to travel in an oblong retrograde loop around it. Kamoʻoalewa roves in an odd looping orbit, varying its distance between thirty-eight to a hundred times as far from Earth as the Moon.

Sabine is using advanced multispectral telescope imagery at a range of five kilometers.

Dilip says, "Looks circular, but with odd white spokes extended radially."

Sabine peers at the shifting view and says, "Not a crater, though. Too regular. The spokes are at ... lessee ... sixty degree spacing."

Dilip comes to sit beside her. "So ..."

"Artificial. Not natural, not human ..."

"Didn't the Chinese send Tianwen 2, a collector probe, out here back in—what?—the 2020s?"

"Launched in '26. They couldn't get it to match with the fast rotation, every half hour. So they just tried a landing on it anyway, even though it's rotating. Never heard from again."

"This thing though—" Sabine pauses, making the perspective calculation on her board. "It's big. Ten meters across, easy."

Dilip frowns. "That old Chinese craft was plenty less than that."

"So this is ..."

"Not theirs. And not ours at all. This answers two big questions. Clearly there is life and civilization elsewhere! It can't have come from the solar system."

"Look at how the shadows of that edge move, as the rotation brings it into view. The circle is higher than the dusty regolith around it. Yep, not a crater. Or a rebound from an earlier impact, or ..."

"But the same pale dusty color as the regolith around it. So camouflaged, maybe?"

Sabine nods. "Hidden from any ordinary spectrum search, can't see it by just looking at its reflected sunlight. So this thing is impossible to see from Earth. It's well hidden, but can see Earth closer than anything except the Moon."

Their craft is named *Dyson* after the great twentieth-century scientist. The onboard nuclear drive, lodged below a cluster of thick cylindrical propellant tanks, gets managed by the robotic crew. "Above," relative to forward acceleration, is the tech-deck where the other crew works to keep the nuke and everything else running right, plus usual maintenance work. The big craft needs as much attention as a newborn baby.

Dyson is a nuclear thermal rocket. Fact is, chemical rockets are just not good enough. Sure, chemical rockets took us to the Moon the first time, but to do that, most of what was launched from Earth was fuel and the tanks to hold the fuel. What we needed was the spaceship equivalent of a pickup truck: a simple, rugged, and basic transportation system capable of hauling the astronauts and a big load of cargo for the Space Force to police cislunar space. And that pickup truck is the nuclear thermal rocket.

A nuclear thermal rocket is fundamentally extremely simple. A nuclear reactor produces heat. If you pass a gas over that heated reactor core, the gas heats up—and you can expand heated gas out a nozzle to produce thrust.

So a nuclear thermal rocket is actually far simpler than the nuclear generators used to produce electrical power on the Earth; most of the parts needed to generate electricity aren't needed. A nuclear thermal rocket consists of a tank, a pump, a nuclear reactor, and a nozzle. That's all.

In fact, space is the ideal place for nuclear power: between the trapped high-energy particles of the Van Allen belts, cosmic rays, and solar flares, space already is basically radioactive. You wouldn't want to crash a nuclear thermal rocket on Earth, so there are operating regulations that don't allow nuclear rockets in orbits that would decay in any time shorter than a hundred thousand years. Their natural home is in space.

Back in the 1960s, NASA had a program called NERVA (Nuclear Energy for Rocket Vehicle Applications) to develop nuclear rockets. The Russians also had their own development project. But these were mothballed. Nixon decided not to follow the Apollo missions to the Moon with a program to send humans to Mars, so the NERVA program was canceled for lack of an application—but not before over twenty different nuclear rockets were designed, developed, and tested. They just never were used in an actual flight.

Then in the 2020s nuclear rockets came back with the DRACO program. Nuclear rockets are so effective because the energy in nuclear bonds is so much greater than that in chemical bonds. For any thermal rocket, nuclear, or otherwise, the exhaust velocity is proportional to the square root of the temperature. So for more thrust per pound of fuel, you must have higher temperature exhaust. How hot can you go? *Dyson* uses the particle bed method and operates at 5,000 degrees Celsius, a temperature way above what chemicals burn at.

In a nuclear rocket, the energy source and the reaction mass are separate, so in principle, you can use almost anything for reaction mass: heat it to a plasma, and let it expand out back. Hydrogen can be found anywhere a spaceship might want to go in the form of water ice, so it makes an attractive propellant. You can use electrolysis to split out the hydrogen for reaction mass and save the oxygen for the crew to breathe, or if you want higher thrust but can afford lower performance, you can use the water directly. Water's a lot easier to store, and you need big, tight tanks to hold hydrogen, and you have to keep it cold, about twenty degrees above absolute zero.

Dyson is fueled using water harvested from the Moon. That makes the hardware simpler and more robust and helps provide the thrust sometimes needed on Space Force duty. But water isn't as good at blocking neutron radiation. So the reactor engine is at the back, below the tanks, which in turn are separated from the crew compartment to provide the best possible crew protection from stray reactor-generated radiation.

August 12, 2049, 9 PM

They coast closer to Kamoʻoalewa. Space Force Huntsville, still puzzled by their detection, has observed a Chinese nuclear craft of unknown design headed toward their vicinity. It had appeared visibly on Huntsville's system as it lifted off from the lunar south pole.

Dyson manages thrust and maneuvers, now slowly gliding toward the asteroid.

Huntsville's flat voice comes on. "We've determined that the Chinese ship vectoring toward you is a new design, a nuke drive with surprisingly high acceleration. We think it may be a stripped-down freight carrier module, with a personnel compartment riding on the main thrust axis."

Dilip says to Huntsville, "Sounds odd. What ETA?"

"Soon, a day or two. Depends on their approach strategy. Maybe a Chinese stealthsat intercepted your report," Huntsville said after the usual several-second delay.

"Look at this closeup spectral scan," Sabine says as she gracefully walks across their control deck in the light-g tug. They keep it at a fifth g to lessen the zero-g body effects.

She had snapped the spectral lines at high rez. Huntsville runs those through their team and in a few minutes says, "The Chinese ship is running an augmented fuel, maybe pure hydrogen. No oxygen lines we can see."

"So they're lugging all the mass needed to keep liquid hydrogen from leaking. Not using water like us. They're coming out at us pretty damn quick too," Dilip says. "Must be a nuke with high specific thrust."

"Let's do a flyby of Kamo'oalewa now," Sabine says.

August 13, 2049, 10 AM

Kamo'oalewa swims on their big screen as a gray rock pile. They stand off at one hundred meters and watch it spin. Spectra show that it's mostly metals with some ceramics. It spins so fast because of the YORP effect, due to the scattering of solar radiation off its surface and the later emission of its own thermal radiation as it rotates away from the Sun.

Sabine points to their big deck screen, set to max magnification. "See? Those shifting networks in the surface."

Dilip frowns. "So? It has a pattern on it?"

"A pattern that's changing. Look at this, from just eight minutes ago." Huntsville already has the patterns, sent live. The flat voice says, "This is active matter. Not passive. Crystals altering, self-organizing into a new pattern. We'll get the AI doing pattern recognition."

"How did it look before?" Dilip asks.

"Static. It's reacting to us. Or to the Chinese approaching. Maybe it reacted to that Chinese mission way back in the 2020s, and that's why they lost comm with it. Where did this thing come from? Interstellar?"

Dilip squints at the display. "And how did it get here? I see no propulsion. It looks like a big disk. I'll ask Earthside . . ." He thumbs on the mic and says, "Operations, need back info. Ask Oracle, when did a star last pass near ours?" He's calling on the Cislunar Highway Patrol System, which had seemed to produce negative feelings and so had been renamed "Oracle," without any irony.

After some delay, the reply is "Our most recent stellar visitor was . . . let's see . . . Scholz's Star. This infograb says it's 'two dwarf red stars orbiting each other, slinging by us.' It came within 0.82 light-years from the Sun about 70,000 years ago, at about 82 kilometers a sec. Pretty fast. In their work on minor objects with long orbital periods and extreme orbital eccentricity, researchers find a significant overdensity of objects toward the constellation of Gemini that may be the result of the passage of this star. Studies of the paths of comets with exaggerated, hyperbolic orbits found that a subset appear to have trajectories that were perturbed by Scholz's Star. It passed through the Oort cloud. So we'll get comets falling into the inner solar system in about two million years. Scholz's Star is a binary; primary is a red dwarf about 86 Jupiter masses. The secondary is a brown dwarf with 65 Jupiter masses. The system has a mass total of 0.15 of the Sun's mass. The pair orbit closely at a distance of about 0.8 astronomical units (120 million kilometers, 74 million miles) with a period of roughly four years. The system is estimated to be between three and ten billion years old. It's speeding away; about eighty star systems are known to be closer to the Sun now."

Sabine is skeptical. "Why send a probe here?"

Dilip replies, "The time over which our biosphere has been observable from great distances, perhaps thousands of light-years, due to oxygen in the atmosphere, is a very long time, billions of years. The first oxidation event occurred about 2.5 billion years ago! An ET civilization anywhere nearby can see there's an ecosystem here, due to the out-of-equilibrium atmosphere. They could send interstellar probes to investigate.

"Sabine, do some trig, and—say the probe moved at a thousand kilometers a sec..."

"That's damn fast for a ship."

"But not for our beam-driven sails."

"Those are light structures for fast interplanetary supply in emergencies. And for interstellar flybys. We're talkin' interstellar here..." Her fingers dance on her arm *familiar*, which winks to show it's on the computations, based on what it's heard, without her further instruction. "Scholz's Star would be within a light-year of us for maybe a year, depending on its angle of approach... So could launch a few probes toward us. It would take about three centuries for them to get close enough for optical and radio observations, but still far enough away not to be easily detected."

"You're assuming this society around Scholz's Star is interested in info coming back to them, centuries later. So their institutions must last that long. So their probe—that thing holding onto this co-orbital rock, because it stays near Earth and comes near Earth every year—has to last centuries. In open space with radiation, vacuum. How?"

Sabine shrugs. "For power, a good reactor."

"How long could that last?"

"Decades easily, but even centuries, with more uranium or plutonium-239—that's maybe bomb-grade, swift stuff indeed. Maybe they knew tech we haven't thought of yet."

"So this thing has been looking at Earth for ... a long time."

"It's got to be somewhat intelligent, just to survive out here."

Dilip covers the mic even though it's off. "Those changing dots down there—a signal? It wants to talk?"

"Earthside has to decide what we do next."

"Let's use our heads, not theirs! And let's call it 'the Lurker.' Maybe it's this close in order to observe Earth."

Sabine works the controls, gathering high-resolution data on the Lurker. She finds no hidden structures, telescopes or antennas. Then she looks down at a panel. "Space Force Earthside sends exhaust velocity readings of a Red Chinese high-thrust rocket that's approaching our position. Big thrust."

They maneuver closer to the Lurker, observing the probe on the asteroid's surface and flurries of messages from Space Force command, about whether to announce the find versus media firestorms et cetera. The consensus seems to be that might lead to hasty thinking. Let's release minimal information, if any, and take no provocative action.

Which is fine, Dilip and Sabine agree, except for the international incident bearing down on them at interplanetary speed.

They hold in place, discuss how to closely approach the asteroid.

"Should we signal it?" Dilip asks.

"Not authorized, for sure."

"Let's not tell them. Let's just inch up on it. Just nearer, maybe turn on our outer spotlights to show we are aware."

Sabine nods. "The Lurker might think that's a signal."

"So we'll blink the lights, no more?"

Sabine nods and together they make it happen. The Lurker's

pattern again changes appearance, but no signal is sent back via radio, microwave or visible.

Desperately overdue, and wanting to be rested when the Chinese arrive, Dilip and Sabin signal Huntsville they are starting their sleep cycle. They instruct their onboard Watch Assist to keep a standoff distance of three hundred meters, record everything, and alert them when anything changes.

August 13, 2049, 9 PM

The Chinese craft comes in at high speed. No comm from them at all. Earthside has decided to withhold the story from the public. The Chinese-Space Force comms have gone silent, shut down. The Chinese rocket turns about and starts a powerful decelerating pulse. Hours later, the craft arrows in to rendezvous at a one kilometer standoff.

By this time, Sabine and Dilip are awake.

"There's a Chinese voice signal, Dilip. It's in spoken Mandarin." It's made into English by the AI translator, complete with grammar and pronunciation errors. This is part of that continuing Chinese attempt to force people to master Mandarin. Their campaign has failed but they keep at it. The Chinese message is just a call sign.

"Let's reply." Dilip opens the mic and says, "This is Dilip and Sabine Bhadra calling from the Space Force ship *Freeman Dyson*. What is your identification and what is your mission? What are you trying to do?"

There is no reply.

After two full minutes, Dilip closes the channel. "I guess we're going to stay quiet."

They observe the Chinese craft deploy a team of telepresence robots, heading toward the Lurker. Space Force Earthside says to stand back and watch. Dilip thinks otherwise. "We'd better send out our bots too."

Space Force agrees. They begin the checklist to deploy their own telepresence robots as the Lurker starts showing visual quick shifting patterns—as if trying to deal with the intruders.

Chinese in space suits and riding an EVA craft detach from the Chinese vessel, joining their robots.

Sabine says, "The Chinese vehicle and their robots are

approaching closer, and the Lurker pattern is getting a more agitated surface. I see puffs of local dust at the Lurker perimeter. They're prying at the edge of the Lurker! Maybe dislodging some anchors? They're trying to pull it away from the surface!"

There's a visible flash from the Lurker and suddenly their screens go blank.

Sabine scans the console. "There's an AI alert... There's been an electromagnetic pulse on all measured bands and wavelengths, optical through radio. We can't see anything. Good thing we hadn't deployed our robots!"

Inside *Dyson*, they are shielded. Its external systems soon reboot and screens flicker back to life.

Dilip says, "The Chinese robots and spacecraft are drifting. And their comm carrier has gone dead. The pulse must have scrambled electronics in their spacesuits and their spacecraft. And their robots." The Chinese taikonauts don't seem to be moving in their vehicle.

Sabine says, "We've got to get them out of there! Into our ship, I suppose. Let's launch our robots and try to open up their ship and extract them."

Their robots deploy normally. Some attach to the Chinese EVA craft, hanging adrift in space now. Some tug drifting space suits toward *Dyson* and into its air lock. When it cycles, Dilip is standing by to render air. He finds that the Chinese respiration systems are still functioning, so they're still breathing. He cracks open their faceplates. They're still alive, but unconscious, and their suit monitors flash and buzz with obvious errors and malfunctions.

Sabine uses the autodoc to try to revive them. "Good thing we standardized these space medical systems in the thirties like the docking systems back in the twentieth. Otherwise the incompatibility would have killed these guys. Let's see if they'll revive in a bit."

Dilip looks over the tools still tethered to some of the spacesuits: spades, cutters and electric pry-jaws. "Clearly they just wanted the tech. Pry it loose and take it home for study."

Sabine nods agreement. "But this isn't some passive space relic. It started transmitting in microwave. Maybe it's talking to us. We'll have to use an AI to see if it's language. We're gonna have to monitor this Lurker."

✳   ✳   ✳

After a few minutes, back on the console, Dilip says, "We're getting a tightbeam transmission from unknown origin, looks like it's further out, away from Earth. I'll have the AI backtrack it and find the location—it's from another co-orbital! The aliens sent more than one Lurker! It's from asteroid 2023 FW13, which shares a similar orbit to Kamo'oalewa, but 9 million miles out. How many Lurkers are out here? We've already found a couple dozen co-orbitals. Are they *all* watching us?"

"Dilip, I wonder how long it has been here? Co-orbitals can be stable for very long times, so maybe we've been observed for a long time. Dating it will require a great deal of remote observation, but that's a problem for the next expedition out here. Maybe this confirms the zoo hypothesis, that they don't want to disturb us."

"Zoo . . . Sabine, say it is trying to communicate; are we going to be able to understand it?"

"We're going to have to stand off and try. And it's going to try, too, now that it is awake. It will be faster than we will; it's been listening to us and learning."

"I wonder if it sent a signal out to wherever it came from?"

Sabine says, "I guess we'll know in a few years. Space Force Command Station message coming in, says back off from the alien Lurker. They're afraid if we linger, it'll zap us like it did the Chinese. Maybe that's right. Let's get out of here, before the Lurker awakens further."

Dyson turns away, heading for Earth orbit and the Space Force station, leaving the Lurkers to the next expedition . . .

✲ ✲ ✲

Gregory Benford is best-known for his Galactic Center Saga novels and *The Berlin Project* (2017). His work has earned him two Nebulas and the Campbell Award, along with four Hugo awards and twelve Nebula nominations. He was a scientific adviser for *Star Trek: The Next Generation*, and his contributions in astrophysics and plasma physics earned him the Lord Prize in 1995 and the Asimov Prize in 2008. He is a Professor Emeritus at UC, Irvine, and an ongoing advisor to NASA, DARPA, and the CIA.

James Benford is a physicist, high-power microwave scientist, author and entrepreneur, perhaps best known for introducing novel technological concepts and conjectures related to the exploration of outer space, including laser-driven sailships, the possible use of co-orbital objects by alien probes to spy on Earth, and technical and safety issues associated with the Search for Extraterrestrial Intelligence (SETI).

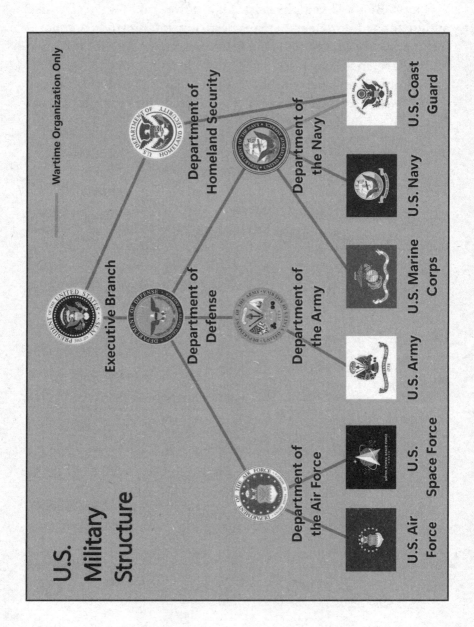

U.S. Military Structure

Wartime Organization Only

Executive Branch

Department of Homeland Security

Department of Defense

Department of the Navy

Department of the Army

Department of the Air Force

U.S. Air Force

U.S. Space Force

U.S. Army

U.S. Marine Corps

U.S. Navy

U.S. Coast Guard

Space Force Nomenclature

✸

With the creation of a new service branch comes a momentous responsibility: that of choosing nomenclature that will shape its culture and perception for decades to come. Notable examples include the names given to service personnel and organizational units, and its motto.

Personnel

The word "soldier" comes from the Old French word *soudier* meaning "one who serves" or "one who receives pay." That word derived from the Latin word *solidarius*, meaning "one who serves in the military for pay" or "paid companion." The Latin word in turn came from *solidus*, a type of Roman coin. Thus, the English language gives us "soldier" to mean anyone who serves in the military in any capacity. Alas, that isn't very specific, so we've added a number of other words to denote people serving in various branches and roles—sailor, marine, and more recently, "airman" notable among them.

A sailor is simply "one who sails," and so was the natural name in the Navy (from the Latin *navis*, meaning "ship" or "vessel") during the age of sail when that word had come to refer to a national shipborne fighting force, and later (by extension) to anyone serving in the Navy, even if they never come near a ship. Likewise, "marine" comes from the Latin *marinus*, meaning "of or belonging to the sea," so that to was a natural choice for a service branch dedicated to marine operations but not to fleets of warships. When the Air Force came along in 1947, the Latin equivalent *aerius* had already been anglicized into "aerial," but in the U.S. we use the spelling "air," so Air Force personnel became "airmen," people of or concerned with the air.

So far, so good, and it was reasonable that when the Space Force came along as a service branch derived from the Air Force, under the same federal department, and initially constituted by former Air Force personnel, some wondered if its ranks would be filled with "space-men." No, they won't, and there are several good reasons. First, it strikes many as outmoded and a bit sexist; second, it and its scholastic cousin "space cadet" have unfortunate connotations inherited (perhaps unfairly) from pulp-era science fiction. Finally, and perhaps most importantly, it sounds more like what you would call someone serving in a space navy—and that's not what the Space Force is. The Space Force is more like the Marines, or more to the point, like the Coast Guard, in that its primary role is not to conduct battles from large fleets of ships but to guard, track, and enforce, mostly from the ground. "Space-man" just doesn't seem to describe that.

An argument might have been made for calling Space Force personnel "spatiors" after the Latin word for space, *spatium*. There are problems with that as well though, not least of which is that the Romans didn't mean quite what we do by "space" and—far more importantly—in English, "spatior" doesn't exactly roll smoothly off the tongue! It sounds a bit like an invective hurled during a shouting match. Ah those Latin roots, perhaps all the good ones are taken?

Thus, on December 18, 2020, word came out that personnel serving under the U.S. Space Force would be called "guardians." Officially, the name both reflects the role of the force (akin to the Coast Guard, but for space) and directly honors decades of defensive space operations in the various U.S. Armed Forces. Of course, like any government policy announcement, this brought its share of opprobrium, with some poking fun with comparisons to Marvel Comics' "Guardians of the Galaxy."

But in fact, the term is far from new. Coast Guard personnel have been called "Guardians of the Coast" since the late nineteenth century due to their role in controlling piracy and smuggling. The term stuck, and has been used informally (alongside "coasties") to refer to Coast Guard personnel ever since, with modern units retaining slogans such as "Guardians of the Gulf" and "Guardians of the Great Lakes."

So influential was the so-called "guardian ethos," that in the early 2000s, moves were made to recognize it as the official name for Coast Guard personnel. This might have become policy had it not been blocked by Coast Guard Admiral Robert J. Papp Jr., who stated that since "Coast Guard" was the name given the branch on its creation in U.S.C. Title 14 (enacted in 1915), members were "Coast Guardsmen" and no commandant had the authority to change that.[9] For the record, and with all due respect, he seems to have been wrong about that— the law has, at least as revealed in a fairly thorough online search, nothing to say about the name or about so conscribing the authority of the commandant. Nevertheless, his policy stands.

So much the better for the Space Force. In 2020, the Space Force adopted "guardians" as its official term for Space Force members. The decision was made after a year-long process that involved input from Space Force members and leaders, as well as a public outreach campaign. The term was chosen because it reflects the Space Force's mission of protecting and defending the space domain.

It probably helped that since 1983, the motto of Air Force Space Command had been the apt and very popular "Guardians of the High Frontier."

Echelon Names

Modern military organizations are large and require efficient hierarchical means of management and control. To this end, each military organization defines its own terminology to name the various layers and components of its organization. The resulting vocabularies are far too complex and diverse to cover in any depth here, but for example, the term "battalion" is derived from the Italian word battaglione, which means "a large battle formation." Similarly, the term

---

[9] Leavitt, Michael P. "Coast Guardsman, Not Guardian." *Flotilla 23-1*, Annapolis, MD: U.S. Naval Academy.

"brigade" comes from the French word brigade, which originally referred to a group of soldiers tasked with a particular duty.

In today's U.S. military, the Army has its brigades, the Navy its squadrons, the Marines battalions and regiments, the Air Force, flights and wings. At the highest level of organization are the numbered armies, fleets, and air forces, each having regional and functional responsibilities. The Space Force has no equivalent, being much smaller, so the next command echelon below field commands is the delta[10], a single level of command which combines the wing and group command echelons found in the Air Force. Each delta is organized around a specific function, such as operations, installation support, or training.

Motto

The Space Force motto serves as a symbolic representation of the values and mission of the organization. The motto is a concise and memorable phrase that captures the essence of the Space Force's focus on space operations, technological innovation, and national security. In this way, it serves as a form of nomenclature that conveys important information about the Space Force to those both inside and outside the organization.

The Space Force officially adopted *"Semper Supra"* as its motto in July 2020, shortly after its establishment as a separate branch of the U.S. military.

According to the Space Force's first chief of space operations, General John Raymond, the motto was selected after a rigorous selection process that involved input from Space Force members and leaders. The process included a call for suggestions from the entire Space Force community, followed by a review of proposed mottos by a panel of senior leadership. This panel then narrowed the choices to a few which were reviewed by General Raymond and his senior staff.

"Semper Supra," is Latin for "Always Above." According to official sources, it represents "our role in establishing, maintaining, and

---

[10] Erwin, Sandra. "Space Force to Stand Up Three Major Commands, Lower Echelons to be Called 'Deltas.'" *SpaceNews*, June 30, 2020.

preserving U.S. freedom of operations in the space domain." Of course, that includes the operation of intelligence gathering assets, and support for soldiers on the ground, so the motto could be construed as either reassuring or menacing depending on which end of the force one is facing.

About "Superiority"

First published in the 1953 collection, Expedition to Earth, *Clarke's "Superiority" is a classic science fictional cautionary tale, warning of what cognitive scientists term "illusory superiority," a cognitive bias wherein one overestimates their own qualities or abilities in relation to others. It afflicts nations no less than individuals and, in this age of propaganda and Dunning-Kruger-driven social media, is as relevant as it ever was. Even more so in space, where relative orbital velocity can turn a gumdrop into an energy-dense superweapon.*

✡ ✡ ✡

Superiority

✳

Arthur C. Clarke

In making this statement—which I do of my own free will—I wish first to make it perfectly clear that I am not in any way trying to gain sympathy, nor do I expect any mitigation of whatever sentence the Court may pronounce. I am writing this in an attempt to refute some of the lying reports broadcast over the prison radio and published in the papers I have been allowed to see. These have given an entirely false picture of the true cause of our defeat, and as the leader of my race's armed forces at the cessation of hostilities I feel it my duty to protest against such libels upon those who served under me.

I also hope that this statement may explain the reasons for the application I have twice made to the Court, and will now induce it to grant a favor for which I can see no possible grounds of refusal.

The ultimate cause of our failure was a simple one: despite all statements to the contrary, it was not due to lack of bravery on the part of our men, or to any fault of the Fleet's. We were defeated by one thing only—by the inferior science of our enemies. I repeat—by the *inferior* science of our enemies.

When the war opened we had no doubt of our ultimate victory. The combined fleets of our allies greatly exceeded in number and armament those which the enemy could muster against us, and in almost all branches of military science we were their superiors. We were sure that we could maintain this superiority. Our belief proved, alas, to be only too well founded.

At the opening of the war our main weapons were the long-range homing torpedo, dirigible ball-lightning and the various modifications of the Klydon beam. Every unit of the Fleet was equipped with these and though the enemy possessed similar weapons their installations were generally of lesser power. Moreover, we had behind us a far greater military Research Organization, and with this initial advantage we could not possibly lose.

The campaign proceeded according to plan until the Battle of the Five Suns. We won this, of course, but the opposition proved stronger than we had expected. It was realized that victory might be more difficult, and more delayed, than had first been imagined. A conference of supreme commanders was therefore called to discuss our future strategy.

Present for the first time at one of our war conferences was Professor-General Norden, the new Chief of the Research Staff, who had just been appointed to fill the gap left by the death of Malvar, our greatest scientist. Malvar's leadership had been responsible, more than any other single factor, for the efficiency and power of our weapons. His loss was a very serious blow, but no one doubted the brilliance of his successor—though many of us disputed the wisdom of appointing a theoretical scientist to fill a post of such vital importance. But we had been overruled.

I can well remember the impression Norden made at that conference. The military advisers were worried, and as usual turned to the scientists for help. Would it be possible to improve our existing weapons, they asked, so that our present advantage could be increased still further?

Norden's reply was quite unexpected. Malvar had often been asked such a question, and he had always done what we requested.

"Frankly, gentlemen," said Norden, "I doubt it. Our existing weapons have practically reached finality. I don't wish to criticize my predecessor, or the excellent work done by the Research Staff in the last few generations, but do you realize that there has been no basic change in armaments for over a century? It is, I am afraid, the result of a tradition that has become conservative. For too long, the Research Staff has devoted itself to perfecting old weapons instead of developing new ones. It is fortunate for us that our opponents have been no wiser: we cannot assume that this will always be so."

Norden's words left an uncomfortable impression, as he had no doubt intended. He quickly pressed home the attack.

"What we want are new weapons—weapons totally different from any that have been employed before. Such weapons can be made: it will take time, of course, but since assuming charge I have replaced some of the older scientists with young men and have directed research into several unexplored fields which show great promise. I believe, in fact, that a revolution in warfare may soon be upon us."

We were skeptical. There was a bombastic tone in Norden's voice that made us suspicious of his claims. We did not know, then, that he never promised anything that he had not already almost perfected in the laboratory. In the laboratory—that was the operative phrase.

Norden proved his case less than a month later, when he demonstrated the Sphere of Annihilation, which produced complete disintegration of matter over a radius of several hundred meters. We were intoxicated by the power of the new weapon, and were quite prepared to overlook one fundamental defect—the fact that it was a sphere and hence destroyed its rather complicated generating equipment at the instant of formation. This meant, of course, that it could not be used on warships but only on guided missiles, and a great program was started to convert all homing torpedoes to carry the new weapon. For the time being all further offensives were suspended.

We realize now that this was our first mistake. I still think that it was a natural one, for it seemed to us then that all our existing weapons had become obsolete overnight, and we already regarded them as almost primitive survivals. What we did not appreciate was the magnitude of the task we were attempting, and the length of time it would take to get the revolutionary super-weapon into battle. Nothing like this had happened for a hundred years and we had no previous experience to guide us.

The conversion problem proved far more difficult than anticipated. A new class of torpedo had to be designed, as the standard model was too small. This meant in turn that only the larger ships could launch the weapon, but we were prepared to accept this penalty. After six months, the heavy units of the Fleet were being equipped with the Sphere. Training maneuvers and tests had shown that it was operating satisfactorily and we were ready to take it into action. Norden was already being hailed as the architect of victory, and had half promised even more spectacular weapons.

Then two things happened. One of our battleships disappeared completely on a training flight, and an investigation showed that under certain conditions the ship's long-range radar could trigger the Sphere immediately after it had been launched. The modification needed to overcome this defect was trivial, but it caused a delay of another month and was the source of much bad feeling between the naval staff and the scientists. We were ready for action again—when Norden announced that the radius of effectiveness of the Sphere had now been increased by ten, thus multiplying by a thousand the chances of destroying an enemy ship.

So the modifications started all over again, but everyone agreed that the delay would be worth it. Meanwhile, however, the enemy had been emboldened by the absence of further attacks and had made an unexpected onslaught. Our ships were short of torpedoes, since none had been coming from the factories, and were forced to retire. So we lost the systems of Kyrane and Floranus, and the planetary fortress of Rhamsandron.

It was an annoying but not a serious blow, for the recaptured systems had been unfriendly, and difficult to administer. We had no doubt that we could restore the position in the near future, as soon as the new weapon became operational.

These hopes were only partially fulfilled. When we renewed our offensive, we had to do so with fewer of the Spheres of Annihilation than had been planned, and this was one reason for our limited success. The other reason was more serious.

While we had been equipping as many of our ships as we could with the irresistible weapon, the enemy had been building feverishly. His ships were of the old pattern with the old weapons, but they now out-numbered ours. When we went into action, we found that the numbers ranged against us were often one hundred percent greater than expected, causing target confusion among the automatic weapons and resulting in higher losses than anticipated. The enemy losses were higher still, for once a Sphere had reached its objective, destruction was certain, but the balance had not swung as far in our favor as we had hoped.

Moreover, while the main fleets had been engaged, the enemy had launched a daring attack on the lightly held systems of Eriston, Duranus, Carmanidora and Pharanidon—recapturing them all. We were thus faced with a threat only fifty light-years from our home planets.

There was much recrimination at the next meeting of the supreme commanders. Most of the complaints were addressed to Norden—Grand Admiral Taxaris in particular maintaining that thanks to our admittedly irresistible weapon we were now considerably worse off than before. We should, he claimed, have continued to build conventional ships, thus preventing the loss of our numerical superiority.

Norden was equally angry and called the naval staff ungrateful bunglers. But I could tell that he was worried—as indeed we all were—by the unexpected turn of events. He hinted that there might be a speedy way of remedying the situation.

We now know that Research had been working on the Battle Analyzer for many years, but at the time it came as a revelation to us and perhaps we were too easily swept off our feet. Norden's argument, also, was seductively convincing. What did it matter, he said, if the enemy had twice as many ships as we—if the efficiency of ours could be doubled or even trebled? For decades the limiting factor in warfare had been not mechanical but biological—it had become more and more difficult for any single mind, or group of minds, to cope with the rapidly changing complexities of battle in three-dimensional space. Norden's mathematicians had analyzed some of the classic engagements of the past, and had shown that even when we had been victorious we had often operated our units at much less than half of their theoretical efficiency.

The Battle Analyzer would change all this by replacing the operations staff with electronic calculators. The idea was not new, in theory, but until now it had been no more than a Utopian dream. Many of us found it difficult to believe that it was still anything but a dream: after we had run through several very complex dummy battles, however, we were convinced.

It was decided to install the Analyzer in four of our heaviest ships, so that each of the main fleets could be equipped with one. At this stage, the trouble began—though we did not know it until later.

The Analyzer contained just short of a million vacuum tubes and needed a team of five hundred technicians to maintain and operate it. It was quite impossible to accommodate the extra staff aboard a battleship, so each of the four units had to be accompanied by a converted liner to carry the technicians not on duty. Installation was also a very slow and tedious business, but by gigantic efforts it was completed in six months.

Then, to our dismay, we were confronted by another crisis. Nearly five thousand highly skilled men had been selected to serve the Analyzers and had been given an intensive course at the Technical Training Schools. At the end of seven months, ten percent of them had had nervous breakdowns and only forty percent had qualified.

Once again, everyone started to blame everyone else. Norden, of course, said that the Research Staff could not be held responsible, and so incurred the enmity of the Personnel and Training Commands. It was finally decided that the only thing to do was to use two instead of four Analyzers and to bring the others into action as soon as men could be trained. There was little time to lose, for the enemy was still on the offensive and his morale was rising.

The first Analyzer fleet was ordered to recapture the system of Eriston. On the way, by one of the hazards of war, the liner carrying the technicians was struck by a roving mine. A warship would have survived, but the liner with its irreplaceable cargo was totally destroyed. So the operation had to be abandoned.

The other expedition was, at first, more successful. There was no doubt at all that the Analyzer fulfilled its designers' claims, and the enemy was heavily defeated in the first engagements. He withdrew, leaving us in possession of Saphran, Leucon and Hexanerax. But his Intelligence Staff must have noted the change in our tactics and the inexplicable presence of a liner in the heart of our battlefleet. It must have noted, also, that our first fleet had been accompanied by a similar ship, and had withdrawn when it had been destroyed.

In the next engagement, the enemy used his superior numbers to launch an overwhelming attack on the Analyzer ship and its unarmed consort. The attack was made without regard to losses— both ships were, of course, very heavily protected, and it succeeded. The result was the virtual decapitation of the Fleet, since an effectual transfer to the old operational methods proved impossible. We disengaged under heavy fire, and so lost all our gains and also the systems of Lormyia, Ismarnus, Beronis, Alphanidon and Sideneus.

At this stage, Grand Admiral Taxaris expressed his disapproval of Norden by committing suicide, and I assumed supreme command.

The situation was now both serious and infuriating. With stubborn conservatism and complete lack of imagination, the enemy continued to advance with his old-fashioned and inefficient but now vastly more numerous ships. It was galling to realize that if we had only continued building, without seeking new weapons, we would have been in a far more advantageous position. There were many acrimonious conferences at which Norden defended the scientists while everyone else blamed them for all that had happened. The difficulty was that Norden had proved every one of his claims: he had a perfect excuse for all the disasters that had occurred. And we could not now turn back—the search for an irresistible weapon must go on. At first it had been a luxury that would shorten the war. Now it was a necessity if we were to end it victoriously.

We were on the defensive, and so was Norden. He was more than ever determined to reestablish his prestige and that of the Research Staff. But we had been twice disappointed, and would not make the same mistake again. No doubt Norden's twenty thousand scientists would produce many further weapons: we would remain unimpressed.

We were wrong. The final weapon was something so fantastic that even now it seems difficult to believe that it ever existed. Its innocent, noncommittal name—The Exponential Field—gave no hint of its real potentialities. Some of Norden's mathematicians had discovered it during a piece of entirely theoretical research into the properties of space, and to everyone's great surprise their results were found to be physically realizable.

It seems very difficult to explain the operation of the Field to the layman. According to the technical description, it "produces an exponential condition of space, so that a finite distance in normal, linear space may become infinite in pseudo-space." Norden gave an analogy which some of us found useful. It was as if one took a flat disk of rubber—representing a region of normal space—and then pulled its center out to infinity. The circumference of the disk would be unaltered, but its "diameter" would be infinite. That was the sort of thing the generator of the Field did to the space around it.

As an example, suppose that a ship carrying the generator was surrounded by a ring of hostile machines. If it switched on the Field, each of the enemy ships would think that it—and the ships on the far side of the circle—had suddenly receded into nothingness. Yet the circumference of the circle would be the same as before: only the journey to the center would be of infinite duration, for as one proceeded, distances would appear to become greater and greater as the "scale" of space altered.

It was a nightmare condition, but a very useful one. Nothing could reach a ship carrying the Field: it might be englobed by an enemy fleet yet would be as inaccessible as if it were at the other side of the Universe. Against this, of course, it could not fight back without switching off the Field, but this still left it at a very great advantage, not only in defense but in offense. For a ship fitted with the Field could approach an enemy fleet undetected and suddenly appear in its midst.

This time there seemed to be no flaws in the new weapon. Needless to say, we looked for all the possible objections before we committed ourselves again. Fortunately the equipment was fairly simple and did not require a large operating staff. After much debate, we decided to rush it into production, for we realized that time was running short and the war was going against us. We had now lost about the whole of our initial gains and enemy forces had made several raids into our own solar system.

We managed to hold off the enemy while the Fleet was reequipped and the new battle techniques were worked out. To use the Field operationally it was necessary to locate an enemy formation, set a course that would intercept it, and then switch on the generator for the calculated period of time. On releasing the Field again—if the calculations had been accurate—one would be in the enemy's midst and could do great damage during the resulting confusion, retreating by the same route when necessary.

The first trial maneuvers proved satisfactory and the equipment seemed quite reliable. Numerous mock attacks were made and the crews became accustomed to the new technique. I was on one of the test flights and can vividly remember my impressions as the Field was switched on. The ships around us seemed to dwindle as if on the surface of an expanding bubble: in an instant they had vanished completely. So had the stars, but presently we could see that the Galaxy was still visible as a faint band of light around the ship. The virtual radius of our pseudo-space was not really infinite, but some hundred thousand light-years, and so the distance to the farthest stars of our system had not been greatly increased—though the nearest had of course totally disappeared These training maneuvers, however, had to be canceled before they were completed, owing to a whole flock of minor technical troubles in various pieces of equipment, notably the communications circuits. These were annoying, but not important, though it was thought best to return to Base to clear them up.

At that moment the enemy made what was obviously intended to be a decisive attack against the fortress planet of Iton at the limits of our solar system. The Fleet had to go into battle before repairs could be made.

The enemy must have believed that we had mastered the secret of invisibility, as in a sense we had. Our ships appeared suddenly out of no-where and inflicted tremendous damage—for a while. And then something quite baffling and inexplicable happened.

I was in command of the flagship *Hircania* when the trouble started. We had been operating as independent units, each against assigned objectives. Our detectors observed an enemy formation at medium range and the navigating officers measured its distance with great accuracy. We set course and switched on the generator.

The Exponential Field was released at the moment when we should have been passing through the center of the enemy group. To our consternation, we emerged into normal space at a distance of many hundred miles, and when we found the enemy, he had already found us. We retreated, and tried again. This time we were so far away from the enemy that he located us first.

Obviously, something was seriously wrong. We broke communicator silence and tried to contact the other ships of the Fleet to see if they had experienced the same trouble. Once again we failed—and this time the failure was beyond all reason, for the communication equipment appeared to be working perfectly. We could only assume, fantastic though it seemed, that the rest of the Fleet had been destroyed.

I do not wish to describe the scenes when the scattered units of the Fleet struggled back to Base. Our casualties had actually been negligible, but the ships were completely demoralized. Almost all had lost touch with one another and had found that their ranging equipment showed inexplicable errors. It was obvious that the Exponential Field was the cause of the troubles, despite the fact that they were only apparent when it was switched off.

The explanation came too late to do us any good, and Norden's final discomfiture was small consolation for the virtual loss of the war. As I have explained, the Field generators produced a radial distortion of space, distances appearing greater and greater as one approached the center of the artificial pseudo-space. When the Field was switched off, conditions returned to normal.

But not quite. It was never possible to restore the initial state exactly. Switching the Field on and off was equivalent to an elongation and contraction of the ship carrying the generator, but there was a hysteretic effect, as it were, and the initial condition was never quite reproducible, owing to all the thousands of electrical changes and movements of mass aboard the ship while the Field was on. These asymmetries and distortions were cumulative, and though they seldom amounted to more than a fraction of one percent, that was quite enough. It meant that the precision ranging equipment and the tuned circuits in the communication apparatus were thrown completely out of adjustment. Any single ship could never detect the change—only when it compared its equipment with that of another vessel, or tried to communicate with it, could it tell what had happened.

It is impossible to describe the resultant chaos. Not a single component of one ship could be expected with certainty to work aboard another. The very nuts and bolts were no longer interchangeable, and the supply position became quite impossible. Given time, we might even have overcome these difficulties, but the enemy ships were already attacking in thousands with weapons which now seemed centuries behind those that we had invented. Our magnificent Fleet, crippled by our own science, fought on as best it could until it was overwhelmed and forced to surrender. The ships fitted with the Field were still invulnerable, but as fighting units they were almost helpless. Every time they switched on their generators to escape from enemy attack, the permanent distortion of their equipment increased. In a month, it was all over.

This is the true story of our defeat, which I give without prejudice to my defense before this Court. I make it, as I have said, to counteract the libels that have been circulating against the men who fought under me, and to show where the true blame for our misfortunes lay.

Finally, my request, which as the Court will now realize I make in no frivolous manner and which I hope will therefore be granted.

The Court will be aware that the conditions under which we are housed and the constant surveillance to which we are subjected night and day are somewhat distressing. Yet I am not complaining of this: nor do I complain of the fact that shortage of accommodation has made it necessary to house us in pairs.

But I cannot be held responsible for my future actions if I am compelled any longer to share my cell with Professor Norden, late Chief of the Research Staff of my armed forces.

✵　✵　✵

British science fiction author **Arthur C. Clarke** was a man ahead of his time—or at least the science of his time. He envisioned geostationary satellites long before they became a reality and wrote about virtual reality before the term even existed. With his sharp wit and playful imagination, Clarke was like a wizard of science fiction, conjuring up worlds and technologies that were both fantastical and prescient.

His novel *Childhood's End* is considered a classic in the genre, and his collaboration (with Stanley Kubrick) on *2001: A Space Odyssey* is an iconic classic on the page and screen for its portrayal of space travel and technology. Clarke's interest in science and technology was reflected in his work, and he was known for his accurate depictions of futuristic technologies and their impact on society. He also served in the Royal Air Force during World War II, which influenced his writing on military topics.

A Fair Defense

✵

C. Stuart Hardwick

Claressa Smallwood wiped her eyes, stared at her tear-streaked reflection and, forcing more measured breaths, willed the last sniffles away.

Get it together, Clare. Don't let Daddy see you like this.

He'd never gotten over Momma, not the loss nor the bills, and the last thing he needed now was to see his only daughter falling apart as they hauled her off to juvie. Not when she was all that kept him going, plodding along like a comic-book mummy trying to read a compass through the wrappings. Only north for him was the future, *her* future, and now she'd taken that away from him, hadn't she?

Should've thought of that before hauling off and belting Patty Steadman. But a girl could only take so much. The new high school had four years of chemistry *and* electronics, but it also had more social strata than a Jane Austen novel. Claressa wasn't rich nor an athlete nor even dance team or band material. She was a nerd, a transfer, a nobody, and if the white kids dissed her on account of being black, the black kids shunned her for "acting too white."

That wasn't *entirely* fair. That sort were the exception more than the rule, but it only takes one bad egg to spoil an omelet. And it's not like the others were going to leap to her defense. Why would they? High school would pass like salmonella and they'd all go on to college or trade school or marriage or whatever and live among adults who knew enough at least to *pretend* to be decent *most* of the time.

363

And that's how Claressa saw it, too, at least till she went and won the science fair. That upset the local ecology, raised her standing just slightly from "not worth the bother" to "worth making an example of."

And Ms. Childress, bless her heart, had thought she was helping, writing to NASA and starting a funding drive. The project *was* good: "Expanding Elastomeric Polymer Nets for Space Debris Remediation." With a little work it could've been great for next year, the kind of project that wins national, gets attention, earns college money and internships.

But not this time. NASA had passed, and to raise that injury to exponential insult, when Ms. Childress (who knew as much about crowdfunding as Pookie, the classroom turtle) delivered the news, Patty's spies had been eavesdropping. One thing had led to another and there she was behind the cafeteria, clocking Bratty Patty with a loaded book bag before the foul-mouthed witch could see it coming.

And now *here* she was, crying in the bathroom of the West Capshaw Police Station where they'd hauled her after pulling her out of English with everybody staring, not on account of her dramatic rendition of Ms. Eliza Doolittle's cockney dialogue, but at her fumbling to collect spilled books under the impatient gaze of the principal and a chubby peace officer with a piece.

Well let them stare. If they didn't respect her performance, maybe they'd fear her new rep instead, little Ms. Al Capone in corn rows. At least the gossip would keep them awake through lunch after they got done boring each other stiff with their halting, monotone readings.

But now she had to go out, and there would be Patty with a smug look and a story no doubt embroidered by claims of a dying tooth, and all the cops and Patty's car-salesman dad who owned half of Madison County and had probably donated the TV in the break room here.

She'd as soon have died right here, melted into a puddle and down the drain to feed some distant algal bloom. But Daddy would be out there too.

"Buck up, Claressa." That's what Momma would've said. "No sense crying over spilled ketchup, just don't track it on the rug!"

The once-white bathroom door had chips through the many-layered paint revealing a sort of insect-blood green underneath.

Claressa drew herself up, gave one last blot with her jacket sleeve, and forced the door open with a too-loud bang. Then before her nerve could falter, she strode down the little hall toward the waiting lady cop and the big room with all the desks and cubicles.

Buck up.

The lady cop opened the outer door and let Claressa pass. Sure enough, Daddy had come. He was sitting quietly, clean and shaved and wearing a tie and sport coat. A good day then; well, so far.

On closer inspection, though, he didn't look like a dad called in on consequence of a delinquent toss-up. He was rocking slightly, not so anyone else would've noticed, looking down just enough to mask the gray starting to creep up from his temples. Claressa ran through the applicable emotions: anger, disappointment, disgust, concern... none of them seemed to fit. His hands clutched his cell phone in his lap, not so he could read it but as if wanting to wad it up.

The bill collector, which he didn't think she knew about. What he looked like he was was... trapped.

The crash had made him a widower, but had taken three horrible weeks to do the job. They'd sent him home with a clean bill of health, a ruinous bill of accounts, and a bottle of pills for the heartache. Through all the vacant smiles and tears, Claressa hadn't pressed, even when the mail and the trash piled up. Even when the plant sent him home that day and he sat on the sofa with the TV off, ashen and rocking like now. She'd let him be, given time to heal.

But he just wasn't healing, wasn't the man he had been, and as she watched him rocking like a little boy, like something shaken and discarded by a dog, her spine prickled with cold dread that he might not ever be again.

Patty and her dad were absent. Instead, there was a military man with what looked like an old-fashioned bus driver's hat tucked under his arm. He stood stiffly, as if sitting in one of the vinyl chairs might soil the pretty blue fabric of his uniform.

As the lady cop shewed Claressa forward, a man in plain clothes but with a badge on his belt stepped up to the uniformed man and said, "Everything's in order, sir." The uniformed man nodded. Claressa's father looked up at the exchange. He saw her, rumpled up and took her hand.

"Baby girl... um, this man's from the Air Force and says he needs to . . . Um, he needs us to . . ." He looked up at the taller man. "What is it you need again, Mr. . . . um . . . ?"

The uniformed man glanced at his watch and stepped after the plain-clothed man, who was clearly waiting for them to follow. "Colonel Frank Hutchins, OSI. I need you to come with me."

"OS . . . what now?" Claressa's father leaned forward slightly and looked away as if listening to an intrusive whisper.

Colonel Hutchins's gaze followed, but finding nothing of interest, he answered, "I'm sorry, sir, I thought they'd explained. I'm from the Air Force Office of Special Investigations, our version of the FBI." He looked down at Claressa. "Don't worry, you're not in any trouble; you're needed to aid in an investigation. Someone thought it would be less conspicuous to work through local law enforcement. I'm sorry for all the trouble, but if you'll both come along, we're under a bit of time pressure."

Apparently so. Behind the station, on a raised concrete platform out past the parking and the transformers and the satellite dishes, a big dark helicopter sat roaring, the *whup, whup, whup* of its rotor accelerating as they approached. They climbed inside, the door slid shut, and they lurched away in darkness, window shades and the wind and roar forestalling conversation or even a good look around.

Slowly, Claressa's eyes adjusted, but by the time her heart stopped pounding enough to find the shade release and wonder what trouble it would cause to slip the harness and press her nose up against the glass, they were turning and rocking and her ears popped as they swooped back down to the ground.

Sunlight flooded in. Two soldiers in camouflage fatigues hurried them out and a short way across broiling concrete to what looked like a small corporate jet. At its steps, the Office of Special Investigations man gave a crisp salute to a younger man in a darker uniform with six large buttons sweeping across his chest like a sash. Claressa and her father were conducted inside and the door pulled up as the engines spooled to life.

This was much nicer than the helicopter, with lots of bright windows and dark blue leather seats in little groupings like in limousines in the movies. As soon as Claressa and her father claimed theirs, they were joined by the young man from outside and a pleasant-looking middle-aged woman with the same dark uniform but a lot more ribbon boards on her chest.

"Welcome aboard, Ms. Smallwood," she said, sitting opposite Claressa. "I'm Major General Lina Gutierrez, United States Space Force. I need to talk to you about your science fair project."

The jet's powerful climb so thrilled Claressa that only after a layer of cloud had obscured the terrain did she realize the general was patiently waiting. She turned, pulled her knees up to her chest, then dropped them again to keep her sneakers off the upholstery.

She ducked her head. "Sorry, ma'am."

General Gutierrez gave a little laugh. "Not at all. Do you think I'm as old as all that?"

She did, in fact. The general had the look of someone long too harried for regular exercise, though well burnished by the sun, and her black, loosely curled, shoulder-length hair shielded telltale gray near the roots. Only the eyes belied age. Light as caramel, they shone with youthful intensity.

Locking them now on Claressa, the general got down to business. She wanted to know all about the project: where Claressa had gotten the idea (the wall-clinging sticky frogs she played with as a kid), where they came up with the formula (Daddy, a chemist on leave from BASF), how they'd tested it (a vacuum chamber made of steel pipe and pressure cooker parts and an arsenal of model rocket motors).

Basically, she wanted the science fair spiel. The problem: space debris tends to degrade into tiny bits too small to track but big enough to blast holes in anything they hit at orbital speed, and they're hard to clean up without causing exactly the type of impacts that cause even more debris. The hypothesis: a lightweight, elastic, self-healing polymer similar to that used to weatherproof modern windows and doors might sweep up such debris while remaining intact, then be collected or tracked and left to deorbit due to its vastly increased drag. The conclusion: rudimentary tests were promising, but there was a lot more work to be done. The polymer needed refinement, in particular to stop it sticking to itself and clumping up into a ball. Next steps: would require money they didn't have and access to NASA test facilities they'd been denied.

Gutierrez said, "Oh, you weren't denied."

Claressa started, "But—"

"You were . . . intercepted."

The general tipped the Hello Kitty-stickered lid from a white cardboard file box strapped into the seat beside her. A box which, until this morning, has been on the shelf of Claressa's closet between her roller skates and a toy accordion.

"Is this it?"

She pulled out the six-ounce jelly jar in which Claressa's elastomeric goop had been displayed at the science fair. Warily eyeing her guests, she carefully unscrewed the lid and prodded inside with a pen knife. She poked around as if for a dollop of butter, but the stuff pulled from the blade as fast as it was disturbed. Finally, she caught a bit on the tip of the blade and pulled up a tendril that, stretched to the limits of her reach, snapped back and healed over instantly.

"How the devil do you form it?"

"With a cheese slicer," Claressa said.

The general raised a suspicious eyebrow and Claressa continued. "We cut it with piano wire and a jet of distilled water. The hydrogen bonds keep it from healing before you can cut it, then the water boils away in the—"

Claressa's dad had squeezed her forearm. "Can I ask where you're taking us?"

"Kirtland Air Force Base."

"Kirtland? That's . . . um . . ." He stared, blinking as if from a tic, then repeated, "That's in New Mexico, isn't it? Clara has finals coming up."

"Kirtland is home to the Space Rapid Capabilities Office and the Air Force Research Laboratory."

"That other man, um . . . that other man said something about an investigation."

The general turned to Claressa. "Ms. Smallwood, you asked NASA for a few thousand dollars and help developing your idea for next year's science fair. I'm offering you the full resources of the United States government to develop it into something we can deploy in space right now, this week. That's the investigation."

Claressa's mouth dropped open. She didn't know what to say. Surprisingly, her father did.

"Now hold on just a minute, um . . . hold on a minute. You come in here all cloak and dagger and whisk us off across the country without, um . . . without a by your leave and we're supposed to believe that's, um . . . that's what, out of the goodness of your heart?"

"No, Mr. Smallwood, out of necessity. We need what you've come up with for national defense, and we need it immediately. It might sound melodramatic, but you will literally be helping your country."

Mr. Smallwood huffed. "It's a science fair project! Um . . ."

"And you will be generously compensated."

He gave no sign of having heard. "It's a science fair project! It's a good idea, but the impact velocities Clare tested aren't remotely realistic and the goop's not stable enough for storage and handling, much less the space environment, um . . . space environment. I'd like to know how it's so godawful vital, that . . . um . . ."

"I can tell you all that once the paperwork—"

"What's that?"

"There are some papers I need you to sign, and then—"

Mr. Smallwood's nodding head skipped a beat and realigned along a new axis. "Sign nothing! That's my little girl's future you're talking about, and I won't, um . . . I won't see it taken away and turned into a weapon!"

"Mr. Smallwood, I can assure you what we'll be working on is purely defensive—"

Again, he huffed. "So was Agent Orange."

"Mr. Smallwood . . ." The general sighed, and Claressa thought she looked as if he'd suddenly turned into a particularly stubborn garden gnome, making further conversation worse than useless. She turned, in fact, and looked down into Claressa's eyes.

"Ms. . . . . Claressa, just about anything can be made into a weapon, that's true, but weapons can protect lives and property as well as destroy them. Come to the lab tomorrow and you'll see." She glanced at the gnome but directed her words as before. "In the meantime, I believe they have all your school things up front. You might want to do some studying. You're going to have a busy few days."

At Kirtland, Claressa and her dad were given a cheaply furnished but well-maintained room and, in the morning, a rather intimidating ride in a big white police SUV. The latter was provided by two camouflage-wearing soldiers who brought donuts and juice and fussed at Claressa's father for not being up and dressed at the prescribed time.

The lab complex was across the base, a cluster of cinder block and steel-clad structures a few blocks from the flight line and all generously provisioned with warnings against unauthorized entry. The soldiers walked them through a keypad-secured door and into a boxy metal building that from the outside might have been a warehouse, but on the inside looked more like the office wing at the front of Claressa's school.

Both impressions faded as they left the glassed-in security station and rode up in an elevator. A young woman in fatigues stood watch outside a conference room. Inside, beside a long wooden table, a wall of glass overlooked an open, multistory laboratory filled with tangles of piping and wiring around a gray central tower with landings like a refinery stack.

Claressa and her dad sat, backs to the window, across from two men and a woman in civilian clothes already at the table. Two more soldiers came in wearing fatigues, one offering to fetch coffee, the other delivering documents that Claressa's dad glanced at and shoved away.

"I'm not . . . um, I'm not signing anything. I know my rights."

General Gutierrez, also now in the same incongruous wilderness camouflage fatigues as the others, stepped through the door with a to-go coffee and assumed the head of the table. He repeated his objection, adding, "And I'm not telling you the formula."

"Oh, we already have that." This was one of the civilians, a young red-headed man in jeans and a white golf shirt. "Spectroscopy had it by oh-nine-hundred, and we ran up a batch overnight. We're getting ready now to put it to the test. Should be interesting."

The general sipped her coffee.

"The paperwork's actually more for *your* benefit, Mr. Smallwood. We have cameras watching me tell you that by executive order of the President of the United States, what you two are about to learn, everything you've developed thus far for your project, and anything you henceforth develop or learn relating to it, is now classified. Releasing it to or discussing it with anyone not authorized in writing through my command will result in your prosecution under the Classified Information Procedures Act."

She turned to one of her soldiers. "I think that ought to cover it?"

The woman nodded.

Claressa's father started up, shouting. "You can't, um—" But he seemed to lose his footing. The soldier to his right caught his arm and stopped him falling against the glass. He didn't seem to appreciate the help and shucked off the hand before dropping back into his chair.

"Clara's worked hard, and um ... worked hard on this, and you just can't ..."

The others might not have understood his emotional response, the tears welling up in his eyes; Claressa did. He'd made the goop before the accident, before the involuntary leave, and Claressa had made most everything else using YouTube videos for guidance and scraps from his workshop and Mr. Fargeson's junk pile down the street. That it had worked and not killed anyone was a miracle not likely to be repeated. And while pride kept his troubles held close, money was principal among them. Her future was his being, college her future, and scholarship money her way into college. If they were taking her project away, they would destroy his very reason for being.

He sat quivering, as if caught between the desires to hide beneath the table and launch himself at the general's throat.

The general sighed and tapped the lid of her cup. "Captain Sims, tell them."

Sims, the serviceman who'd just helped Claressa's father, was the same young man from yesterday on the plane. He swiveled toward Claressa and her dad and interlocked his fingers before him, gesticulating with his index fingers as he spoke.

"You probably know that GPS depends on satellites. Each carries an atomic clock, and positions on Earth's surface are determined by triangulation and careful timing of the signals coming from multiple satellites."

Claressa's father said, "Yeah, so?"

"So at least twenty-four satellites are needed to provide sufficient visibility to all points on Earth, and we normally maintain a few spares. Right now we're at twenty-two. Total."

"Beg pardon?"

"Someone's disabling our satellites. We don't know how, exactly, but we can see the interceptors pacing them and approaching. Once they do, we lose the satellite. We've already gone through our on-orbit reserves, two new models sent up as spares and four older ones decommissioned but still functional. Any more losses and the constellation will become seriously compromised. The immediate concern is that precision munitions will become vulnerable to jamming, maybe useless. The opening salvo in an asymmetric war."

"Well, then shoot them down. Isn't that what you folks are here for?"

"That would create debris clouds that would compromise the entire orbit. Plus these hostiles are the size of coffee makers, nearly impossible to hit, and even making the attempt might reveal capabilities we would prefer to keep hidden, given that this might be a prelude to a larger attack."

Claressa's dad looked down. "Well, I guess you're screwed then. What's it to do with us?"

"We've fast-tracked four replacement satellites, but that's all we have in the pipeline. It could take months to get another batch ready. We need a way to protect these in the meantime. Some sort of defensive pack we can strap to a finished satellite that won't compromise its operation."

General Gutierrez turned in her chair.

"Mr. Smallwood, Claressa, this may be a *prelude* to war or it might be the war itself. GPS has become vital to far more than targeting smart bombs and helping taxis find their way. It's integral to farming, construction, flood control, energy distribution, weather forecasting, logistics; even ATMs and cell phone networks depend on the atomic clocks on those satellites."

"We're not . . . um. We're not helping you militarize space!"

"That ship sailed long ago, Mr. Smallwood and, not to put too fine a point on it, you *need* the military. In the U.S., it's twelve percent of the federal budget, about the same as Medicaid. It would be great if we could shift that money elsewhere, space exploration maybe, or the eradication of poverty, however you buy that exactly.

"But there are people out there who, whatever we build, whatever we do to provide for the general welfare, are ready to step up and take it or smash it if we let them. That's just the way life is. They wait for their chance to knock us down with another Pearl Harbor, another 9/11, and our eyes and ears in the sky stop it happening. And when we must, they let us put bombs through windows instead of carpet-bombing cities like in the old days. And because both those things are true, those who would attack us cool their heels, and we have peace without the sword of Damocles of Mutually Assured Destruction hanging over us like during the Cold War.

"The price of peace is eternal vigilance, haven't you ever heard that? It's a high price, paid through a power that sometimes tempts the best and the worst among us, but it's a bargain nonetheless. There are wolves at the door, Mr. Smallwood—no, real human enemies who are hidden and far more dangerous than wolves—and we need your help driving them off. That's all.

"Your daughter's idea for sweeping up trash is just what we need to neutralize these hostiles without creating more debris. It doesn't have to be perfect, or cheap, or even particularly safe. It just has to work. Long enough to stave off a shooting war down here on the ground."

"I don't know . . . Um, I don't know . . ."

On the other side of the glass, a buzzer echoed through the chamber.

On the table, a speaker phone Claressa hadn't noticed till now announced itself with an amplified clatter and a disembodied voice: "We're ready."

The woman unmuted the phone long enough to say, "Roger. Standing by," and her colleagues huddled around her laptop. "Here we go."

The echoing sound of pumps, a bang that shook the glass and made Claressa's heart jump, and a momentary and muffled whoosh. Then there was silence till the phone squawked again and the tinny voice said, "Check from index thirty-two ninety."

The laptop keys clattered. The woman looked up, crestfallen. "It didn't work."

"Hah!" Claressa's dad scoffed. "Don't need the formula, eh?"

"It's not the chemistry, sir," said the man who'd spoken earlier. "This test was a control using your sample. It just doesn't work under our more realistic conditions. We fired a pancake of your goop through hard vacuum at three hundred meters a second. It appears to have struck the target and disintegrated. That's what we were afraid of. It's useless for our purposes." He looked up at Claressa. "And for sweeping up trash, too, I'm sorry to say."

Claressa's dad stared, befuddled. "Maybe it's, um . . . maybe it's gone bad after what? Eight, nine months?"

Gutierrez sighed. "Or maybe we really are screwed."

❁   ❁   ❁

The meeting broke up after the general admonished her experts to "figure it out," and an underling to "see that he signs so we can get him into the lab."

The latter, at least, was not difficult. While the others went off after coffee, donuts, and facilities, Claressa chastised her father for rejecting the documents without first reading them. She skimmed them for him. The Space Force was offering money, she said, and while she had no idea if it was a fair price, he was out of work and to judge by the recent phone calls, out of money. Maybe the government *was* stealing her idea, but she would have more of them. Fat lot of use ideas would be if they ended up out on the street.

He started a few times as if trying for the right angle to argue from. In the end he just sighed. Reluctantly, grumbling, he signed. Probably, she thought, it was less because of anything she'd said than that his goop hadn't worked and he didn't know why . . . and cooperating with these brainiacs in their fancy government lab was the only way he ever would.

The brainiacs returned, led by the red-headed man, who introduced himself as Dr. Walter Carlson and, with a toothy grin, offered Claressa a saucer-sized blueberry donut. "From a shop in front of the BX," he said, "better than crap from the machines."

Paperwork signed, the Smallwoods were issued badges and guidance on which doors they weren't any good for, and Dr. Carlson showed them down the hallway to an equipment-packed room recognizable as a chemistry lab by the spatially labyrinthine glassware and the juxtaposed odors of gunpowder and bleach.

The first order of business was to confirm the formula the Kirtland team had derived by mass and nuclear magnetic-resonance spectroscopy, then run up a new batch under Mr. Smallwood's direction in order to exactly reproduce the goop he'd made at BASF and so hopefully Claressa's experimental results.

Second and third test shots, using the goop made at Kirtland overnight, ended the same as the first. Mr. Smallwood's new batch would take a few hours to "cook," so he and Claressa left the chemists for a short ride across base to see a mock-up of one of the new GPS satellites.

It was bigger than Claressa had imagined, a cube the size of eight dishwashers all stacked together, covered with tarps and gold plastic sheeting, gunmetal-blue solar panels stretching out left and right the width of a badminton court. As they walked around it, a studious young man with a dark complexion, Master Sergeant Lee Turley, pointed out where the kicker rocket would be during launch, where the antennas and thrusters were located, and where, in the confines of the tall fiberglass faring that would protect it during launch, there would be any room left over to squeeze in defensive countermeasures. Very little, was the answer, perhaps enough for eight stacked gallon cans in the middle of two of the six faces.

Claressa's dad shook his head, impressed with the engineering on display despite his desire to appear aloof, but no doubt wondering, like Claressa was, how anything useful could be packed into so tight a space.

"Have you thought about the interface for, um . . . the interface for power and data? You have test jacks or something we can use?"

Looking up at the satellite, Turley answered, "Yes sir, that's actually—" He spun around. "Mr. Smallwood?"

A worker, directing the operation of an overhead hoist, had backed into Claressa's dad who'd ignored the insult, instead staggering forward like a robot kicked in the ass but not given any program except to keep its feet. Turley grabbed his arm and quizzically met his vacant gaze.

"Sir? Are you all right? Sir?"

"Wha? What?" Mr. Smallwood startled and pushed the hand away. "What are . . . Where am I?"

Turley turned to Claressa. "Is he . . . is he drunk or something?"

Claressa harrumphed. She'd heard those men this morning while her dad was hunting socks, joking about the beer cans in the trash. Cans he had nothing to do with. And she saw the way the others looked at him, not just today but for all these months since the accident. People were so stupid, popping off, forming opinions without knowing what they were talking about or lifting a finger to find out. Sometimes she just wanted to punch someone, and she was still just young enough, she figured, to maybe just get away with it once.

"My daddy is not a drunk!" she said, belting Sergeant Turley good in the stomach. Or at least she would have. He'd caught her hand and now stood impassively staring.

"No, ma'am. I'm sure he's not. I'm sure . . . I didn't mean anything by it."

This was, Claressa thought, the most mature reaction she'd ever received from an adult.

Claressa's cheeks burned. "I'm sorry," she said, but the damage was already done.

The MPs drove her and her father back to the first building. Mr. Smallwood was taken to see the chemists. Claressa was taken to see the general, who kept her waiting while phone calls were made—calls she could hear through the anteroom just well enough to tell they were about her and her father.

The aide let her in. The general frankly asked, apologizing, about alcohol and drugs. Claressa attested that her father had not been prescribed and was not using so far as she was aware, any drug of any kind that would upset his equilibrium. When the general asked if there was anything else she could think of "that might explain your father's odd behavior," she had no answer. It was his equilibrium itself that was the problem.

And so, with a brief stop to wash her face, Claressa was taken to join him and the others eating lasagna in a mess hall employing the exact same collapsible furniture as her school. She couldn't help thinking, with his cell phone locked away, he seemed particularly on edge—rather like a junkie needing a fix. The comparison did nothing for her nerves.

In her absence, another test had been performed, this time with the nice, fresh goop cooked up under her father's supervision and an impact velocity of one hundred meters per second, more closely replicating her science fair experiment. The results had been exactly the same—disintegration.

This, Claressa knew, could not be right. She wiped sticky cobbler from her lips and said, "Let me see your setup, how you set up the experiment."

With Gutierrez's consent, and after everyone had finished eating, the civilians led the Smallwoods back across base to the cavernous, four-story laboratory. At its center stood a towering three-story vacuum chamber that could be flash evacuated using a steam condenser in the basement. Inside was an electromagnetic rail gun that could accelerate test articles to near orbital speed, though in the last test it had barely been set to idle. At the base of the tower was a conical target chamber of thick steel and concrete, surrounded by water tanks to absorb noise and the energy of any catastrophic breach should one occur.

Past a gap in the tanks, what looked like a bank-vault door stood open, and inside the gleaming steel interior, two soldiers were scraping what was left of Claressa's science fair dreams off the splattered floor and walls. In their midst, a sort of small metal soccer ball stood on a pole. This was obviously the target, crowned with the tattered, leathery remains of what should have been a pliable, translucent wrapping of self-adhering goo.

Claressa couldn't believe what she was looking at. She'd assumed the grown-up, college-trained military brainiacs would have known better than she had, all those months ago in her improvised garage-floor workshop. "How'd you make your pancake?"

"What?"

Claressa's dad said, "She means the projectile."

"Oh. In a hydraulic press, why?"

Claressa clapped. "That won't work. I started out using a rolling pin, but the pressure causes cross-linking and stiffens the goop. You end up with praline instead of bubble gum."

"Then how'd you do it?"

"A turntable and a power drill. Let centrifugal force pull the bonds open so it stays soft till after impact. We used waxed paper to keep it from sticking. Daddy says the molecules have lots of side branches that interlock like Velcro. Sticks to everything, especially itself, and is prone to polymerization, but it's stable enough if you just don't squeeze too hard."

"Of course," said her dad, leaning in through the open hatch, "you'd need stabilizers and, um . . . need stabilizers and plasticizers to tune it for space and the particular application."

The redhead, Mr. Carlson, Claressa recalled, shook his head. "A few minutes of plasticity would be enough." Subdued for most of the day, he suddenly had a gleam in his eye. "Guys," he said to his colleagues in the chamber, "you finish here. We're going to build a turntable."

✿　　✿　　✿

By dinner, Carlson and the base's merry band of guerrilla engineers had built a contraption that could spin out disks of goop a millimeter thin and big as a sombrero. They needed one that big to prevent its own inertia from squishing and embrittling it during acceleration. By midnight they had the right balance and had managed one test, successfully plastering an eighty-centimeter projectile disk cleanly around the target. When they opened the door to look inside, the goop was still pliable, drooping and quivering beneath the target globe like gelatinous alien snot.

Carlson let out a whistle and raised his hand to give Claressa a high five, but turned at a bang as the stairwell door flew open behind them.

"Ms. Smallwood? Ms. Smallwood, it's your father!"

"Daddy!"

Claressa's father lay sprawled on the landing halfway up the stairs. A guardian knelt over him, shining a cell-phone light in his eyes.

"They're responding now, ma'am, but I'm pretty sure they were fixed when we found him." He was talking to someone on speaker. He tapped off the light and held the device to his ear. After a moment he said, "Yes, ma'am, we'll do that."

As another guardian checked over his legs, Mr. Smallwood cried out and bolted awake, blindly batting hands away. "The house . . . the house! You can't . . ." Then he looked around, evidently bewildered by his surroundings.

"Daddy, it's me. We're here with the Space Force, remember?"

As reality dawned, he relaxed somewhat against the helping hands. "I know where we are, I'm not senile. I just took a wrong step is all."

The rebuff stung. Something *was* wrong, something way more than a simple wrong step. From the top of the staircase a young man's voice echoed—one of their police escort's mentioning the beer cans at the "BOQ," and from below came the sound of a woman, asking about something that sounded like "foreclosure." Had Sam Smallwood's prideful denials finally come to that? Were they about to be out on the street? Was that why he'd been so agitated, so irritable? Why he'd fallen? Was she to blame too?

He shucked off another hand and climbed drunkenly to his feet, to the dismay of all those around him.

"Sir, sir! You may have broken that foot!"

"You could have a concussion!"

He fought and twisted like their old poodle Beatrix when confronted with the bathtub, but a downtrodden, middle-aged, unemployed chemist was no match for three Space Force Samaritans in their prime of life and he knew it.

"All right, all right," he said at last, and acquiesced to being hoisted between two broad shoulders. The men carried him down and Claressa followed. General Gutierrez stopped her at the door, giving Claressa's shoulder a gentle squeeze.

"They'll get him checked out. Let's give them space and I'll have someone drive you over. In the meantime, there's nothing like staying busy to set your mind at ease. Why don't we let Mr. Bently show you the materials science lab—"

"My father's not a drunk!"

"I didn't say—"

"He's not a drunk and he doesn't do drugs! He's just . . . it's just, since . . . since . . ."

Claressa's voice cracked as her eyes filled embarrassingly with tears. "Are we gonna lose our house?"

The dam burst. All these months, Claressa had been lying to herself, pretending everything was all right, pouring herself into schoolwork and the science fair and ignoring her father's deteriorating condition, covering for and shielding him while hoping it was just his grief. But it wasn't. Something bigger was wrong, the sort of something that could leave her all alone in the wide world, or worse . . . and she'd known it and let it go on for months when she might have told someone, anyone, and tried to get him some help.

She tried to say something like that to the general, but her voice box wasn't working. For the first time in her entire life she felt utterly lost and exposed, and deep in this fortress of order and impersonal formality with the weight of the world suddenly foist upon her.

She just stood there, hopeless, face wet with tears, terrified and ashamed. She squeezed her eyes shut, but then opened them wide in surprise. Major General Lina Gutierrez of the United States Space Force was holding her tight, patting her back, telling her everything would all be all right.

❖ ❖ ❖

Claressa's father had indeed broken his foot, but if his fall had in any other way thrown him farther off his azimuth, the fact was not obvious as yet. The orderly had brought breakfast of sausage and eggs, and he'd rewarded Claressa for buttering his toast with a bite and a hearty hug.

"Go on," he said. "I know you want to see it work, and they're taking me for tests anyhow. You'll be bored here, and you're more, um . . . you're more inventor than I am. Go invent."

Claressa agreed and kissed his cheek and stole another bite before bouncing to the door.

She was as terrified as she'd been last night, as frightened of what was to come. And yet, if not happy exactly, this morning she felt strangely invigorated. At last they would know. They were asking the right questions, here and over in the laboratory. Everything now was going to work out, if not well, at least as well as it could. The world wouldn't all fall apart for lack of trying.

She turned to her father, twisted her fingertips into a finger-heart, then turned to the door and snapped them before her waiting escort.

"Come on," she said, "the world's not gonna save itself."

With the goop finally sorted, it was time to work on delivery. This was something Claressa had given a lot of thought to, but she wasn't an engineer and hadn't known anything about the interceptors or the satellites or the weight, power, and other integration requirements.

The Kirtland team had all that knowledge, however, and it didn't take long to settle into a productive working relationship. Cynthia Clay, integration specialist with Northrop Grumman, would set Claressa a challenge to which she had already thought up a solution. Cynthia's team would then explain half a dozen reasons that solution wouldn't work, and Claressa, with the irrepressible creativity of youth, would propose something more practical. Then that would be shot down and the cycle would repeat.

This went on over and over again for two days while Claressa's dad was in the hospital. By the time all his tests had been run, all the wrinkles had been ironed out of the countermeasure design and the chemistry of the goop, and it was up to other teams to bring it all to fruition.

The design they'd come up with was, Claressa thought, eminently practical and actually pretty clever. A usefully large pancake of goop would never survive launch, much less fit inside the rocket fairing. So instead of a pancake, the goop would remain packed in an aluminum cylinder about the size of two stacked paint cans. Aluminum was used simply because it could be quickly fabricated and would need no special testing. Lubricated with liquid paraffin and sealed against vacuum, the packaged goop would be affixed atop a simple base module built around commercially available, off-the-shelf cubesat components.

At launch, this would all hang alongside the GPS satellite like a lamprey, mounted to its chassis by an electrically actuated "shoulder joint" pivot and fixed against the satellite by the self-same strap already securing one of the two solar arrays. Each satellite would be launched with two countermeasures, one on each side, and servicing drones could affix the devices to three of the four models of satellite already in orbit.

The brainiacs had already come up with the necessary sensors and software upgrades. After deployment of the solar arrays, the countermeasures would be free to move. When an interceptor came into range, a countermeasure would swing to face it. A small RDX squib would cut a retaining wire tying the countermeasure to its base and securing the walls of the goop bucket. This would also release a valve, freeing high-test hydrogen peroxide to flow across a catalyst and flash into steam, some of which would be tapped to pressurize the peroxide tank, the rest of which would be exhausted through two canted, rearward facing nozzles.

The countermeasure would then rocket away at nearly three g's, well below the compression limit at which the goop would become embrittled, and would spin itself up as it did so. At a certain rotational speed, which it would reach when clear of the host satellite, a second tie would break, freeing the walls of the goop bucket to peel away and be flung off into space along with all traces of paraffin as the goop spun, pizza-dough style, out into a broad, flat pancake. By the time it reached its target, computer modeling showed the pancake could be over three meters across and moving three hundred meters per second.

None of this was the clever bit. The clever bit was all chemistry and materials science, worked out between Mr. Carlson, Mr. Bently, and Claressa's dad, largely on napkins at his bedside. Fragmented carbon nanofilaments mixed into the goop would block the passage of radio waves. When the pancake hit the fan, as it were, it would engulf any target up to a certain size completely, forming a rubbery, translucent Faraday-cage balloon, isolating it from outside radio control and obscuring any optical sensors or communications links.

The fibers would also strengthen the membranous goop, helping it form a larger, more robust pancake, while chemical stabilizers and elastomizers would extend its flexibility and heat resistance enough so that as the interceptor fired its thrusters to try and reestablish control, their exhaust would only inflate the goop like a balloon while painting the inside with soot, further blinding the interceptor. Over a period of half an orbit or so, UV light from the sun would then excite a chemical photoinitiator in the goop, triggering long-chain polymerization and converting the rubbery balloon into a tough, hard shell durable enough to survive for a few weeks while its added drag pulled the interceptor down toward a fiery doom.

Ion thrusters in the base module could further manipulate the interceptor, push it away from its target, and help accelerate its demise. There was even a nonpropulsive pressure relief in case an interceptor tried to use engine exhaust to overinflate and rupture the shell to free itself.

The countermeasure was, in short, foolproof, except only a fool would assume that. You could never know what you didn't know, and the proof would only come in the doing.

Dr. Laura Rubin was trim for someone touching middle-age, a bit dour, as if unaccustomed to smiling, but with crow's feet and cheek lines suggesting that when smiles came, they were hearty. She pulled the privacy curtain back and directed Claressa to a bedside stool.

Her father took her hand and Dr. Rubin leaned in with a light to check his pupils.

"Tell me about this accident."

Claressa told all she knew, that her dad had hit a patch of black ice driving her mom to a Christmas party. Her dad filled in that the car had flown down an embankment, that the best airbags could only do so much. He'd known the place, knew it far better now, blamed himself for the fatal lapse . . . He knew the hospital, the doctor, and other relevant details, but his delivery was punctuated by the habitual pause and repetition that had grown so noticeable of late, like an old-fashioned phono-record skipping, as if his brain had developed a short and was constantly rebooting itself.

With an effort, Claressa held her tears at bay. Light was finally shining on her dad; she wouldn't do anything that pulled it away. "Is he . . . has he had a stroke?"

"No, I don't think so. His scans reveal no ischemic or infarc—that is, there are no obvious areas in his brain damaged by a blocked or reduced blood flow. There are traces of what might be glial scarring; that's just a sign that the brain suffered an injury and healed, which stands to reason after a car crash like he suffered. But I don't think . . .

"Claressa, Mr. Smallwood, what you are experiencing are what we call absence seizures, sometimes called petit mal seizures. It's rare to see onset in adults, and it obviously can be very dangerous if it happens at just the wrong moment, if you're climbing stairs or—"

"Well, that explains . . ." Mr. Smallwood said.

"What's that?"

"At the plant . . . I was overseeing LRC2, a chemical production line, not my usual work, um . . . not my usual work, but I'm the senior chemist and it was a new line. Nothing too complicated but you . . . um, but you have to watch the pressure inside the separator and, well, I let it blow out, somehow. They thought I'd, um . . . They thought I'd been drinking and put me on leave. Of course I never tested . . . but . . . there's a lot of liability and money involved . . . I, um . . . I . . ."

"I was going to say, 'or when driving to a Christmas party.'"

"Come again?"

"Mr. Smallwood, have you ever been treated for diabetes?"

He thought a moment, his gaze appraising, suspicious. "A blood test once maybe, why?"

"Because right now, you're hypoglycemic and showing elevated insulin levels and increased C-peptide levels. Your pancreas looks healthy except . . ."

"Except what?"

"Mr. Smallwood, I have a hunch. I think you might have a pancreatic tumor. I don't mean cancer. A benign tumor throwing your metabolism into chaos."

"You think I have diabetes?"

"No, Mr. Smallwood, quite the opposite. And insulinoma can be tiny and hidden in the structure of the pancreas, difficult to find on an MRI. Even so, it can crank out enough insulin to force your blood-sugar levels to crash, enough to induce absence seizures in an otherwise healthy, adult brain."

Mr. Smallwood's mouth fell slack. For a moment, Claressa though he was having a spell.

"You mean . . . wait a minute, you mean the crash didn't cause the, um . . . the crash didn't cause the seizures?"

"If I'm right, the seizures may have caused the crash."

"But that would . . ."

Claressa watched as her father's face transformed. She ran through the applicable emotions, joy, loss, relief . . . what fit was something bittersweet, cathartic relief mixed with loss and acceptance.

"You mean . . ." Tears filled his eyes and the hand holding Claressa's shook violently.

"I don't want to promise," Dr. Rubin said. "I mean we really have to run more tests, get you under the new high-res scanner their working on over at Sandia. But if I'm right and we're able to remove the tumor, both the hypoglycemia and the seizures might resolve."

Dr. Rubin furrowed her brows. She clearly didn't understand her patient's emotional reaction. Claressa did.

"You mean," said her father, wiping tears with the heel of his free hand, fighting to breath without giving in to sobs. "Um . . . You mean I didn't kill her."

"Ms. Smallwood, may I have a word?"

A police guard was escorting Claressa from the laboratory building where she'd come to say goodbye to Dr. Carlson, Ms. Clay, Mr. Bently, and others from the various labs who'd dropped by for cake and to see the wunderkind who'd just helped save the quarter-trillion-dollar GPS system and, as some of them knew, possibly prevented World War III.

At General Gutierrez's voice, the guard paused. Gutierrez caught up and said, "We'll just be a moment," nodding through the door of a vacant conference room they'd just passed. The guard put her back to the wall and clasped her hands behind her.

"Yes, ma'am."

Claressa and the general stepped inside and the general latched the door behind them.

The general had her morning coffee. She took a water bottle from the sideboard and set it before Claressa. "For the road," she said, "airplane water . . ." She scrunched up her nose in disgust.

"Ms. . . . Claressa . . . First, I have to remind you that everything you've seen related to the project and this laboratory is classified. You are not to discuss it with anyone, ever, you understand that, right?"

"No, ma'am, I mean yes, ma'am, I understand."

"But I also want you to know that anything you've learned more generally—about chemistry, spacecraft, how engineering is done in a crisis, I don't know, teamwork, problem solving, those sorts of things—these things are all part of your tool kit now. These are things you can take with you throughout your life."

"Really?"

The general nodded, "And I think you'll find they're more than you realize. You're a smart girl, Claressa. There are more good ideas ahead of you, even though, as you've seen, ideas don't always work out quite as we conceive them."

While her dad went through further testing, Claressa knew, two of the four new GPS satellites had been fitted with countermeasures and flown to Vandenberg Space Force Base where crews had worked around the clock to integrate them with waiting boosters and launch them into space. The enemy had been waiting, too, and no sooner had the new machines reached orbit than interceptors had closed in for the kill.

But the countermeasures had worked, rendering the interlopers harmless, useless, and doomed to burn up within the month. Contractors were now rushing to equip upcoming satellites with the same system, and robotic servicing flights were in the works to retrofit most of the rest of the constellation.

The attempt had revealed at least one parking orbit in which tiny interceptor sats now waited like ducks in a gooey shooting gallery. They could wait. The enemy had lost their advantage, and they couldn't realistically regain it without betraying their launch site and ultimately, their masters and agenda. The immediate threat was gone, and the whole, globe-spanning intelligence apparatus of the United

States, in space and on the ground, would now turn to neutralizing it for good.

This was nothing like Claressa's naive "save the world" dream of cleaning up orbital space, but it was thrilling to know she might really have saved it, just in a very different way.

Claressa nodded.

"I've arranged for your father to get his job back."

"Really! That's great!" Claressa jumped up and hugged the general, who stiffened at first, then relaxed and waited till she again took her seat.

"And I've arranged to put your compensation in a trust. It's enough to send you to college and help ensure your father gets the care he needs, and more if you spend it wisely."

Claressa's face beamed. "Really?" Tears threatened to fall. "That's . . . thank you!"

"And as for your house . . . I'm not completely sure a U.S. Space Force general has the legal authority to blackball a regional financial servicing firm, but I didn't get these for tiptoeing around." The general fingered the star on her collar. "You talked to Dr. Rubin?"

"Yes, ma'am."

"Your dad's going to need some help for a while, Claressa . . . to make sure he makes his appointments and pays his bills and takes his medication until he kind of gets stable. Can you help him do that?"

Claressa nodded.

"Good girl."

Gutierrez handed Claressa a business card. "I know these are old-fashioned, but you can put me in your contacts and let me know if . . . if you ever need any help."

Claressa looked up, eyes wide. "Ms. . . . General, why are you doing all this for us?"

Gutierrez paused as if deciding how much to reveal, then she let out a sigh. "When I was little, my teacher used to call me a retard. She stuck me in the back of class and told my parents I should be put in a special school. But I wasn't, and you know why?"

Claressa shook her head, "No, ma'am."

"My dad came to see the teacher. He asked all about the class, how all the work was done on the blackboard, how I was sat in the back for misbehavior and always in trouble for getting up. Then he had me take my seat, stood in the front, and asked how many fingers he was holding up."

"Oh my gosh! You couldn't see?"

"I couldn't see. I didn't know I needed glasses. I didn't know how everyone else got by so easily. I'd just stand at the sharpener or fool with the terrarium, trying to memorize the board before I got yelled at. And that worked just well enough to keep a lousy teacher from noticing I couldn't see across the room."

"Oh my gosh! That's terrible!"

Gutierrez nodded.

"Neither of my parents had a college degree. Neither had any power. But my dad got elected to the school board and made sure every kid got an eye exam. And I grew up with an exceptionally good memory, if I do say so myself.

"And that's your answer, Claressa. I can't solve all the world's problems, I can only do my bit. But I can help one man get the care he needs so one smart little girl gets her chance. Make the most of it, Claressa, and one day you'll do more still."

Claressa sat up straight and beamed.

"And when you do, Claressa..." Gutierrez tapped the business card where Claressa had it pressed against the table. "...do give me a call. We can use someone like you."

✧   ✧   ✧

Winner of the Jim Baen and L. Ron Hubbard Writer's of the Future awards, **C. Stuart Hardwick** is a regular in *Analog* magazine, known for hard sci-fi that soars through the cosmos, exploring the depths of human nature and the mysteries of space and time. His evocative prose, enriched by scientific rigor, ignites the imagination and leaves an indelible mark on the human mind.

When he's not at the keyboard or on his bicycle, Stuart can often be found building or dismantling things with equal glee, helping electrons find their way across the lonely Texas power grid, or developing new novel-writing software when he should, just maybe, be writing new novels instead. More, including free stories, at www.cStuartHardwick.com.

Notes from the Editor

✸

The U.S. Space Force protects the U.S. and its allies' freedom to operate in space, keeping it secure, stable and accessible for military and commercial purposes and enabling new waves of innovation.

There are three ways to serve in this vital new endeavor: enlisted members participate and support operations, officers plan and manage personnel, and civilians perform a mix of both support and management of Space Force operations.

Learn more at:

https://www.spaceforce.com/about

https://www.spaceforce.com/careers

Baen Books has long been recognized as a leading publisher of military fiction and military science fiction with a strong reputation for publishing and promoting works in these genres, making it a prominent and influential publisher in the field. Their catalog includes many well-known authors and series in the military and military science fiction genres that you may enjoy, with many available for free.

www.baen.com

For more information about any of the authors in this work, plus some surprises, visit

spaceforceanthology.cstuarthardwick.com